State of Desire

CATHERINE MERRIMAN

State of Desire

MACMILLAN

First published 1996 by Macmillan

an imprint of Macmillan General Books
25 Eccleston Place
London SW1W 9NF
and Basingstoke

Associated companies throughout the world

ISBN 0 333 65130 8

1 3 5 7 9 8 6 4 2

A CIP catalogue record for this book is available from
the British Library

Phototypeset by Intype, London
Printed by Mackays of Chatham PLC, Chatham, Kent

Acknowledgement

The Author wishes to acknowledge the award of a Bursary from the Arts Council of Wales for the purpose of completing this book.

16 July 1993

Well, Michael, it's exactly a year today, since you died. I've got a glass of wine on the table here, and I'm toasting you.

No more firsts. No more first Christmases. No more first birth-days. No more first Rugby internationals. I didn't watch any last season, by the way. Wales were on a losing streak. You'd have been mortified.

Why am I writing this now, when I haven't felt the need to write before? Because there's a milestone feel to the day, I suppose. It's a taking-stock day. Maybe even a hello-goodbye day. And because there was a pen and pad here in front of me.

Over the year I've done all the stupid things bereaved people do. Funny how you can know, and warn yourself about them, but they still happen. I've crashed the Polo. Twice. First just a week after the funeral, when I demolished the gritting bin down in the village, though of course it was empty, so no great harm done. The second time was much worse, up at Brynteg roundabout, when I ran into the back of a car waiting to turn right into the Jet garage. Thank God I didn't kill anyone. I've lost two years' no-claims bonus. Sal says the bereaved are a bloody liability on the roads, and we should all be banned from driving for six months.

Alex has got your old Escort, by the way. He passed his test last

1

December, at the second attempt. Amazingly, he hasn't hit anything yet. He misses you but in an uncomplicated way, I think, as if you were a close friend he'd lost, rather than a parent or authority figure or whatever. That's what you were good at: being his friend, without trying to be a second father to him.

I've tried to make all sorts of idiotic changes in my life, but luckily none have come to anything. First I thought I'd give up my job. I think I felt guilty about not being poorer. I got a lump sum and a small pension from the education authority. Sal says people often muddle up feelings about money with grief. Either they feel guilty because their sense of loss isn't reflected financially, or the sense of loss gets misplaced into irrational panic about poverty. Anyway, I tried to resign, but Frank very sensibly said three months' notice was the least he would accept and within a month I'd changed my mind. I can't think now what possessed me. I love that print shop; I must have been trying to hurt myself.

Then I thought about selling the cottage. For weeks I wandered around the place saying, 'It's all so meaningless, now he's gone.' Sal and Alex kept pointing out how much more meaningless anywhere else would be, but I was desperate to change something huge; because life as it was felt so unlivable, I suppose. But when I enquired at the estate agents' – yes, I got that far – they warned me that there were already a dozen houses for sale in the village, and that everything was sticking because of the threat of the opencast. Oh, you don't know about that, do you? You'd be furious. I'm fairly furious too, but mostly with myself for not grasping what was happening sooner. Sal says she's told me several times, but I obviously wasn't listening. Bereavement makes you horribly self-obsessed. British Coal want to opencast the top of the mountain behind us. Most of Gwern Hill, in fact. There've been meetings in all the villages, none of which I've attended, and nobody wants it, not even the county council. They turned the plan down. But British Coal have pushed an appeal to the Welsh Office, and they're holding a public inquiry in September.

Until that's settled no one's going to buy houses here. So I was saved from that stupidity too.

I haven't had an imaginary illness for four months. I was convinced I had breast cancer last autumn – just a cyst, as it turned out, and I should have known because the lump appeared almost overnight. The hospital doctor stuck a needle into me and aspirated the fluid. Goodbye, lump. But I can tell you the colour of fear – it's a dirty yellow-grey. Then in February I decided I'd got multiple sclerosis, because of a tingling sensation down the underside of my forearm. A tiny trapped nerve in my elbow, Dr K generously suggested, though I doubt it was even that, because it disappeared the moment I left his surgery. We had a chat about you. He says you must have had some virus, like rheumatic fever when you were a child, which damaged your heart valves. I asked if you would have lived longer if you hadn't been a PE teacher and he said he doubted it, and being so fit may well have extended your life. Brynteg school gave you a beautiful memorial service, by the way, when term started in September. Very moving – half the kids were in tears, boys as well as girls. I know they love a weep, but they don't do it for everyone. They raised pots of money, which I suggested they spend on sports equipment, so the school's finally got those cricket nets you wanted, and some spectator benches with *In Memory of Michael Parsons* engraved on them.

Nobody tells you what bereavement is like, Michael. Nobody warns you. Before you died, I imagined grief as a deep sadness, a huge weight on the heart. It is, but that's only part of it. That's what it settles into, later. But early on – the anxiety, Michael, the terrible anxiety. And the restlessness. Nobody tells you about this, or explains it. There is nothing to be anxious about, because the worst has already happened, and yet anxiety is definitely what it is: I was leaping out of my chair when the phone rang, my heart drumming in my chest, as if I might be going to hear news of you. I couldn't sit still; I had to roam, pace floors, do things – anything. My thoughts were always on you, turning memories over and over, dissecting and examining

3

them as if desperate for clues about you. Condolence cards that say, 'Sympathies on your loss' have it, you know, exactly right: although my brain knew you had gone forever, my body didn't. My body thought you were still here, but lost. I've felt it before, I've just realized; that time I thought I'd lost Alex in Aber market. The grip of panic, of fear, of senses super-acutely alert, the urge to move, take action, search, visualize, restore. That is what grief is like. But with the sadness, the awful crumbling knowledge that any search is hopeless, on top.

I threw away the last of your clothes this spring. Or rather, Alex did. Those two Gortex jackets that hung in the hall. Most of your stuff I got rid of last summer. I made myself – clothes are so emotive, so empty and limp and sad without a body to fill them. I worried I might end up cherishing them for ever. I gave Alex your socks at the time, just the plain black and navy ones, but I kept spotting them in the wash and experiencing appalling pangs of hope, so in the end I binned them too. The jackets, though – I thought they'd be useful. Visitors could wear them. But then in the spring I realized that a whole winter had passed and no one had, and Alex came into the kitchen carrying them one day and said we should give them to Oxfam, for all those refugees shivering on hillsides, so I said yes, and he did.

Life is still occasionally unbearable, but not all the time. That's it – time doesn't heal, but the things that occupy time do. Or rather, they give the impression of healing, because they occupy. I'm still having problems trusting who I am, because the feelings I've had over the last year have seemed so real and convincing. I'll think I've settled down and more or less found myself again, and then a couple of months pass and I realize that I'm different, and I think, no, *this* is the real me; and then I change again. It's disorientating. But being aware now of the changes, and the possibility of further change, must be a good sign.

At the moment I'm experiencing hurtling feelings. I can't think of another way of describing them. The feelings have energy, which is pleasurable, but they also have a loose-cannon quality about them. I've got all this life in front of me and I could do anything. I could be anyone. Without you there's no one to fix me down or expect anything of me. There's just me, and what I want or need to be or do. Sal says I'm feeling like this not just because of losing you, but because Alex will be leaving home soon so the nest will be doubly empty. But I don't know. I wonder if I'm not just coming back to life. Feeling at last that I'm going somewhere; hurtling somewhere.

I have regrets, Michael. Well, I suppose there will always be regrets. And I expect anything unresolved always grows bigger once you realize it can never be resolved. I'll make a Sal-edict – people should only die when everything in their lives is perfect.

But they don't, do they? Actually, I don't know why I've brought this up now. I hadn't thought it so important. At least, I thought I hadn't. Just sad. Funny what comes out when you have a couple of glasses of wine, and let yourself run on.

I'm toasting you, Michael. A year today. And toasting myself. To hurtling. I wonder where I'll end up.

Chapter 1

Jenny Parsons leant against the broad window-sill in her cottage sitting room and dialled her friend Sal's telephone number. She was wearing a cotton dressing gown, although the time was three in the afternoon, and drew it more tightly around her body. A light July rain was spattering dust into worm-streaks on the small window panes. She ducked her head to catch a glimpse of sky, a narrow grey strip between the lintel and the green hillside that filled the window view. In her ear the ringing tone stopped. She turned back to the room.

'Sal?' She fixed her eyes on a four-foot bas-relief gold Buddha on the wall to the right of the deep stone fireplace. The ornament looked solid and heavy; in fact, it was fingertip light, made of cheap lacquered fibreglass.

'Hi, Jen.'

'Sal.' Now she stared at the carpeted floor. 'Thank God. Listen. Sal . . . I've . . . I can't say it. Yes, I can. I've just had sex. With Gareth.'

There was a pause. Then Sal's voice, dry and hard: 'Congratulations.' Another pause. 'Is that what you want me to say?'

'Actually I feel a bit shaky.'

She heard Sal exhale. Then say, in a lower tone, 'Who's idea was this? Yours or his?'

'Mine. Yes. I started it. He was fitting a shower over the bath . . . and you know how small my bathroom is, and . . .'

Sal cut in. 'Jen?'

'Yes?'

'Come over.'

'Um . . . maybe. Later. I've got to get rid of him first.'

'What?'

'He's still here. Upstairs.' She heard Sal make a hissing noise. 'I had to speak to you . . . He was like a stranger . . .'

'This happened in the bathroom?'

'No, no . . . The silicone round the bath has to set . . . we were in my bedroom. Michael's bedroom . . .'

'Hey, Jen, don't cry.'

'I'm not. I'm not. It's just my breathing.'

'Well, don't breathe funny, OK?'

A board creaked upstairs. Jenny started and glanced up at the ceiling beams. 'I've got to go. I can hear him. Oh, God, I'm so stupid.'

'Ring me later. Or come round.'

'I will. I will. Sal . . . thanks.'

Jenny put the phone down, left the sitting room and padded across the hall quarry tiles. At the bottom of the stairs she stopped in front of a cane-framed wall mirror and fingered smooth her short brown hair. Her eyes looked huge, opaquely dark. I'm wearing my waif look, she thought, how pathetic. Poor little me. Poor stupid little me.

Upstairs, Gareth was sitting on the end of her double bed with his jeans on, pulling on black socks. His chest was still bare. She sat down on the duvet cover at right angles to him.

'Sorry about that. I just remembered . . .' Her mind went blank. She frowned.

Gareth glanced at her with a smile, said, 'It's OK, Jen,' and returned to his socks.

Jenny watched him. I always thought he was attractive, she

7

thought, even when Michael was alive. I teased Michael about it. Is he attractive? She looked at the familiar parts of him: his hands, stubby-fingered and capable, tugging on the socks; his thick, sand-coloured hair, cut short in no particular style; and what she could see of his face, his regular, masculine profile. And then at the unfamiliar: the paler flesh of his upper arms, yellowish in this light, the muscular curves of his shoulder and flank. She couldn't decide. The familiar was too familiar: the unfamiliar too unfamiliar. She moved her gaze away, staring at the latched wooden door in front of her. He's married, she thought, with four kids, two of them teenagers, and he carries condoms in his wallet.

Gareth swivelled and rested his hands on her shoulders.

'All right, girl?' he said. 'You're not regretting this now?'

She smiled without looking back. His voice, yes, she did like his voice. Soft, humorous, easy-going. The way he called her girl, or girlie. Unthinkingly, inoffensively. 'I'm afraid I might be,' she said.

He slipped his hands under the neckline of the robe and stroked the bare skin of her shoulders. 'Hey, lovely,' he murmured. 'It's no big deal.'

The front of her robe opened. Jenny looked down at her breasts. The nipple areola was smooth now. Mole dark. The breasts themselves soft and quiescent. A moment ago they had been full and heavy and hard. These breasts are thirty-nine years old, she thought. No, I didn't have them till I was fourteen. That makes them twenty-five. They're younger than me. She felt suddenly, irrationally, protective of them.

Gareth was kissing her shoulder. Light butterfly kisses. His hands slid under her arms to stroke the undercurve of her breasts. Jenny watched her nipples respond, the dark skin puckering.

One of his hands moved down her abdomen. 'Lean back, lovely,' he murmured.

8

'No.' Jenny pushed his hands away. Abruptly she stood up. 'Alex will be back soon.' It wasn't a lie, just a stretched truth.

'Ah, right.' Gareth pulled away, and retrieved his blue sweatshirt from the far side of the bed. He shook it the right way round.

I pulled that off him, Jenny thought, with a shudder of disbelief. Just twenty minutes ago.

'I'm glad it was you.' She sank down again on the bed. Suppose, instead of Gareth, a stranger had been fitting the shower? Where had the arousal, the swamping urge to act, come from? Could she have suppressed it? She felt hot. 'Really,' she said.

Gareth pulled on the sweatshirt and stood up. 'Ay,' he said. 'No harm done, eh?'

She looked up. She wanted to apologize.

His voice was soft. 'I said, it's no big deal. I'll get my gear.' He kissed her on the cheek. A quick, platonic, no-worries kiss. 'Remember now, girl, no showers till tomorrow.'

Jenny smiled. 'I'll remember.'

'And warn Alex.'

'I will.' She nodded; her panic had evaporated. He was Gareth again, as he had been when he'd arrived that morning: Michael's best friend, her good friend. Still, after Michael's death, her good friend. An arm round the shoulders in the pub; a lift to the garage or to the school for a parents' evening; a dancing partner at village rock nights; a kiss and a bearhug on New Year's Eve. Just Gareth.

He was in the bathroom now, down the corridor. She listened to him packing his tool bag, and reached behind her for her clothes.

*

'What're you doing here?' Alex asked, as he let himself in the back kitchen door at four o'clock. Jenny was scrubbing new potatoes at the sink.

'Gareth's been fitting the shower. I took the day off. I told you.'

'Hey, great, a shower!' Alex wrenched at the elastic band at the back of his neck and shook out his shoulder-length hair. Hair inherited from his father: thick, ropy, straw-coloured. He was wearing a white shirt and his old grey school trousers, required uniform for his supermarket holiday job.

'You can't use it till tomorrow. The sealant's got to set.'

'Oh, right.' Alex leant across the kitchen table, peering to see the front-page headlines on the daily newspaper. He pulled back. 'Has Lizzie rung? She said she'd ring this afternoon.'

'No one's rung. Brush your hair, it looks stupid like that.' She imagined Lizzie ringing, interrupting the afternoon an hour ago. Lizzie was Gareth's daughter.

Alex combed his fingers upwards through his hair from the temples. Jenny glanced back at him. He looked even sillier now. She suppressed the impulse to say so, and concentrated on the potatoes.

'I said I'd take Lizzie into Aber tonight,' said Alex, moving to the work surface and switching on the kettle. 'But the front end of the car's banging.'

'Oh, no,' sighed Jenny.

'Can't be anything too serious, or the MOT bloke would have spotted it. Think I'll get Mark up to take a look.'

'Who's Mark?'

Alex spooned coffee into a mug. 'From down the pub. Play pool with him sometimes. Knows what he's doing.' He poured boiling water on to the coffee and tipped milk in after it. 'I'm gonna change,' he said, picking up the mug.

Jenny turned and called after him, 'I'm going out later. To see Sal.'

'OK.' The kitchen door swung shut.

Jenny transferred the potatoes to a saucepan, covered them with water, and then made herself a small coffee with the hot water left in the kettle. She carried it outside. The rain had stopped. There had been just enough, she convinced herself, to make watering the flower tubs along the front path unnecessary. Her eyes rested on the white roof of Alex's Escort, which he hadn't bothered to bring through the gate on to the hard standing. It was parked in the narrow lane, in a two-car passing bay the other side of the stone garden wall. Jenny gave an inner sigh. Out of the eighty pounds a week Alex earned at the supermarket he was meant to be saving fifty. The plan this year was six months working to fund six months travelling in the new year, and then university next September, assuming he passed the A levels he'd just taken. But in the first four weeks at the supermarket he'd managed to save only fifty pounds in total because of bills for his car.

She turned her back on the flower tubs and the car. Most of the cottage garden lay behind and above the building. She walked up steep steps through a small terraced lawn. Smaller this year than ever before, encroached by unpruned shrubs, white flowering ground elder, and magenta banks of fireweed. The prettiness of neglect. The garden had escaped from her this year. Even the tubs, below at the house, had been left to their own devices, and contained only runtish self-seeded nasturtiums and last year's antirrhinums – though these had been a flukish success, surviving the winter and now flowering strongly and prolifically.

She walked up the damp lawn to a hardwood bench under a rustling silver poplar. She and Michael had planted the tree the day after their move here in a fit of new-garden enthusiasm. After ten years, the tree was now more than twenty feet tall, its trunk the thickness of a telegraph pole.

She sat down on the bench and gazed out over the village.

11

Her village. The village of Pentre. Her eyes slid across the view, from left to right. Pentre lay in one of the few west–east valleys of south-east Wales. A pleat-like pass between two much larger north–south valleys, tight and gorge-like in its upper reaches, where a forest of beech trees clung with clenched finger-roots to the sheer slopes, the pleat opening and softening as the land fell eastwards until the fields melded with those of the Usk Plain. Pentre was on the eastern edge of Valleys' Wales: four miles from industrial Brynteg, at the windy head of the valley, and the same distance from the rural market town of Abercwm, which nestled comfortably over the river Usk. The sides of the valley at this mid-way point were no longer sheer, but still steep. Each house in the village, unless actually on the valley floor, looked out over the rooftop of the house in the lane below. All ascending lanes curved or zigzagged and many were too steep to bicycle, up or down.

From where Jenny sat the floor of the valley was hidden below the slope of the land. She could hear the faint drone of cars and lorries on the main road that wound up to Brynteg, but not see it. What she could see, staring at the steep fields between the scattered houses opposite and the bracken-blanketed hilltop above, was the terrain of her own past. There, to the right, almost on the skyline, where the hillside – the Darren – began to curve away to face the Usk plain, was the slate roof of her and Pete's first house. Pete, Alex's father. The house had been a near-derelict hovel in those days, set in three acres of rough grazing. Twenty years ago she and Pete had bought it for five thousand pounds – a loan from Pete's father, who was a dentist in Maidstone. And after visiting his purchase he'd instantly also paid for a new roof. You kids, he told them, washing his hands of the folly, can do the rest yourselves. Though they hadn't, as it turned out.

Looking up at the house now, a bright white rectangle under its neat slate roof – twice the frontage it had been – Jenny found the old smallholding hard to visualize. Hard to imagine, too, how she could have lived, and, to begin with at least, enjoyed living in such squalor. Such unremittingly damp squalor. Moisture rose from the hilltop as if the land were sponge and the walls blotting paper. Flagstones turned black after an hour of light rain. Mould grew everywhere: under carpets, on books, in the back of cupboards, in the lower corners of every room. The concrete walls of the outside lavatory were silvered every morning with slug trails.

But Pete and she had been young, undomesticated, and had seen themselves as adventurers, not settlers. Back then the Welsh hills were full of young people like themselves: English dropouts, playing at self-sufficiency or self-enlightenment, or, like Pete, safety-netted by his parents' solid prosperity, just playing. Sweat lodges at Talgarth. Rain dances in Cwmdu. Cannabis harvests at Bronllys. Days that began at noon, and ended at dawn. Never mind the invasion of blackspot mould, just hang up another Indian bedspread.

But then she'd fallen pregnant. Pete had been enthusiastic at first. Talked of alternative parenthood, a new adventure – perhaps a tribal, wigwam style of life in one of the Mid Wales communities; but while he talked and fantasized, Jenny caught buses to antenatal classes and discovered the Welsh: midwives, health visitors, other pregnant young women. She made peace with her parents, who visited from Staines at weekends, lodging in local pubs because the house was still unfit for visitors. They declared themselves entranced by South Wales. She was driven by them to places she never knew existed, just a few miles from the smallholding. The mile-long steelwork sheds at Ebbw Vale, belching fire into a yellow dusk. The dark six-sided tower and green fish-filled moat of Raglan Castle. The lakes and waterfalls of Llangorse and Talybont. Her parents rhapsodized about the landscape – the towering beechwoods, the lush, unsprayed, flower-filled lanes, the drama of the hills, the magnificence of the views. The contrasts and the colour. And Jenny, although she had always seen and appreciated the land's beauty, now began to feel pride. Began to feel a resident. While Pete saw parenthood as an opportunity for change, for new adventures somewhere else, she felt herself consolidating. Digging in.

Even so, it took Pete three years to leave. Alex was at the local playgroup and Jenny had already met Sal who couldn't get her own son into Abercwm playgroup, and so came the four miles out of town to Jenny's. When he was stoned Pete still fantasized – now an overland trip to India before Alex reached school age – but, when sober, took no steps to realize the fantasy. Then one cold damp winter's day, with the flagstones inky and the blackspot rampant, he announced that he'd had enough. He was returning to Maidstone. Jenny and Alex were welcome to accompany him, if they wished. The decision was Jenny's. Jenny was frightened by the idea of coping alone in her Welsh valley, but even more frightened by the thought of starting again with a different, more conventional, compromised Pete beside her, in Maidstone. So she stayed.

Facing her now, directly across the valley, was the tiny terraced cottage she and Alex had moved to after Pete left. Bought with the twenty-five thousand she had made on the sale of the damp smallholding, after returning Pete's father's five thousand. The front door was still the dark green she had painted it – Holly Green, according to the catalogue – the lumpy render walls still creamy white. Apart from a satellite dish attached above a bedroom window the terrace looked much the same as when she'd left it. There she and Alex had lived for six years.

Until she'd married Michael. His rented cottage of those days was at the far western edge of the village, where the houses thinned to a straggle along the winding village road. Not visible from here. She'd first spoken to Michael when Alex was six, and she twenty-six, the day his wandering collie was hit and fatally injured by a speeding car outside her house. The dog wore an address tag and Jenny had run up the road and banged on his door. She had been in tears, the teenage girl driver was in tears, Alex was in tears, and Michael, the quick, wiry man who answered the door, was furious. He swore at the weeping driver, at the dying dog, as he cradled it in Jenny's doorway, and even at Alex for saying, 'Mum, its legs are kicking, it's all right, really, isn't it?'

Two days later he had called back to apologize. Jenny said she understood. She didn't tell him that her own tears had not been for him or his dog, but for what could have been. For the picture that had trembled in her mind – the twitching body not of a dog, but of a child, by the roadside. Michael apologized to Alex too, gravely and sincerely, and later that evening Alex told Jenny that he thought the shouting man must have really been sad that his dog had been killed, and that he was probably nice underneath. Jenny said she thought so too.

Michael had been twenty-nine then, with an ex-wife who lived and taught in Cardiff, but no children. Jenny and he were married three years later, and Gareth, who played cricket with Michael every Tuesday night in the summer and drank with him every Friday night throughout the year, was best man.

From here Jenny couldn't see Gareth and Siân's house. It was this side of the valley, four hundred yards down the steep village lane.

Alex was going out with Lizzie tonight. What would he think if he knew what his mother and her father had just done?

An insect fell from the silver leaves above into her coffee mug. A pale green shield beetle. She watched it paddle in frantic circles around the surface of the coffee. Suddenly repulsed, she tossed coffee and bug out on to the grass.

What, if anything, did her actions signify? Should she feel guilty? Ashamed? She searched her senses but detected neither. Just a numbness, tinged with apprehension. Fear of herself, perhaps, of what she was capable of.

But Gareth was the right person, she reassured herself, as well as the wrong. He was the wrong person because he was a friend, and had a wife and children who could be hurt. But right, also – since it was a mistake, and would never happen again – because of that friendship. Because he understood who she was and what had happened to her, and would keep confidence.

Inside the house the telephone rang. She rose automatically. The ringing ceased. Lizzie, she guessed. She looked at her watch, remembered her visit to Sal, and hurried down the steps to the house.

Chapter 2

Jenny let herself into Sal's Abercwm house through the back kitchen door, which was always left unlocked. Houses did occasionally get burgled in Abercwm, but not often enough for Sal to change this lifetime habit. Jenny didn't view Sal's behaviour as foolhardy – she herself, in the twenty years she'd lived in the Pentre valley, knew only one family, personally, whose home had been burgled. She rapped on the back door as she opened it, called, 'Sal!' and then bent to stroke Sal's fat tabby cat, which had jumped off a work surface to greet her and was swaying in an ecstatic, humpbacked arch at her feet.

'Hi, Mooch.' She tickled the cat's ears. 'Sal?' she called again.

'I'm changing.' Sal's voice came from upstairs. 'Help yourself to something.'

Sal's kitchen was as familiar to Jenny as her own, though considerably smaller – as was the house itself, being a narrow Victorian end-terrace in a street lined with modest, though graciously proportioned, rows of terraces.

The kitchen was also untidier than Jenny's. Sal's idea of a viable kitchen was a functioning cooker, enough adjacent flat surface to chop an onion, and a fridge big enough to serve as a larder. The rest of the surfaces were cluttered with domestic detritus: a tree of clean mugs, piles of magazines, a knitting bag – interestingly adapted from a failed homemade sweater – the

17

cat blanket and bottles and jars waiting for the journey to the bottle bank. A pile of dirty crockery stood on the draining board.

Jenny opened the fridge to the right of the sink, and removed an opened white wine bottle. As she closed the fridge door a grubby card Blu-tacked to the front fell to the floor. The note read, in printed Gothic script, 'If food be the music of love, eat on.' Jenny couldn't remember Sal's fridge door without this loosely attached appendage. She picked it up and refixed it.

She took a clean wine glass from a rack above the draining board and filled it. Then, because she couldn't stop herself, reached across the dirty crockery for a small saucepan that was caked with the remains of a tomatoey sauce and ran water into it. She pushed the pan back on to the draining board to soak.

She turned to study Sal's notice board on the opposite wall. Below its permanent fixtures – snaps of Sal's two children, favourite cartoons and cards, and local emergency services list – Sal pinned recent non-private correspondence. There was a letter on yellow notepaper from – Jenny lifted the page – Carly, Sal's twenty-two-year-old daughter, a photographer in London. Next to the letter was a postcard of treeless mountains and a lake. Jenny peered closer and saw a small gold 'Greetings from Scotland' inscription. She bent it over. It was from Pauline, Sal's lover. Attending a conference. Pauline attended numerous conferences, some educational – she was a teacher – and some political. An exhaustingly active woman. If Pauline had been in Scotland, this explained why Sal hadn't been to Bristol to stay with her last weekend.

There was a thunderous noise overhead – Sal's stairs were poorly carpeted – a moment's silence, and then Sal appeared at the kitchen doorway. She was wearing black leggings and a huge green T-shirt. Her hand lifted imperiously.

'My news first. Sorry, can't wait.' She grabbed a glass and held it out. 'Give us some wine. Ginormous news.'

Jenny said, 'Right,' smiling, and filled the glass.

'Come through,' said Sal, turning for the sitting room.

Jenny followed. Already her desire to unburden herself had lost its urgency. And anxiety. Sal made her feel safe. Sal made her feel supported. Sal understood about mistakes, and regrets, and life being a bugger. In Sal's presence, she could forgive herself anything.

Sal put down her wine glass and flopped into one of the armchairs. She swung her legs over the chair arm and crossed her plump calves. Her feet were bare. Jenny sat down opposite.

'Nathan rang. Just after you did. You'll never guess.' Sal's hard Cardiff voice softened with bliss. 'He wants to come down here. To stay with me. He's going to take a year out, like Alex. He's thinking of staying here, the whole year. Oh, boy . . .' She rolled her eyes to the ceiling.

'Sal,' breathed Jenny. The glow of this quite overwhelmed her own news. Nathan, Sal's son, hadn't lived with her for four years, since he was fourteen. Phil, Sal's ex-husband, had taken the boy with him when he left for London, daring Sal, who was already Pauline's lover, to fight to get him back. Although she didn't know Nathan, Pauline had urged Sal to go for it, not to be cowed, try to retrieve what was hers. Jenny had been much less sure. Nathan was not a passive or unresourceful child. If he'd wanted his mother badly enough, she'd felt, he'd have returned to her. In the end, knowing she was disappointing Pauline, Sal had agreed. 'People before politics,' she'd said. 'I want to know him all his life.'

And now, it seemed Sal's reluctance to fight had paid off, because he was coming back.

'Great news for Alex,' said Jenny. 'Most of his friend are off to university. God, you must be so excited.'

'I kissed the telephone,' said Sal. 'And the duvet, and my nightdress . . .'

'Oh, no,' said Jenny, laughing, 'I didn't think. Were you

19

asleep when I rang?' Sal was a nursing sister at a hospice and often worked nights.

'Forgiven,' said Sal. 'Actually I wasn't. I'd set the alarm for three. Anyway, Nathan rang five minutes later.' She swung her feet to the floor, picked up her glass, and took a swig of wine. 'He says he needs a job. Says he'll do anything except go down a coal mine, and I said no danger of that because there aren't any left. I've already rung old Foster at the Ruckshop – you know, outdoor pursuits – and tried bullying him. His grandson used to work there, but I haven't seen him for a while. Big boots and knives, just up Nathan's street. The pay's a joke, but no worse than anywhere else. No vacancies at your place, I suppose?'

Jenny shook her head. 'We're not even replacing Probert, our guillotine man. Just training up someone else.'

Sal sighed, but happily. 'Well, Mr Foster said his grandson's taken the whole summer off, so to send him for an interview next week.'

'Nathan's coming next week!'

'Yessy, yessy.' Sal hugged herself. 'On Saturday. Roll on Saturday.' She let her arms drop. 'I hope it works out. I might be screaming at him by Sunday.'

'Nonsense.' Jenny spoke emphatically, though she remembered that Nathan had not always been easy. At primary school he was labelled hyperactive. Abercwm Comprehensive called him bright but wild.

'Yes. Nonsense.' Sal smacked her knee. 'Nonsense, nonsense. Right.' She looked up. 'Got that out the way. Now your turn. So. You've been ravishing plumbers.'

Jenny sat back. Frowned the flippancy away. 'I didn't ravish anyone. Or perhaps I did. God, I don't know.' She ordered her thoughts. 'I don't know what happened. I've been getting these extraordinary sensations. Waves of cold prickles, starting at the back of my thighs, going right up to my neck. Like an enormous shiver, except I'm not cold.'

'Wow. Sounds like your hackles rising.'

Jenny considered. It was an excellent description. 'Why should my hackles be rising?'

'I don't know. Adrenalin, isn't it? Is that what started this with Gareth?'

'I think so. It happened while I was watching him. At the time I didn't feel it as sexual. But then . . . suddenly it was . . . and he must have sensed it . . .'

'Takes two to tango.'

'Just for a moment, it really seemed what I wanted to do. But when we'd done it I knew it wasn't, that I'd lost control. I felt so panicky. That's why I rang you.'

'It's done,' said Sal. 'No point regretting it. You can't undo it.'

'He seemed horribly practised. He carries condoms around with him. He used one. Perhaps he forgot I'm sterilized.'

'Bloody hell,' said Sal. 'You pounce on a man for sex and then complain when he gives you a good, safe time.'

'I shouldn't have done it.'

'Agreed. End of story. It is the end, I presume?'

'Oh, God, yes.'

'You did actually make that plain?'

'I think so. Yes. Definitely. He said it was no big deal. I remember that.'

'OK. So no harm done.'

'Except I feel shocked. And guilty.' Jenny gave an embarrassed laugh. 'Well, actually I don't, but I feel I should. Because of Siân.'

'I wouldn't worry about Siân. The woman's an idiot.'

'She isn't. She just doesn't listen.'

'There you are, then. No danger of her finding out. There

wouldn't be anyway. Gareth's not stupid. And it sounds like you're not the first.'

'Yes,' said Jenny. 'Amazing, that. I'd never have thought . . .'

'You're so naïve. They're at it all the time.'

'Michael wasn't. I know he wasn't. And I bet Phil wasn't either.'

'OK, some of them are at it all the time. Gareth's a boyo. A sweetie, but still a boyo.'

'He's got kids,' said Jenny. 'Four of them.'

'No wonder he uses condoms,' said Sal. 'But what have kids got to do with it?'

Jenny sighed. 'Well, nothing, I suppose.'

Sal reached forward and patted her knee. 'Maybe you should try to look at this positively. Life force stirring. Hormones on the move. Something like that.'

'What would Michael think?' Jenny's eyes filled with tears.

'If Michael was alive,' said Sal, 'he'd say to Gareth, "You bugger, what are you doing, screwing my wife?" But since he's dead, it's really none of his business, is it?'

'Oh, hell.' Jenny blotted her eyes with the ball of her hand.

'For God's sake, Jen,' said Sal. 'He *liked* Gareth. They were best mates. And he loved you. Why the hell should he mind?'

Jenny nodded. 'You're right. In fact, I know he wouldn't. He wasn't jealous.' She tried to smile. 'It was really hard to make him jealous. But it doesn't stop me minding.'

'Well, channel it, channel it. And . . .' Sal jumped up and leant across a large cluttered table in front of the window. 'I have just the thing.' She picked up a thick, glossy brochure and tossed it into Jenny's lap.

Jenny stared at it. 'What's this?'

'Not bedtime reading, anyway,' said Sal, sitting down again. 'It'll give you nightmares. It's British Coal's evidence. In support of the opencast. If you're coming to life at last, get stuck in there. The inquiry's in two months. I'm going to give evidence.'

22

'You're kidding.' Jenny opened the brochure and flicked over a couple of pages.

'Look at page one,' said Sal. 'Go on, frighten yourself.'

Jenny turned to page one. She knew what an opencast was. Or thought she did. There were several small workings down the Brynteg Valley: wide, shallow, layered holes where near-surface coal was being removed. But after a minute she lifted her head. 'I can't understand a word.'

'Nonsense,' said Sal. 'That's what they're counting on. Here . . .' She got up and moved to the arm of Jenny's chair. 'You just need a few key words translating. Blaen Dyar is the mountain behind you. I know you think it's Gwern Hill, but it isn't, because British Coal have decided it isn't. I think they're hoping it'll slow objectors down, not instantly recognizing the name. Then the word "void" means "hole". The hole, or rather holes, they're going to dig. There'll be two of them. "Overburden" is the pile of earth they dig out of the hole. The spoil.'

'I thought they dug coal out of the hole?'

'A common misapprehension. No, it's mountain they dig out.'

'But . . .'

'Oh, all right. There is some coal. Obviously. Every so often they hit a seam. Imagine it like a multi-layered cake. What they're after are the thin layers of icing. But most of what they dig out is cake. So to speak. They store it in piles to put back later. Seventeen years later, in this case.'

'Seventeen years!'

'It's a biggie, this one. Look at the land area. They give it in hectares, so you can't visualize it. But it's really two square miles. That's one mile by two, Jenny.'

Jenny read down the page. 'My God. Is this a misprint?' She pointed. 'A hundred metres deep. Can that be right? That's more than three hundred feet.'

'Told you. You should have been at the open meetings. They're planning to hollow out the mountain.'

Jenny lifted her eyes from the page. 'I live at eight hundred feet. The mountain's top's only just over a thousand feet. That means . . .'

Sal grinned. 'That if you were a very fit mole, you could tunnel *down* to it from your house. Scary, huh?'

'Unbelievable.' It seemed completely outrageous. 'Are people actually allowed to remove the tops of mountains?'

'Well, people aren't,' said Sal. 'But British Coal are. As you know, they have a God-like status in these parts. Or, at least, they think they have. If it's black and it burns it's theirs.'

'What did people say at the open meetings?' asked Jenny. 'No one wants it, surely?'

'You're bloody right they don't. Specially the ex-deep-mine colliers. Very bitter. They think opencasting's all about revenge and spite. God's against it too – or at least the Rector was. I swear his speech scanned.' Sal put on her strongest, most rolling Valleys' accent. ' "Blackest, blackest rape", he called it. I was just about to say the same. Well, similar. That it was all about man's insatiable desire to ram powerful machines into large black holes. The farmers are up in arms too because of the grazing disappearing, and because they're afraid the water courses will alter or be fouled. And everyone else is pissed off with the thought of coal dust giving us asthma, and ten hours six days a week of filthy lorries going up and down the main road. Not to mention nearby houses falling down with the blasting. You don't get any compensation, you know, for living next to an opencast. Not unless your house is shaken to pieces. If you need to move, and can't sell up, it's just tough. I asked one of the smarmy young British Coal men whether they'd like to live on top of an opencast, and he went stiff-faced and said he wouldn't mind at all. Lying bastard. That's what galls me, the fact that they won't give an inch. Won't admit any downside at all. I can guess where he lives – in some plush executive box in the Vale of Glam. Toads.'

'I suppose they think they've got a chance because the land's scruffy,' said Jenny. The huge plateau top of Gwern Hill had been opencasted during the war, after which it had simply been left to green over. Most had, quite successfully, though a little hadn't. She frowned, thinking about this. It was puzzling. 'Explain something to me,' she said. 'If Gwern Hill has been opencasted before, how come they can do it again?'

'They go much deeper now. They just scratched the surface last time.'

'Jesus.' Jenny sighed. 'There are ponds up there, aren't there? Bilberry fields. Acres of heather. And the marshes. It sound terribly destructive.'

'All for the chop,' said Sal. 'Except the marshes. I've a feeling they're planning to store them to replace later. In plastic bags, I think.'

'You're joking. In bags? For seventeen years?'

Sal considered. 'Doesn't sound very likely, does it? Perhaps I misheard. No, I don't think I did.' She shrugged. 'Honestly, they just say what they like. Nobody can realistically hold them to anything.' She leant back. 'Destructive, mmm.' She tapped her lower lip. 'You know, when Phil was here the only things he'd do in the garden were destructive things. Breaking up the ground, hacking hedges back, attacking clumps of nettles. He never planted anything, and he'd never housekeep, you know, weed or mow.'

'Michael quite liked weeding.' Jenny felt impelled, as usual, to spike Sal's more sweeping anti-male arguments. The impulse used to feel self-protective. These days, it felt as if it somehow protected Michael, too.

Sal continued as if Jenny hadn't spoken. 'And what he really liked was cutting down trees. Remember those two by the side wall? They *had* to come down, so he didn't need to feel guilty

25

about it. He loved that. Ropes and axes and saws. Half the men in the street queued up to help.'

'I suppose Alex used to dig holes in the garden,' Jenny said, making a small concession. 'When he was little.' She thought back. 'Well, sort of *wear* holes. With little cars. He'd sit in the dirt for hours, making brrmm brrmm noises. The bottom of the garden ended up like a moonscape.'

'That's interesting. You're saying opencasting is a kind of infantilism. Mmm.'

Jenny laughed. So did Sal. Jenny closed the brochure. 'Even if I read this, it's a bit late now, isn't it?'

'Of course it isn't. There's still the inquiry.'

Jenny shook her head firmly. 'I couldn't cope with that. An open meeting is one thing. I'm not speaking at an inquiry.'

'Why the hell not?'

'All the people . . . it'd be terrifying.'

'Chicken. I'm going to. Come on, they need local objectors. Otherwise it'll just be the county council and big groups like Friends of the Earth. They need little people.'

'I don't know anything.'

Sal slapped the brochure. 'That's why you've got to read this. Anyway, you know you don't want it, don't you? They're going to fence off that land for seventeen years, for Christ's sake. Two square miles of it. The whole of the mountain top. An area that's now common land. Blast out two bloody great holes and create two bloody great heaps of spoil. What more d'you want?'

'But that must be true for all opencasts, and it doesn't stop them happening. What's the point?'

'Not all opencasts are at a thousand feet, right on top of a mountain. Not all are so vast. And take a look at the map on page three when you get home. Part of it's in the National Park.'

'Is it?' said Jenny. 'Christ, it would be, wouldn't it? The boundary cuts across the hill. And you can see everywhere from up there. The Black Mountains, even Herefordshire, on a clear day. That means that they'll be able to see the opencast.'

'That's my girl. See, you have got something to say. You're a resident, so you know.'

'Actually,' Jenny said guiltily, 'I haven't been right up to the top for ages.' It was an hour's steep slog from her cottage. She tended, on walks, to go round, not up, the mountain. She brightened. 'Though Alex has. The boys used to ride their mountain bikes up there.'

'Nobody'll be riding anything up there for a whole generation if British Coal get their way. And afterwards no one will want to. You know what their restored land looks like. Glorified motorway verge. Gullied prairie. You think about it.' She tapped the brochure. 'Show that to Alex, too. Be good to get some kids to object.'

'OK,' said Jenny, though she couldn't imagine Alex getting involved. Or any of his friends. They were all either too innocent, too cynical or too fatalistic. These days commitment – even enthusiasm – seemed to be out of fashion.

Jenny left through the front door, the British Coal brochure tucked under her arm. Outside, the July evening air was cool and clear. The sun had set, but it was still barely dusk.

Within seconds whatever had relaxed within her in Sal's presence started to recurl and tighten. Walking the fifty yards to her car her heart began to thud, as it sometimes did, for no good reason. Since Michael's death she had grown used to experiencing the physical symptoms of alarm, without actually feeling alarmed.

She neared the Polo. On the opposite side of the road a man was sitting in a parked white van, studying something on his lap. She stopped at the door of the Polo, staring across at him, and felt a cold prickling shiver start at the back of her thighs.

Her senses seemed to become abnormally acute. She bent to insert the key in the door, and was aware of the weight of her breasts, pressing against the material of her brassière. The man had short fair hair. She couldn't make out his face. Or his age. Between twenty and forty. A man, going somewhere, on his own, in a small white van. The shiver reached her buttocks and lower back. She climbed into the Polo, closed the door, and rested her hands on the steering wheel.

Across the road the man's head lifted. He was young, thirty-ish. He started the van's engine and pulled out into the carriage-way. Jenny watched the van drive down the road, getting smaller and less significant, until red brake lights winked at her, as it disappeared into a distant right turn.

The shiver had reached her shoulders and neck. She waited till the sensation faded, then bit her lip, and twisted her own ignition key.

Chapter 3

Late Monday morning, in one of the small offices above the barn-length ground floor of Treherbert & Sons, printers of Abercwm and Hereford, Jenny was supervising Karen, an ex-machine worker who had recently been promoted upstairs. Karen was twenty-one, looked sixteen, and wanted so much to please and succeed that her posture in front of her computer monitor resembled that of a robotic mannekin, her body angular and rigid with anxiety. Twice this morning Jenny had had to suppress a powerful impulse to grasp her thin shoulders, push them down six inches, and shake the girl into relaxation.

Karen was laying out a wedding invitation on the screen.

'That's fine,' said Jenny. She pointed with a pencil to the middle line of text. 'But give the names of the bride and groom separate lines. After "their daughter", move down and centre to "Julia". And after "to" put "Mr Charles Bottomley", centred, on his own line.'

While Karen adjusted the layout Jenny picked up a magnifying glass and inspected a letterhead she had been handed an hour ago. A home-produced effort. Through the magnifying glass a fuzziness around the letter A was clearly apparent. Bubblejet printed, she guessed. Definitely not laser.

'I think we'll re-do this,' she said aloud. 'The client hoped

29

it could just be photographed, but I don't think so. I'm sure we've got an almost identical font.'

'Is this right?' Karen asked. Her eyes stared at the screen as if hypnotized.

Jenny put the letterhead to one side and checked the screen. 'Yes. Fine. Well done. Relax, Karen. Blink.'

Karen laughed, blinked and looked away from the screen.

'You'll get terrible headaches if you stare at it like that,' said Jenny. 'Move back a bit. Loosen up. Don't let it mesmerize you.'

Behind them the door of the office opened. Jenny glanced over her shoulder. 'Hi, Frank. Just a tick. Save it now,' she said to Karen.

Frank Meredith, the manager of the Abercwm office, entered the room. He stood, watching, behind the two women. A tall, brown-suited man in his late forties, not overweight, but heavy-limbed. He held himself diffidently, as if his height and size were a matter of permanent minor embarrassment to him. His features were not handsome – his forehead was too high and his lips too thin – but neither was he ugly. He and Jenny usually had lunch together at a local pub.

Jenny watched Karen at the keys, then nodded, and stood up.

'There. Wasn't so bad, was it?' She reached for her cardigan.

Karen gave a smile of triumph and shook her head. She would have spoken if Frank hadn't been standing behind them.

'Right,' Jenny said, turning to Frank. 'I'm with you.'

Frank leant forward and said, 'Well done,' to Karen. It was a simple, if formally delivered, congratulation. Karen responded with a look of mute terror. Frank tried to help Jenny with her cardigan, but while he was working out which bits of material to grasp, she managed it herself. He held open the office door for her instead.

Jenny rattled down the narrow wooden stairway, which

smelt strongly of paper dust and print solvent. Frank's slower tread followed her. She pushed open the heavy fire door at the foot of the stairs and felt her hearing batten down against the machine noise. She walked quickly along the tiled length of the print floor, past the rhythmically pounding Heidelburg printers, battleship grey and as tall as a man, then past the unattended mangle-like guillotine, which was switched off while Marston, the new operator, was at lunch. Along the walls on either side of the room were huge open wooden shelves bearing stacked parcels of virgin paper, the raw material of the business. Paper of different weights, colours, sizes, qualities and constitutions. On the left-hand side of the room, below the shelves, was a forty-foot worktable on which stood the finished products: piles of invitation and business cards, newsletters, menus, letterheads, posters, compliment slips. Some piles waiting for their brown-paper wrapping, some already sealed, a sample copy of their contents glued to the top of the parcel.

Beyond the guillotine Jenny glanced at a near-empty shelf to her right.

'We need more recycled,' she called back to Frank.

'What?' He increased his pace.

She waited until they were at the door. 'More recycled.'

Frank nodded. 'It's on order.'

They were outside. They walked down a short paved alleyway into a narrow cul-de-sac backstreet. An untidy, workshop backstreet housing a number of small businesses. To the right of the printers was a panel beater's barn; to the left, a photographer's studio.

Frank moved round Jenny so that, as they walked down the street, he was between her and the road. He always took this outer, kerbside position. Michael had said that it was to protect her against lions. 'He can't help it,' he'd said. 'It's completely ingrained.' Jenny had laughed – Frank was so far removed from her image of primitive man that the idea seemed ludicrous. Yet

31

in essence – in the recognition that internalized in Frank's psyche was a dated chivalry towards women, acquired, presumably, in his youth, which nothing could now shift – Michael was right. And in the observation that the strength and rootedness of this attitude was beyond Jenny's comprehension. Although Frank was only ten years older than Jenny, their differences were generational. Frank was a graduate of the fifties: a small-town, apprenticeship-based fifties at that. Jenny was a child of the sixties: a city-based, cosmopolitan sixties. Frank had never hitch-hiked anywhere. Never dropped a tab of anything stronger than aspirin. Never attended a pop festival. Never worn loon pants or flares. Never, indeed, Jenny had been astonished to discover, even worn jeans. He had been a teenager before teenagers had been invented. Before rebellion was permitted. He'd inherited, unquestioningly, what must have been his parents' outlook on the world: a natural courtesy to inferiors, deference to superiors, and respectful acceptance of the established order. Frank liked her, Jenny knew, without either really knowing or understanding her. Each protected the other; Frank protected her because the protection of women was, as Michael had perceived, insepar-able from his relationship with them, and Jenny protected Frank from her past – unexceptional though this was – because she knew he was shockable.

At the pub Frank ordered a beef roll and lemon squash; Jenny also had the beef, but with a glass of dry cider. They carried their drinks and plates out the back to a small, high-walled beer garden. There were three picnic tables on the grass, none occupied. Jenny sat down. Frank did the same, folding himself carefully into the bench seat opposite her. He placed his knife and paper napkin neatly to the right of his plate. He would take three times as long to eat his roll as Jenny: cutting it into finger-food chunks with the knife, wiping his fingers and mouth with the napkin after each mouthful.

'How is Karen coming along?' he asked, lifting the knife and inspecting the roll. 'Did you make progress this morning?'

Jenny took a long draught of cider. She was always thirsty after working. The air of the upstairs offices, she guessed, despite the heavy fire doors, must carry invisible paper dust. She said, 'Ah,' appreciatively, and put the glass down. 'Not bad, actually, except she's so nervous. Lacks confidence. But an excellent keyboarder. I'm trying not to overload her. She's very keen. I'm sure she'll be fine.'

Frank started to cut his roll into four. He put the knife down and gazed at her ruefully. 'You're very good with these youngsters, aren't you? They seem to loosen up with you.' He picked up one of the beef roll quarters.

Jenny picked up her own roll. 'I wouldn't have called Karen loose this morning.' She knew what Frank meant, though. She shrugged. 'I've got a child that age. And you're too polite. You alarm them. Anyway . . .' She smiled. '. . . I'm not the boss.' She bit a hunk out of the roll and chewed. She wondered if Frank knew that some of the younger staff made jokes about him. Not cruel jokes, because he wasn't disliked, but jokes nonetheless. They mocked his courtesy, which to them seemed laboured, old-fashioned and hilarious. They mocked his fastidiousness. She had actually witnessed Barry, one of the two youths on the shop floor, doing his Frank-nibbling-a-biscuit impression. It was well observed; even she'd smiled. And they mocked him as unworldly because he was unmarried and lived with his widowed mother.

Frank took a bite out of his beef roll quarter. Jenny looked away. She didn't like watching him eat. He chewed too long, with his thin lips too neatly closed.

She lifted her gaze above the beer-garden wall, above the low slate roofs of the nearby houses, to the massive acorn-shape of the mountain known as Southern Hill, high and close enough to be visible from most of Abercwm. The lower slopes were steep and dark with dense woodland, the smooth rounded moor-

33

land summit rising in an almost perfect pale parabola from the trees. Beyond this hill, invisible from Abercwm, was the plateau range that included Gwern Hill. Or Blaen Dyar, as she would have to start calling it.

She nodded towards the view. 'I think I'll take a look at the Blaen Dyar area after work.'

Frank finished his mouthful. 'Where?'

Jenny gestured. 'Up there. Behind the mountain. Where they're planning the opencast.'

'Ah, yes.' Frank became alert. 'We've had leaflets in about that. From Friends of the Earth. And posters from an Action Committee.' He gazed up at the hill. 'So it's going to be up there, is it?'

'Frank.' Jenny smiled at him. 'There's been talk about this for months.'

'Has there? Yes, I suppose I have seen articles in the *Gazette*.' He shook his head. 'I'm not very familiar with that area, I'm afraid. Mother and I don't tend to go that way on our Sunday drives, you know.'

'Yes,' Jenny sighed. 'I don't suppose you're unusual, either.' This was because of Gwern Hill's south-westerly location, on the very edge of industrial Valleys' Wales. People rarely drove south-west, purely for recreation. They drove north, into the Black Mountains, north-west, to the Brecon Beacons, north-east, to Golden Valley and Hereford, or east, to the Forest of Dean. Jenny's hairdresser, a woman in her late twenties, claimed never to have set foot in Brynteg, despite it being less than eight miles away. The Valleys' world was a different, higher, colder, poorer world. Brynteg residents came down to Abercwm for the market and the shops. Or for days out. Abercwm folk didn't visit Brynteg, or the Valley towns beyond, for days out. When – if – they went, they went for a clear purpose: to visit relatives who still lived there, to tramp wind-blasted scrapyards in gumboots for cheap car parts or to rummage in bargain factory shops on trading estates. School parties visited industrial heritage sites and descended abandoned coal mines. Their parents, by and large, preferred not to. The scenery in much of the Valleys was green and attractive – even spectacular, in places. Located elsewhere, it would have been appreciated, even treasured. Here, though, it was handicapped by being surrounded by, and in competition with, even more green and spectacular land.

'Though the lake's up there,' Jenny remembered. 'Gwern Lake. That'd be just outside the opencast fence. And people do go up there with model boats, don't they? And to walk. But that's about as far as they get. You should try it, though, Frank. The views are terrific.'

'And the opencast is going to be where, exactly?'

'From about a mile above my village to Gwern Lake. On the mountain top between. A vast triangle, really. All the land that was opencasted before, plus quite a lot more. I must go up myself, to get the feel of the place. Sal wants me to speak at the public inquiry.'

'Does she.'

Jenny smiled down at her plate. She knew Frank disliked mention of her friendship with Sal. The Jenny he liked to imagine her as – the vulnerable, feminine, possibly fawn-like Jenny, who needed protection from lions – wouldn't have a friend like Sal. A friend who was loud and assertive. A woman who made no effort to be ladylike. In Jenny's eyes, Sal was beautiful precisely because of this, and because her efforts were in other, more worthwhile, directions; but Frank, she knew, merely saw a dumpy, sharp-tongued woman. He would have been even more disapproving if he had known that Sal was lesbian, but Jenny had deliberately protected him from this fact.

'I don't think I will, mind you,' she said.

'I'm sure you don't need that sort of stress,' Frank said.

Jenny mentally added on 'so soon after Michael's death', and said, 'Actually I've been feeling better recently. Much more

35

energetic.' A picture of Gareth, naked, flashed into her mind. She pushed it away. Sweat dampened her armpits. Frank would be appalled, horrified, if he knew. She took a small breath. 'More outward-looking, I think.'

Frank folded his arms on the wooden slats in front of him and leant towards her. 'Come to dinner then. With Mother and myself. At home. Wednesday week. It's my fiftieth birthday.'

'Oh, Frank,' said Jenny, smiling. 'Is it really?'

Frank looked regretful. 'Afraid so. Will you come? Mother'd love to meet you again.'

Jenny remembered liking Frank's mother on the two occasions they'd met. Or admiring her, rather. She remembered a tall large-boned woman with – unlike Frank – an athlete's graceful bearing. A woman who gave no sign of being dependent, either emotionally or practically, on her son. Though their last meeting had been several years ago. She must be nearly eighty now.

Jenny stared at Frank, and then said, 'What a nice idea. I'd love to.'

Frank's face lit up with delight. Just for a moment he looked handsome. He grasped her hand, pressed it to the table top, and released it. 'Wonderful,' he said. 'Wonderful.'

Chapter 4

After work Jenny drove to her bank to use the cash machine. She parked on double yellow lines outside the brown dressed-stone building and, as she climbed back into the car with the money, caught sight of a familiar male figure further up the busy street. Gareth. He was walking towards her, one hand tucked in the pocket of his zip-up jacket the other tapping a rolled magazine against his thigh. His lips were pursed in a whistle. He hadn't seen her. She started the Polo's engine, half urging their gazes to meet, half frightened that they would, awkwardly, revealing their friendship as spoiled.

He was very close now. She saw his gaze fall on the car. His lips widened to a smile. Without slowing his pace he veered across the pavement, ducked his head to the open car window, and grinned, 'Hiya, lovely.' And then was gone.

She sat for a moment, the words, 'Hi, Gareth,' a whisper in her throat. Weak with thankfulness. The encounter had been entirely normal. She slipped the car into gear. Had Gareth, she wondered, been at all anxious about meeting her? She saw his grin again and how it had sprung to his lips, unforced, with no hint of self-consciousness, and was sure he hadn't. She felt lucky, undeservedly lucky, as well as relieved.

She drove out of Abercwm and a mile from the town left

37

the main road at a junction signposted to Gwern Lake. She crossed a humpbacked canal bridge into a straggling centreless village, and, as the land rose, the scattered houses gave way to dense broadleaved woodland. She had to negotiate three steep, dark, hairpin bends before breaking out of the trees on to a shrubby hillside. The last time she had driven this route – which normally she wouldn't, since there was a single-track lane directly from Pentre up to Blaen Dyar and the lake – had been several years ago, when she had taken Alex straight from shopping in Abercwm to cheer on the Milk Race, which used this twisting, killing incline as part of their Birmingham to Cardiff cycle run. She remembered standing on the roadside near the lake at the top as streams of police cars and laden escort vehicles cruised by, followed by the cyclists themselves, sweating peacocks in multicoloured Lycra, powering their machines up the one-in-six gradient. There had been a festive atmosphere, the police clearing the tarmac of on-coming traffic and pedestrians with hands clothed in animal glove puppets. A television helicopter had thwacked the air overhead.

Today, although the road was a wide, well-maintained B road, the carriageway was empty. She rattled across a cattle-grid on to the mountainside proper. To her left now was rising treeless moorland. To the right she looked down into a deep scooping valley, one of several that fringed the Blaen Dyar plateau, narrow tributary valleys of the wide Usk plain. The view gave her a thrill of pleasure. It was a pastoral valley studded with small stone-built farms, a cul-de-sac valley, one lane in, same lane out. This made it somehow charmingly private, an idyll which could be spied upon, as she was doing now, but not – except by invitation – entered.

She was skirting the rim of the valley bowl. On her left now, as she approached the plateau summit, Gwern Lake appeared, its diamond shape glittering in the late afternoon sunshine. A man-made lake, a quarter of a mile long and half as wide, originally dug in the peat to store ballast water for the quarrying cable trams that, more than a century ago, had ascended and descended the hillside. Now, with the old tram road courses scarcely discernible in the heather, Gwern Lake was just a surprising felicity; an unfenced, unsupervised, uncommercialized – save for a small gravelled car park – stretch of deep fresh water.

Jenny swung the car right at the very top of the hill, turning away from the lake, and on to a narrow single-track lane that ran, eventually, beyond a mile-wide plain of moorland, several disused quarries and the scattered ruins of cottages, down to her own valley, and the outskirts of Pentre. She was now in Blaen Dyar. This road, she knew from the map at the front of the brochure Sal had given her, constituted the northern limit of the opencast site. Everything to her left would be fenced off by British Coal. Everything to her right – a much smaller area, since the land fell within a few hundred yards into the scooped valley she had just half circled – would be spared.

A quarter of a mile on she parked on a long concrete platform at the side of the lane. This was actually the floor of a demolished shed, but was used as a lay-by. All around now was a man-made, worked landscape, though softened by nature over fifty years. Small spoil heaps from the last opencasting had been left to weather and green themselves as best they could. In this area heather and bilberry had taken hold and now flourished, the springy shrubs muting and rounding the contours of the land. The scene was unusual and not unattractive; children especially, in Jenny's experience, loved it, with its hillocks and craters, its secret hidey-holes, its sudden pools and bogs.

She climbed out of the car and locked the door. Six sheep grazing nearby immediately panicked and cantered away, their hoofs skittering on the tarmac. One was wearing last year's fleece like a loose cloak slung around its shoulders. Self-shearing sheep, Jenny's local farmer called them. They had long undocked tails too, unlike their fat lowland relatives.

The sun was still high. Although there was a stiff breeze Jenny decided she didn't need her jacket. She started walking away from the road, up a wide track so rough and stony it resembled a river bed more than a right of way. She had to watch her feet constantly over the boulders.

Fifty yards on she passed a white sign, stuck in the ground beside the track, which read 'Property of British Coal. No Vehicles'. A sign clearly ignored, since twenty yards on she came across a heap of builder's rubble, including some plastic sheeting, fly-tipped in a hollow to the side of the track. She stared grimly at the mess. The person who had done this was not just a mindless, despoiling vandal, she thought. He was – given the current battle over the future of the land – a traitor.

The horizon directly ahead – a wide bank of bilberry – was now very close. She puffed up the incline and stopped at the top. In front of her stretched a wild moorland world of bilberry, tussocky scrub grass and heather as far as the eye could see. No roads, no paths, bar the thinnest of sheep tracks and no obvious landmarks. Somewhere out there, she knew, hidden from view, were a couple of large, still ponds and numerous small pools.

She turned right, following a sheep track. After a few hundred yards the track met another and the merged path then dipped sharply at the same time as the land to her left rose. She was entering the floor of Black Cliff valley, a wound from the war-time workings that had never healed, a gash in the land flanked by a fifty-foot high spoil cliff; a cliff more than two hundred yards long, too steep and unstable, even after half a century, for nature to green.

She was in the wound now, the cliff itself to her left. The dark near-vertical face looked soft and crumbly. Alex had slid down it on his bottom, on to the dank bare soil of the valley floor, at the age of nine. Every child who had ever seen it had doubtless done likewise. Even Jenny had done it, at the age of twenty-nine. Once, up here with Alex in thick mist, she had witnessed a lone motorcyclist ascend the cliff. A feat that had seemed so impossible, and which had been achieved so absurdly quickly, that she had doubted, the instant the scream-ing noise had been cut off by the mist, that she had actually seen it. Alex had breathed, 'Wow,' and she had snapped, 'Idiot,' but had nonetheless felt herself uplifted, and knew that she was glad to have witnessed someone's astonishing private heroics, however illegal and foolhardy.

She turned and ran up the much lower bank to her right to look down the way she'd come, and out and across the Usk valley. The wind was sharp now, rather than merely stiff, but the visibility perfect. She swept her eyes in a semicircle from left to right, along the horizon: the Darren plateau, beyond and above Pentre, then the humped range of the Black Mountains, fjorded with steep farming valleys, then the Abercwm amphi-theatre peaks, and behind them, bluely, the hills of Hereford-shire. Far to the right, but in the foreground, were the slopes of Southern Hill. All was green, from the mint green of young moor grass to the black green of cloud shadow over bracken. And between where she stood now and the panorama of hills, was the fertile, rolling, Usk plain. She felt an echo of the aston-ishment she had felt twenty years ago, on coming to south-east Wales, and first seeing the landscape. The sense of outrage, almost, that she hadn't known about it. A secret that, for some reason, had been kept from her.

A hang-glider with a blue sail drifted into view around the shoulder of Southern Hill. Above the sail, on the same traject-ory, wheeled a large bird. It had jagged wing tips: a buzzard. Against a blue and white sky, a hang-glider and a buzzard, both exploiting the same thermal, were performing a small aerial formation dance.

It came to her that she was standing on land that – if British Coal won their case – would soon cease to exist. She looked down at the bilberry at her feet, trying to imagine the mountain hollowed out, and for a moment felt giddy, vertiginous. Like spotting, when swimming, a sea-bed far below, and feeling, just for a panicking instant, unsupported by the water. She had to adjust her stance on the bilberry carpet. Was she standing now over one of their voids? Over what would be a vast three-hundred-foot-deep hole?

The idea seemed, quite simply, impossible. Out of the question. Who had the right to demolish mountains? What arrogance to suppose that you could apply, with any hope of success, for permission to hollow out a mountain. Who had the authority, assuming you did have the arrogance, to grant that permission? How deep into a planet could the earth be owned? And how awesomely powerful must be the force that was capable of destroying, and consuming, a mountain . . .

She lifted her eyes from the ground and stared at the view. Had British Coal seen this? Properly seen it? The men who must have been up here, prospecting, digging their boreholes. Had they ever stopped and raised their eyes?

A pang of grief welled up inside her. Grief not for the land, but for her own loss. For Michael. A related emotion had triggered it. Acute pangs came less often these days, but with undiminished intensity. The emptiness within her would suddenly become so active, so tuggingly hollow, that she would feel, just for the duration of the pang, a danger of implosion. Her body had to fight against it. She waited, tensed, enduring the sensation, knowing it would pass.

It faded. The wind and the emotion had watered her eyes. She blinked, her body shivering in the evening chill, and set off quickly down the slope to the car.

Chapter 5

At home she had to leave the Polo outside on the lane; Alex's Escort was swung broadside across the cottage hard standing. There wasn't room for two cars unless they were tucked in extremely neatly. She parked in the small lay-by behind a bright red pick-up truck that didn't, she knew, belong to either of her neighbours. She viewed it suspiciously – it was an excessively large vehicle, with huge lorry-sized wheels, and had been driven not quite to the end of the lay-by, making parking behind it difficult. Parking places were limited in the narrow village lanes. This lay-by was reserved – not legally, but by tradition – for her own visitors and those of her immediate neighbours. Any vehicle left here longer than half a day, and certainly if it remained overnight, would have its ownership keenly investigated.

Entering the cottage garden she guessed the ownership of the pick-up solved: Alex was leaning against the door of his car, and below him a young man in jeans and a blue check shirt was squatting on his heels by the front wheel. The young man had his hands on the upper curve of the tyre and appeared to be trying to wrench it towards him.

'Hi, Mum.' Alex waved a beer can at her.

Jenny stopped. A huge black dog had appeared round the

43

front of the Escort and was padding towards her. A German Shepherd.

'It's OK. It's Sheba.' Alex tilted a thumb towards the squatting man. 'His dog. This is Mark.'

'Hello, Mark.' Cautiously Jenny held her hand out for the dog to sniff. The animal had a long, immensely thick coat. Not uniformly black, she now saw, but streaked dark brown and tan along its lower flanks. It resembled a bear more than a dog. Except for its eyes, which were liquid, oily-brown, and expressively canine.

'This is my mum,' said Alex to Mark.

'Hi, Alex's mum.' The young man turned his head and gave her a quick, preoccupied smile.

'Jenny.' She walked closer. The young man had short light-brown hair. 'Is that your lorry outside?'

'It's not a lorry,' Alex scoffed. 'It's a Hilux. Four by four. A pick-up.'

'Whatever,' said Jenny.

'It's mine.' Mark got up. 'Bearing gone there,' he said to Alex, 'as well as the bushes.'

'Shit,' said Alex.

'They do kits. No problem. Ta.' Mark received a beer can.

'You've only just had the car MOT'd,' Jenny complained.

'Cowboys, eh?' Mark grinned. The dog had gone to sit by him. His left hand rested on her shaggy head.

'Mark's going to do it,' said Alex. 'Bushes don't cost much, do they?'

'Nope.' Mark pulled the tab on his beer can and took a swig.

How old is he? Jenny wondered. Mid-twenties? Older? The sleeves of his check shirt were rolled to the elbow. His forearms were honey-coloured and muscular. He made Alex look very young and slight.

'I know you,' said Mark suddenly. He grinned, waving his beer can at her. 'I remember you, from way back. Used to live the other side, didn't you? At Kellow's place? On your own. Hey . . .' He gave a delighted laugh. 'You gave me a glass of water once.'

'Did I?' said Jenny, astonished. She had no memory of meeting this young man before.

'Ay. Used to be a hippie chick, didn't you?'

'A hippie chick?' echoed Alex.

Mark chuckled. 'Came down off the mountain. Ay, that's it. Long hair, you had. Not when I had the water. Before. Wore long dresses and kept all those herbs in your kitchen. The little kids were scared of you.'

'Oh no,' laughed Jenny. 'I never heard that.'

'Yeah, well, kids like to spook each other.'

'I don't remember long dresses,' said Alex.

'They went out,' said Jenny.

Mark smiled. 'And then you had your hair cut off.'

'That wasn't long before Michael and I moved here,' said Jenny. 'Only the year before.'

'No? Well, you'd had it cut when I got my water.'

Jenny tried to remember this young man visiting, and failed. 'How old were you?'

Mark shrugged. 'Fourteen, fifteen.' He nodded. 'Fifteen. Was with Wingnut and Damien. April time.'

'Why did I give you water?' So he wouldn't have looked like this. Ten years ago. Just a school kid.

'I asked for it. Me and me mates had a bet. Used to pass your place from the school bus.'

'Are you sure it was me?' said Jenny. Though perhaps she did remember something now, very vaguely. A blond boy, much fairer than the man in front of her now, interrupting their tea.

Mark nodded emphatically. 'Oh, ay. Prats, we were. I was dared to take something.'

Jenny blinked at him. 'And did you?'

Mark grinned. 'Just the water.' He turned to Alex. 'Hey,

45

must have been you there. Didn't make the connection. In the kitchen, eating your tea. Squinty-eyed runt.'

'Oi,' said Alex. Jenny laughed.

Mark touched his beer can against Alex's chest. 'You said . . .' He put on a babyish whine, '. . . "What does he want, Mam?" and your mam said, "A glass of water," and it sounded so dull I bottled out.'

Jenny laughed again. Her heart was fluttering in her chest. Though the feeling, unusually, was not unpleasant. She said, 'So you lost the dare. The bet.'

Mark hesitated. 'Suppose so. Must have.'

'You're shivering, Mum,' said Alex. 'Go inside.'

'Am I?' Jenny looked down at herself. 'God. Yes.' She lifted her arm. The hairs from her wrist to the cardigan cuff at her elbow were erect. 'I was up the top. Where they're planning the opencast. I must have got colder than I thought. I was taking a look at the views.'

'Ay,' said Mark. 'Gonna be up behind here, isn't it?'

'Yes,' said Jenny. 'Terrifying.'

Mark smiled but said nothing. Alex drained his beer.

They wanted to talk car repairs. Jenny moved back and said, 'Well, nice to meet you, Mark.'

'Ta-ra,' said Mark.

Inside, in the kitchen, she hung up her jacket. Then checked the kettle for water and switched it on. She propped herself against the work surface and pressed the flats of her fingers hard against her cheeks. The shiver still prickled her shoulders. She squashed her lips together, blowing steadily through them. In her mind's eye she still saw the young man. Almost microscopically, as if his image was etched on her retina. Blue eyes. Dark blue, the colour of his shirt. Chameleon eyes, perhaps, as some blue eyes were, that stole hues from outside. And humorous eyes; a thin line of skin below his lower lids had puckered when he smiled. Round his neck, just above the V of the open

shirt, but just below the small hollow at his throat, a thin gold
chain had curved . . .

She snatched her hands from her face and made an
impatient, derisory noise. The kettle had boiled; she concentrated on making her coffee. Sitting down at the table to drink
it she noticed a postcard, addressed to Alex. She lifted it up.
From Pete, in Brittany with his wife and their two children,
Alex's half brother and sister, aged ten and eight. Alex had
holidayed with them in the past, but this year – simply because
he felt himself too old for it – had declined.

She turned the card over and stared at a picture of a boulder-
strewn beach, white-flecked sea and cloudless sky. Yellow granite
sandwiched between blocks of blue; this time an unnatural,
unbelievable tropical blue. She was still staring at the card when
Alex came in.

'Why d'you leave the door open?' he complained. 'Thought
you were cold.'

'Oh.' Jenny looked up and refocused her eyes. 'Yes. Sorry.'
She raised the card. 'Regretting saying no, are you?'

Alex banged the door shut and said loftily, 'Of course not.'

'Mark's gone, has he?' Jenny put the card down.

'Yup.' Alex moved to the sink and started washing his hands.
He turned with sudden enthusiasm. 'And guess who rang just
before he turned up. Nathan! Sounded just the same. He's trying
for a job at the Ruckshop. Got an interview this afternoon.'

Jenny smiled. Sal had rung last night, sounding dreamily
happy. 'Yes. Sal's been pulling strings.'

'He's coming over later. And Lizzie. After tea. That's OK,
isn't it?'

Jenny shrugged. 'Fine. How's he getting home? Can he
drive?'

Alex dried his hands on a tea towel. 'Not sure. Don't think
so. He's coming on the bus. He could stay over, couldn't he?'

'It's your floor.' The cottage had a tiny third bedroom but

Alex's friends never used it. She pushed herself back in the chair. 'It must be years since he's seen Lizzie.' Nathan had visited Sal regularly over the years, so Alex had met up with him, but it had nearly always been in Abercwm.

'Four,' said Alex. 'And she says that the last time she saw him he had two black eyes. You remember . . . we'd gone into town and got smashed, and those boys jumped us at the chippie.'

'Don't remind me.'

'It wasn't our fault.'

'No. Well, being smashed was.' Nathan had so often been in trouble; though in truth it hadn't always been his fault. And boys were at their worst at fourteen. Infants on testosterone. And his parents had been breaking up.

'Wonder if he'll recognize Lizzie?' she said.

'Lizzie?' Alex was scornful. 'Course he will. She hasn't changed.'

'Oh, Alex,' laughed Jenny. 'She was thirteen.'

'So?' Alex looked mystified. Jenny wondered if he ever really looked at his best friend.

'Next Wednesday,' she said, suddenly remembering her own date with a friend. She rose and scrawled a note on the wall calendar. 'I'm having dinner with Frank.'

'You're kidding,' said Alex.

'Will you drive me, please? I'll get a taxi back.'

'Where to?'

'His house. It's his birthday. His mother'll be there too. They're giving me dinner.'

'Oh, wow,' said Alex. 'Dinner with the Frankfurter.'

'I'll take some wine, I think. Just in case.'

'You tell him to get a life.' Alex's tone was suddenly belligerent.

Jenny looked at him. 'Hey. Hey. What's this about?'

'Nothing.' Alex's lower lip jutted at her. 'Think he fancies you, do you?'

'Oh, Alex.' But she was touched. He was being loyal to Michael. Gently she said, 'I've no idea. I certainly don't fancy him. But I'm allowed to go out with whom I please. Frank's celebrating his fiftieth birthday. That's all there is to it.'

Alex sighed. He leant back against the sink and stroked the side of his beer can against his cheek. Then lowered it. 'I know. I think it's Nathan ringing. He asked about Michael. I said we were both OK but we missed him. I just said it like, as if, you know, it was no problem, but then afterwards I thought, last time I saw him Michael was here. And it kind of reminded me . . .'

'That's one of the hardest things, isn't it,' said Jenny. 'Speaking about it with someone for the first time . . .'

'Stupid,' said Alex.

'No, it isn't. But I'm allowed to go out with Frank without you insulting him.'

'Sorry.' Alex nodded. Then looked up and said, 'It's good that Nathan asked straight off, though, isn't it?'

'Very good,' agreed Jenny. 'Gets it over with.'

Alex pushed himself away from the sink, threw his can in the bin and peered at the clock on the cooker. 'Shit,' he said. 'I've been outside an hour. Gotta ring Lizzie.' He started for the door. He pulled it open and suddenly threw his head back and laughed, as if his spirits were completely restored. 'Hippie chick,' he chuckled. 'Shit, Mum . . . hippie chick.'

Chapter 6

'Y ou ought to paint this room black,' said Nathan, standing in the middle of Alex's rear-of-cottage bedroom. He reached up and tapped the low sloping ceiling. 'Look cool in black. Matt black.'

'And you'd be completely invisible,' Lizzie said, tucking her legs, clad in red and black striped leggings, up beside her on Alex's high brass bed. 'Apart from the triff waistcoat, of course.'

Alex grinned. He was sitting on the bed too, at the pillow end; he pulled his knees up so Lizzie could lean back against his shins. Nathan had turned into a remarkably black person. Black shirt, black jeans, black boots, even black leather fingerless gloves, the poser. His hair had always been black, of course, but Alex had never seen it so long and wild. Very little of his friend's face was visible behind the shaggy curls, and the little that was was shadowed with dark stubble. Though probably only a day's growth – Nathan's father Phil had had to shave twice daily, Alex remembered, to look smooth-chinned. The waistcoat Nathan was wearing, of dark red silk, just made the rest of him look blacker. And slighter. Alex had forgotten how skinny Nathan was.

Nathan turned on Lizzie accusingly. 'You used to be blonde. Long hair, down to your bum. Quite fancied you, I did, once.'

Lizzie laughed, flicked her head, and patted her thick auburn bob. 'Blonde's boring.'

Nathan and Alex exchanged pitying looks. Alex reached forward over his knees for the back of Lizzie's head and swept her hair up the nape of her neck. 'Blonde roots, see,' he said, flicking at her scalp. Lizzie said, 'Get off,' and pushed his hands away.

Nathan prowled the room. There were two wooden chairs, one in front of Alex's huge shallow-drawered school-master's desk, and another with its wheel-back to the window, but he showed no inclination to sit down. He pounced on a tin box on the floorboards at the end of the bedstead.

'Hey,' he said. 'Where d'you get this lot?' He carefully lifted out a brass-coloured dumb-bell.

'Used to be Michael's,' said Alex. 'From years back. When he played rugby.'

'Yeah?' Nathan put the weight down, rolled up his right shirt-sleeve to the shoulder, and picked it up again. He raised it to chin height, showing Lizzie his biceps. 'Impressive, huh?'

'Not bad,' said Lizzie. 'Not as big as Alex's.'

Alex leant forward, planted a smacking kiss on the crown of her head, and smirked at Nathan.

'I see,' said Nathan, nodding wisely. 'Like that, is it?'

'No,' said Lizzie, with an arch smile. 'It isn't.'

Alex smiled too, but avoiding Nathan's eyes. Nathan pumped the weight up and down. He broke the short silence by asking, 'So where's the action round here these days?'

'What action,' said Lizzie.

'Same as ever,' said Alex. 'Oh, 'cept there's a new pub in Ponty. Groups out the back at weekends. We usually go to Aber, though.'

'The Garden Bar's OK,' said Lizzie. 'You know, by the bus station. Or the King William.'

'I go away for four years,' Nathan groaned, lowering the weight back into the box, 'and evolution stops.'

'There's the Cockroach,' said Lizzie, sounding defensive. 'That's new.'

'The Cranefly,' explained Alex. 'Goes in for happy hours and cocktails. Where the old Grosmont used to be.'

'Sounds a rave,' said Nathan. 'Where d'you score? I mean . . .' He caught Alex's eye and grinned at the ambiguity. 'Blow, you know . . .'

Alex shrugged. 'King William?'

'He doesn't score,' said Lizzie.

'Because he's a sensible person,' said Nathan, nodding at her.

'Because he's tight,' said Lizzie.

'You don't either,' complained Alex, thumping a knee into her back.

'Because we're both sensible,' Lizzie agreed, and blew him a kiss over her shoulder.

'Want a spliff now?' Nathan finally sat down, in the chair by the desk. He dug in his waistcoat pocket.

Alex sat up straight, pushing Lizzie forward. 'Better close the door properly,' he said. 'And open the window.' The sound of the television downstairs seemed suddenly louder. 'Mum knows the smell.'

'Won't mind then, will she?' said Nathan.

Alex wasn't sure, but knew he didn't want to find out. He swung his legs off the bed and padded across the room in his socks to close the door. On his way to open the window he laughed.

'Mark called her a hippie chick.'

'Who's Mark?' Nathan was sticking cigarette papers together on the wooden desk top.

'Oh, play pool with him sometimes. Bloke in the pub.'

'Is he going to fix your car?' asked Lizzie.

'Yup.' Alex jumped back on the bed. 'He was up here earlier.'

He thought. 'He might know where to score dope, I suppose. He knows everyone.'

'Must meet him,' said Nathan. 'Sounds useful.'

'Mmm,' said Alex. Mark, it came to him uncomfortably, might not take such positive view of Nathan. To change the subject, he said, 'Did you get that job?'

Nathan nodded. 'Walkover. Only part-time, mind. Market days, Tuesday, Friday, Saturday. Suits me.'

'He didn't object to your hair?' asked Lizzie.

'Tied it back.' Nathan stopped what he was doing and used both hands to scrape his hair back into a pony tail. He tilted his head to one side and said in a high camp voice, 'Have a nice day, now, ugly dude trippers.'

Lizzie and Alex rocked against each other. Nathan was transformed to a nerdish, moonfaced, stubble-chinned adolescent. He had a surprisingly pudgy face, Alex thought, for someone otherwise so thin.

Nathan released his hair, which sprang back over his shoulders.

'I'd love to have hair like that,' sighed Lizzie. 'So wild.'

Nathan looked smugly at Alex, and lit up the joint. He dragged on it till it drew strongly, then held it in front of him and regarded it with narrowed eyes. 'Your mum looks different,' he said, as if something had reminded him of Jenny. He switched his gaze to Alex. His voice was tight, his lungs full of smoke. He exhaled. 'Good though. She all right now?'

Alex drew his knees towards his chest. 'Think so. Calmer. Sometimes she shivers, even though it's not cold. But she listens now. Less distracted.'

'I remember that,' said Lizzie. 'I'd say hi in the street and she wouldn't hear me. Or see me, even. Weird. She does now, though.'

'She's going to dinner with the Frankfurter next week,' said

Alex. 'So she must be feeling OK.' As explanation he added, 'He's a bloke she works with.'

'Why Frankfurter?' asked Nathan. He inhaled deeply and passed Lizzie the joint.

'Because he's long and boring and colourless and called Frank,' Alex said.

'Obvious,' said Nathan. 'And he fancies your mum, right? Does she fancy him?'

'Course not.'

'You hope.'

'I know.'

At midnight Alex left Nathan spreading a sleeping bag on the bedroom rug and walked Lizzie home down the steep village road. Her parents' house was a three-storey dressed-stone building, once a pub, too large and squarely built to be described as a cottage. The only lights on were the porch light and one of the front first-floor rooms, Gareth and Siân's bedroom. Just outside the low front gate Alex whispered, 'So what d'you think of Nathan, then?'

Lizzie laughed quietly, looking away from him, at the illuminated porch. 'I think he's a bullshitter.'

'Yeah.' Alex smiled to himself, pleased. Generously he said, 'OK, though, isn't he?'

'Quite hunky,' said Lizzie. 'Unusual looking.'

Alex frowned. He hadn't intended Lizzie to remark on Nathan's physical attractiveness. 'He didn't know you when he first saw you. Just for a minute. Funny that. My mum said he might not.'

'You don't notice things.'

'I do.'

'No, you don't. You're lazy. You see what you want to see.'

'D'you think I ought to paint my room black?'

'No, I don't. It's a stupid idea. Nobody paints rooms black any more.'

'Maybe they do in London.'

'Well, they do here, but only if they're fifteen. It's kids' stuff.'

'Mmm,' said Alex.

When he got back to the cottage Nathan was already bedded down on the floor.

'Nicked one of your pillows,' he said.

'Fine.' Alex switched off the main light, so the room was lit only by the bedside lamp. He kicked off his shoes and pulled at his T-shirt.

'What's with you and Lizzie, then?' asked Nathan. 'I didn't come with you, in case . . .'

'Me and Lizzie?' Alex snorted. 'Don't be stupid.'

'She got a boyfriend, then?'

Alex hesitated, wondering why Nathan wanted to know. He pulled his socks off and unbuttoned his jeans. 'All last term she fancied this boy from Brynteg. But he's gone to the States for the summer, and then he's off to uni. Everyone's pissing off.'

'Our turn next year.'

'Yeah. Hope I get in somewhere. How d'you think you did?' He climbed over Nathan on to the bedstead.

'Dunno. Got three Cs in my mocks.'

'I got a C and two Ds,' sighed Alex.

'Yeah, well, sciences are easier.'

'If you can do them.'

'True.'

'I'm going to Oz in the New Year,' said Alex, plumping up his one remaining pillow. 'If I've saved enough. Got two friends out there this year, and one of Dad's cousins lives in Perth. I really fancy surfing.'

'Your mum won't mind you going?'

Alex hadn't actually considered this. 'Hasn't said so.' No, it wasn't an issue. 'If I wasn't going, I'd be off to uni, wouldn't I? Same difference.' He reached out to the bedside lamp. 'I'm gonna turn this off, OK?'

'Yup,' said Nathan.

Alex switched the light off. The curtains were undrawn, but the sky outside was moonless and opaquely black. For a moment there was silence. Then Nathan's voice said, 'Michael died at the school, my mum said.'

'Yeah. Last week of term.'

'Were you there?'

'What d'you mean? I was in the building, yeah.'

'But not . . . I mean, you didn't . . . you know . . .'

Alex pressed his head back on the pillow. Then said, 'I was in French. I was taken to the headmaster's office. So I wouldn't hear anything from other kids, I suppose. The ambulance had already gone. Then Mr Barnes told me he was dead and took me down to Mum in Aber.'

'Shit.'

Nathan sounded genuinely shocked. Alex told himself that anyone would want to know details of disasters that happened to friends.

'Did you see him after?' Nathan asked.

'No,' said Alex.

'Not in the undertakers, you know, the chapel whatsit?'

'Mum did, but I didn't. I didn't want to. OK?'

'Hey,' said Nathan. 'Just asking.'

'Yes,' said Alex. After a moment he said, 'It's OK. I'd want to know too, I expect.'

'Never seen a dead body,' said Nathan.

'No,' said Alex. 'Well, me neither. Mum said that to begin with, at the hospital, he still looked like him. But that later he didn't. She said that that was OK. She's not religious or anything, but she said it was like something important had left him.'

'Wow.' Nathan sounded impressed; almost envious. 'Why didn't you want to see him?'

Alex stared up at the blackness. 'Don't know.' He was lying. Although he hadn't known at the time, he did now. He hadn't wanted to visit Michael, he had worked out, because he hadn't loved him. It would have been an act of fraudulence. He had his own father, a father who, despite his many faults – prime among them being that he was a deserter – he guessed he probably did love. A father whose dead body he could imagine wanting, or needing, or at least feeling he had the right, to visit. But not Michael, whom he'd liked, and trusted, but not, he knew now, loved. He no longer felt guilty about not loving him. Other people, he'd gradually realized, as he mediated between his mother and the concerned, unbereaved world, hadn't expected it of him.

He was not, however, going to share this with Nathan. 'I didn't need to,' he said. 'That's all.'

'Right,' said Nathan.

Chapter 7

August

Frank's house – or rather, Frank's mother's house – was a substantial detached house of a type common to the more affluent streets of Abercwm: walls of dark purplish dressed stone, large sash windows, and a slate roof edged with decorative barge-boarding. The style was reminiscent, Jenny always thought, of Victorian railway stations, or private nursery schools. The house lay in a quiet cherry-tree-lined avenue on the north side of town, only a field's length away from open farmland.

Mrs Meredith let her in. Frank's mother looked much as Jenny remembered her; a tall, once strong woman, now in her late seventies, with thick streaky-grey hair swept into a knot at the back of her head. Her eyes were watery, but still strikingly alert. She wore a grey silk dress, with fine folds of bodice gathered into a silver brooch at one shoulder. Seeing the dress, Jenny was glad that the coolness of the evening had prompted her to wear her dark green velvet blouse-and-skirt suit, rather than the less formal cotton dress she had been considering.

Frank emerged from the kitchen to greet her. 'Happy birthday,' she said. 'I've brought you this.' She lifted the wine bottle.

'How kind,' Mrs Meredith answered for him. She took

Jenny's jacket. 'You could open it now, Frank. Give it a little time.'

'I will, Mother.' Frank smiled benignly at both of them. 'What will you have now? Sherry?'

'That would be nice.'

'Lovely,' said Jenny.

Mrs Meredith led her through a dark panelled dining room into an airy wrought-iron conservatory with a marble floor. Tall brass tubs containing climbing plants stood to left and right of double garden doors. These were wide open; a pair of white wicker armchairs and a sofa faced the lawn.

'I remember this,' cried Jenny, looking up to admire the ceiling dome. 'Goodness, those are young grapes, aren't they?'

'A nightmare to maintain. So much of the glass has become brittle.' Mrs Meredith patted the cushions on the wicker sofa. 'Please, my dear.'

Jenny sat down. Through the open doorway she could see the garden: a large perfectly flat oval lawn, surrounded on three sides by wide beds of silver and green foliage. Only a few flowers, all white. The plants were meticulously ordered: large, shrubby perennials at the rear of the beds, in places completely shrouding the brick perimeter wall, sloping to low ground cover at the edge of the lawn. The overall effect was of a shallow, green, silver-and-white bordered bowl. Not a square inch of bare ground was visible.

'I'm so glad you felt able to come.' Mrs Meredith lowered herself stiffly into one of the chairs and, seeing the direction of Jenny's gaze, looked out herself across the close-mown grass. 'When my husband died, I took up gardening.' She turned back with a smile. 'Do you have a garden?'

'I do,' nodded Jenny. 'But nothing as . . .' she wanted to say 'organized', but the word seemed unflattering, '. . . elegant as this. The ground's very steep, and rather exposed. We're so high.'

59

'Gardens renew themselves,' said Mrs Meredith. 'And they reward you for what you put in.'

'And punish you if you neglect them,' smiled Jenny.

'But it's never too late, is it? And even a neglected garden is green, and alive.'

'Mother is a green person.' Frank joined them, bearing two brimming sherry glasses. 'Green and grey. There used to be roses all along the far wall.' He distributed the glasses before waving a hand at the furthest flower bed. 'But you had them removed, didn't you, Mother?'

'Your father liked them. I never did. They get too much disease. And they look so cruel in winter.'

Frank sat down in the other armchair and crossed his legs. Jenny averted her eyes – his legs were too long, and he crossed them in the way a skirted woman would, keeping his knees tight together and his shins parallel. She sipped her sherry, which tasted creamy and expensive. Dressed like this, in this strange, formal house, with these strange, formal people, she felt interestingly detached from reality. The occasion felt both inhibiting and liberating.

'Frank,' Mrs Meredith said, sitting up. 'Where's your sherry? Come on, dear, it's your birthday.'

Frank hesitated, smiling, and then said, 'Well, why not?' He rose, and left the conservatory.

Mrs Meredith leant toward Jenny. 'He's too strict with himself. Turning into a fuddy-duddy.' She shook her head. 'Maybe I've encouraged him to spend too much time with me.'

Jenny did not think, despite Mrs Meredith's words, that she was genuinely regretting anything. There was too much satisfaction in her voice. Mrs Meredith, Jenny decided, must have always wanted Frank to live with her. No son stayed with his mother nearly all his adult life without her approval, tacit or otherwise. And, apart from a few years in Birmingham in his late twenties, Frank, she knew, had always lived here. He, presumably, had been equally happy with the arrangement.

'Frank has told me,' Mrs Meredith went on, 'that you are against this opencast that's being planned. Up on the hill.'

'I think everybody is,' said Jenny. 'I've just caught up with it rather late.'

'I remember the workings there during the war.'

'Really?'

'Indeed. People in Abercwm had dust on their washing. Especially those on the south-west side.'

'Good heavens. Frank?' He was just returning with a sherry. 'D'you hear that? In the war the dust blew on to washing here from the opencast.'

'Of course,' said Mrs Meredith. 'Things were, doubtless, more lax then. It was mined under emergency measures. They evicted people from the land, farmers, villagers. Quite ruthlessly, I believe. The houses were demolished and the land dug up. They promised to restore the area and let the people back when the war was over, but I don't think it ever happened.'

'No,' said Jenny. 'It didn't.'

'I understand,' said Frank, 'that they've promised there'll be no dust this time. Techniques have improved, I'm sure.'

'Doubtless,' nodded Mrs Meredith.

'I don't know,' said Jenny. 'Apparently it's the dust you can't see that's dangerous, rather than the dust you can. I can't believe there won't be any. It's always windy up there, and the workings are going to be so huge. They say they'll spray with water, but how can they spray such a vast area?'

Neither Frank nor his mother responded. Jenny laughed. 'Sorry. Getting on my high horse.'

'And why not?' said Mrs Meredith. 'People should get involved. People should care.'

'Absolutely,' Frank agreed.

Ten minutes later they withdrew into the panelled dining

room to eat. Mrs Meredith sat at the head of the dining-table, Frank to her right, Jenny to her left. The main course was beef in a sweetish sauce – Jenny thought she detected a malty hint of treacle – garnished with watercress, and served with new potatoes and peas.

'Did you cook this?' she asked Frank. She was, she discovered, quite ravenous. She picked up her glass, which Mrs Meredith had filled with red wine.

'A joint effort,' said Frank. 'Mother started it off during the afternoon.'

'Well, cheers.' Jenny raised her glass. 'It's delicious.'

They toasted the excellence of the beef, and then Frank's birthday. Mrs Meredith refilled Frank and Jenny's glasses. Frank had only half drunk his sherry – the glass stood abandoned on the sideboard – but seemed to be enjoying the wine. When he had drained the second glass Mrs Meredith picked up the bottle again.

'You're trying to get me tiddly, Mother,' Frank said.

Mrs Meredith poured steadily. 'It's your birthday.' She had hardly touched her own wine.

'My mother,' said Frank to Jenny, 'can be a very controlling person.'

'I have your best interests at heart, my dear.'

'I wouldn't deny it. You see, Jenny, I live with a benign dictator.'

Mrs Meredith looked amused. Frank's face was flushed, as if he had been overly bold, but was proud of it.

'There,' said Mrs Meredith, 'he's become a little reckless, hasn't he? Isn't it an improvement?'

Jenny felt Mrs Meredith was showing off her son to her. Was she indeed a controlling person? Who, she suddenly wondered, had first suggested this dinner?

Frank took a forkful of potatoes and another swallow of wine. 'Of course, Mother was wild,' he confided, 'as a girl.'

'Wild?' said Mrs Meredith. 'I don't think so. Impulsive, yes.'

'She rode a horse to Lampeter once,' said Frank. 'Purely on a whim.'

'From where?' asked Jenny.

'From Cwmdu,' said Mrs Meredith. 'Where my parents lived.' She shrugged. 'I was missing my sister. She was married, I hadn't seen her for a year. So I climbed on my pony and rode to Lampeter.'

'How old were you?' Jenny asked, astonished.

'Oh, about fourteen. Old enough to be brave, and to follow a map, but young enough to be thoughtless. I didn't tell my parents, I'm afraid. We sent a telegram from Lampeter when I eventually got there. I was in trouble when I got home, not surprisingly.'

'That's amazing,' said Jenny. 'You can't imagine anyone doing that these days, can you? How long did it take you?'

'Two days. It's about fifty miles, I think. It was a different age, of course. Very few cars on the roads. I don't think I saw one. When it grew dark I simply stopped at a farmhouse and asked if I could graze the pony in their field. They agreed – not an unusual request in those days. I shared a bed with their daughter, in the farmhouse. At first light I rode on. Then I rested my pony for a week at my sister's before riding it back again.'

Jenny was touched by the story. Frank's face expressed pride and filial indulgence. Mrs Meredith started to collect the empty plates. Jenny wondered if Mrs Meredith was saying, see, we're not so stuffy, this family has its unconventional side too . . .

A familiar coldness started at the back of her thighs. She felt the shiver move upwards across her buttocks, prickling the skin of her lower back. She reached for her wine glass and rested her hand on the stem. She stared at Frank, who was helping his mother clear the dishes. Did Mrs Meredith want her to care for this man? His face was relaxed, the angles soft in the dim lighting. Not unhandsome. But bloodless. And old. She picked up her wine glass and sipped. Her shoulders were trembling. I am too young for him, she silently told Mrs Meredith. I'm moving away from death, not towards it.

But still, her diaphragm felt tight. She put the glass down carefully.

Frank carried the plates out of the room. Mrs Meredith said quietly, 'How old are you, my dear? If it's not an impertinence. I know you have a grown-up child.'

For a frightening moment Jenny thought she had spoken those inner words aloud, and Mrs Meredith had heard them. Then knew she hadn't. But how alarming.

'I'm thirty-nine,' she said. 'I was a little wild myself once. I had Alex when I was twenty. Three weeks before I was twenty-one.'

'And are you friends, you and your son?'

'I think so. Yes. I shall miss him terribly next year when he goes to college. He's been with me . . . well . . . all my adult life.'

'I'm sure,' said Mrs Meredith. 'But you have other friends, of course.'

'Oh, yes,' said Jenny. 'Of course.'

'You will have no reason to be lonely. Frank, you know, is very fond of you.'

Jenny murmured, 'Yes,' just as Frank returned. She pushed herself back in her chair.

Frank placed a glass bowl on the table containing fresh raspberries and balls of melon in a pale pink syrup.

'Mother's favourite,' he said. 'Does anyone want cream?'

Mrs Meredith declined. Jenny shook her head too. Frank served out.

Jenny normally liked both raspberries and melon, but found her appetite had disappeared. And the wine seemed to have given her palpitations. She forced a few of the fruits down.

After the dessert Mrs Meredith announced that she was retiring for the evening.

'That was delicious, dear,' she said to Frank. She tipped her head to include Jenny. 'But I think I shall go upstairs now. Will you excuse me?' She rose.

Frank started to protest but was silenced. 'And no coffee, I think.' Mrs Meredith extended her hand to Jenny. 'So nice, my dear, to have met you again.'

Jenny felt her hand firmly and coolly grasped. Frank escorted his mother to the door and kissed her goodnight. He walked back to the table, smiling.

'I think that was a tactful withdrawal. She doesn't usually retire till nearly ten.' He sat down in the chair Mrs Meredith had vacated, next to Jenny. She thought she had never seen him look so confident and relaxed.

He rested his elbows on the table and steepled his hands, touching his lips with his fingertips. Then took his hands away. 'I've been imagining you here for quite some time. Mother said she didn't think you'd come, so soon after . . . But I told her you would. I was right, wasn't I?'

Jenny frowned down at her empty fruit bowl. Had she misunderstood something? Frank seemed to be reading much more into her presence here than was, surely, justified. She suddenly imagined him naked. In this dark shiny polished formal room, naked. Then herself. Her shoulders shivered. Where did this feeling come from? Not from Frank. No. Her breasts had become hard inside her bra.

'I've come here because you asked me to,' she said steadily. 'Because it's your birthday. A special birthday.'

'Absolutely.' Frank sounded indulgent. 'May I kiss you?'

'A birthday kiss?'

'A birthday kiss.' He leant forward. Jenny kissed the pursed flesh of his lips quickly, laughed, and withdrew. Frank's hand now rested on the curved wooden back of her chair.

'Thank you,' he said, without moving away. He stared at her. 'You are beautiful, you know. So . . . fragile-faced. So feminine.'

Jenny tried another laugh. 'I think you've had too much wine.'

'Very possibly. Will you kiss me again?'

Jenny watched his face approach and almost recoiled. At the last minute she closed her eyes. His lips pressed against hers, more firmly than last time. Again it was she who pulled away.

'Are we going to have coffee?' she asked.

Frank jumped up. 'Of course.' He swept the fruit bowls away with euphoric energy.

Jenny waited until he had left the room and then wiped her lips with a napkin. Her throat ached. She felt as shaky as she had after having sex with Gareth. A wave of impatience swept over her. She muttered, 'Stupid, stupid, stupid,' to herself.

After five minutes Frank returned with a small, steaming coffee pot. She hated the way he was still smiling to himself. She rose, picking up her leather bag.

'I have to go to the bathroom.'

'Just off the hall,' said Frank. 'Shall I show you?'

'No,' said Jenny. 'I'll find it.'

The bathroom was large, with a pale cork floor and a gilt mirror above a blue-veined Armitage wash-basin. Jenny locked the door, turned to face the mirror, and started to undo the velvet buttons of her blouse. Her fingers were trembling and stiff, the material clingy and difficult. She could hear the hiss of her own breathing. She finally undid the last button, shrugged the blouse off and hung it from one of the basin taps. She undid her bra and let the straps fall down her shoulders. She stared at herself in the mirror. The skin of her breasts was flawless. Protected, hot-house skin. Yet the flesh beneath was so hard and active. Difficult to believe it wasn't muscle. She touched her nipples, first one, then the other, with the flat of her palm and watched the dark skin respond. That energy, that awesome energy, that Gareth had aroused in her – no, that she had aroused in herself, watching Gareth – was present again. Coiled

66

somewhere deep inside her. She could feel thin tendrils unwinding from it, insinuating themselves like fuses, into delicate, sensitive, arousable parts of herself. But this time she would remain unignited. Frank had not aroused her. And she did not want Frank. He had nothing to give her. That was unkind, but true.

And she was angry, she realized. Yes. Acknowledging it made tears spring to her eyes. She stuffed her bra into her handbag. She thought of walking back to Frank now, confronting and denying him. She stared swimmingly at herself. I am too beautiful for you, she told Frank. Too young, too alive. She touched her breasts again. The ache of unfocused desire was so powerful she had to close her eyes. She stepped back to steady herself. Oh, Michael, she thought, dear Michael. Surely, you would have wanted me now.

No. She opened her eyes. If she didn't collect herself, she would start to cry in earnest. She put on the velvet blouse again, buttoning it carefully. Smoothed the fabric over her breasts. Then used the lavatory and returned to the dining room.

'White or black?' Frank was standing with the coffee pot poised at the sideboard.

Jenny sat down. 'White.' She looked at him, and felt the energy within her subside. 'My taxi will arrive at ten.'

Frank glanced at a wall clock above the sideboard. 'We have half an hour, then,' he said.

He made no further advances to her, and paid her no more compliments. She felt, as they drank their coffee, that he was still basking in what had passed before. Her taxi arrived promptly. On her way out he kissed her again, but only on the cheek, a farewell embrace.

When she got home Alex and Nathan were in the kitchen, drinking tea, Alex sitting at the table, Nathan standing restlessly beside him.

'What're you doing here?' Jenny asked him.

'Picked him up after dropping you off,' said Alex. 'We've been watching a video.'

'Oh, yes?' Jenny hung up her jacket. 'Anything I'd like?'

'Doubt it. *Hellraiser.*'

'You're right. Pity. I could watch a video now.' Nathan was staring at her. Alarmed, she glanced quickly down at her blouse. The alarm died; the buttons were all safely secured.

'And how was the Frankfurter?' Alex lifted his tea mug.

'He was fifty.'

'Fifty? Hey, wow . . .' Alex smiled up at Nathan. 'That makes him more interesting, doesn't it? A fifty-year-old Frankfurter.'

Nathan grinned.

'Shut up,' Jenny said. 'I don't insult your friends. *And* you.' She stabbed a finger at Nathan.

Nathan dropped his eyes, but his grin widened.

'Who called one of my girlfriends a pernicious dwarf?' Alex enquired.

'Oh, yeah?' said Nathan. 'Who was that?'

'Someone called Leanne.' Jenny filled a tumbler with water at the sink. 'She wasn't his girlfriend. And I wasn't insulting her. She was pernicious.'

'She was, actually,' admitted Alex. 'She kept calling Lizzie over, because she knew we were friends. They had a fight at the bus shelter. She tried to ram Lizzie's head through the glass. The sixth-form girls stopped her.'

'The boys didn't do anything, of course.' Jenny pulled a savage face. 'Thought it was a tremendous laugh. Poor Lizzie.'

'I only went out with her once,' Alex told Nathan. 'It was all in her head.'

Jenny sipped at her glass of water and moved towards the door. 'I'm going to bed. You're staying over again, are you, Nathan?'

Nathan glanced at Alex, who said, 'Yeah. If that's OK.'

'Fine,' said Jenny.

She left the room. Nathan and Alex heard her footsteps ascending the stairs. Nathan said, 'She ever thought of having a toy boy?'

'Fuck off,' said Alex.

'Joke.' Nathan laughed. 'I got a thing about velvet.'

'Dunno why she dressed up for Frankfurter,' Alex said grumpily.

'Your friend Leanne.' Nathan pulled out a chair the other side of the table and sat down. 'That common, is it? I mean, girls fighting?'

'Na,' said Alex. 'Psycho, she was.'

'So what about the boys? You still have to be careful in Aber?'

Alex shrugged. 'Suppose so. Some boys you keep out the way of. The Brynteg lads are OK, 'cos they're watching their backs too. And you're careful who you chat up. You know.'

'You haven't been in any fights, then?'

'Nope.' Alex chuckled. 'Me and me mates, we run fast. No.' He shook his head, more seriously. 'Haven't had any trouble for a while. Why . . . you get fights in London?'

Nathan nodded. 'A few. Too many. I dunno.' He shrugged. 'It's just . . . there's two groups, you know, round our place. If you're not in one, you're in the other. Even if you're not, you know? A couple of blokes, they're mental. Get a few drinks inside them, all they want to do is smash faces.'

'Just as well you're down here, then.' Alex grinned.

'Mmm,' said Nathan.

Alex stared at him. 'Is that why you're here? Hey, is that . . .'

Nathan shook his head quickly. 'No. No. But . . . it's the reason Dad agreed. I got cautioned.'

'For what?'

'Carrying a knife.'

'Shit.'

'Everyone carries knives,' said Nathan carelessly. 'You say you're not going to, but then you got to. There's lunatics out there.'

'You ever pulled one?'

'Nope. No. I don't go looking for trouble.'

'You told your mum this?'

'You're joking. Don't you dare tell yours, either.'

'Course not.'

For a moment neither of them spoke. Nathan picked up his tea. Alex wondered if his own face was still expressing shock. Did all boys in London walk around carrying knives? Did Nathan think him naïve? An innocent? He knew boys here who owned knives – he had a couple of sheath knives himself – but no one who carried one. Or was Nathan exaggerating, to excuse his own behaviour?

'It's nothing, being cautioned,' Nathan said. 'It's just Dad, he went ape. He thinks I need some time out. To cool off, like.'

Alex made an effort to look relaxed. He leant back in his chair and locked his hands behind his head.

'But of course,' he said. 'You're cool already.'

'You got it.' Nathan's face split into a grin. 'Supercool.'

8th August

Darling Michael,

Since I last wrote to you I have had sex with Gareth. And, I have a horrid suspicion, encouraged Frank to fall in love with me. I'm sorry. Not for you. For myself.

Actually I'm not worried about Gareth; I've met him twice in the last three weeks and he's acting as if nothing has happened. The first time was outside the bank; he said 'Hiya' as he passed, and it could have been 'Boo'. No hint of undercurrent. The second time was just yesterday in Dixons, when he bent my ear about his boys' computer, which has broken down, and which he can't get anyone to mend. I found it almost impossible to believe, as he chattered on about colour chips and the catastrophic effect of Coca-Cola on keyboards, that he'd ever lain naked on top of me.

Did you know Gareth was a womanizer? He is, isn't he? It occurs to me now that perhaps you did. Men must have their secrets too. I suppose that's why he's so relaxed with me, because sex is just sex to him – nothing to take too seriously or suffer angst over. Of course, Gareth assumes women are strong and know exactly what they're doing. I doubt he'd admit that, but he does; when you're on the receiving end you can feel it. So he doesn't see himself as responsible for us. That must be why he's comfortable living with Siân, even though everyone else thinks she's a steamroller. Is this a South Walian trait? Because of generations of dominant Valleys' mams? I don't know. But it makes him unpatronizing. He knows we're different, and he wants to play around with us, but he looks us straight in the eye while he does it. Whatever his faults, that at least makes him attractive.

Which is more than can be said for Frank. Oh dear. Of course, he's a different sort of Welshman. So stuffily middle-class he could be English. I'm sure he has a horror of the Valleys, even though he's lived next door to them most of his life. Maybe precisely because of that. He doesn't want to see ugliness or poverty, or even industry, because at heart he's a snob.

After those two kisses at his birthday dinner I suddenly like him a lot less. You can probably tell. In fact I'm beginning to think that most of my liking for him over the years has been false. I've just enjoyed being liked by him, assuming he'd never act on it. Now he has, I'm forced to look at him and my feelings about him properly, instead of in that lazy, basking way, and I don't like what I find. In many ways he's exactly the opposite of Gareth. He's not physically attractive, which Gareth still is. Or at least fit, which – as you know – is for me so much of male beauty. Frank is not a physical man, never has been; I don't like to imagine him without his clothes. His long white body. Ugh. And he's old. But worst of all is his prideful, indulgent, condescending manner. He thinks he's being gentlemanly, but he's a generation out of date. Possibly two. Women are either up there on their pedestals, or down there, below his angle of view. Today at work he presented me with a bunch of flowers. Cornflowers. They looked so perfect they could have been plastic. Blue and white. I told him, very firmly, that he mustn't, but he simply didn't hear me. There's a frightening arrogance about that sort of deafness.

I suppose all this has come about because he can sense the tension in me. A tension I feel as sexual, though it may be more than that. Whatever, it is a great shiny compressed thing and it is rooted where I imagine my womb to be, and it's capable of exciting me sexually. Whatever it is, it is energy. I am not sleeping well at the moment and yet I'm not tired in the daytime. Sometimes I feel as if I'm waiting for something enormous to happen. I've just had a most curious thought: if this energy suddenly burst out of me, undirected, into sex, or opencast action, or anything at all, what would it look like?

Nathan has come back. Sal is ecstatic. He's staying all year, supposedly. I keep remembering what a handful he was as a kid. Sal says it's hard to get him to sit down even now. He looks wiry and impish. Stylish too, in a dark, quicksilver, Celtic way. Alex is seeing quite a lot of him.

I'm half-way through reading a 200-page brochure Sal gave me about the opencast. She's keen that I give evidence at the inquiry. She says that throwing myself into fighting British Coal will channel my energies. (I've told her about Gareth.) But I know I haven't got the courage.

All the same, I drove up to Blaen Dyar ten days ago and tried to imagine that I was standing on the glass top of a 300-foot hole. I nearly lost my balance. I've worked out that the 'voids', as they're called, would be deep enough to sink twenty of our cottages in, stacked one on top of each other. And after working that out, I keep seeing this image: a colossal void, filled to the brim with Welsh houses. Whole rows of terraces, piled in on each other. As if someone's lifted the end of a valley up and slid them in. Weird.

The views from up there are stupendous. It's easy to get blasé about views, living round here, but these are really special. By the end of my stroll I felt tremendously outraged and tearful. Have you ever thought that perhaps other humans don't see what we see? So arguing aesthetics with them is pointless? No, that's defeatist, they have eyes like ours. I want to show everybody what will be lost if the land is fenced off and destroyed. I think that's what I feel strongest about. But it's not something I could put into words.

You'd have given evidence, wouldn't you? The occasion wouldn't have daunted you at all. So sensible and rational and unneurotic. You and Sal would have ganged up on me.

Oh, Michael. The night I had dinner with Frank I longed for you. I longed for my body's arousal to be for you. I would have seduced you with it, I promise, I would have been irresistible.

I wish you hadn't died just when you did. I wish I had known – we had known – never to let omissions ride. That's what makes them problems. And that's how they stay, when people die on you while you're letting them ride.

Oh, shit. Forget it. I'm going to empty the washing machine.

Chapter 8

'I've been writing letters to Michael,' Jenny said, pouring tonic water into a tall ice-filled glass. It was Monday, and she and Sal were having an early evening drink in the riverbank garden of Abercwm's Castle Inn. Their table was just yards from the river's edge. In front was a picture postcard view of wide, winding river, the water so shallow in places that its surface rippled and eddied over river-bed stones. The day had started grey but was now a warm, still, hazy-sunned evening.

'I've told him about Gareth.' Jenny put the tonic bottle to one side. 'Do you think I'm mad?'

'No,' Sal said. 'Probably a great idea. Just don't leave anything lying around. Did it make you feel better?'

Jenny considered. 'I'm not sure. It slightly stirs things up.'

'Maybe they need stirring up.'

'Mmm.'

Sal looked at Jenny as if expecting her to elaborate. Jenny couldn't. She looked down.

'And I told him about Frank.'

'Oh, yes?' Sal laughed. 'I'd forgotten. How did the dinner *à trois* go?'

'He bought me flowers the next day. I think it was a bad idea.'

'Christ, Jen.' Sal's eyes became circles. 'You didn't seduce him too?'

'Don't be ridiculous.' Jenny sipped her drink. Then put the glass down. 'Perhaps I should've. Might have frightened him off. I think he's courting me.'

'Courting you? Courting? What a sweet expression.'

'It's a Frank sort of expression.'

'Well, he's a safer bet than Gareth. You like him, don't you?'

Jenny sighed. 'Actually, I don't think I do. And I certainly don't fancy him. He's fifty, for goodness sake.'

'My,' said Sal, primly. 'How ageist.'

'Well.' Jenny was suddenly irritable. 'Men don't fancy women of fifty, do they? At first sight, I mean. Not if the women look fifty. Why should they expect us to fancy them? I'm not saying I couldn't like someone of fifty.'

'But you're saying that, in this particular case, you don't?'

'Honestly, Sal, it felt like a conspiracy. Mrs Meredith hinting that Frank and I could make a match. And I suppose she's right. Ten years is nothing. Except it is.' Jenny felt her irritability tip into distress. 'When I think of it, I feel insulted. I do.' Her voice broke.

'Hey,' said Sal, alarmed. 'Don't get upset.'

Jenny swallowed, and cleared her throat. 'Sorry, sorry, I'm all right.' She flapped her hand, and managed a smile. 'Honestly. Just feeling fragile.' She choked on a laugh. 'Frank said that. How fragile I looked. As if it was a bloody compliment. Stupid man.'

'D'you want a gin in that?' Sal still looked anxious. 'Go on. I'm having another.' She got up, lifted her own near-empty glass, and drained it. Sal, unlike Jenny, didn't have to drive home.

'No.' Jenny's distress had already subsided. 'I'm OK. Honestly.'

Sal checked her face. 'Fair enough. Back in a tick.'

While she was gone Jenny sipped her iced tonic. The tension

within her melted away. The scene here was soothingly peaceful. She gazed downriver. This evening the view seemed particularly quiet. No breeze ruffled the alders on the opposite bank. The river waters tinkled, unbusily. About a hundred and fifty yards away, in the shallows of one of the river bends, a pale amphora-shaped object was stuck vertically into the riverbed. The object was difficult to identify – the sunlight had caught the water's surface, and the mirage-like shimmer dazzled the eye. Something left behind by a day fisherman, she guessed.

Sal returned with a full glass and plonked it on to the table.

'You fancied Gareth, didn't you?' It sounded as if she'd been pondering their conversation while buying her drink. 'How old is he?'

'Thirty-six.' Jenny turned back to the table. 'He was a father at nineteen.'

'Oh, wow,' said Sal, sitting down. 'A real Valleys' boy.'

'Except he's still with Siân.'

'Mmm.' Sal sipped her gin. 'D'you know. I think my Nathan fancies his Lizzie. He called her a babe.' She made a gagging noise.

Jenny smiled. 'Good taste. Lizzie's a sweet, sensible girl. Though I think she and Alex see too much of each other. They cramp each other's style.'

'Maybe they'll get together one day.'

'Maybe. Or maybe they know each other too well. I don't think Alex sees Lizzie at all, physically.'

'Well, perhaps I should encourage Nathan.' Sal sighed. 'Not feeling too pro him right now, actually. Found a load of knives in his bedroom. He'd got them all in a box under the bed. And before you ask, I was only looking for underpants.'

Jenny picked up her drink. 'Don't worry. Lots of boys collect knives. My brother did. Alex has got a couple. Doesn't mean a thing. They just lie in a drawer somewhere.'

'But now he knows I've seen them he's hung them up on

the wall. I imagine Pauline coming over. She'd have the castration squad on to him. He says they're purely decorative.'

'I'm sure they are. It's just their age, Sal, they're weapon-obsessed. Alex can't kill a wasp, but he knows all the gun types in films, AK this and Uzi that. Like they can recognize any make of car from five hundred yards but can't remember how long it takes to boil a potato. Don't worry about it. God,' Jenny put her glass down suddenly, 'I'm shaking.'

Sal stared at her. 'Christ, you are.' She gestured at the glass. 'Put it down properly. Are you still upset?'

'No. It's one of my shivers. I told you. They just sweep over me.'

'Maybe it's the change.'

'Thanks. They're cold flushes, not hot. Shit.' Jenny winced, touching her front. 'Makes my boobs go hard.'

Sal leant forward, studying her. 'This is fascinating. Were you thinking about sex?'

'No.' Jenny made a contemptuous noise. 'I hardly ever think about sex. It's as if sex is thinking about me.'

Sal stared at Jenny's chest. 'Why didn't you lose your tits after you had Alex, like a normal person?'

'No idea.' Jenny shifted position, plucking at the front of her blouse. She laughed quietly. 'This happened at Frank's. They felt like rocks, for about an hour, till I left. I was jolly glad I had a woman taxi driver.'

Sal snorted into her drink and put it down quickly. 'What the hell are you saying?'

'Er . . .' Jenny smiled uncertainly. 'Don't know. Just what I felt . . .'

'Are you saying you did find your night with Frank exciting?'

'No.' Jenny was emphatic. 'Actually I think I was angry. Though it did occur to me at one stage to take my top off.'

'What?' said Sal, suppressing a laugh. 'To zap him with your killer tits?'

77

Jenny grinned, though she knew she was blushing. 'In a way.'

Sal grinned too. She shook her head. 'You're amazing. And if it had been a male taxi driver . . .?'

'Well, nothing. I suppose it would just have taken me longer to unwind. To come down. To relax. Sorry.' Jenny shook her head, frowning. 'I don't have the words, I can't explain.'

'I think you've done alarmingly well.'

Something downstream caught Jenny's eye. 'Good God!' The distant amphora shape in the shallows had just sprouted wide grey wings and a stiletto beak, and was lifting ponderously into the air. It trailed long stiff legs.

'It's a heron!'

'It's often there.' Sal sounded unimpressed, but then she drank here regularly. 'That's its fishing bend.'

Jenny watched the heron rise above the alders and set off, head tucked back deep into its shoulders, in a westerly direction.

'It's going my way,' she said. 'I wonder if it's the same one people see in Pentre?'

'Could be,' said Sal. 'Only four miles away, isn't it? Probably less, as the heron flies.' She smiled to herself.

'D'you know,' said Jenny, talk of distances reminding her. 'That coal dust can travel four miles. Minimum. Dust from the old opencast fouled washing here in Aber during the war. Mrs Meredith told me.' She pulled a sour face. 'And she and Frank also told me what a good girl I was to be fighting the new opencast.'

'Absolutely,' said Sal. 'You plucky little woman, you. Glad you reminded me. Have you decided what you're going to say at the inquiry?'

Jenny shook her head firmly. 'Oh, no. Sorry. I did tell you. I can't speak.'

Sal looked mystified. 'I thought you just said you were fighting the opencast.'

'Not speaking . . . Just, well, being against it.'

'Oh, big deal.' Sal looked exasperated. 'How's that going to help? Sending out objecting vibes, are you? Don't you want to stop it?'

'Of course. I went up there. It's . . . sacrilegious. But . . .'

'Have you finished reading the brochure?'

'Almost.' She caught Sal's eye. 'I'm more than half-way.'

'Oh, Jen,' Sal pleaded. 'This is where your energies should be going. They want to steal your mountain. You'll be nearly sixty before you're allowed on it again. Sixty. And by then it'll be a man-made, sanitized place. And that's assuming they don't apply for an extension. Which they always do. This is our last chance. If we win, they've no one else to appeal to. We must fight.'

'I know,' Jenny said. 'I know.'

'Please think about it,' said Sal. 'Promise me you will.'

Jenny sighed. 'All right,' she said, reluctantly.

Chapter 9

The next day Jenny took the brochure into work with her. She told Frank she was planning to read it at lunch time and he said, 'At the pub, why not?' to which she could think, in the few seconds she had to reply, of no convincing objection.

On the way there at one o'clock she realized something she'd failed properly to notice yesterday, when they'd also lunched together. That this week Frank, while he had so far obeyed her request not to buy her gifts, like the flowers last week, had now taken to touching her. Just in small ways: his arm had brushed hers on their way out, steering her through the office doorway, and now, ascending the steps to the pub, his palm pushed at the underside of her bare elbow. Yesterday, she recalled, he had done exactly the same, though she had dismissed it then as an isolated, insignificant event. Standing at the pub bar, however, as they waited to be served, she knew it wasn't, and that she was affronted; yet she didn't know how to tell him to stop.

They lunched in the back beer garden as usual. Once they had eaten, Jenny spread the opencast brochure across the wooden slats.

'Mother has suggested that we take a drive up that way soon,' Frank said, nodding at the brochure, and wiping his fingers on a paper napkin.

'Mmm.' Jenny stared at the text under her left hand. Then glanced right, to the facing page: six close-up photos of grass, apparently. She was into the ecology section. Her brain, she knew, would take nothing in, with Frank sitting opposite her.

'I meant to tell you . . . I've remembered the last time I was up there.' Frank smiled to himself, squinting at a point over Jenny's head. 'I had to visit a supplier over at Ponty. Yes. Must have been '83. That very cold winter. Gwern Lake was frozen over. Most extraordinary. There'd been a freezing fog overnight . . . everything was white with hoar frost. The sky was deep blue, over this arctic, petrified, sparkling mountain top.' He laughed, sounding astonished. 'Even the lake. The surface of the southern end had frozen in wavelets. Like ripples of dazzling white sand.'

'Good heavens.' Jenny remembered '83 well; a stunning, six-week diamond of a winter. 'What, you stopped, did you?'

'Oh, yes. Yes. Everyone was. Just pulling to the side and getting out. I told you, it was breathtaking. And even with the people . . . so silent.'

A lump of sentiment caught in Jenny's throat. She felt vindicated. She wasn't the only person to have seen the Blaen Dyar land itself – as opposed to the views, about which there could be no argument – as beautiful. 'Well,' she said, tapping the brochure, 'if this goes ahead, it won't be silent again for a long time. The opencast will be just the other side of the road. And I'm sure I've read something in here about noise.' She licked a finger and riffled back through the pages. 'Here. Ah. No. Actually they're a bit coy about noise.' She laughed scornfully. 'They just say "the level will be within limits adopted on present sites". How helpful.' She read on. 'Oh, and blasting will be between ten and four on weekdays, and ten and noon on Saturdays. "Preceded by audible and visible warnings". Christ.'

'Mother has read in the local paper,' said Frank, pulling a wry face, 'that British Coal have already bought a number of

81

properties up there. Ones close to the site. There is a letter to the Editor estimating how much money they must already have spent. It amounted to a very great deal.' He gave her a sad, apologetic smile. 'It doesn't look, I'm afraid, as if they expect to lose.'

'Of course they don't.' Jenny tried to make her voice cynical rather than bitter. She closed the brochure with a thump, and sighed. 'I ought to give evidence. I know I should. I've even told Sal I'll think about it. It's just that the idea terrifies me.'

Frank's long face stiffened. 'Of course it does. You mustn't let anyone bully you.'

Jenny sighed again. Frank was criticizing Sal. But also belittling herself.

'I would like to,' she said, not looking at him. 'If I were braver.'

Frank reached across the table and rested his hand on her forearm.

'You are brave.' He squeezed her wrist. His fingers had surprising strength. 'Of course you are. But others will make all the points. The county council are objecting, they have experts. Nothing depends on one person.'

'No.' Jenny heard Sal countering that argument – that if everyone took the same line, there'd be no objectors at all. And she knew Sal was right, and Frank wrong.

She looked down at Frank's hand on her arm, and thought how impossible, how burdensomely impossible, the simple words 'Please take your hand away' were. Because of what would suddenly be acknowledged between them. Because of what would then exist, exposed, an awkwardness created entirely by Frank, but a complication much more for her, given their respective desires and positions, than for him. She felt resentment churn in her stomach. Since he had created this himself, out of nothing, let him suffer the disappointment of being misled by it. He was not her responsibility. She refused to be forced into saying anything, when she would be the one to lose by it.

He finally removed his hand himself, to pick up his glass. Jenny dropped her arm to her lap, and kept her body close to herself for the rest of the lunch hour, so it couldn't happen again.

She thought more about giving evidence during the afternoon. And driving home, was uncomfortably conscious of the Blaen Dyar plateau hills to her left, along the southern skyline. Keeping vigil; as if expecting, in their infinitely patient, monolithically undemanding way, something from her. She caught herself sighing. She had to acknowledge that, paradoxically, Frank's support for her reluctance to speak at the inquiry had done more to undermine it than Sal's contempt had. Though, still, the mere thought of mustering an argument and standing up in public to articulate it, made her hands tense on the steering wheel. Was I always this gutless? she thought bleakly. Wasn't I braver and more confident before Michael died? The answer, of course, was yes, but knowing it didn't help.

Her insides were still tight as she turned off the main road into Pentre. She drove cautiously past Gareth's house, where there was a blind bend, and on up through the village. The lane steepened as she neared the cottage.

The entrance to the hard standing was blocked. The gate was wide open but a large red pick-up truck had been reversed on to the concrete between the gate-posts. She parked across the lane, undid her seat-belt, and exhaled deeply to relax herself before getting out. Then walked across the road.

There was movement in the pick-up's cab. A dog's head, dark and massive, turned to watch her approach. Jenny hesitated, wondering which side of the vehicle to pass. There was less than a foot's gap right or left. The window on the passenger door was wound down about six inches. She squeezed by on the driver's side, aware of the dog's eyes following her.

Alex's Escort was jacked up and skewed across the hard standing. The lower half of a male body, clad in blue jeans and brown leather lace-up boots, protruded from the empty front wheel arch. The man was lying on his back, working on something beneath the car. One leg was lifted slightly at the knee.

Jenny approached. The check material of the man's shirt had rucked and separated above his jeans' waistband, and in the exposed triangle of bare skin she could see the neat blind eye of a navel, and below it, a thin disappearing line of hair.

'Is that Mark?' Of course it was Mark. Mark who'd said he knew her, though she hadn't remembered him.

'Your son's a tit,' said Mark's voice. 'Doesn't he ever service this?'

'I doubt it.' Jenny could only manage a murmur. She continued to stare at his half-body. She was experiencing a hallucination. The body appeared brighter, in sharper focus, and much more significant than the car or concrete or tools around it. As if some exterior, urging force were spotlighting it for her. *Here it is. Here it is. Here it is.*

A prickle ran up the back of her thighs, but got no further. The embryo shiver died. As if it, too, had heard the message, and knew it wasn't needed. That desire and object, this time, did not conflict. *Here it is.* Here was what? She clasped her hands together at the front of her skirt. She sensed a huge ripe emotion unpeel inside her.

She needed to say something. She said, 'Are you going to be long?' and hoped her voice sounded ordinary. Though why should it? His body was extraordinary. *Look at me. Here I am. Look at me.* She nearly laughed.

He was easing himself out. She stepped back and composed her face. His chest appeared, then his shoulders and head. He was wearing transparent plastic goggles. He got to his feet. His smile, beneath the goggles, was friendly.

'Hi. Done the bushes, any road. That'll stop the banging.' He wiped his hands on a rag, lifted the goggles off his head between his wrists, then leant forward and brushed grit from the front of his short hair.

'Alex will be delighted.' He was talking to her as if nothing odd was happening. And, of course, in reality, it wasn't. With more confidence she said, 'You weren't hoping to catch him, were you? He won't be home till after nine.' She stared at his hands. 'D'you want to wash?'

'Ay, ta, won't be long.' He turned to retrieve the Escort's wheel, propped against the pick-up's bumper. He rolled it across the concrete, lifted it on to the hub, and squatted to replace the wheel nuts.

'The kitchen's the far end. I'll leave the door open.'

Mark nodded, and reached for the wheel brace.

Jenny took her keys out of her jacket pocket, walked round to the back door, and unlocked it. The air inside the kitchen was cool and undisturbed. She crossed to the work surface and reached for the kettle, then changed her mind. She turned round, stared at the front window, and waited.

After a couple of minutes Mark passed the window. His boots scraped on the grille outside. She smiled at him as he entered the room, and nodded at the sink. 'There's Swarfega on the window sill.'

'Ta.' He tossed the Escort car keys on to the kitchen table. At the sink he unscrewed the cleaner tub lid with the tips of his fingers and scooped out the green jelly.

'Would you like a coffee?' Jenny watched him rubbing the jelly into his hands, working it with his thumbs into his knuckles and the sides of his fingernails. 'Or tea?' Now she reached for the kettle.

'Ay.' Mark glanced round. 'If you're making one. Tea. Two sugars.'

There wasn't enough water in the kettle. She had to stand very close to him to fill a jug under the cold tap. His rolled-up sleeve brushed her forearm. She left the tap running for him to rinse the jelly off his hands. He didn't look, or feel, or smell, like one of Alex's friends. Reassured, she took two mugs off their hooks, put a tea-bag in one, and instant coffee in the other. While she waited for the kettle to boil she said, 'I'm sorry Alex isn't here.'

'Wasn't expecting him.' Mark finished rinsing his hands and looked around for a towel.

'Use the roller.' Jenny indicated a striped towel hanging to the left of the sink.

'Oh, right.'

The kettle boiled. Jenny made the tea and coffee. She picked up Mark's mug and held it out to him.

'An improvement on a glass of water. I hope.'

Mark took the tea, looked down at it, and grinned. For a moment Jenny thought he was embarrassed. Then saw he was trying not to laugh.

'What is it?'

He shook his head, looking up now, but avoiding her eyes. 'Nothing.'

But he was still smiling; he was lying, Jenny knew. A lie – a deliberately transparent lie – was provocative. A flirtation, even. She sipped her coffee, and saw, suddenly, a picture of hot, frantic entwined bodies. She had to put the mug down. She leant back against the work surface and carefully folded her arms.

'You often do favours like this for people, do you?' she asked.

'Now and then.' He finally looked straight at her. The blue of his irises seemed paler today. He had bold eyes. She wondered if he was actually good-looking and couldn't decide; his physical presence was so affecting that the details of his features seemed irrelevant. She tried to think of a question that would match the boldness in his eyes, without making herself sound foolish. She decided on a question she actually wanted the answer to.

'Are you married, Mark?' What would she do if he was? Would it matter? Yes. She felt the panicky edge of disappointment.

Mark shook his head with an amused smile. 'Nope.'

The panic melted. 'Got a girlfriend?' she asked.

He grinned. 'Swarms of 'em. Honeypot, I am. Come Saturday night, have to pick 'em off me.'

She laughed. One of Alex's friends would have either stonewalled the question, looking cloudy-eyed at such presumption, or would have answered politely and truthfully, adolescent to adult. Mark's reply was evasive; but an adult-to-adult evasion.

He lifted his mug to his lips, drained it, and put it down next to the kettle. He was less than a yard from her now; blood thudded in her ears. In her mind's eye she saw herself act: putting a hand on his chest, stopping him, holding him here. Telling him: you are the man I think I've been looking for. I need you. Please.

But in the real, inhibited, shockable world, nothing happened; her hands were frozen immobile, still crossed at her waist. A terrible anxiety seized her: that having found this person, this man she knew she was looking for, she was nevertheless, through sheer cowardice, going to lose him.

But he hadn't moved away. He was still very close. His attention seemed unfocused. Was he about to say something? Waiting for her to say, or do, something? Or was he working something out?

The grip of anxiety loosened. The silence was becoming awkward. Gloriously awkward. It was starting to whisper. Like the sound of a quietly dripping tap that, once heard, swells to Niagara. Now it was roaring. Something was about to happen.

Mark caught her eye and said in a low steady voice, 'When I was fifteen, I was a liar.'

'Oh, yes?' Jenny heard herself give a gasping laugh; a ludicrous, but marvellous, sound.

Mark nodded. He looked very tense.

'I told the boys I'd done this.' He touched his palm, very lightly, to her left breast.

Jenny breathed in and out, feeling the movement of her body against his hand. What courage. She felt a small bud of triumph blossom inside herself, knowing his bravery had been also partly hers. She kept perfectly still. In a level voice she said, 'And did they believe you?'

'Oh, ay.' He pressed his palm harder against her. There was relief in his face; he must, surely, be awash with it. 'Convincing, I was. Think I believed me too.'

She smiled. She glanced down at his hand and told herself that she too must now be as brave as he.

She forced herself. 'Just that, was it? Nothing more?'

She saw him hesitate. Felt his hand tremble. Gareth's hands had not trembled. Excitement, not fear, she knew, made young men's bodies tremble.

She said, 'I'd like us to make love,' and admired the voice she'd finally found: a calm, clear, brave, unembarrassed voice. She heard the words again, echoed in her head, and added, with no effort at all, because she knew his answer, 'You'd like it too, wouldn't you?'

Mark stared at her as if checking and rechecking her words. Then jerked his head and said, 'Ay. Shit. Ay.'

She took him upstairs to the small spare bedroom. Both kitchen and sitting room downstairs faced the front garden and, in the daytime, without drawn curtains, weren't truly private. She congratulated herself on being capable of clear thought, as well as clear speech.

The spare room double bed was high, with carved wooden head and footboards, and the bed itself, under its heavy Afghan wool rug, was double mattressed and lumpy with piles of spare bedding. She stood beside it and let Mark kiss her on the mouth, because he seemed to want to. Then guided his hands where she most wanted him, under her T-shirt and bra. Her desire had become liquid, and her breasts so swollen with it she was surprised to find them dry.

It seemed to her, a few minutes later, on her back across the hummocky mounds of bedding, with Mark inside and above her, that she and he fitted together perfectly. As she had known they would. Even with their bodies untidy, half-clothed, rushing at it. She was the lock, and he her key. Or was he the lock, crushing around her, and she his key? The distinction was blurring . . . whichever, she thought dimly. Gareth had been neither. Frank could never be.

His face was at her shoulder. He smelt young, hot and familiar. She could be inhaling herself. Their flesh feverishly busy. Opening each other up.

She climaxed suddenly. A million eyes in her body snapped open, stared at the world in astonishment, and shut tight again. Then opened again, stunned blind. The air channels behind her eardrums blocked and unblocked. The soles of her feet sang.

She felt him climax too. Her muscles hugged at him, contracting around him, once, twice, thrice. Then rested.

After a moment he pulled away. She opened her eyes and heard the bed springs creak as his weight lifted from her. She stared up at the pale grey ceiling.

'OK?' He was speaking. Not expecting an answer, just registering his presence. Making sure she hadn't died of pleasure.

89

CATHERINE MERRIMAN

The idea amused her; she shifted her head. He was doing up his jeans. His face was pale and his skin damp with effort, but his eyes bright and pleased with themselves. And why not? she thought; she was pleased with him too.

She sat up, loosened her T-shirt so it fell back over her breasts, and pulled her skirt down. He started to tuck his check shirt back into his jeans.

'Don't.' On impulse she stopped him. This might never happen again. His only existence, once he'd gone, might be in her memory. She drew him towards her, until his thighs brushed her knees, and started to unbutton his shirt. 'Can I see you?' She hesitated. 'D'you mind?'

'Help yourself.' He undid two of the buttons himself.

She pulled the check material aside and stroked the flats of her fingers up his abdomen, over his ribs – the ridges well sheathed, a man's, not a boy's ribs – to his chest. His skin was sticky. She checked his expression. He liked his own body; he was proud of it, was enjoying showing it off to her. It was a working body. A good, strong, working body. She pressed her palm against the light-brown diamond of damp hair on his breastbone.

'I can feel your heart beating.'

'Yippee,' Mark said. 'I'm alive.'

'Yes.' She smiled. 'You are.' She undid his jeans button, and drew the zip down.

'Shit,' said Mark, with a mock-anxious laugh. 'You want to do it again?'

'No.' She laughed back up at him. 'Not right now.' He was so easy; she could be talking to herself. She moved her eyes slowly up his torso, from the soft brown curl of his pubic hair, over the expanse of living breathing glowing skin and muscle and bone, to the small scooped hollows above his collar bones. Mark stood patiently relaxed, letting her enjoy him.

90

'OK.' She felt brimful of him. She glanced up at his face – of course he was good-looking, how could she have been unsure of it – and, feeling suddenly choked, tugged his jeans closed.

Chapter 10

After Mark left Jenny ate a salad supper, mowed the small front lawn and most of the steep side lawn, until the evening midges drove her inside, and then sat at the kitchen table to read the last third of the British Coal Statement of Case brochure. She knew she needed to shower, but was putting it off. Sometimes, when she shifted position in the chair, she imagined she could still smell traces of Mark, a heady masculine perfume beneath the pungent new-mown grass scent rising from her shoes.

Alex returned at dusk. He burst through the back door carrying a clanking black plastic dustbin bag over his shoulder. He was in his work clothes, but with his hair loose. He swung the bag with cavalier aim on to the table.

'Careful.' Jenny pulled the brochure clear.

'Sorry.' His cheerfulness was undimmed. He dug in the bag and with a conjuror's flourish produced a four-pack of beer. Then another of cider. Then a six-pack of lager.

'Twenty-five p. a can,' he said, tearing at the cardboard of the six-pack. 'Not bad, huh? They're dented. Well . . .' He held one up, which looked perfect to Jenny, and squinted at it with a mock-expert eye. 'Kind of dropped.' He grinned. Then opened the fridge door behind him and squatted to start stuffing the cans inside.

'Better rescue your dinner,' Jenny said. 'The salad in the blue bowl. You got a lift, did you?'

'Yeah.' Alex pulled out the salad bowl and put it on top of the fridge. He glanced back at her. 'Hey, has Mark been round? I left him the keys. Is the car fixed?'

Jenny passed her hand over the glossy pages in front of her, smoothing them flat. 'He was here when I got home. He's replaced the bushes, whatever they are.' She kept her eyes on the brochure. Two circular diagrams filled the lower half of the right-hand page. Concentric rings, entitled 'Wind Direction Rose Graphs'. They looked more like bull's eye targets to her.

'Great.' Alex gave a satisfied sigh. He snapped open a lager can. Foaming beer shot across the table. 'Shit,' he laughed, and swung round to the sink.

'Alex.' Jenny pushed her chair back. 'You are paying Mark for this work, aren't you?'

'Well, for the parts. Obviously.' He sucked foam noisily from the top of the can.

'But not for his time?'

Alex shook his head. 'He's loaded, Mum, honest. He wouldn't take it. Goes out Saturday night with a hundred quid in his pocket.'

'Really?' Though she didn't actually find this surprising.

'Or more. He works at the steelworks. There's a gang of them. Go to Llanwern, Port Talbot, all over. Sort of repairs flying squad. I think he's a welder.' He pondered. 'Or is it hydraulics? Anyway, gets loads of overtime. And he doesn't pay anything for the flat.'

'What flat?' This volley of information was alarming. Of course Alex must know more about Mark than she; but having it shot at her felt risky: akin to playing factual Russian roulette.

'The flat over the garage.'

'What garage?'

93

Alex groaned. He spoke very slowly. 'The . . . village . . . garage. He's Mark Bevan, Owen Bevan's son.'

'Good God.' Mark was suddenly, shockingly, located in the real world. Owen Bevan's son. Owen, proprietor of probably the biggest business in the village, the garage and filling station. Not that she knew Owen well, or his wife. Their children – there were three, no, four of them – were all adult, and much older than Alex. As parents, she and the Bevans were nearly a generation apart. Mark would be their youngest. Their only boy.

Alex was saying, 'Sheba's the guard dog. She gets shut in the garage shop at night. Hey, guess what, she's going to be mated soon. Can we have an Alsatian?'

'What?' Jenny took a moment to catch up. 'No. It'd chase sheep. And the house is empty all day.'

'Two hundred quid, he says he can sell the pups for. Each.'

'Certainly not, then.'

'If she has just five, he'll have made a grand.'

'I'm sure it's not as simple as that.'

''Tis. He's done it before. His dad breeds terriers, so they know what they're doing. He's potty about Sheba.' Alex picked a lump of feta cheese out of the salad bowl, tossed it into his mouth, and laughed crudely. 'Blokes in the pub reckon he'd do it himself, if he could.'

'Shut up.' Jenny pulled her chair back up to the table and, as if to close the subject, turned over a page of the British Coal brochure. She didn't want to hear any more about Mark. She felt lucky that what she had already learnt hadn't spoilt him. Or frightened her. She needed to be able to trust him. 'Please don't tell anyone,' she'd asked him, as he was leaving the cottage. 'I don't want Alex to know.' And he'd replied, swinging himself up into the cab of his red pick-up, 'Anything you say.' As easy as that. 'Anything you say.' She did trust him. She believed him. *Anything you say.* A pleasure-echo tugged at her womb.

Her elbow knocked a loose leaflet from the brochure to the

floor. It must have been tucked between the pages. She picked it up and examined it. It was a shiny folded sheet, a little longer than A4. On one side were two landscape photographs in long horizontal strips across the page, one above the other. She stared at them.

'What is it?' Alex had seen her expression. He put the salad bowl down and leant over her shoulder.

'Look, look.' Jenny stabbed at the foreground of the upper photo. 'Do they think we're morons? What's that?'

'Er . . . silver birch, I think.' Alex peered closer at the picture. 'And gorse? Difficult to tell.'

'Because it's a gloomy picture,' nodded Jenny. 'Shot in black and white, on a grey day. Now look at this one.' She tapped the lower strip photograph, which was in bright colour.

'Millions of horrible baby Christmas trees,' said Alex. 'In glorious sunshine.'

'These are before and after shots,' wailed Jenny. 'That . . .' she pointed at the upper picture '. . . that was heathland. Beautiful, scrubby, birch and gorse heathland. And that's what they restored it to.' She turned the leaflet over and read the title. *Opencast Mining in Great Britain.* 'Oh, Christ. In the whole of Britain, is this the best they can manage? A visual con? Heathland to conifer plantation? What are they going to do to us?'

'Calm down, Mum.' Alex sounded anxious. 'It won't happen. We'll beat it.'

'How? God, you can't trust people to do the right thing, can you, not where money's involved. How can they do this, when they've closed all the deep mines? It's . . . it's malice. Spite. We must fight it.'

'Right,' agreed Alex. 'So we'll fight. Please, Mum. Calm down.'

'OK. OK.' Jenny made an effort. She showed Alex a calmed-down face. 'OK. But . . . I must give evidence. I know I must. When I was up the top last week I knew it. I wish I could take the inquiry there. The Inspector must have visited, but I bet he never saw what I saw. I bet he was only shown fly-tipping, and old gullied spoil heaps.' She groaned. 'I just can't bear the thought of having to speak.'

'Don't then,' said Alex. 'Show them pictures. Photos. Hey . . .' he pushed at her shoulder, his voice lifting, '. . . even better, a video. Yeah, you could make a video.'

'I haven't got a video camera. Anyway, I wouldn't know how.'

'Don't be stupid, Mum. Anyone can use a camcorder. They're designed for dodos. You can hire them, loads of people do. For weddings and things.'

Jenny looked at him. Perhaps the idea wasn't ridiculous. 'D'you think they'd allow video evidence? They'd need equipment, wouldn't they?'

'Just a telly and a VCR,' said Alex. 'Of course they'd allow it.'

'I don't know . . .' She thought. 'They have sound on them don't they? So I could just do a voice-over? I wouldn't have to speak?'

'Course they do. Where've you been?' Alex sounded exasperated. 'I'll do it for you, if you really can't. I bet I could hire one in Aber. No, hey, genius idea – Mark's got one. I remember, he did an eighteenth at the pub. I'll ask if we can borrow it. Shit. I'm brilliant. He can edit too . . .'

'Hang on, Alex, hang on.' Jenny lifted her hand. Her heart was suddenly hammering. He was going much too fast. What was he suggesting? That they involve Mark? Good God. She mustn't be hustled. What did this mean? She thought. He was handing her, if she chose to take it, a pretext for her and Mark to meet again. A cast-iron excuse to associate. Or, at least, communicate. If she wanted to.

She did want to. The idea was irresistible. Excitement surged in her. 'OK,' she said. 'But perhaps I ought to ask him, not you. I mean, since I'm the one that wants it . . .'

'I'll be seeing him.' Alex spoke as if she were being dim. 'I've got to pay him for the bushes, haven't I?'

'Oh, yes. Of course.' She nodded. Silly of her; she was getting carried away. She made herself relax. 'It's a clever idea. Congratulations.'

Alex mused. 'Maybe Nathan and I could make a video too . . .'

'No,' said Jenny instantly. 'I'd never get my hands on the camcorder. I thought of it first.'

'You didn't, I did.'

'But for me. I've got first claim.'

Alex laughed at her. 'Keen, now, aren't we? OK. You first, if he'll lend it.'

'Be persuasive.' Before she could stop herself, she said, 'Tell him it's for me, not you.' The look Alex gave her made her flush. 'I gave him a glass of water once, remember.'

'Oh, right,' nodded Alex. 'He owes you.'

Chapter 11

The next day Alex called in on Nathan after work. He knew the back door of Sal's house would be open, but nevertheless rang the front-door bell.

It looked as if Nathan had spent all day in the sitting room. On the coffee table were several dirty mugs and crushed beer cans, plus a ketchup-stained dinner plate and an ash tray full of stubs. The room smelt of tobacco smoke and fried bacon.

'You just had breakfast?' It was now six in the evening. Sal, Alex assumed, was still at work.

'Yup.' Nathan grinned. 'Second today.'

'Waster.' Alex swung his leg over the arm of Sal's tweed sofa.

'Wanna beer?' Nathan didn't wait for an answer, but disappeared into the kitchen. He returned with two cans and tossed one to Alex. Behind him Sal's tabby cat appeared, stared around the sitting room and then stalked in straight-legged disapproval back into the kitchen. Alex pulled the tab on his beer and twisted his watch. 'Just a touchdown, this. Got to see Mark.'

'Oh, yeah?' Nathan strode to the alcove television beside the fireplace and prodded the set on. He stared at the talking face of a female newsreader, before switching off again.

'Don't you ever sit down?' sighed Alex.

'Sure.' Nathan jumped into an armchair and swung his legs over the arm. 'Sitting, OK? What you seeing Mark about?'

'Got to pay him for work on the car. Gonna try and borrow his video camera too. Mum wants to use it.'

'Oh, yeah? What for?'

'She's going to make a video to show at the opencast inquiry.'

'Oh, right.' Nathan lost interest. 'Mum's doing something for that.' He sniffed. 'Pointless.'

'You think.'

Nathan gave a lordly wave. 'Direct action, that's the only thing that'd work. You have to show 'em you mean business.'

Alex felt provoked to say, 'Direct action like what?'

'Do something. Don't just spout off.'

'You mean do something up on the mountain?'

'Maybe.' Nathan sounded defensive. 'Maybe.' His face relaxed to a laugh. 'Difficult up there, mind. Who'd know?'

'You can see it from everywhere.'

'Well, yeah. But not what people are doing on it.'

Alex considered. The idea of doing something practical rather appealed. He certainly wasn't prepared to give verbal evidence. You'd have to prepare notes, like for an essay. 'Paint,' he said suddenly.

'Eh?'

'People drive up there. There's roads along three sides of the site. We could paint messages. "Opencast starts here". Something like that. Most people haven't a clue where it's going to be.'

'Not bad,' conceded Nathan.

'There are signs up there too,' said Alex, thinking. 'You know. "Property of British Coal". "No vehicles". That sort of thing.'

'Smash 'em up.'

'Maybe shoot 'em up.'

'With what?'

'Air gun?'

'Don't make me laugh.'

'Shotgun.' Alex felt reckless.

'Where'd you get a shotgun?'

'Mark's got one.'

Nathan's pupils seemed to dilate. 'Would he lend it?'

'Dunno. Maybe. I could say we wanted to go ratting.'

'Hmm.' Nathan shrugged. 'Well. Or we could just axe the signs.'

'Or . . . repaint them. Use them ourselves. "No opencast". You know.'

' "British Coal are the pits".' Nathan giggled. 'Shotgun sounds more fun, mind.'

Alex laughed. 'True.'

'Is there anything else up there?'

'Not on the site. No fences. There were test vehicles, but they've gone now.'

'What about a fire?' Nathan had swung his legs off the chair arm and actually appeared to be thinking. 'You'd see a fire from miles away. Something really smoky, like old tyres.'

'Hell of a way to lug old tyres,' said Alex. 'Suppose you could choose somewhere close to the road. Black Cliff valley, maybe. There's often junk near there anyway. People fly-tip.'

Nathan was scratching his stubble. 'Where's their HQ? British Coal's HQ?'

'Don't look at me.'

Nathan leaped up and bounded over to Sal's table. He rummaged in a pile of papers, found a leaflet and flicked through it. 'Aberdare. Miles away.' He tossed the leaflet aside and walked slowly back to his chair. 'We ought to write to them. Threaten direct action. Sabotage. And we ought to call ourselves something. Like we're an organization.'

Alex grinned at him. Was he serious? 'Guardians of Blaen Dyar?'

100

'Warriors of Blaen Dyar. Hey, we could write in Welsh! That'd put the wind up them.'

'What's "Warriors of Blaen Dyar" in Welsh?'

'Don't ask me.'

'And you a Welshman.'

'You live here.'

'Lizzie'd know,' Alex said. 'She did Welsh for GCSE.'

'We could write letters to the press, too. Warning letters. Beware the Warriors, et cetera.'

'Not in bloody Welsh, we couldn't. One mistake, they'd know.'

'OK. English, then. Cut the letters out of newspapers. Just have the name in Welsh. Hey . . .' Nathan rubbed his hands together. 'This could be a giggle.'

Alex wondered if he should remind Nathan that the objective wasn't, actually, to have fun. Still, enjoying themselves, coincidentally, wouldn't be a sin. 'We'd have to tell Lizzie,' he said. 'Could be serious, if we wrote to the press. Wouldn't want her blabbing.'

'She's against the opencast, isn't she?'

'Oh, yeah,' nodded Alex. 'I mean, she'd be OK . . . just . . .'

Nathan reached for his cigarettes and lit up. 'Right.' He rolled the cigarette to the corner of his mouth and looked business-like. 'So what we got? We got . . .' he counted on his fingers '. . . road painting. Shooting up signs . . . OK, or repainting them. A bonfire. Threatening letters.'

'What do we do first?'

'What's the most illegal?'

'They're all illegal, aren't they?'

'Bonfires aren't illegal.'

'They are,' said Alex. 'Danger of grass fires.'

Nathan looked scornful. 'Up there? Thought it was all bogland?'

'Some is, some isn't. Most isn't. But it doesn't matter what it is. People who see fires still report them. Still get the fire brigade out.'

'Well, that's good, isn't it?' said Nathan. 'At least it's noticed.'

'Yeah,' said Alex, confused now as to what the point had been. 'Suppose you're right.'

'Painting roads'd be a doddle,' said Nathan. 'Illegal, but a doddle. Do it at night, no problem. Same with the signs.'

'Sending threatening letters is definitely illegal,' said Alex. 'Quite heavy, in fact.'

'We'll do that last, then,' said Nathan. He jumped to his feet and paced to the window. 'We need the right gear.' He walked back to the table and stubbed out his cigarette. 'Camouflage trousers. Black and white. You know. Urban guerrilla togs. You can get 'em in the market.'

Alex sighed. 'We're not urban guerrillas.'

'Don't quibble. The urban guerrilla look is cool. I could get balaclavas from the shop, too.'

'I don't need a balaclava.'

'Course you do. You want to be a warrior, you got to look a warrior.'

'My mum'd go mad.'

'So'd mine.' Nathan chuckled. 'Really spook her.'

'She'd approve of direct action, though,' said Alex.

'Yeah,' admitted Nathan. 'You're right. She would.'

'Don't tell her, will you,' Alex warned.

'Course not.'

At eight Alex left to find Mark. He and Nathan hadn't fixed anything definite, except that each would search their respective cupboards and sheds for paint.

Driving out of Abercwm, Alex wondered if Nathan's enthusiasm would last. He had, he was sure, no real passion for the cause itself; the idea of dressing the part had seemed to appeal to him most. He was treating the thing as a game. A fantasy game, possibly. Time would tell.

In Pentre Alex drew up outside the village pub, the Bridgend, which was where he expected to find Mark. Before leaving the car he pulled on a green sweatshirt over his white work shirt. He was still wearing his grey trousers and lace-up shoes, but this was the village pub, not a pub in Abercwm, so it didn't worry him.

Inside, in the red and brown front saloon, there were half a dozen men clustered round the bar, and two women at a window table. The Bridgend pub was often quiet. Compared to pubs in neighbouring villages, many of which had dining rooms and employed chefs, it was considered dull and old-fashioned. Alex had been coming here to play pool in the back room and drink – first soft drinks, then beer – since he was fourteen. He was as comfortable in these surroundings as in his own sitting room at home. Which was why, at weekends, he drank in Abercwm, since part of the pleasure of going out was the buzz that came from not being quite comfortable.

Mark wasn't in the front room. And no one was serving. Alex slipped down a side passage, passed the ladies' and gents' toilets, and entered the back bar. This was a large lino-floored room containing the pool table. Four young men were playing.

'You seen Mark?' Alex called. They hadn't. He went over to the deserted bar and leaned across it.

'Roy?'

Roy, the landlord, appeared from a side door carrying a box of potato crisps. He was a heavy man in his fifties with a pronounced limp, the result of an accident at Ebbw Vale steel-works, which had ended his career as a crane driver. By the time he'd been signed back fit, two years after the accident, the whole plant had closed.

Roy put the boxes down and said, 'What'll it be, Alex?'

Alex debated, and then said, 'Better not, thanks.' He'd had

103

two small cans with Nathan; and only last month he'd been stopped and breathalysed in the village. 'Just looking for Mark. Have you seen him?'

'Haven't lad. Not tonight. Could be working late.'

'Oh. Right.' Alex felt deflated. He'd been looking forward to seeing Mark. Reluctantly he backed away. 'It's OK. Nothing important.'

Outside the pub again he tapped the Escort key in his palm and stared down the village road. He didn't want to give up and go home. If he walked just fifty yards on he'd be able to see the garage, and any vehicle parked on the forecourt. He hesitated, then pocketed the key, and set off down the road.

Past the post office he could see the garage: a two-storey flat-roofed brick building. The pumps and glass-fronted shop were unlit, but behind the pump canopy a light was shining from a big upstairs window. To the left of the building a narrow driveway led to the rear workshops. There was no gate to the entrance, but a vehicle – Mark's red Hilux – was parked across it.

Alex crossed the road. He had never visited Mark in his flat before, but guessed access was through a frosted glass door on the right of the building. Passing the plate glass of the filling-station shop he peered inside. Sheba was not yet at work guarding the tobacco shelves and the workshops behind. He walked on and rapped smartly on the glass door. It swung inward. A small lobby and steep stairs led upwards.

He knocked again, and this time heard a dog bark. He shouted, 'Mark? You there?' and started up the stairs.

A door on the left at the top opened. Mark and Sheba looked down at him. Mark said, 'Shit, Alex,' but in a mock-weary voice, and left the door open for him as he withdrew.

Alex said, 'Hi, Sheeb,' and entered the flat. There was no hallway; he had stepped straight into a large rectangular living space. Sitting room and kitchen combined. It had a front-facing picture window, half the height and almost the full length of the room. The sitting area was furnished with a black leather three-piece suite. He stared around. 'Thought you were going to the pub.'

'Too shagged. Only just got in.' Mark was in his socks; his boots were lying, as if just kicked off, on the grey carpet. He padded to the strip of kitchen units along the back wall, opened a white cupboard above the marbled work surface and removed a large tin.

Alex, still looking around, said, 'Shit, long day.' Black shelving on the other side of the room housed stereo, video equipment and a TV. The door behind him must be into the bedroom.

'Got called out at four this morning,' Mark said, stabbing the spike of an opener into the top of the tin. 'Haven't finished yet, either. Got to be back in P'Talbot by eight tomorrow morning.'

'Shit.' Alex watched Mark's face as he sawed the tin-opener round the can. The rims of his eyes were pink, his chin unshaven. The dog was pushing her nose against his thigh. 'Can they make you work such long hours?'

'You bet.' Mark looked at him and chuckled. 'An' I love it. Suckers for jobs against the clock, we are. Time goes fast. When you're finished you get a buzz you can fly home on.' He picked up a tin bowl from the floor, rinsed it under the tap, and heaped dog meat into it. 'Don't want to be unsociable,' he said. 'But I'm feeding Sheeb and giving her a run, and then I'm crashing out.'

'Won't keep you.' Alex dug in his pocket and pulled out two ten-pound notes. 'Wanted to thank you for doing those bushes. Would twenty cover them?'

'Expect so. Haven't paid Dad yet. Took 'em out of stores.' Mark lowered the bowl to the floor. 'There you go, girl.'

Alex put the bank notes on the work surface. The dog took her first bites of food. She ate with surprising delicacy, he thought, for such a wolfish-looking animal.

'Fussy bitch, she is,' Mark said with a smile, noticing he was watching. He sounded proud.

Alex looked across to the door to the left of the front window. The bathroom, he guessed, over the stairwell. He hesitated, shifting his weight to his other hip. 'Actually, I got another favour to ask you.'

'Oh, ay?'

'You know the opencast British Coal are planning?'

'Yup.'

'Well, the public inquiry's next month, and Mum wants to make a video to show at it. But she hasn't got a camcorder. Have you still got yours?'

'I have.' Mark frowned down at Sheba, who was still eating pickily.

'Well, I was wondering . . . She says she wouldn't know how to work one, but I told her it was easy and I'd help her if we could borrow one. Don't suppose we could borrow yours, could we?'

Mark didn't lift his gaze. He appeared to be thinking. Slowly he shook his head. 'Nope.'

'Oh,' said Alex.

'Tell you what.' Mark looked up. 'I won't lend it, but I'll do it for her. You know what she wants?'

'Oh . . . right, well.' Alex swallowed his disappointment. He had been looking forward to using the camcorder. But Mark's offer was too good to refuse – he supposed his mother would agree. 'Er . . . The views, I think, mostly. It's a two-way thing. Anywhere you can see from up there will also be able to see the opencast. And she wants to do a commentary, so she doesn't have to speak at the inquiry. She wants it all on the video.'

'Might be OK,' shrugged Mark. 'If it's not too windy. Could always dub it.' He reached behind him, opened a drawer, and took out a chain dog lead. 'Look. You tell her, if she gets down here at two on Sunday I'll take her up and we'll shoot something. But tell her not to bother if it's raining, or if the visibility's duff.' He wound the chain round his palm. 'Now I got to take Sheeb out.'

Alex followed him down the stairs. Out on the forecourt he said, 'She pregnant yet?'

'No.' Mark bent to attach the lead. 'Just coming into season. Be a week or so yet.' He dropped to his heels, and took the dog's black head in his hands. 'Going to see Spartan up at Brecon, aren't we, girl? You'll like him. Big black randy boy.' He rubbed at Sheba's cheeks as if he were drying her with an invisible towel. The dog panted happily into his face.

'Mark?' said Alex, suddenly remembering. 'Have you still got your shotgun?'

Mark laughed, getting to his feet. 'Your mum wants to borrow that too, does she? Back up the video?'

Alex grinned. 'No. Nathan and I . . . we wanted to go shooting.'

'Who's Nathan?'

'A friend. Down from London for a while. Used to live here.'

'You've nowhere to shoot.'

'Got a garden.'

'Grow up. It's a shotgun. You'd take your neighbours out. Buy an air rifle.'

'What d'you use yours for, then?'

Mark smiled. 'Not a lot, these days. Killing things, now and then. Looking out for Sheba.'

'What?' said Alex. 'You got it upstairs? In the flat? I thought they had to be in a special cupboard.'

'Ay. Steel box in the bedroom.'

'What d'you kill? Rabbits and things?'

'Been known.'

'Where? On your dad's land?' Owen Bevan owned fields above the garage, mostly bracken-infested rough grazing. 'Couldn't we shoot there too?'

'Nope.'

'Why not?'

Mark laughed. 'Pushy, aren't you? You ever fired a twelve bore?'

Alex shook his head. Hopefully he said, 'Used an air rifle.'

Mark snorted. 'You'd have to fire it, wouldn't you? Your brain's in your fingers, first time. Just itching. First time I took it out I shot the phone lines down. Missed the magpies, killed the lines stone dead. Nearly broke me nose with the recoil, too.'

'Shit,' said Alex.

'Ay, and then when I creeps back into the yard Dad's waiting, and flattens me in the mud.' He grinned. 'Glory days, huh?' He prodded a finger at Alex. 'Think you could carry a loaded gun and not fire it? Or your butty?'

'Course.'

'Bollocks.'

Alex thought Mark was being exasperatingly adult and responsible. 'You took a gun into school once,' he complained. 'Mr Granger told me. You shot it out the art-room window.'

Mark chuckled. 'He still there, is he? OK bloke, he was. It was only a piddling Gat gun. And Mr Granger fired it. To unload it. Good shot, too. Dented a Tango tin at fifty feet.'

'You could have been suspended.'

'Yup. Lucky, wasn't I?'

'But you won't lend me your gun.'

'Nope.'

Alex looked at the dog, and then at the shop she protected. 'Would you use it, if you thought Sheba was in danger?'

'Course,' said Mark. 'Anyone takes on Sheba, they got me next.'

Alex stared up at the window of the flat. It was growing dark. The light shone out warm and bright.

'Wish I had a place like this.' He was suddenly painfully envious of Mark. Not just for this flat. For everything: his job, his money, his vehicle, his independence. For the way he looked, his physicality. Even for his responsibilities. His guardianships: of Sheba, of the garage. It seemed almost romantic.

Mark said, in a different, quieter voice, 'How long ago was it your dad died?'

Alex shook his head, stuffing his hands into his trouser pockets. 'He wasn't my dad. My step-dad. More than a year ago. July last year.'

'Your mum. She OK now?'

Alex shrugged. 'Seems all right. Sometimes . . . she kind of over-reacts. But maybe that's just her. I can't remember what she was like before Michael. He was calm. Very calm. Sort of slowed her down. But in a good way. He was OK.'

'Ay.' Mark nodded. 'I remember him from school. Cricket mad, wasn't he?'

'That's him.'

'Tough, going out like that.'

'Yeah,' said Alex.

Chapter 12

'Sal?' said Jenny, into her work telephone mid-morning on Friday. 'Guess what. I'm going to give evidence at the inquiry.' She grinned into the mouthpiece.

'Attagirl,' Sal said.

'As long as it can be video evidence. Alex has come up with a brilliant idea. I'm going to make a video. Show them the Blaen Dyar views and what it's really like. They'll allow that, won't they?'

'Can't see why not. Great idea. Where're you getting the camera?'

'Oh, one of Alex's friends has got one.' Jenny heard the carelessness in her voice. 'He'll shoot the views, and I'll do a voice-over. I've planned it out already, more or less. We're going up on Sunday.'

'Fantastic.' Sal's voice was so warm Jenny felt treacherous. After Sunday, she told herself. I'll tell her then. When – if – there's anything worthwhile to tell.

Sal went on, 'You should ring the Secretariat and say what equipment you'll need. Hang on, I'll give you their number.'

Jenny heard the rustle of papers. She made a scribbling motion to Karen, sitting beside her.

'It's a Newport number,' said Sal.

'OK.' Jenny received a pencil from Karen and wrote it down.

'Got that. Listen . . .' She passed the pencil back. 'Two things. One, I need to know if they ask questions. British Coal, I mean.'

'Ah,' said Sal. 'I asked about that. Apparently British Coal cross-examine experts and major objectors, like the county council, but not private individuals. We only get clarifying questions.'

'Like what?' said Jenny, instantly alarmed.

'Simple facts. Like where you live, or when or where you took your video, say. Nothing you'd need to do homework for. They won't try to intimidate you, honestly. It's all about presenting themselves as Mr Nice Guys.'

Jenny nodded slowly into the receiver. 'That sounds OK. I suppose.'

'What's the second question?'

'Oh . . . a general one. I just thought . . . when do we know the result of all this? I mean, whether we or British Coal have won?'

'The Inspector has to write a report. Then it has to go round the Welsh Office. Then the Secretary of State has to prepare his statement. It'll be some time next year.'

'Oh, right. Hardly instant.'

'You said it. Jen, are the boys doing something, d'you know?'

'Who? Alex and Nathan? About the opencast?'

'Yes.'

'Not that I'm aware of. Why?'

'Well, I'm standing here looking at my message pad. There are doodles all over it. Pictures of masterful-looking action heroes in combat gear going pow and wham. With "Warriors of Blaen Dyar" scrawled underneath.' A grudging admiration entered her voice. 'They're actually rather good. I didn't know Nathan could draw.'

Jenny said, 'I haven't heard anything. Glad they're at least thinking about it, though. Alex usually assumes that right will prevail, in the long run, so he doesn't need to get involved in anything. I'm never sure if I find his faith touching or infuriating.'

'Useless lot,' Sal said. 'They pretend they're cynics when really they're pig ignorant.'

'Times are hard,' Jenny said. 'You can't blame them.'

'Well, you can,' said Sal. 'But it doesn't do any good.' Her voice picked up to brisk. 'Anyway, you make that phone call, OK? Sorry, Jen, must go.'

'Me too.' The door behind Jenny had opened. 'Bye.' She put the receiver down.

Frank walked up behind her and rested his palms lightly on her shoulders. Jenny was aware of Karen's swift sideways glance. She knew she should ask Frank to remove his hands, but couldn't say it. Instead she stood up, so they fell away, and bustled over to one of the filing cabinets.

'What d'you want, Frank?' She pulled out the middle drawer and flicked busily through the hanging files.

'Just to say I won't be able to make lunch today.' Frank's expression was tenderly apologetic. Jenny's insides clamped into a furious, impotent knot. 'An errand for Mother,' he went on sadly. 'Can't be helped.'

Jenny picked out a file at random, opened it and frowned at the contents. 'Fine.' She glanced up at him. 'No problem.' She returned her gaze to the file. The papers were upside down, but it was too late to reverse them. She snapped the file shut and replaced it.

'Just one of those things,' Frank said. Karen looked up from her work and gave him a polite smile.

Jenny manoeuvred around him to get back to her chair. 'Fine,' she said again. She sat down, stared at the screen in front of her, and placed her fingers on the keyboard.

'Well,' said Frank. She heard him shuffling behind her. 'I'll leave you to it, then.'

Jenny said, 'You do that.' But then felt forced to add a quick smile over her shoulder, because the words sounded so rude.

Frank lifted his hand in acknowledgement. The door closed behind him. Jenny leant back in her chair and closed her eyes.

'You and Mr Meredith,' said Karen, cautiously. 'Is it true? Are you, you know . . . seeing each other?'

Jenny snapped her eyes open. 'Is what true? No. Of course we're not.'

Karen looked confused. 'Sorry. I just thought . . .'

Jenny leant forward abruptly, catching her hand on the keyboard. The screen in front of her cleared.

'Oh, bugger. I've crashed it.'

'No, you haven't.' Karen reached across, rattled a few keys, and the information was restored.

'You're getting good at this, aren't you?' Jenny sighed, and stared at the screen. 'I had dinner with Frank on his fiftieth birthday because he asked me to and because, at the time, I considered him a friend. Now, I'm not so sure.'

'I think he's sweet on you,' said Karen. 'He sent those flowers, didn't he? I think he is. Everyone thinks so.'

'Oh, God,' groaned Jenny. 'Do they? I mean I know he is. I just didn't realize it was that obvious. I'll have to do something.'

'I'm sure he's a very kind man,' said Karen, tentatively.

'Are you?' said Jenny. Karen, of course, saw them as a viable couple: Frank, a middle-aged bachelor, herself a middle-aged widow. The cow, she thought drearily, how dare she?

'Ooh,' said Lizzie, as if she'd just remembered something. She put down the comb she'd been tugging through Alex's thick fair hair and rummaged in the drawer of her desk. 'I've got that translation for you.' She handed Alex a sheet of paper.

It was six thirty in the evening and she, Alex and Nathan were in Lizzie's tiny bedroom. Nathan was cross-legged on the low single bed picking at Lizzie's acoustic guitar, while Alex sat at her desk. Lizzie had been practising French plaits on his hair. Somewhere else in the house a younger brother and sister were arguing loudly above the plinky-plonk music of a computer game, and downstairs a rich female soprano voice was flexing itself through operatic scales. Lizzie's mother, Siân, was a principal singer for the Abercwm Operatic Society. The house was always full and noisy. Alex loved it; there seemed, paradoxically, more privacy here than in the relative silence and emptiness of his own house.

He tried to read Lizzie's handwriting on the sheet of paper, but it was impossible while she was still combing his hair. 'Hang on,' he said. 'Ow. God, you're rough.' Lizzie stopped. On the paper in front of him he saw the words *Rhyfelwyr Blaen Dyar*. Slowly he said, 'Ree-vel-were bline dee-err. Is that right?'

'More, rhr-vel-we'rre bline dee-arrr,' Lizzie said. It suddenly sounded authentically Welsh. 'Emphasis on the "vel".'

'Let's see.' Nathan put the guitar down. Alex tilted his chair back and handed him the paper.

'Wow.' Nathan stared at it. 'Her-vel-we'rre bline dee-arrr. Shit.'

'I'm not going to be able to say that,' said Alex.

'All to the good,' said Nathan. 'People aren't going to suspect you're a member of a group you can't pronounce, are they?'

Alex grinned. 'Suppose not.'

'D'you know what "Blaen Dyar" means?' asked Lizzie.

'Source of the Dyar,' said Alex immediately. 'Whatever Dyar is.'

Lizzie nodded. 'Blaen is river source. Or valley head. Dyar's an old word. It's marked as obsolete in my dictionary. It means sad, cruel, or loud.'

'Hey,' breathed Nathan. 'The source of the sadness. Not bad.'

'If sadness was a river,' said Lizzie.

'Better and better,' nodded Nathan.

Lizzie was peering at Alex's forehead. 'You've got a black-head.' She pulled his head round. 'Turn this way.'

'Get off.' Alex pushed at her.

'You two are disgusting,' Nathan said.

'Jealous,' said Lizzie. She picked up a crimper from the shelf above her desk. 'Straighten your hair for you, if you like. Bet it's amazingly long.'

'No, thank you,' said Nathan.

Lizzie bent over Alex, waving the appliance in his face. 'Can I crimp yours? Ah, go on.'

'No.'

'You know you like it.'

'No.'

Nathan hummed, loudly and tunelessly. Lizzie smiled and put the crimper back on the shelf. She nodded at the piece of paper Nathan had tossed on to the bed cover. 'So where're you going to write that? Is it going on the roads?'

Nathan looked at Alex. Alex said, 'Er, not sure yet.' Lizzie, to date, had only been told about the road painting. Alex suspected that she'd be dubious about warning letters to British Coal – as indeed he himself was, now, after seeing some of Nathan's drafts. 'He must Die, who Massacres the Mountain,' was one. 'The Sentence for Rape is Death' was another. Infuriatingly, although Nathan had obviously put thought into these messages, he'd yet to explore Sal's garden shed, in which Alex knew there was paint. Alex's own house search had turned up nothing except three part-used tins of black gloss, which would be useless on tarmac.

'Has Gareth got paint?' he asked suddenly. 'Bet he has.'

'What kind?' Lizzie enquired. Nathan had picked up her guitar again and was strumming quietly. 'Hey,' she said. 'That's "Knocking on Heaven's Door". Pretty good.'

Nathan's playing became louder and more ostentatious.

'Something pale that doesn't take hours to dry,' said Alex. 'Emulsion, I suppose.'

'Spray paint,' said Nathan, bending over the guitar in intense concentration. 'Car paint.'

'No one's going to have enough of that lying around,' said Alex. 'You said yourself we shouldn't buy anything.'

'What about your mate Mark?' said Nathan. 'Got a garage, hasn't he?' There was an edge to his voice, mentioning Mark's name. Before they had arrived at Lizzie's, Alex had told him that Mark wouldn't lend them his shotgun.

Alex said patiently, 'You said we shouldn't involve other people. He'd want to know what it was for, wouldn't he?'

'I dunno,' said Nathan. 'Would he?'

'Yes,' said Alex. 'He would.'

Nathan shrugged. Alex wondered why he sounded so antagonistic. Almost as if he was in some sort of competition with Mark.

'I think we ought to keep everything between the three of us,' he said. 'It's only paint.'

His voice and Nathan's guitar playing were drowned by a high human note of extraordinary penetration, emanating from downstairs.

'God,' said Lizzie, wincing. 'Embarrassing. Sorry.'

'Madhouse,' said Nathan, grinning broadly.

'She's not even that good,' complained Lizzie.

'Not bad either, though,' said Nathan. 'Kind of Wagnerian.' He tilted his face upwards, closed his eyes, and held out his hands in front of him. 'I see straw plaits.' He traced a curvaceous womanly shape in the air. 'Billowing white marquee dress. A huge horned helmet...'

'I think it is Wagner, actually,' Lizzie admitted.

'... and, hey,' Nathan opened his eyes, on a mental roll, 'you on this...' he waggled the guitar '... me on my bass. Alex

116

on drums. "The Warriors of Blaen Dyar".' He flung his arms wide. 'It's showtime, kids.'

Lizzie bent double, snorting.

Alex said, 'I don't play drums.'

'Oh, God.' Lizzie laughed harder.

'Bet Mark does,' said Nathan. 'Heh heh.' His shoulders shook.

'Oh, piss off.' Alex knew Nathan's needling was unmalicious, but his butterfly mind was exasperating. 'The paint,' he said emphatically. 'Lizzie?'

Lizzie collected herself. She nodded. 'I'll have a look. Dad's got drums of it in the lock-up. Bound to be something pale.'

'Great,' said Alex. 'Thanks.'

'Oh,' said Nathan. 'And I forgot. I got these.' He reached over to his leather jacket and yanked something out of a pocket. 'Here.' He tossed two dark woollen objects across the bed. Alex spread one out. A navy blue balaclava.

'Where d'you get these?'

'Nicked 'em from work,' said Nathan.

'Was that wise?'

'Old stock. No one buys balaclavas in August. He won't miss them.'

'This isn't a game, you know,' said Alex.

'Would I have nicked them,' Nathan asked, 'for a game?'

Alex said, 'Probably.' Nathan and Lizzie laughed. Alex found himself smiling too.

'So when're we going to do this painting?' he said. 'And are you coming with us, Lizzie?'

'Doing it at night, are you?' She pondered. 'Maybe.'

'You can be look-out.' Nathan spoke with deep conde-scension.

'Oh, ta.' Lizzie stuck out her tongue at him. It was a self-conscious gesture. Alex knew she was flirting, and was embarrassed. And irritated.

'How about Sunday night?' he said, trying to push things on. Nathan shrugged.

'You know what next week is?' Lizzie said.

'Shut up,' said Alex and Nathan as one. Lizzie sniggered. Thursday was A-level results day.

'Could you get the paint by Sunday?' Alex asked.

''Spect so.'

'Right. Sunday night. OK, Nathan?'

Nathan lifted his hand high above the guitar, and brought it down into a crashing chord. In a sepulchral voice he said, 'Sunday night.'

Chapter 13

Jenny arrived at Bevan's garage on foot, at exactly two o'clock on Sunday afternoon. The weather was warm in the valley but would be cooler on the hilltop, so she wore a long-sleeved shirt over her jeans. She carried a jacket, in the pocket of which was an exercise book containing a draft of her video script, and two maps, one a large scale of the Blaen Dyar area, the other a relief map of south-east Wales.

Owen Bevan was on the forecourt, doing something with a screwdriver to one of the petrol pumps. He was in his late fifties and a much slighter and craftier-looking individual than his son. Jenny never used his garage except occasionally for petrol. It had a capricious reputation: the deal you got, in workmanship and price, depended on whether Owen saw you – on the day in question – as friend or fodder. Jenny had never dared take the risk.

'Just borrowing your son for a while,' she said, smiling at him guilelessly. 'He said he'll take a video for me.'

Owen nodded at her, looking unsurprised. 'You tell him what to do, lady, he'll do it. Handy with that camera, he is.'

'It's most generous of him.' Jenny looked up at the sky which, between grey-bellied towers of cumulus cloud, was a deep clear blue. The day had started crisp and almost autumnal and, although the sun was now hot, there was still very little distance haze. 'Good day for it, I think,' she added.

Mark emerged from a door to the right of the shop. He was swinging a grey object – the camcorder – from his left wrist. Sheba was at his heels.

'Put her in the shop, Dad.' He smiled at Jenny and nodded at the red pick-up, parked across the workshop driveway. He was wearing a red-and-yellow sunburst T-shirt. Oh, gaudiness suits him, Jenny thought meltingly, crossing the forecourt. His hair was damply dark, as if he'd just showered.

She heard Owen say, 'Here, Sheeb,' and saw the dog stop, stare a moment after Mark, and then lower her body and slink away.

Close to, the pick-up seemed very high and lorry-like. Mark placed the camcorder in the passenger footwell.

'Give you a push up, if you like.'

'I'll manage.' Jenny threw her jacket in, clambered up beside it, and put a foot each side of the camcorder.

Mark walked round the vehicle and climbed into the driver's seat. He slammed the door shut and rested his hands on the steering wheel. Jenny stared at his forearms. His wristwatch was gold, white-faced, with a brown leather strap. The hairs on his arms were golden too. Anticipation of this moment had been curling her insides for days. She wanted to crush her lips to his skin.

'So.' Mark turned to her. 'Where we going, exactly?'

'Um . . .' She shifted her eyes from his arms to the cab footwell and found one of the maps. It was already folded to show the Blaen Dyar area. 'The highest point, I suppose. Or the edge of the summit plateau, anyway. There isn't really a peak. There . . .?' She thrust the map in front of him, indicating a cross she'd made in biro.

Mark inspected it, and nodded. 'Right. Take the Black Cliff track.' He returned the map to her and started the engine.

120

As they bumped off the forecourt Jenny reached for her seat belt and secured it. She had never sat so high in a single-decker vehicle; the motion felt ship-like, as if the cab were afloat four feet above the tarmac.

At the main road they turned left, and then after a few hundred yards swung right into a narrow lane, the start of the mountain ascent. A line of new, cottage-style houses with double garages and neat gardens gave way to steep fields and high banks of greenery. Then the lane became a dark lush tunnel, the banks topped with unruly hedges and overhanging hazel, oak, holly and sycamore.

The pick-up was noisy in low gear. Jenny watched Mark steer one-handed, the other resting on the gear shift. Vibration caused the map on her lap to slide to the floor; she didn't bother to retrieve it. The thrumming noise seemed to insulate them from the world outside. Jenny could contain herself no longer. She ran the tips of her fingers along the upper curve of Mark's golden forearm.

He smiled out through the windscreen. She leant towards his shoulder, so she could whisper and still be heard over the engine. 'Your dad says I only have to tell you what to do, and you'll do it.'

'Does he.' Mark's smile became a grin. 'Generous bastard, Dad is.'

Jenny released her seat belt. She moved closer still, lifted the loose dazzling sleeve of Mark's T-shirt, and pressed her lips against his shoulder. His flesh was cool and dry.

Mark glanced sideways at her, not at her face but at her body, as if studying what she was wearing.

'Undo your blouse, then,' he said. 'Let's see you.'

Jenny laughed, pulled away from him, and sat back.

'Go on.' Mark sounded as if his request was entirely reasonable. As if, since they both knew what this outing was about, any coyness on her part was humbug. He released the gear stick

121

and touched his knuckles to the side of her right breast. Jenny wasn't wearing a bra and knew, the moment his hand discovered this, that she was going to undress for him. His fingers brushed her nipple. The noise of the engine seemed to become louder and more cocooning.

She started to unbutton the shirt. Mark withdrew his hand and replaced it on the gear stick.

With all the buttons undone Jenny still hesitated. 'We might meet another car.'

'Ay, give 'em a treat. Open it.'

Jenny kept her gaze on the empty winding tunnel-road ahead and opened the shirt. The last time she had sat in a moving car with her breasts uncovered had been twenty years ago. With Pete. At dusk, during a journey from . . . yes, Brecon. Pete had adored her breasts and had announced, in a fit of euphoric magnanimity, that everyone, the whole world, deserved to see them. She'd been less stoned than he but had obliged, knowing it would excite her.

As it did now. A muscle began to tick, then thud, low in her abdomen. Her stomach flesh tightened, her diaphragm lifted, pushing into her breasts.

The trees and high banks outside ended abruptly. Sunlight streamed into the cab. They had reached the cattle-grid that divided the farmland fields from mountain grazing. Mark changed down a gear to rumble the pick-up across the metal bars. From here, though the incline of the land itself was steeper, the road straightened and levelled out, traversing the western face of the bracken-shouldered mountain. Pentre lay beneath them to the right, the main road that bisected it clearly visible hundreds of feet below, curving up through the lines of doll's houses like a grey, white-lined snake.

The engine note dropped to a steady drone. Mark's free hand fumbled with the button on Jenny's jeans. With her eyes still on the road she shifted her buttocks forward, so he could get at it. She felt herself start to loosen and unfurl, in anticipation.

He tugged the zip down. She pushed her head back against the head-rest, wanting to close her eyes, but not daring to. His fingers pressed against her pubic bone. She lifted her hips towards him.

She had to let her eyelids fall. Her body strained for him, now he was inside her. She wanted more, to feel herself stretched, the hollowness inside her filled, crammed . . .

'Shit.' His hand was snatched away. She opened her eyes. There was a bright blue alien speck on the road ahead. A distant car. She sat up, wrenching at her shirt fronts, wrapping them tightly across her body. Blindly she stared off to the right, across Mark, away from the mountain and the road into the bright emptiness beyond. Which became, as her eyes recovered focus, the huge valley view. They seemed to be teetering over it; Mark had pulled the pick-up half off the road, on to the very edge of the fall.

She felt a gut-churning wave of fear, but managed to relax into it. To be frightened of heights in such an extravagantly three dimensional land was absurd. She heard the car pass and Mark chuckle, as he swung the pick-up back on to the tarmac.

'Did they see anything?' Her voice was jerky. She zipped her jeans. Her thigh muscles were trembling. She started buttoning her shirt.

'Na,' said Mark. 'Course not.' He sounded deeply amused.

Jenny made herself smile too. She was being disingenuous – the risk had been part of the excitement. She reminded herself that being here, in this vehicle, with this man, was no crime. No secret, even.

They passed above a series of abandoned limestone quarries. The edge of the road ran just a yard in from the cliff face, only a low steel barrier separating them from the fifty-foot fall. Before Jenny had come to terms with her fear of heights she had been terrified of this route. Until she had learnt to go with the fear, to realize that without it the rewards were diminished, and so to stop wishing it away.

They left the quarries and moved inland. The road became flat and fast, waist-high bracken either side. They rounded the last obscuring spur; Blaen Dyar lay ahead.

'Good God,' Jenny said.

The land had turned purple. As if an astonishing heavenly paintbrush had been swept across it, tinting it with soft, rich, smoky hues. The mountain's annual blossoming. The heather was in flower.

'Oh, wonderful,' she breathed. 'What a bonus.'

They passed two parked cars, one pointing inward at the heather, the other outward at the valley views. Jenny did up the last of her shirt buttons.

A mile on, past a cluster of ruined cottages, they came to the lay-by where she had stopped three weeks ago. Mark slowed almost to a halt and swung the pick-up off the road, on to the boulder-strewn track. Jenny had to clutch the handgrab above her window as they lurched up the incline. Passing the white 'No Vehicles' sign, Mark pointed gun-fingers at it, said, 'Kerpow,' and blew imaginary smoke from his fingertips. Jenny steadied the video camera with her feet as it tried to slide across the cab floor. It would have been as fast to walk, and much more comfortable; Mark, though, she knew, was enjoying showing off his vehicle.

After a quarter of a mile, where the track veered right towards Black Cliff valley, he stopped and switched off the engine.

'Across there, eh?' He nodded directly ahead, into the bilberry and heather.

'I think so.'

They got out. Mark swung the strap of the camcorder over his shoulder. The heather plants here were large and ancient, with twisted woody stems like bonsai trunks, and flowering so prolifically it seemed vandalism to step on them. Jenny noticed marsh grass this time too, with spikes like porcupine quills, the colour fading towards the tips, each spike skewering a dry brown flower cluster. And ice-green lichen fronds that broke when you trod on them, as crisp as coral.

A few hundred yards from the pick-up, at the crest of a purple ridge, Jenny turned to survey the valley behind them. The panorama already stretched due west to due east.

'It's hard to tell, isn't it? Are we near the top yet?'

Mark ran up beside her and looked towards Pentre.

'Nope. Should be able to see the Beacons, above the Darren. Been up here with the school.'

With the school, Jenny repeated to herself, as she followed him down the ridge side. But with an inner smile.

They walked on. Jenny put a foot in a tiny pool hidden beneath the heather. The water was intensely cold. It felt not like rainwater but like some deep visceral fluid, welled up from the saturated heart of the hill.

'Hang on.' She stopped to take off her shoe. Mark waited on a heather dune ahead. As she squeezed the canvas out she saw him scanning the hilltop with narrowed eyes. With, it suddenly occurred to her, professional, appraising eyes.

She put the shoe on again. 'You are against the opencast, Mark, aren't you?' She felt the edge of a laugh . . . she hadn't asked . . .

'Mean a few jobs. Two hundred, maybe.'

'They won't be reserved for locals, you know. All the work's being contracted out.'

'Ay. And the pay's rubbish. Driving jobs, mostly. But . . .' He smiled. 'There's machinery. They'll need maintenance . . .'

She started walking again. 'So what are you doing up here, helping me?'

'What d'you think?' He laughed, and ran up to the top of

125

the next heather dune. He put the camcorder to his eye, and swung it through 180 degrees. A red light glowed on top of the machine.

'Here,' he said. 'You can see Pen-y-Fan. This'll do.' He took the camera from his eye.

Jenny joined him on the ridge and stared north-west. 'Hey, wow.' Distant blue peaks had appeared behind the mid-distance bulk of the Darren. 'I must put those in my commentary. I wonder if you can always see them. How far away are they?'

'Fifteen, twenty mile.' Mark was strolling off to her left.

'Where are you going?'

He was jogging down into a small crater-like hollow behind them. The far wall of the hollow was a miniature waist-high peat cliff. He crossed to it, patted the soil with his palm, and put the camera down.

He turned round and beckoned. 'Come here.'

Jenny smiled, glancing quickly around the deserted heather dunes, and walked down to him. Mark reached for her hips and pulled her close.

'Someone might come,' she whispered.

'Ay,' he said.

'And it looks scratchy.' But her arms were round his waist. She ran her fingertips up either side of his spine, feeling the muscle edge, where flesh met vertebrae. She dug her nails in.

'Ow.' Mark jerked her away.

'Sorry.' She hadn't meant to hurt him; she had just felt, at that moment, a grabbing exultation.

Mark swung round and studied the floor of the hollow. He yanked his T-shirt off and spread it out neatly on top of a rectangular clump of heather. Then caught her eye, urging her on, and dropped to one knee to unlace his boots.

Jenny kicked off her canvas shoes. The ground beneath her feet felt like raffia matting. Mark looked up at her. His irises were heather blue, the colour of the world around them. In one movement she pulled the shirt off over her head and tossed it at his T-shirt.

Something flickered in Mark's face. As if her half-nakedness, achieved so suddenly, had startled him. He stood up.

'What's wrong?' She glanced around.

'Nothing.' He shook his head quickly. 'Nothing's wrong.'

'Right.' She started to unzip her jeans. Mark put his hands on his own waistband, but got no further. He stood barefoot in his jeans, completely immobile, staring at her. She smiled, stepped forward and plucked at his belt buckle. 'Hey,' she murmured. 'You started this.'

And then nothing was holding him back; he had grasped her to him and was sighing hot breath into her neck. She melted against him, touched. Something had checked him, forced him to relinquish the lead. He does understand me, she told herself, as they stepped out of their remaining clothes. And how to empower me.

And then they were down on the heather, on the shirt and the T-shirt.

This time, at the end, she was aware, dimly, of falling towards him, of being held, as her body flared, by strong hands under her armpits, pulling her forward. Of a soft tugging bite at one heavy, hanging breast, then at the other. She heard a deep groan that she knew was hers, but which seemed to come not from her mouth or throat or larynx, but from the whole of her. The whole singing instrument of herself.

Chapter 14

Alex and Lizzie drew up outside Sal's house just after eleven thirty p.m. In the boot of the Escort were two half-gallon tubs of pale yellow emulsion paint, part-used, two brushes, and two torches. Nathan was outside on the pavement waiting for them, in grey, black and white urban camouflage trousers – new from the market, Alex wearily presumed – and carrying a bundle under his arm. The Escort only had two doors, so Lizzie had to get out to let him in. Nathan tossed the bundle on to the back seat and fell in after it.

'Are you pissed?' Alex asked, as Lizzie slammed the passenger door shut. 'For God's sake.'

'Pished?' said Nathan, grinning. 'Never.' He rummaged in the bundle and handed a can over the seat to Lizzie. 'Fancy a Bud?'

Lizzie said, 'Hey, thanks,' and took it.

He tried to hand one to Alex. 'Don't be stupid,' Alex said.

'Captain Sensible tonight, is it?' said Nathan. 'Good-oh.' He snapped open a can.

'I'm not going to do this,' said Alex, looking right and left before pulling out into the high road, 'if you're going to be a dork.'

'A dork? Me? I'm just in the mood. Honed to fighting pitch.'

'We're going to be painting, dickhead, not fighting.'

'Honed to painting pitch.' Nathan made an explosive, choking noise.

Lizzie turned in her seat to look at him. She took a swig of Budweiser and leant towards Alex. 'It's OK. He's putting most of it on.'

'I hope so,' muttered Alex.

Within ten minutes they were ascending the hairpin bends up to Gwern Lake. Since leaving town they had encountered no other traffic. Alex was relieved; he'd been worrying that his decision to start painting so early might be proved foolish. That he might have been over-influenced by the thought of a seven a.m. start at work tomorrow. But the roads were dead now. Sunday night dead.

They emerged from the trees on to the hillside. There were no house or street lights, left or right, just a bright white line in the middle of the dark curving road, guiding them up the mountain. A waist-high softly defined wall of bracken edged both sides, giving way, as they approached the plateau summit, to the more sculpted outlines of heather and rock. The lake appeared on their left, just a fleeting pale shimmer from inside the car. Alex slowed and, beyond the lake, opposite the mountain road junction, bounced the Escort into the entrance track of the gravelled car park. The track curved and then widened to an area as big as a football field. It was quite deserted. He drove across to white bollards at the lakeside and parked facing the water.

He switched off the engine. For a moment the three sat in silence, staring at the view. A half-moon hung in the sky directly ahead, silvering the still water. Beyond, and to both sides of the lake, was the dense humping blackness of the mountain, and beyond that, distantly and far below, the white and yellow pinprick light clusters of Usk valley villages. The mountain ridge horizon was topped by a purple-black sky.

Alex watched the water. 'Expect a hand to come up, don't you?'

'Magic,' said Lizzie.

'A land of dark, mysterious deeds,' Nathan whispered. Then added cheerfully, 'Like road painting. This the first stop, is it, Cap'n?'

Alex smiled through the darkness at Lizzie, before reaching for the door catch. 'Yes,' he said.

They climbed out of the car. Lizzie had her own torch and flashed it towards the road. 'Where're we painting, exactly? At the junction with the mountain road?'

'That's what I thought,' said Alex. 'The opencast fence will be just a few yards in from there.'

'What're we painting? "Opencast starts here"?'

Alex shook his head. 'Just "Opencast", and an arrow above it. That's all we need.'

'Facing which way? For which drivers?'

'For the traffic coming up. Traffic going down'll be leaving the site. We'll do one for them the other side of the mountain.'

'Been thinking about this, haven't you, Cap'n?' said Nathan admiringly.

'Unlike some,' Alex said.

'Ooh.' Nathan was standing just behind Lizzie, and let his head fall forward on to her shoulder. He stood up abruptly, clutching at the sides of his jacket. 'Where's my balaclava?'

'For Christ's sake,' groaned Alex.

'You got no style.' Nathan yanked a woolly object from his pocket and pulled it over his head. Lizzie shone her torch at him, and giggled.

'You look a nerd,' said Alex.

'Ah,' said Nathan, wagging his finger. 'But an unrecognizable nerd.'

Alex opened the car boot. He couldn't see anything because

the interior light didn't work. Lizzie was shining her torch beam on earth banks to their right. 'Lizzie,' he said.

'Sorry.' She swung the beam back. 'I was just looking over there. That's where the adders' nests are, isn't it?'

'Adders?' Nathan rose on tiptoe and picked up one foot, then the other.

'Yes,' said Lizzie. 'It's a breeding site. We were shown it on the school walk.'

'The school walk?' Nathan reverted to a normal stance. 'What school walk?'

'At the end of the summer,' said Lizzie. 'The whole school goes for a walk. Well, a sort of nature ramble.'

'How quaint.' Nathan turned to Alex. 'Can this be true?'

'The fifth and sixth years don't,' said Alex. 'They've finished by then. A few cop off too. But maybe two hundred or so go. A van meets them somewhere for a barbecue.'

'Shit. Two hundred kids tramping the hills. Bet they see a lot of wildlife.' Nathan chuckled.

'Won't be walking here again if there's an opencast,' Lizzie said.

'No,' said Alex. 'And I don't suppose the adders'll think much of it either. They don't like noise.'

'"Tis quiet, isn't it?' said Lizzie. 'Listen . . .'

They stood still, listening.

'Spooky,' said Nathan, breaking the silence.

Alex handed him a torch and put the other in his jacket pocket. He lifted one of the paint tubs out. With a screwdriver he levered off the top.

'I've stirred it already,' said Lizzie. 'Sorry it isn't a gel.'

'Looks fine,' said Alex. 'Right, how are we doing this? One painter and two lookouts?'

'Sounds OK, Cap'n.' Nathan snapped his torch on.

They walked towards the road. 'You take the Aber side,

Lizzie,' Alex said. 'Nathan, you go up there, beyond the junction. I'll do the painting.'

'Hey,' Nathan said. 'Boring.'

'You can paint the next one. We'd do three, I thought. It's a kind of triangle, the site. So we do one here, one on the top road just outside Brynteg, and the other where the Brynteg road meets this road, over the hill. We won't bother with the mountain road. Not enough traffic.'

'How do we signal if we see a car?' Nathan asked.

'Shout "car", dickhead. You'll see their headlights long before they'll be close enough to hear you. There's no one else up here.'

Nathan clicked his heels, saluted, and set off up the road.

Alex watched him go, and then turned to Lizzie. 'You could stay here, really. You can see down both the main road and the lane then.' He stared after Nathan, who had stopped at the roadside. Now he was squatting, peering at something with the torch. Alex groaned. 'What's he doing now?'

Nathan came running back. He held out his hand, shining the torch on it. Lying on his palm was a small, limply fragile, long-stalked toadstool.

'Is this what I think it is?'

Alex inspected the toadstool cap. 'No. It hasn't got a nipple. And it's too big. It's a bit early anyway. Give 'em a month or so.'

Nathan stared out across the hilltop, into the Blaen Dyar blackness. 'This is what it's all about, isn't it? Destroying the natural habitat of the magic mushroom. Disaster. I remember, you get thousands of them up here.'

'I'm sure there'll be plenty left,' said Alex. 'Can we get on?'

'Right.' Nathan tossed the toadstool away. 'Shit . . .' A clattering noise made them all jump. 'What was that?'

They swung their torches towards the mountain lane.

'It's ponies,' said Lizzie. Six pairs of eyes glittered at them.

The animals had come off the hill on to the road, and were standing facing them, shaggy heads tossing in the torchlight.

'Do they bite?' asked Nathan.

'Don't be stupid,' Lizzie said. 'Look, there's a foal with them. How cute.'

The ponies hesitated, then swung away and shuffled off down the lane. Three white humps rose from the verge, became alarmed sheep, and cantered noisily into the bilberry.

'Bloody hell, large mammals everywhere,' said Nathan.

'My mum used to say there were dinosaurs up here,' Alex said. 'She called it the lost world. Because of the quarry cliffs on our side. From the village Blaen Dyar can look kind of cut off.'

'Been at the mushrooms, I expect,' said Nathan.

'Can we get on?' Lizzie gave an ostentatious shiver.

'Right,' said Alex.

'To your stations, men.' Nathan tramped away from them.

Alex put the paint tub on the tarmac, squatted to remove the lid, and dipped his brush into it.

'Hang on,' said Lizzie quickly. 'I think a car may be coming.'

Alex wiped the brush clean. 'From where?' He stood up.

'Up from Aber. It's miles away, but . . .'

'Right. No problem. Just move back into the car park. Car!' he shouted up the road. A distant torch beam waggled acknowledgement.

He grasped the paint tin in one hand and Lizzie's arm in the other. They hurried across the tarmac into the car park. Lizzie switched off her torch.

The ascending headlights were clearly visible now. One car only, travelling at moderate speed.

'Oh, shit,' breathed Alex. He tugged Lizzie further into the car park. 'It could be a police car.' It was difficult to see more than a general body shape in the dark, and behind undipped headlights. But he had the impression that the vehicle was white, and had some attachment to its roof.

'They might see your car.' Lizzie sounded panicky.

'No, they won't. It's too far from the road. At night all you can see is what's in front. Honestly.' He glanced up the road. 'Where the hell is Nathan? Hope he's got out the way.'

'What's a police car doing here?'

'It's a main road, isn't it? And the quickest way over the mountain.' And the pubs only closed an hour ago, he thought. Oh, bugger, we did start this too early.

The car was only a hundred yards from them now. 'It is a police car,' Lizzie said. 'Alex. It's slowing down.'

'They can't see us,' said Alex. 'I promise.' Lizzie was right, though, it did appear to be slowing.

It crawled past the car park entrance. Alex moved a couple of steps nearer the road.

'Careful,' Lizzie squeaked.

The car was stopping some way ahead. Its brakes bathed the tarmac in red light. A figure was beside the car, bending down to it.

'It's Nathan,' groaned Alex. He turned and strode quickly into the dark of the car park, towards the Escort. He had to get rid of the paint. Lizzie jogged at his side. He'd left the boot open, so all he had to do was lower the paint and damp brush into it, and gently squeeze the lid closed.

'I'm going back there,' he said, when the boot-lid had clicked. 'We've done nothing wrong. Come on.'

'I don't want to.' Lizzie's voice was frightened.

'Hey.' Alex put his arms round her and gave her a quick squeeze. 'It's OK.' He released her. 'Come on.'

He walked out of the car park and up the road. Lizzie followed. Two policemen, one holding a hand lamp, were standing beside the police car talking to Nathan, who was still wearing his balaclava.

The policeman with the lamp saw Alex and walked down to meet him. 'You know this gent?' he said, flashing the torch back at Nathan. The officer was young, with an impatient, edgy look. 'Says he's an urban gorilla.' He swung round and barked. 'Take that thing off.' Nathan snatched the balaclava off his head.

'We were looking at the view,' said Alex. 'Just walking.'

His words were ignored – the policeman had spotted Lizzie. 'Young lady here,' he called back to the car. He moved past Alex and shone his lamp into her face. Alex heard him say, in a lower voice, 'These boys friends of yours, are they, love?'

'Yes,' said Lizzie in a small voice. She raised a shielding hand.

'Stay here a minute.' The policeman gestured her aside. 'You go up there,' he said to Alex, pointing the beam at his partner and Nathan.

Alex hesitated, not wanting to leave Lizzie.

'Go,' said the officer.

'It's all right,' said Lizzie.

Alex walked up to the car. Nathan was giving his name and address to the officer in an unabashed voice. The officer had a square face with a rugby player's flattened nose, and was at least thirty. Alex preferred older policemen and relaxed a little.

'Name?' The policeman looked at him.

Reluctantly, Alex gave his name. 'We haven't done anything wrong. Just driving around.'

'Uh-huh,' said the policeman, writing. 'So you've got a car up here, have you?'

Alex groaned to himself. 'Yes.'

The policeman glanced up. 'Where is it?'

'The car park.'

The policeman closed his notebook and reached into the car for a torch. 'Perhaps you'd show me. You come too,' he said to Nathan.

Alex led the way back down the road. At the far side of the tarmac the other policeman was still talking to Lizzie. Her face was tilted upwards, and she was shaking her head. Alex felt uncomfortably responsible for her. She looked very young and vulnerable.

They reached the Escort. The policeman walked round it, then shone his torch into the interior. In the beam Alex could see at least two Budweiser cans.

'Mine, officer,' said Nathan instantly. '*Mea culpa.*'

'Who's the driver?'

'Me.' Alex dug in his jacket pocket. 'And it's my car, and I haven't been drinking.' He held out his driving licence.

The policeman looked at it, then handed it back. He moved to the rear of the car.

'Open the boot, will you, please.'

Silently Alex unlocked and opened the boot. He watched the torch beam illuminate his spare tyre, a jack, an empty oil can, the two paint brushes, one damp, though barely yellow, and the paint tubs.

'What's this?' asked the policeman.

'Paint,' said Alex. 'Yellow paint.'

'He's going to paint his bedroom,' Nathan said. 'Be pretty, officer, won't it?'

The policeman didn't reply. His partner and Lizzie were approaching. Lizzie walked quickly to Alex's side. Alex took her hand and held it tightly. Both officers regarded the paint tubs.

'Right.' The officer with the broken nose took the car keys from the boot lock. 'You . . .' he indicated Alex '. . . come with me. You other two, stay here.'

'I haven't been drinking,' insisted Alex. He knew he was going to be breathalysed.

'Then you've nothing to worry about, have you?'

Alex sighed, released Lizzie's hand and followed the officer back up the road. At the car the officer produced an object the size and shape of a personal cassette player.

'Have you done this before?'

'Yes,' said Alex, resentfully. 'And I was OK then, too.' He wondered if the policeman knew how humiliating this procedure was.

He blew steadily into the tube, and stopped when the officer told him.

'I wasn't lying, was I?'

'You weren't.'

The officer returned the breathalyser to the police car and escorted Alex back to the car park. His partner was just putting his radio away.

'May I suggest,' the older policeman said, handing Alex his car keys, 'that you three go home now. And take your paint with you.'

Nathan started to argue, 'There's no law . . .'

Alex cut across him. 'We'll go home. We were anyway.'

'You do that. Goodnight, boys, miss.' The officers strolled away.

Alex watched them leave the car park and then said, 'Get in,' to Nathan and Lizzie. The police car wouldn't leave until the Escort did. Nathan and Lizzie obeyed. He climbed into the driving seat, slammed the door shut, and started the engine.

No one spoke on the mountain descent. Then, as they reached the trees, Nathan said, 'Fucking pigs.'

'It was your fault,' hissed Alex. 'Why didn't you get out of the sodding road?'

'There's no law against walking on the road.'

'In a fucking balaclava.'

'Just wanted to give them a scare. I didn't know it was a police car.'

'You're such a pillock.'

'Shut up,' said Lizzie tightly. 'Both of you.'

'Yeah,' said Nathan. 'And what were they talking to you about?'

There was a pause before Lizzie said, 'Just . . . you know . . .'

'Use your brain,' Alex snapped. 'Wearing your fucking rapist gear.'

'Oh, shit.' Nathan gave a laugh of astonishment. 'Shit . . . I didn't think . . .'

'No, well, you don't, do you?' said Alex bitterly. 'You've spoilt everything. They've got our names and addresses now. Anyone paints anything up here, they'll be calling on us.'

'Garbage. They didn't know what it was for. It was just tubs of paint.'

'You've ruined it. If we do anything now, they'll know it's us. It's all ruined.'

Nathan was quiet a moment, then said in a contrite, cartoon-character voice, 'Sorry, folks.'

There was another silence, before Lizzie said, to Alex, 'It was bad luck as well. He wasn't to know it was a police car. And maybe we should have done it later. It was risky, wasn't it?'

Alex sighed. He was cross with himself, as well as with Nathan.

'I know,' he said. 'I know.'

'At least we didn't get caught,' said Lizzie. 'If we'd started painting they'd have stopped when they saw it. So maybe we were lucky, really.'

'She's right,' said Nathan quickly. 'Course they'd have stopped. If it had been half painted.'

Alex knew they were right. He thought how scared Lizzie would have been if they'd had to hide from the policemen in the dark, with the crime half committed. How agonizingly responsible he would have felt then.

'You're still a pillock,' he said to Nathan, but unrancorously.

'I know,' Nathan agreed sadly. 'But I can't seem to help it.'

Lizzie gave a short laugh. And so, after a few seconds, did Alex.

Chapter 15

On Monday evening Sal and Jenny met again for a drink at the Castle Inn, as they had the previous week. This time, however, they sat inside, at a table in one of the window bays. Outside, the weather was foul; heavy rain rattled the window panes. Jenny heard it as appropriate mood music; she had just told Sal about her new sexual relationship, and Sal was not taking it well.

'What's his name?' Sal pushed herself forward in her seat. Her fists were clenched.

'Mark.' Jenny met her friend's glare. Ill-humour, she thought, did not become Sal. It made her face fleshier. Her shape more ungainly. Her voice cruder. Cowish, even.

'So. You get to take your video, and in return he gets to fuck you.'

'No,' said Jenny. 'I get my video, and we both get to have sex. If you must put it like that.'

'Jesus Christ,' snapped Sal. 'Who is this boy?'

'He's not a boy.'

'You said he was one of Alex's friends.'

'Someone he knows. He's much older.'

'How much older?'

Jenny picked up her drink. 'Twenty-five.'

'Oh,' cried Sal. 'A mature man.' She fizzed air through her teeth. 'So who is he? Do I know him?'

'I don't think so. He lives in the flat above Bevan's garage. He's Owen Bevan's son.'

'And you just decided, wham bam, I'm going to have this one, did you?'

Jenny reflected. 'In a way. Once I knew it was possible.' And when was that? she wondered. When he told me about the glass of water? Good God. It might have been.

'He'll tell everyone,' said Sal. 'Your name will be harlot.'

'He won't.'

'Course he will. That's what boys do. They tell their mates.'

'He's not a boy. And he won't. I've asked him not to.'

Sal hooted.

Jenny leant forward, irritated. 'Why are you so angry? I've told you because I'm happy about it. You didn't make a fuss about Gareth.'

'You regretted that.'

'I see. So if I'm unhappy about something, or regret it, that's OK. But if I'm pleased . . .'

'Don't be silly.' Sal's voice was still hard, but had lost its furious edge. 'I'm concerned for you. That you're . . . out of control. That this isn't you. It isn't, Jen. You're behaving reck-lessly. Stupidly.'

Jenny nodded. 'Not stupidly. But I do feel reckless. And I do sometimes feel out of control. But I felt much more out of control with Gareth than I do with Mark. It's just sex. Good meaningless sex. It's sex which might have meaning that I couldn't handle.'

'Meaningless to whom? Would it be meaningless to Alex?'

'He won't find out. Even if he did . . . it's my life, not his.'

'You don't believe that. Else, why the secrecy?'

Jenny sighed. Sal was right, of course. 'I'm being instinctive. Taking what I want. What I need.'

'You sound like a man. You've left out "regardless of anyone else".'

Jenny made an exasperated noise. 'What's so wrong with having an affair?'

'You'd call it an affair, would you?'

'All right. Having sex. Whatever.'

Sal was silent for a moment. Then said, 'I just think you'll regret it. I know you're trying to fill a hole in your life. You're empty, that's understandable. But you can't fill holes by shoving pricks in them.'

Jenny wanted to say, *But you can. Joined to Mark, I am whole.* But knew that, said aloud, it would sound preposterous. She said, 'If it's what I want to do, and so does he, why shouldn't I?'

'Just be careful which pricks you use, Jenny, that's all. Just be fucking careful.'

'I don't think I'm into safe sex at the moment. I'm sorry.'

'I wasn't thinking of that. Though maybe you should be. But first Gareth, then this one. I don't want you fucking around with every kid you come across. I'm warning you.'

Jenny stared at her, and then laughed, suddenly understanding why Sal was so angry. Christ. She was worried about Nathan . . .

'I'm not interested in kids. Sal . . . how could you imagine . . . I've got Mark now, anyway . . .'

'You're mad.' But Sal's voice was grumpy now, rather than angry.

'And I've got a smashing video. I'll show it to you when Mark's tidied it up. He's really good. We only had to do it twice, and that was because I made a muddle of the voice-over the first time.'

'Still panting heavily, were you?'

'Ha ha. I forgot one of the Black Mountain valleys. And guess what, we got a buzzard, being mobbed by jackdaws. Or rooks. Crow family, anyway. I previewed the whole thing through the eyepiece. One long sweep of the horizon, like it's on a tripod, really steady. Then another sweep, coming back, of the near-ground, so you can see Gwern Lake and the heather in bloom and Sunday drivers looking at the view. And lots of shots of sheep looking sweetly pastoral, of course.'

'How long is it?'

'Short. Less than ten minutes. But you can see a lot in ten minutes. And say a lot. It's brilliant. He's got such steady hands.'

'As you'd know.'

Jenny giggled. Sal gave her a grudging smile. 'He's bringing a copy over later in the week. I'll lend it to you. You'll be impressed.'

'I don't doubt it,' Sal sighed.

At eleven the next morning Frank poked his head round Jenny's office door. Jenny was alone; Karen was downstairs showing a client paper samples.

'Ah,' said Frank.

'Hello,' said Jenny, steadfastly not turning round. She was laying out a menu card for the Bombay Queen Indian restaurant. She heard feet shuffle, and the door close. Then Karen's chair was pulled back. Frank sat down next to her.

She reached the end of her line, suppressed an irritated tick, and took her hands from the keyboard. Frank had been out all day yesterday, attending meetings at the Hereford branch. She had enjoyed his absence.

She sat back and gave him a polite, employee smile.

'I took your advice on Sunday,' he said. 'Well. Mother and I did.'

'Oh, yes?'

'And I think we saw you. It was you, wasn't it?'

'I'm sorry?' She was lost. What was the man talking about?

'Mother and I. We went for a spin to Gwern Lake, and

then, as you suggested, across Blaen Dyar. Quite an experience, especially above the quarries. I think we saw you. In a red van? A truck? You pulled over for us.'

Jenny swallowed a stone in her throat. It lodged half-way down, pressing on her breastbone. But she had been covered up. It was all right. Mark had said so. She swallowed again.

'You were being driven by some young man.' Frank was smiling.

'Yes,' said Jenny. 'Yes. One of Alex's friends. We went up the top to make a video. He has a camcorder. I told you I wanted to give evidence at the inquiry. I'm going to show them a video. I think it's rather good.'

'Ah.' Frank nodded several times. 'I see. How interesting.' He shifted position. 'This young man. Um. You know him quite well?' He gave a short apologetic laugh. 'That's what Mother said. That you seemed to know him well.'

Jenny double checked her memory. Mrs Meredith couldn't have seen anything compromising. Only, possibly, the expressions on her and Mark's faces, as the vehicles passed. What expression would she have been wearing, as she held her unbuttoned shirt over her subsiding breasts, and over her open jeans, and her wide-open, suddenly deprived body. What could an expression – glimpsed only for a second – betray? And how dare – how dare – Frank question her?

Coldly she said, 'I do know him quite well. Very well, in fact.' Her anger tightened to a hard lump. This interrogation was outrageous. 'He is an acquaintance's son, actually. I've known him for years. And . . .' She let the edge of her outrage show, she was entitled to it. '. . . I don't honestly see what business it is of yours.'

Frank lifted his hands in instant capitulation. 'I'm sorry. I am sorry. You're right, of course. I knew there'd be a simple explanation.'

143

'What d'you mean, a simple explanation?' Jenny's voice rose. 'Frank . . . what are you talking about?'

Frank placed a hand on her shoulder.

'Please don't,' said Jenny.

He withdrew his hand. 'Jenny. You and I. You know how I feel about you.'

'Do I? OK,' she conceded. 'But you're assuming far too much.'

'I'm your best friend. I care about you, Jenny. The night of my birthday—'

'The night of your birthday, what, Frank? I came to dinner with you. It was your birthday. End of story.'

'You kissed me.'

'I kiss lots of people on their birthdays. You asked me to kiss you.'

Frank's expression was compassionate. Almost pitying. As if she were a child, denying her emotions. As if he understood the reasons for this denial.

'It's been more than a year,' he said gently. 'No one would blame you.'

'Blame me for what?'

'For . . . wanting to make a fresh start.'

Jenny looked away. Argument was hopeless. Unless it involved cruelty, which was impossible if she wanted to keep her job.

She took the easy way out. 'I'm not ready for anything. I don't know what I want. Really. It's too soon. It wouldn't be fair on you.'

'Let me decide that.' Frank's voice was urgent. 'I'm not asking anything of you. Just that we remain friends. See each other out of work, now and then.'

'That's not what you're asking.' Oh, God, she thought, he sounds encouraged. 'You know it isn't. You're asking a lot more than that.'

144

Frank leant very close to her. She could smell his body. It smelt faintly sour, like old fruit.

'I've loved you a long time,' he said. 'I've wanted to tell you, so often. I never said anything, while Michael was alive.'

'For Christ's sake.' He sounded as if he expected praise for such restraint.

'I know,' Frank persisted, 'that on the night of my birthday, you felt something. I could see it in you. Maybe you didn't recognize it here,' he tapped his temple, 'but you felt something, I know.'

'You're mistaken,' said Jenny. 'If you saw anything, it had nothing to do with you.' He reads everything wishfully, she thought. Huge for tiny. Positive for negative. Him and his bloody mother.

'Is there anyone else?' asked Frank. 'You'd tell me if there was, wouldn't you? I think I deserve to know.'

Jenny stared at him, and then shook her head. What the hell was he saying? That he was Michael's natural successor? Bastard. She got up. In as steady a voice as she could manage she said, 'I don't think you're hearing me, Frank. And I don't think you see me properly, either. I'm not the person you think I am.'

'I see you very well,' said Frank. 'And I hear you. I promise.'

Words were futile. Jenny moved to the door. 'I'm going downstairs now. And at lunchtime I'm going shopping. Please . . . please forget about this. Don't make it difficult for me to stay. I like working here. I don't want to have to hurt you.'

'I'm not hurt,' said Frank, rising. 'I understand. I've spoken too soon. We'll say no more about it. But I'm here.' He gave her a small, tender, understanding smile. 'I'll always be here.'

Jenny left the room. Oh, God, she thought, as her feet thudded down the stairs. Yes. He's said it. He'll always be here.

*

'Disaster,' said Jenny on the phone to Sal that evening. 'Frank has declared his love for me.'

'No shit?' said Sal. 'What a bummer.'

'It's not funny. I may have to change jobs. The man's blind and deaf. He can't take a hint. In fact, I doubt he could take a bloody body blow.'

'The genes are linked. The "My God I'm Irresistible" and the "My Penis is Standing Up" gene. They're all the same. When you do finally get through to them they bash your head in and claim provocation.'

'I doubt it'll come to that with Frank,' said Jenny.

'You never know.'

'No need to sound so cheerful. I don't want to leave. Oh, hell.'

'Give him a cooling-off period. Take some holiday.'

'I can't. I took a fortnight in June, remember, with Mum and Dad. Though maybe Frank's got some holiday due. That's an idea. Where's my diary?' She flicked through the large appointments book she kept by the phone. 'Oh, yes. Whoopee. He has. *Frank to Italy*. In a fortnight.'

'Can you stick it till then?'

'Have to, won't I? I expect so. He's promised to cool it. But it's harassment, you know. He can say what he likes to me, and I can't to him. I never thought of Frank as a bully but he is, quietly. Patronizing and arrogant.' She sighed. 'And I used to think he was a gentleman.'

'Welcome to the real world, sweetie.'

'Am I giving off vibes, d'you think?'

'I'm surprised you haven't had more offers, actually. Poor little widow, all alone, must be desperate for it.'

'He says he's loved me for years. And, get this, that he deserves to know if I'm seeing anyone else.'

'So you've told him about bollock brain, have you?'

Jenny frowned, hurt. 'Please don't call him that.' It was as if Sal was objectifying and insulting part of herself. 'Of course not.' She winced, contemplating the thought. 'God, what would he think of me?'

'Why should you care? You want his illusions shattered, so shatter 'em. Tell him you're bonking the balls off someone young enough to be your son.'

'That's not true. He isn't.'

'Near as dammit. Go on, tell him. Watch his illusions crumble.'

'It would be too horrid. I couldn't.'

'My arse. You mean that although you don't want him, and, indeed, despise him . . . shut up . . .' – Jenny had made an objecting noise – 'you still want him to think well of you.'

'No,' said Jenny, belligerently. 'No. Not necessarily. But I want to keep my job. I couldn't tell him the truth, and stay.' The belligerence deflated. 'All right. I couldn't tell him, full stop. But don't ask me why. I just couldn't.'

'Fine. Jenny, can we leave your sex life, just for a moment? Do you know what the day after tomorrow is?'

Jenny said immediately, 'A level results day.' And, she thought, but didn't say, the day Mark's coming round. The prospect of both events made her mind tremble. 'Alex has got his list of college numbers by the phone already. He's convinced he won't get his grades. He's practising begging.'

'Remind me. What does he need?'

'Two Bs and a C for Southampton. Three Cs for Plymouth. I'm trying not to think about it. How's Nathan getting his results?'

'His dad's phoning them through. He doesn't seem at all worried. Says even if he doesn't make it this year he'll get in somewhere for next.'

'I'm sure he's right. He did sciences, didn't he?'

'You know they're planning a night on the town that evening, don't you? Places or no places. Along with the rest of

147

junior humanity, presumably. It'll be mayhem. Nathan says Alex is staying over here, with a few others from out of town. I'm definitely working that night. I can't bear to see them pissed, it brings out the nurse in me. Cheyne-Stokes breathing and stomach pumps. God, I wish spirits weren't so cheap.'

'We were as bad. Or, at least, the boys were.'

'Maybe. But it was only beer then.'

'And dope.'

'Speak for yourself. But nobody dies of hash overdoses. And, anyway, it's dope too, now. And worse.'

'I don't feel in a position to lecture. You just have to make sure they know the facts, and trust that they're basically sensible.'

Sal sighed. 'Alex probably is. I'm not so sure about Nathan. I can't keep alcohol in the house any more.' She sounded depressed. 'D'you think it's my fault? He needs to prove his masculinity or something?'

'Expect so,' said Jenny. 'Bound to be.'

Sal gave a barking laugh. 'Thanks, Jen. Quite right.'

'I can hear Alex's car,' said Jenny. A vehicle door slammed outside. 'Yes, it's him.'

'OK,' said Sal. 'Well, good luck with Frank. Hang in there.'

'I will. Thanks.' A human shape – Alex – passed the window. Jenny put the phone down. She walked through to the kitchen. Alex was hanging up his jacket.

'Just been talking about you to Sal. About Thursday.'

'Oh, yeah? Ah, Mum . . .' Alex sounded glad she had brought this up. 'If I get my grades, are you going to give me anything?'

Jenny smiled. 'I hadn't thought. What did you have in mind?'

'Not sure,' said Alex. 'One bloke, he's getting a CD player.'

'My God. I thought students bought those with their grant cheques.' She opened the fridge. 'D'you want a drink?'

'A beer. Thanks. Yeah, well, but I won't be getting a grant cheque this year, will I?'

'I'm not buying you a CD player.' She removed two beer cans. 'Christmas, maybe.'

Alex took his can. 'Could I have a tattoo, then?'

'What?'

'Nathan's got this magazine. About tattooists in Blackwood. They do these Celtic knotwork designs. Really classy. Armlets and things.'

'For heaven's sake.' Jenny poured her own beer into a glass. 'A, they hurt, and B, you'd regret it. You didn't get your ears pierced because you were squeamish. Tattooing's much worse. Blood everywhere.'

'How d'you know?'

'Everyone knows. It's fashionable. Hollywood stars have their boobs tattooed.'

'Mark's got one.'

Jenny nearly said, no, he hasn't. Stepping dizzily over it, she said, 'Where?'

Alex clapped the outside of his right shoulder. 'There. Sort of a cow horn design. Looks good.'

Jenny was astonished. How extraordinary that she hadn't noticed.

'He's older than you,' she said.

'He had it done when he was sixteen.'

'When he was doubtless an idiot. It's illegal at that age. He'll regret it one day.'

'Bet he won't.'

Jenny blew out with exasperation. She opened the fridge again, took out a bowl of pasta and tuna, and thumped it on to the table. 'It's your body. Do what you like. But I'm not treating you. Have your nipples chained together. Have "cretin" tattooed across your forehead.'

'They won't do faces or hands.'

Jenny laughed. 'Get some plates and forks. I'll tell you what . . . if you get grades good enough for Plymouth I'll sub your night out. OK?'

'By how much?'

'A tenner?'

'Oh, Mum . . . we'll be getting videos after. Sal's lending us her place for the night. Ten quid's nothing.'

'All right. Twenty. But please don't buy spirits. To take back to the house, that is. Sal doesn't like it.'

Alex rolled his eyes. 'I can't stop people buying spirits.'

'You don't even like them,' Jenny complained. 'All you do it tip them into kids' drinks and then throw the lot up. It's so stupid.'

'It's called a lad's night out,' Alex said patiently. 'It's about being stupid. Don't be such a dirge.'

'Someone might choke on their vomit,' said Jenny. 'It happens.'

'Not with ten mates kipping beside them it doesn't.'

'Poor Sal,' sighed Jenny. 'I'm glad we don't live in town.'

Chapter 16

Alex got a B, a C and an E. He rang Jenny at lunchtime on the Thursday to tell her, and to say that he'd phoned Plymouth and they'd agreed to accept him for his deferred place anyway, despite being a grade down. He sounded breathless and a little shaky.

'Darling, that's wonderful.' Jenny's own insides liquefied with relief. 'You got them all. The E was for French, was it?'

''Fraid so. B for History, C for English.'

'Well done. Really, well done. Have you rung your father?'

'Just about to.'

'And how did Nathan do, d'you know?'

'Got a B and two Ds, same points as me. He's pleased. He'll definitely get in somewhere next year.'

Jenny was relieved, both for Sal's sake and for her own. Even between best friends, children's achievements – or failures – could cause awkwardness. The fact that Alex and Nathan had never attended the same school had been, she always thought, a big plus in her and Sal's relationship.

'So you'll both have something to celebrate tonight. That's still on, isn't it?'

'Course. Going round to Nathan's for tea first.'

'Well, there's a twenty-pound note for you in the box on my dressing table. You'd better take that now.'

'Ah, great, Mum. Thanks.'

'And when will I see you again? Tea tomorrow?'
'Be back midday, I expect. Not working tomorrow.'
'OK. Go easy tonight.'
'Yes, Mum.'
'No spirits at Sal's.'
'No, Mum.'
'Don't sigh. It's only because I love you. And well done, darling.'
'Thanks, Mum.'

At home after work Jenny watered the flower tubs, mowed the front and side lawns, swept the kitchen floor, and vacuumed the sitting-room carpet. Since lunchtime and Alex's phone call her energy level had felt inexhaustible. Once or twice, as she worked, she thought she could actually hear the mechanics of the inner motor that was producing the energy, making a zooming noise at the edge of audibility. And several times, as she mowed, watered, vacuumed and swept, she stopped and mentally hugged herself, reminding herself why she was happy. It was extraordinary how important Alex's success seemed now – up to a week ago she would have denied any anxiety about it.

And, as so often, one happiness seemed to inspire others. A host of smaller, immediate, here-and-now felicities presented themselves: the cottage was looking gratifyingly pretty just now – and the garden, despite its wildernesses. And the view of the valley, seen with a fresh, energetic eye. She was lucky, she told herself, no, privileged, to live here.

And on top of all this, of course, like an extravagant gift thrown in by an already generous fate, was the prospect of Mark's arrival, in less than two hours. Bringing with him her videotape, and himself.

*

She had a shower at eight, put on a blouse and skirt, and heard his pick-up in the lane while she was still upstairs. She ran down to greet him. He was about to reverse into a tight space in the lay-by across the road.

'You can park here,' she called, opening the garden gate.

Mark raised a hand and pulled across on to the hard standing. Sheba was sitting, very upright and stately with her ears pricked forward, on the passenger seat. Mark cut the engine and swung his door open.

'Alex not home tonight?' He was wearing a tan jacket over a white shirt and black jeans.

'No,' said Jenny. 'He's celebrating in Aber.'

'Oh ay, A levels.' He reached into the vehicle and took out two videotapes. 'Do all right, did he? Stay,' he said to the dog. He slammed the car door shut.

'Not brilliant. But good enough.' She noticed Sheba's eyes, following her master's movements from behind the windscreen. The dog's expression was one of intense, unconditional adoration. Jenny smiled to herself and said, 'D'you want to bring her in? She could use the garden.'

Mark shook his head. 'On heat, she is. Can't let her run loose. She's used to the car.'

'She's a beautiful dog.' Jenny knew a compliment would please him. 'Such a kind head. Alex says you're letting her have pups this time.'

'Yup. Goes to Brecon getting next week. Be due end October. You want one? Cost ya.'

'So I've heard. No thanks.' Jenny led the way along the front of the house to the kitchen door. 'I'm out at work all day. And too many sheep round here. I couldn't cope with a sheep chaser.'

'Ah,' said Mark. 'You got to train 'em right. Let 'em know who's boss.'

Jenny entered the kitchen. 'Good at that, are you?'

153

'I am,' nodded Mark, wiping his feet on the mat. 'Ask anyone.'

Jenny couldn't help grinning. 'Nothing,' she said, seeing his expression. 'I'm just pleased to see you. Why've you got two tapes?'

'Ah . . .' Mark frowned down at the cartridges. 'Show you now.'

'You've got more than one version, have you?'

'Kind of.'

He looked diffident. Jenny was touched by the idea that he had been working on the tapes. The original, she thought, had looked pretty good. 'Don't worry,' she said, 'I'm sure I'll like whatever you've done.' She jogged his elbow. 'Come through to the sitting room.'

Most visitors, on first entering the cottage sitting room, made some appreciative comment. The room's features – the oak beams, the deep fireplace with its brick-lined bread oven, and the adjacent blocked-off spiral staircase – were the main reason Jenny and Michael had chosen the cottage. Jenny guessed Mark would make no comment, and she was right. He deposited one of the videotapes on top of her television, slid the other into the VCR below, then took off his jacket and slung it over the back of one of the grey-and-blue armchairs.

'Would you like a drink?' Jenny stood at the sideboard. 'We're not in any rush, are we?' His white shirt had fancy pearl buttons, she noticed; he ought to be wearing a bootlace tie. She bet herself he owned one.

'No rush.' Mark reached into the pocket of his jacket, took out a quarter-bottle of whisky, and waved it at her. 'Have some of this, if you like.' He sat down on the sofa.

'Oh, OK.' Jenny picked up two small glasses and put them on the coffee table. The table was one of her more bizarre possessions – the black top was a lacquered octagon, supported by four sinuous Chinese dragons – the table legs – whose lizard heads overlooked the table top. It had been given to her at Alex's birth by a sentimental hippie overcome by her motherhood, who insisted it would bring her and Alex good karma. From its surface, he insisted, plain food became ambrosia, water nectar, and the duffest dope would blow your mind. Alex called it 'Mum's mad hippie table.'

'Where's the remote?' asked Mark. Despite his agreement that there was no rush, he seemed anxious to get on.

Jenny retrieved the remote control from a shelf above the television and switched on the set. 'Bit old-fashioned here, I'm afraid,' she said, walking back. 'Have to turn the telly on by hand.'

Mark didn't answer, but took the remote from her, his eyes on the screen. The police programme *The Bill* was showing. A patrol car was speeding down a suburban street with its blue light flashing.

'Sit down,' he said. There was an echo in his voice of the tone he used with Sheba.

'Yes, sir,' Jenny murmured. He was definitely tense. Was her good opinion really that important to him?

She picked up her glass of whisky, then lowered it and half-rose. 'I think I need water.'

'No, you don't.' Mark pulled her down again. He pointed the remote control at the VCR. 'Watch,' he said.

His arm, returning the control to the table, brushed against hers. She smiled at him, saw his gaze occupied by the screen, and dutifully leant back to watch. The police car disappeared in a haze of grey dots. The dots merged to a uniform dark grey screen. A voice off, male and familiar, said, 'Come here.' At the same time the dark retreated, allowing light to filter into the edges of the picture. The dark acquired shape and rich colour, became a man's brightly clad torso.

'What's this?' she asked, with prickling alarm. Mark didn't reply. The man on the screen was moving away from the camera.

155

Now he was full length, side on. He was Mark. Surrounded by greens and violets: tufty, springy greens and violets. A woman with short dark hair entered from the right of the picture, a smiling woman, wearing a loose long-sleeved shirt and jeans. The man put his hands on her hips and pulled her towards him.

'Stop this!' Jenny lunged for the remote.

Mark caught her hand and held it tight. 'Wait.' His voice was low and contained. 'It gets better.'

'Stop it!' The woman on the screen had her hands under the back of the man's T-shirt. Jenny wrenched her eyes from the couple and twisted her head, her whole body, away from the television. She squeezed her eyes tightly shut.

Mark released her, picked up the remote, and clicked it at the VCR. The couple disappeared, replaced by a white puppy cavorting with a toilet roll.

'What's the problem?'

Jenny had to gasp for breath. 'You . . . my God . . . that's a bastard thing . . .' No wonder he had seemed tense. A greater horror struck her. 'Christ . . . you've seen this already, haven't you?'

'Course I have.' Mark began to grin. He was relaxing. Now his bombshell was unstoppably detonated.

'What . . . how long . . . how much does it show . . .?'

'Well . . .' He nodded to himself, considering. 'All of it, I suppose. Starts there, at the beginning, and ends . . . at the end.'

'How could you film us? Without asking me? Jesus Christ.'

'You might not have agreed.'

Jenny tried to laugh; her throat was shaking. 'You're dead right.'

'Why not?'

'It's disgusting. The idea's disgusting.'

''Tisn't. You haven't seen it. You ashamed? You regret doing it?'

'No. Of course not. But . . .'

156

'Well, then. Watch it.' He stabbed the remote control at the VCR again. 'Just watch.'

The couple reappeared, framed against their green and violet backcloth. The man was pulling off his T-shirt, spreading it on the ground just behind them. He knelt to unlace his boots. The woman stared down at him. Her face was in profile. Her cool, hungry expression made Jenny feel faint.

'I don't think I can watch this,' she whispered.

'Yes, you can.' Mark moved closer and slipped an arm around her shoulders. 'You're the star. Relax. Enjoy it.'

The woman on the screen pulled her shirt off over her head. The man stood up quickly, still wearing his jeans. The couple faced each other, side on to the camera. There was a smudge on the man's upper arm. His right arm. That's his tattoo, Jenny thought dazedly. Why, although I was looking at him so intently, couldn't I see it?

The woman said something inaudible, glancing around, and the man shook his head. Then a voice – the man's voice, sounding very distant – said, 'Nothing. Nothing's wrong.' The woman started to unzip her jeans. The man hesitated. Jenny suddenly, grimly, understood.

'Were you camera shy?' The thing was monstrous. A treachery. As if her own flesh had conspired against her. 'Or did you just want me making the running?'

Mark's eyes were on the screen. 'Not sure,' he said, sounding truthful. 'Just . . . happened.'

The woman tugged at the man's belt, twice, and then the couple seemed to fuse, their torsos pressed together. The woman's face was turned to camera. Do I really look like that? Jenny wondered, half appalled, half amazed. So uninhibited. So completely overcome.

'You've lost it from there,' Mark said. His hand squeezed her shoulder.

The couple were kicking off the rest of their clothes. They

were quite naked now. Their entwined shape bent and curved, and partially separated, as the man went down on the discarded clothing. He pulled the woman down on top of him. Their bodies made a Y-shaped diagonal across the screen. As the man lay back it looked as if his eyes had closed.

'And that's where I lose it.' Mark gave a short, bashful laugh.

The screen woman moved rhythmically over the man. Her back and most of her right side was visible, one breast, her right flank, a kneeling leg. The man's hands gripped her thighs, high up, close to her groin. The woman grasped the hands, detached them, and pushed them firmly against her breasts.

Jenny had no memory of doing that. Of guiding him in any way. And yet the woman was indisputably herself.

Now the woman's back was arching as she moved. Her face was in quarter-profile; hard to see her expression. She looked self-involved. The man's face was barely visible either, deep in the pile of clothes and heather. Though twice his chin rose, tipping upwards in effort. His arms, outstretched to the woman's breasts, seemed to be both supporting her and forcing her away.

After a while something about the woman's movements became steady and acutely controlled. She was no longer a stranger; Jenny knew exactly what she was doing. The man on screen seemed to sense the change in her too; his knees rose and his hips pushed against her.

The woman slumped forward and was caught by the man, his hands under her armpits. He held her a moment, then drew her up his chest till her shoulders overhung his head. His face lifted to mouth her breasts. Jenny heard the first human sound since the man's words at the beginning of the tape: a hollow, root-stirring female groan.

Then the man's arms collapsed and the woman was down in the crook of his shoulder, her head twisting away from him. His face was buried in her hair, and both were still.

After a minute Jenny said, 'You deliberately put the clothes there.'

Mark said nothing. He was still watching the screen. The couple beginning to stir. Rising from the vegetation. Starting to pick up clothes.

'I suppose you think you're very clever,' said Jenny.

'Nothing clever about it. Shit, you can bunny, can't you?' He turned suddenly to her, his face pushing at her neck. He slid his hand up her thigh.

'It's got you all excited, hasn't it?' Savagely she pushed his hand away. Smoothed her skirt. There was something contemptible about aroused men. Their overbearing neediness. Their blindness. He was still nuzzling her neck. He seemed completely unaware of her anger.

She reached forward for the remote control, fast-forwarded the tape to blank screen, and pressed Pause.

'Where's my inquiry tape?'

'Up there,' Mark mumbled. 'On the telly.'

'Why did you take this?'

'Why not?'

'It's dangerous.'

'Crap.'

'You can't keep it,' Jenny said. 'You'll show it to someone.'

'Don't be stupid.'

'You haven't, have you?'

'Yeah, course. Showed it in the pub.' His shoulders trembled. 'Sheba's seen it. Not impressed.'

Jenny was adamant. 'I can't let you keep it. It's too risky.'

Mark sat up properly. His weight lifted off her shoulder. 'I'm not going to show that – ' he stabbed a finger at the television ' – that, to anyone.'

'Why not? I'd have thought it was just the thing to entertain your mates.'

'Would you show it to yours?'

159

'That's different. Anyway . . .' Now she was angry rather than shocked. It was a despicable video. But interesting too.

'It's a video,' said Mark, 'of you fucking me.'

'And you don't like that? Don't tell me you don't like it.'

'I like it. Course I like it. But I wouldn't show it around.' He put his arm across her waist and tried to lean over her again. 'Hey,' he murmured. 'Come on.'

Jenny knew that, right now, she was too angry for sex. But that she would probably feel different later. 'No,' she said. 'But you can draw the curtains.'

Mark sighed, sat back, then reluctantly got up.

'I like you in the video,' she said, making her voice cruel. 'I wouldn't mind my friends seeing you. You looked very obedient.'

'Fuck off.' Mark tugged the curtains across the window. Jenny picked up her whisky, drained it, and poured herself another. She felt herself gathering strength.

'How many times have you watched it?'

He sat down again and smiled. 'A few times.'

'And have you done this before? With other women? Am I part of a library?'

He snorted. 'Course not.'

'So why me?'

'Made it easy, didn't you?'

'So you had it planned from the start?'

'No. Well . . .' He corrected himself. 'The possibility, ay. I know how to set things up. So . . . if I were lucky, you know . . . with where I could put the camera. And I was. Just lucky.'

'And why, if you thought I wouldn't agree to it being made, have you shown it to me now?'

Mark picked up his whisky and considered this. Then said, 'I reckoned . . . maybe it was the idea you wouldn't like. But when you saw how it turned out, you wouldn't mind. Being, you know . . .'

'I beg your pardon? Being what?'

'Well . . .' He shrugged. 'Kind of wild. You know.'

'Wild?' Jenny laughed. 'I'm not wild.'

'Suit yourself. Just telling you what I thought.' He nodded at the VCR. 'You want to see it again?'

Jenny was staring at him. Another man who thought she was someone she wasn't. Though he had reason, maybe. Yes. She picked up the remote control, and pressed rewind.

'Why not?' she said, aggressively.

This time she concentrated on watching the male figure. Mark's actions and reactions, reassessed in the knowledge that he knew he was filming himself. As long as he remained aware of the camera, he must have been affected by it. He seemed, early on, simply to be stalled by what he was doing. Or was his hesitancy more calculated? Had he anticipated then that he would show this to her? And did he understand that some images might be more acceptable than others? How clever was he? And how much of her shock was because she had so seriously underestimated him, had failed to credit him with initiative, rather than because of what he had actually done?

She was aware of his body beside her on the sofa, shifting position. His fist, resting on his thigh, curling and uncurling. His expression rapt, attention focused on the screen couple who were on the ground now. The man had become unconscious of the camera. Jenny watched the screen figure closely, saw his head lift. His insensible, trance-like expression. She felt a grim ticking of excitement.

'I like that.' Mark nodded at the screen. The woman's back was arching, her breasts lifting, straining against the man's hands.

'It's how I come,' Jenny muttered. 'It's not for your benefit. I'm trying to force myself into my breasts.'

'Oh ay?' Mark gave an astonished laugh.

'That's just how I think of it,' said Jenny sourly. 'It pulls the right strings.'

161

'Does seem to,' agreed Mark.

They watched, this time, until the screen went black. Jenny looked at the VCR counter, which indicated fifteen minutes, and then pressed Pause on the remote. She sat forward on the edge of the sofa, swivelled so she was facing Mark, and placed her palm on the fly of his jeans. Anger vied with arousal. She wanted both to caress and hurt him.

'Let's screw,' said Mark.

'Not just yet.' She pressed her hand down.

His body tensed. He pushed the back of his head against the sofa.

'Let's play a game,' she said.

'What game?'

She thought. Anything would do, as long as it delayed things, to punish him, but kept her – kept both of them – in the mood. 'The Truth Game,' she said. 'I ask you questions, and you answer them truthfully.'

'What's in it for me?'

'Um . . . If I believe you,' she improvised, 'you get an article of clothing taken off. From me or you, you choose. But no touching till the end.' Mark had closed his eyes while she was speaking. She pressed harder on his fly. 'OK?'

Mark opened his eyes. 'Be careful. OK.'

'Right. Here we go. The questions are about you, Mark. First question. When did you lose your virginity?'

Mark winced. Jenny lifted her hand slightly.

'When I was sixteen. The weekend after my birthday. I think.'

'What d'you mean?' Jenny asked scornfully. 'You think?'

'I was pissed. At a party in Aber. Afterwards she said we didn't do it, but I reckon we did. Most people believed me, anyway.'

'God. I can imagine. And I believe you. No one would invent

such an unedifying story. All right. What article of clothing do you want off?'

'Your top. How long's this going on?'

'As long as I say.' Jenny pulled her blouse off over her head.

'You're wearing a bra.' Mark sounded cheated.

'So I am. Don't touch. I mean it.' She replaced her hand on his crotch. Mark tensed again, then relaxed.

'So how many girls, women, have you slept with, since that first one? Not counting me.'

Mark said mulishly, 'Why d'you want to know?'

'Because I'm interested. Because,' she said fiercely, 'you tricked me into taking part in something you knew I wouldn't agree to. So now you can bloody well do what I say.'

He sighed, and said, 'Three.'

'Only three?' Jenny removed her hand in surprise. Then put it back again, rather too swiftly.

Mark jerked backwards and said, 'Shit.'

'Sorry,' she said. 'I expected more.'

'Had two steady girlfriends,' he said defensively. 'I didn't play around when I was with them.'

'And who was the other one?'

'That's another question.'

'No, it isn't. It's a supplementary.'

Mark winced, squeezed his eyes closed, then opened them again. 'A girl I met in Spain. Back in June. She was like you.' His voice took on a spiteful edge. 'Just wanted me to bang her for a fortnight. So I did. OK?'

'OK,' said Jenny. 'That'll do. What d'you want off now?'

'Your bra.' He moved restlessly. 'Can we hurry this up?'

'No.' Jenny reached behind her back and unhooked her bra. Before she slipped the straps down her shoulders she said, 'You're sure now? No touching, remember.'

'I'm sure.'

Jenny pulled the bra away. Mark stared at her breasts, but made no attempt to touch them.

'You're very good, you know,' Jenny said admiringly. 'Except when you take sneaky videos.'

Mark looked away. 'Sorry. Shouldn't have done it.'

'Unconvincing.' Jenny walked her fingers down his jeans zip. 'I was going to ask if any of your casual sexual encounters had been bad. But you haven't had—'

'Some better than others,' Mark interrupted.

She laughed. 'Are you enjoying this?' She pushed down with her fingers.

'Pass.' His voice was tight.

'How diplomatic.'

'Take something else off.'

Jenny kicked off her shoes. Mark hissed through his teeth.

'What d'you like best about sex?' Jenny asked.

'Coming.'

'Oh, very good. All right. What d'you want off now?'

'Undo my jeans. Shit.'

Jenny unbuckled his belt, released the waist button, and unzipped his jeans. He was wearing black and white striped boxer shorts. How well co-ordinated. Under his black jeans and his smart white shirt. She leant over him.

'What d'you like a woman to do,' she whispered, 'when she's having sex with you?'

'Anything,' Mark whispered back.

'Think,' said Jenny. She slipped her hand inside his boxer shorts. Mark pushed his body back against the sofa and closed his eyes. His face had become pale, his skin waxy. He opened his eyes again.

'Lose it,' he said. 'I like them to lose it.'

'What's this "lose it"?' Jenny asked. 'You said it before. What d'you mean?'

'Get into it. So there's nothing else. Lose it.'

164

'Why d'you like that?'

'It's beautiful. And so I can lose it too. Ah, shit . . .' He tried to sit forward. Jenny pushed him back. His breathing was shallow and fast. He closed his eyes again.

'What, you can't lose it till the woman does? Suppose she doesn't?'

'Then I don't.' His voice was a whisper. 'Not really.'

She studied him.

'But I think you're losing it now, Mark, don't you?' She started to undo the pearl buttons of his shirt. 'Stay still,' she said, as he shifted.

She undid the buttons and opened the shirt. She watched the rise and fall of his chest muscles. His eyes were still closed. 'You're right,' she murmured. 'Losing it is beautiful.'

She leant over him till her lips were an inch from his. Finding it, losing it; they were the same. She whispered, 'You can touch me now.'

He left at midnight. Sheba had guard duty at the garage, and he had to be in Port Talbot by eight in the morning.

After he'd gone Jenny removed the videotape that he'd left in the VCR, stuck a piece of Sellotape over the broken tab at the back, and recorded fifteen minutes of an Australian film on to it. Afterwards she re-ran the tape, to check the over-recording had taken, and then went to bed.

28th August

Darling Michael,

I've been putting off writing. I've been waiting, I think, to be finished with Mark, so I could write about past rather than present events. I haven't actually finished with him but the time has still, effectively, arrived. It's now ten days since I last saw him. Ten days in which he's made no attempt to contact me, and I have made none to contact him. I've realized that with no excuse to meet, we're not going to. He expects me to make the running, which is absolutely correct of him; but without an excuse I can't. It is impossible. I'm like a silly teenager who can't plan for sex because it's got to 'just happen'. Though I'm surprisingly unmiserable about it. As if, at least for the moment, I've had enough.

Sal will be pleased. Her disapproval has persisted. It makes me sad, and a little cross. I realize how dominant I've allowed her to become. How dominant she expects to be. Like a mother hen: I'm the chick stepping out from under her wing, and she's pecking me on the head trying to get me back under again, into a place where she's always right, and knows what's best for me. Even if I have been foolish – and I don't necessarily accept I have – I have to learn to do things for myself, and I never will, if she's always mothering me.

Frank is now away in Italy. Last week he behaved more acceptably in the office – he's stopped touching me – but his long, tender, moose-like gazes are still infuriating. I feel very resentful – I really don't feel responsible for igniting his ardour, and I loathe his assumption that we are intimates. I suppose I'm getting my just deserts for tolerating his patronage in the past, in exchange for his chivalrous devotion, which I took as platonic and safe . . . No, I refuse to blame myself. It's Frank's fault, for being so misleadingly fatherly and sexless. If he'd been younger and more attractive I'd have been more careful. But, of course, he's the same as any other man underneath. I should have known.

Mark, too, thinks I'm someone I'm not, you know. Funny – I go in for this, don't I? But because I was once 'a hippie chick' he thinks I must also have been wild and promiscuous. He thinks being a hippie was all about peace-and-love orgies and no-strings sex, which, of course, it never was, except in the media and the minds of definitely unhip men. He'd be astonished if I told him that I've only ever slept with four men, and two of them are himself and Gareth.

A quirk of fate: d'you know, in those years after Pete left, only one male approached me sexually, before you? A fifteen-year-old boy, who entered my house with sex on his mind, and in the wishful belief that it was on mine. A boy who chickened out, in the end, but who was at least bold enough to try. A boy who was Mark.

I've misread him, too, mind. He's not as laddish as I first thought. That story, and his looks . . . but he's not. He's a hard-working, skilled young man and one day he'll have his own business – or his father's – and be a name in the village. You know the Bevan-type families, whose boys go into skilled manual work not because that's all they can do, but because they value it as real work and see it as a springboard to being their own bosses, beholden to no one. Born entrepreneurs. Straight up-and-down lads, you used to say, all heart and guts.

Oh, shit, I've just realized, you must have known him. You must have taught him.

Michael, do you understand what I've been doing? I don't, fully, but I'm sure you must. Do you mind? Christ. Listen to me. Here I am, telling you, my husband, asking you about my lover.

The question is confused. If you were in a position to understand of course you'd mind. But if what I were doing were, say, the actions of another widowed woman, not your wife? You wouldn't give it much thought, really, would you? It wouldn't honestly interest you much. I'm not complimenting you now – remember that argument we had about Sal's break-up with Phil? About how, although we were friends with both of them, you were always three steps behind events, because – and I know you denied this, but it's true – you simply didn't care enough to keep up. Because the disaster wasn't ours and, whatever happened, you would still be getting up, going to

167

work, teaching the kids, coming home, getting on OK with Alex and me, running across the hills in the evening, drinking in the pub with Gareth. Your life was unaffected by their unhappiness, so you could lose touch with it. Even though Sal was my best friend and we both liked and felt sorry for Phil. You could be very selfish, emotionally.

I'm sorry. I'm not trying to justify anything – by listing your faults, excuse my own. But you could be detached, couldn't you? So now you're permanently detached, do I have to worry about what you'd think? I do, for some reason, want you to know. Should I be worried? Or am I trying to tell you something?

Mark has a video of him and me on top of the mountain, making love. He took it surreptitiously and showed it to me last time we met. Seeing it shook me. I can't cope with surprises. Maybe it's the reason I'm not desperate to see him now – if he could shock me like that once, he might again. He left the tape behind and I erased it but, of course, I realize now, he must have an original. The tape I wiped was a standard tape, and much too big to have ever been in a camcorder. I asked Alex – pretending I was asking about the inquiry tape – and he says that original tapes are tiny, and played back by connecting the camera directly to the television. You can then make copies on normal tape, using the telly's VCR. That was obviously what I had. No wonder Mark was so unbothered about leaving it with me.

I'm not panicking, because although his deceit was – is – unnerving, he didn't keep the video secret and wanted to share it with me. And he was even right that once I'd got over my shock and anger I enjoyed watching it. But however much I trust his motives – and I do, oddly – it doesn't alter the fact that the tape is dangerous. Simply in itself, for the pictures it contains. But there's nothing I can do about it – even if I forced him to hand over the original I'd never be sure he hadn't made other copies. He took the video and it exists, and what's done is done. I have to let it go. A price – small, I hope – I've had to pay for him. I can't believe he'd show it to anyone who mattered. He has no reason to hurt me. And I don't even believe he'd show it to someone who didn't matter, because of how he comes across in it.

Actually, he looked beautiful. He is beautiful. There is something essentially pure about him. Or, at least, I was – am – attracted to that part of him which seems essentially pure. Or maybe I only see that part. But I see it clearly. I still love to think about him. I can excite myself, simply by visualizing him. And I never felt, after seeing him in real life, any regrets, or guilt. Just physical and mental satisfaction. Or do I mean satiation?

I looked beautiful too. I have proof, see – or I did have – that, given the opportunity, I'm good at sex. Bunnying, Mark called it.

I'm sorry. That was uncalled for. I haven't been having sex with Mark to get back at you. It may look and sound like that, and it would be simple and neat if it was, but I'm sure that's not how it is. I do deeply regret that at the time you died we weren't making love, and I do sometimes feel bitter and sad about it, but I do not feel angry or vengeful or bitter towards you when I'm with Mark. I don't feel I've been looking to him for the sex we weren't having. I'm a grown-up person, and I know the situation we had is common among grown-ups and would have been temporary; it was the end of the school year and you were just too busy and tired to relax. I was frustrated about it, but I wasn't agonized, and neither were you. You were too busy and tired. If you'd lived, it would have been of no consequence. Your death gave it a significance it doesn't deserve. And I've not, I'm positive, been acting on that false significance.

I have been looking for something in Mark, and finding it, but it isn't you or your body, or revenge on you for what you weren't giving me. I couldn't name what it is I have found, but I'm sure it isn't that. I haven't thought about you when Mark and I've had sex. I think about me.

Chapter 17

September 1993

Sal and Jenny waited near double doors in a cavernous foyer area in the belly of the county council offices. It was the afternoon of the last Thursday in September. The foyer was a cruciform area with no windows, lit by a diffuse white light from behind its low suspended ceiling. A dozen giant-sized green leather armchairs faced each other in two rows of six in the centre of the foyer. The only other furnishings were four large white No Smoking notices attached to the pale unplastered brick walls, and a huge acreage of grey carpet.

Jenny peered through one of the glass door panels into the inquiry room. It was the size of a school sports hall. Sal, who had visited the previous week with another objector, had just identified for her the players within. On a raised dais to the far right, behind a line of thin tables, sat the Welsh Office staff. Three of them. The middle figure was the inquiry inspector, a wispy-haired man in his fifties; on his right sat the secretary, a sturdy, wholesome-looking youngish woman; and to his left was another official, male, late thirties, who was possibly a deputy inspector. Below the dais, on the floor of the hall, were two flanking rows of desks, behind which sat representatives of the two main inquiry combatants: on the left, three officials

170

from the county council, as major objectors to the opencast appeal, and, on the right, three representatives of British Coal, the inquiry applicants. All six were men, and it seemed to Jenny that, of the two groups, the British Coal contingent was younger and more sharply suited. In the centre of the room was a small square table bearing a microphone and a reading lamp, and at it, facing the dais and the twin batteries of floor-level desks, sat a man in a green corduroy jacket: a witness giving evidence. From outside the room his voice was barely audible. Some distance behind him were two rows of spectator chairs, only eleven of which were occupied. The rest of the hall, a large space behind the chairs, was completely empty.

Jenny thought she recognized one of the spectators: an elderly man with a thatch of springy grey hair. She pointed. 'Don't we know him?'

Sal nodded. 'Howard. Abercwm Friends of the Earth. He's here every day. Provides a taxi service for objectors without cars.'

'There aren't a lot, are there?' Jenny frowned. The proceedings actually looked rather low key. She didn't know whether to be relieved or disappointed.

'Most people are at work. I told you it wouldn't be daunting.'

'My telly,' said Jenny suddenly. 'Where's my telly?'

'Behind the county council desks.' Sal pointed through the doors. 'Over there.'

'Oh, yes.' Jenny saw a tall trolley bearing a television at head height. A shelf below held a VCR.

She looked at her watch. Sal was due to give evidence at three thirty. Hers was listed for three forty-five. It was now three twenty.

'Should we go in?' she whispered.

'Let's wait till the bloke at the desk's finished,' said Sal. 'It's a long walk to those chairs.'

'I think I want to go to the loo.' Jenny pulled back from the door.

'I'll come with you.'

Sal led her across the empty foyer and down a wide corridor to the ladies'. Jenny was conscious, as they walked, of the white-noise hum of air-conditioning in her ears.

'God, who'd work here?' she said. 'The atmosphere's horrible. Dead and noisy. Not a single window. We could be anywhere.'

'Corporate architecture. Designed by the same bozos who restore land, I dare say.' Sal sniffed the air. 'Mmm. Yum. We'll all get legionnaires' disease.'

In the ladies' the roar of the air-conditioning was even louder. They used the lavatories and washed their hands quickly. Rather than add to the noise by using the blowers, they dried their hands on tissues from Jenny's handbag.

Walking back to the double doors Sal said, 'So, you per-suaded Frank not to come and cheer you on?'

Jenny pulled a face. 'Actually it wasn't difficult. Someone's got to mind the shop. He wanted to take me out for a celebratory meal tonight but I told him you and I were going to the pub. I'm afraid I've had to invite him too, but he won't come. An evening in the Bridgend isn't his scene at all.' She peered through the glass door panel. The man in the green jacket was still talking.

'I haven't been there for ages,' said Sal.

'I haven't either. Alex still plays pool there.'

'Is he coming tonight?'

'Not till after ten. He's working. Have you asked Nathan?'

'Not seriously. A drink with Mother? The humiliation.'

Jenny took a small breath and said, 'Mark could be there. If he's not working.'

Sal said nothing.

'It's his video,' Jenny said. 'I should tell him how it went.'

172

Sal moved closer to the double doors. She stared through the glass, her eyes narrowed, and said, 'I thought you weren't seeing him any more.'

'I haven't seen him. I just said he might be there.'

Sal glanced back at her. The hardness in her expression dissolved. With a snort she said, 'Honestly, Jen, you should see your face. Just don't let me drink too much, or I'll be rude to him.'

Jenny smiled. 'No, you won't.'

There was movement in the inquiry room; they heard the scrape of chair legs and the murmur of voices. The green-jacketed man was returning to the spectator seats.

'Now,' said Sal.

They pushed at the double doors, which squealed on their hinges. Heads turned towards them. Howard from Friends of the Earth lifted a friendly hand. The room proceedings felt, from inside, much more formal than they had looked from outside. They walked across the wide expanse of floor and sat down in the nearest chairs. A heavy man in his forties with a Cossack moustache and wearing a blue blazer was walking to the witness table. Jenny was aware of her heart pounding.

Sal hissed in her ear, 'They must be running late.'

The witness was asked to introduce himself and gave his name as the Honourable Jeremy Lyons. He identified himself as chairman of a salmon-fishing association. He then read out a two-page statement. It voiced fears that toxic coal waste might pollute the Usk river from tributaries originating at Blaen Dyar. He listed particular fishing syndicates whose waters might be affected, and what each was worth. The figures ran into hundreds of thousands of pounds.

'Great stuff,' whispered Sal, when he'd finished. 'Money talk. Their sort of language.'

The inspector thanked the speaker for his evidence, sounding sincere and gracious, and then asked the British Coal representatives if they had any questions. A blue-suited young man from the desk nearest the witness table stepped forward holding a large map.

'May I, sir, ask Mr Lyons to mark the stretches of water he is concerned about?'

The inspector nodded. The young man took the map to the witness. The two spoke quietly, the young man nodding and drawing lines on the map with a felt-tip pen. Then he withdrew to his desk.

'See,' Sal whispered. 'They don't argue. Just ask simple questions. Nothing frightening.'

Jenny nodded. Her mouth was dry. The inspector thanked the witness again, who rose, returned to his seat to pick up a coat and briefcase and left the hall.

'Ms Sally Barnes?' the woman on the dais called, looking around the floor.

Jenny touched Sal's arm. Sal stood up, yanked the tail of her shirt down over the seat of her skirt, and walked to the witness table. Jenny knew, from her belligerent, rolling stride, that Sal was nervous too. She watched her sit down and smooth out her papers. The inspector prompted her with a smile.

Sal gave her name and address in a breathless voice and started reading from her prepared typescript.

Jenny looked down at her lap. She knew Sal's evidence almost by heart, having typed it out for her on the word processor at work. The trick had been to find an angle that the big guns – the local authority and national environmental organisations – weren't covering. Something different from the straightforward issues of dust, health and environmental damage. This was Sal's second attempt. The first had been a tirade. A declamatory rant about vindictive governments out to punish workers they perceived as enemies by destroying the deep-mine coal industry and substituting opencasting. 'This is a political speech, you realize,' Jenny had said cautiously, asked to comment on it.

'Not an argument about Blaen Dyar. It's not even an argument against British Coal.' Sal had sighed and said that she'd guessed it was unusable. This second attempt wasn't specifically about Blaen Dyar either, but she had at least directed her criticisms at British Coal. Her argument, essentially, was that their promises and assurances regarding the opencast were worthless.

'They say, for instance . . .' Sal's voice began to settle down, becoming stronger and steadier, '. . . that they will finish open-casting and have restored the land in seventeen years. But we know that once British Coal has a foothold anywhere they invariably ask for extensions, either in time or in area . . . We've every reason to suppose that once on site, they will apply here . . . And they don't have to agree or deny this now, because they're under no obligation to reveal future plans. The proposed time span of seventeen years is therefore meaningless . . .'

Jenny noticed the middle British Coal man jot something on a piece of paper and show it to the colleague on his left. The two exchanged small smiles. Jenny felt a wave of dislike for both men, and a surge of protective affection for Sal.

'They say there'll be no dust,' Sal was saying. 'They don't prove it, they just say it. Even though the mountain top is over a thousand feet high and persistently windy. Even though we know that fifty years ago, when the mountain was first open-casted, there was dust as far away as Abercwm. They're going to blast their way three hundred feet into it, scoop out the rock and soil with giant diggers, transport it around the site in mammoth trucks, and build two huge overburden hills . . . and yet they claim there will be no dust. They say this because they can – because nothing happens to them if they're proved wrong . . .'

She sounded fluent and impassioned now. '. . . And if there is dust, if the incidence of asthma and other bronchial disease does rise locally, will they stop opencasting?' She paused, look-ing around. 'They won't, will they? They'll simply, as they've

175

done elsewhere, deny that their dust is to blame. Or question the statistics. We have no sanctions. The assurances they give us here are meaningless.'

The young British Coal man nearest Sal was staring at her with a fixed, blank-eyed expression. Jenny put her videotape on her lap and wiped her sweating palms on her skirt.

'They say,' Sal declared, 'that when they eventually stop opencasting, they'll restore the site attractively. I don't believe them. Nobody believes them. We'd like to see examples of attractively restored upland. It is easy to pull a mountain to pieces, but quite another thing to put it back together again. Opencasted land is dead. Restoration is much harder and more complicated than they pretend. Suppose they can't breathe life into the land again? Suppose they can't successfully restore it? What redress do we have? The answer appears to be . . . none.'

Jenny wondered if all this was a waste of time. She stared at the inspector. He had a kind, intelligent face. An old-fashioned face. And he looked sympathetic. Did he have to be a good actor? How many times over the last few weeks had he heard the same arguments? And speeches that were irrelevant, or inarticulate, or abusive, or preposterous? According to the local paper, one witness was objecting on religious grounds, claiming Blaen Dyar to be an ancient druidic holy place. Had the inspector listened with as much apparent attentiveness to him?

Sal was winding up. 'I believe,' she said, 'that if British Coal win their case here, we will be lumbered with a vast opencast operation which is dirty, unsightly, noisy and unhealthy, which employs precious few local people, which denies access for a generation to a huge area that is now common land, and which will be a first foothold in a much larger and longer operation. British Coal have made promises, but promises were made fifty years ago, and we know they weren't honoured. British Coal's evidence, I believe, is not objective or accurate or honest and is simply what you would expect anyone to say to win their case. I ask, therefore, that the inquiry reject their appeal.'

She stopped. The microphone picked up the rustle of paper. She scraped back her chair.

'A moment, Ms Barnes.' The inspector peered down at the British Coal desks. 'Any questions?'

The young man at the end desk folded his arms across his chest and without conferring with, or even looking at, his colleagues, said, 'None.'

The inspector said to the secretary, 'We have a copy of Ms Barnes' evidence, do we?' and received a nod. He smiled at Sal. 'Many thanks for your time and trouble.'

Sal walked back to her chair.

'Brilliant,' whispered Jenny. She could hear Sal's chest wheezing.

'Smarmy bastards,' she hissed, her voice shaking. She scowled at the British Coal desks. 'They know I'm right . . . look at them.'

Jenny wanted to hug her friend, knowing she'd worked herself up with her own words. And that she had detected contempt from the British Coal desks. But Sal would loathe any suggestion that she appeared vulnerable, or in need of protection.

The Secretary was speaking. 'Jenny Parsons? Ms Jenny Parsons?'

'Me,' said Jenny, and stood up. Her heart immediately hammered against the wall of her chest. The secretary said something in the inspector's ear. He nodded.

'You have video evidence for us, I believe. Mr Grant?' He addressed a man in a brown suit behind the county council desks, who rose, shot Jenny a cheerful wave, and began wheeling the television trolley to the edge of the main arena. Jenny didn't know where to place herself, and hovered between the chairs and the witness table.

'Do you wish to introduce the video?' The inspector's voice was encouraging.

'Er . . .' Jenny looked at the tape in her hand, and shook her head. 'I don't think so. It's self-explanatory, really.' Her voice, unamplified, sounded thin and lost.

The brown-suited Mr Grant came up behind her. 'You want to give us the video, love?' His voice was very friendly.

'Oh, yes.' She handed it over. 'It's all ready to run.'

'Right you are.' He adjusted the position of the trolley, checking that all parties, including spectators, would be able to see the television screen, and slotted the video into the VCR.

'I expect you'll need the volume up high.' Jenny was suddenly drenched in panic. The room was so huge, the screen so small. The air so deafeningly dead. No one would be able to see or hear anything.

'It'll be fine, love.' The man indicated the witness table. 'Sit there, why don't you, while it's running.'

Jenny sat down shakily. She turned the chair so she could see the screen.

There was a roaring sound from the television set. Mr Grant twiddled a knob and the roar was silenced. She heard her own voice.

'My name,' she heard, 'is Jenny Parsons, and I live with my son in the village of Pentre . . .'

A picture had appeared on screen. A view of green and purple moorland in the foreground, and beyond, a long lumpy mountain ridge. Sharper pale mauve peaks rose in the far distance.

'I am standing now on the northern high point of the plateau site,' her voice went on, 'and we are looking west. My aim in this video is, first, to show how visible an opencast site up here would be, since everywhere shown on screen can in turn see us, and second, to show something of the site itself, and what we locals would lose if it were fenced off. What we are looking at now is the Darren, above the village of Pentre, and, beyond, the peaks of the Brecon Beacons.'

Slowly the picture panned right.

'Here,' her voice continued, 'we can see the Usk valley, as the shoulder of the Darren slopes down into it, and . . . here . . . the southern face of the Black Mountains . . .'

Jenny remembered that it was at this point, on the first take, that she had made a mistake, forgetting to name one of the Black Mountain valleys. Mark had told her to continue anyway, so he could hear the whole of the commentary and plan his camera sweeps accordingly. He'd stood with one of his feet touching hers, and told her to pause if he pressed against her. The system had worked perfectly – that was how, on the second take, they had slotted in the buzzard. She'd said, afterwards, 'Good at teamwork, aren't you?' and he'd grunted, 'Be out of a job, else.'

The Abercwm hills were on screen now, the peaks that formed the natural amphitheatre around the town. Her voice was naming each peak. The colours of mountains, valleys and sky, viewed here, in this sterile, man-made environment, seemed astonishingly rich and vibrant. Much more so, Jenny thought, than when she had watched the video at home. Because, she supposed, at home she was surrounded by richness and vibrancy. Here, she saw the landscape with starved, unspoilt eyes. It looked even more exotic, more special, more magnificent, than she'd dared hope.

On screen the diamond shape of Gwern Lake appeared, a dozen colourful dots – parked cars in the car park – necklacing the near end. Her voice-over pointed out that the lake was only yards from the eastern edge of the opencast site.

Now the camera started its slow east–west track back. The near-ground of Blaen Dyar appeared. The hillocks and hollows of the old workings, clothed green-grey with bilberry and purple with heather. The mountain road snaked across the screen and

179

at intervals parked cars studded the verges, bonnets aimed at the views. Scattered groups of sheep, looking timelessly tranquil, grazed the bilberry dunes. Over one hillock the camera zoomed upwards and into close-up, showing a low-flying buzzard, a large yellow-legged bird of prey with an awkward, tilting flight, being mobbed by crows. The buzzard's mewing cries were audible on the tape. Then the camera pulled slowly down and back, and the shoulder of the Darren came into view. The picture now was identical to that at the start of the video.

The screen went blank. The video was over. For a moment there was silence. Then Mr Grant stepped forward and switched the television off. Jenny felt an intense pressure in her chest. It could be either a suppressed sob, or a laugh. She wished Mark had been here to see his work. She wanted to tell him that she had been moved by it.

The inspector was looking down at the British Coal desks, asking if there were any questions. The blue-suited young man nodded, lifted a map, and walked over to Jenny.

He smiled politely. 'Could you show us where you were when you shot the video, please?'

He was wearing a strong musky aftershave. The scent of it transformed him from an anonymous office-dressed interrogator to a self-aware, striving young man. The pressure inside Jenny's chest emerged as a laugh. She coughed to cover it. Then frowned over his map, which was drawn on a huge, clearly detailed scale. The contour lines whorled like giant fingerprints across the Blaen Dyar plateau.

'There,' she said. The high spot she and Mark had stood on actually bore a number. She felt the laugh rebuild. She imagined pointing a millimetre to the south of it and adding, *And that's where we filmed ourselves earlier, naked, having sex.*

The amplified voice of the inspector broke in to say, 'Excuse me? What height can we say the film was taken from?'

The young man leant in to Jenny's microphone. 'Four

180

hundred and six metres, sir. That's fine,' he murmured to Jenny, enveloping her again in musk, and returned to his seat.

Mr Grant had removed the videotape from the VCR. He passed it, after a nod from Jenny, to the inquiry secretary. Jenny was thanked by the inspector. She turned to face Sal, tipped her head at the double doors, and mouthed, 'Let's go.' Sal nodded and rose.

Out in the empty foyer Jenny stopped abruptly, waiting for Sal to catch up. She stood completely still, her fingers steepled against her lips. Behind her she heard the double doors squeak on their hinges. She closed her eyes and enjoyed the liquid warmth coursing her body, the trickle and flood of relief, triumph, euphoria. She detected desire, too. She opened her eyes. Something was suddenly clear. The state of desiring was the grail. What defined you, ultimately, as a whole human being. She had just seen one video, and been reminded of another. Now they had merged. What she had seen, what had excited her, had been Mark.

'I feel amazing,' she said, as Sal drew level. She gave a laugh, which emerged as a loud, wild noise. 'Bloody wonderful.'

'Well, we are, aren't we?' Sal tugged her on.

They swung down the corridor. A kind of bliss crept over Jenny. 'Wasn't the video good? Before it started I was convinced it would all look tiny and lost and insignificant. But it didn't.'

'The place looked staggeringly significant,' Sal assured her.

Jenny nodded. It had, it had. 'And your evidence was terrific too. You sounded passionate. And angry. They need that. Proof that people really care. That it's not just dry argument. Or a game. You annoyed the British Coal men.'

'Because I was telling the truth.' Sal looked pleased now, not upset. They passed a long reception desk and left the building through automatic glass doors. On the tarmac path to the car park Sal inhaled deeply.

'God. Back on planet earth.' She grasped Jenny's arm,

suddenly euphoric. 'I'm gonna get pissed tonight. So are you. We deserve it. I'll stay over. I can, can't I?'

Jenny grinned at her, equally elated, and said, 'Course you can.'

Chapter 18

They split a bottle of red wine over pizza at Jenny's cottage and walked down to the Bridgend pub at dusk. Jenny's mood was still floatingly euphoric; the wine made her brain fizz.

Mark was not in the front bar of the pub. But Gareth was, elbow on the counter, chatting to Roy, the landlord.

'Bloody hell.' Gareth waved them over. 'Sal girl, long time no see.'

'Gareth.' Sal stood on tiptoe and pecked his cheek. Gareth wrapped his arms around her and returned the kiss, smackingly. 'Hey, girl, great to see you.' He put her down. 'What you two having?'

'Uh uh.' Sal flapped her purse in his face. 'Our shout.'

'We're celebrating,' Jenny told him. 'We've been down the county council offices. Giving evidence at the inquiry.'

'Oh, ay?' Gareth gave a surprised laugh. 'What you do that for?'

'Two red wines,' said Sal to Roy, 'and' – she jerked a thumb at Gareth – 'whatever he's drinking.' She turned back to him. 'Because, Mr Too-Lazy-To-Get-Off-His-Backside, some of us are public-spirited. Some of us care.'

'Ay,' said Roy, fervently. 'You tell him, missus.'

'You can shut it,' Gareth said.

Roy winked at Jenny. 'That's what's needed round here. People who do more than blather.'

Jenny laughed. She heard a raised male voice coming from the hatch to the back bar. Not Mark's voice.

'Pardon me, butt.' Gareth leant belligerently across the bar. 'And who's got a sweetie from the Coal boys hanging on their front wall, eh?'

'What's this?' Sal looked from Gareth to Roy.

'Courtesy of our friends,' Gareth said. 'Aerial photograph.'

'Have you?' Jenny asked Roy. 'Where?'

Roy chuckled and tipped his head toward the front-bar door. On the wall hung a large framed colour photograph, three feet by two.

Sal walked over to inspect it. 'Wow.'

'Ay,' said Roy. 'Frame, glass an' all. No obligation, they said.'

'You been bought, mun,' said Gareth. 'Shame on you.'

Roy grinned. 'I'm not the only one.'

'Ah,' sighed Gareth. 'Know what they're doing, those boys. And that inquiry – it's a farce now, I'm telling you. All for show. Ta, girls, cheers.' He picked up the pint Roy had pulled for him.

'That's a very cynical and defeatist attitude,' said Sal. 'And most convenient, for an idle person.'

The corners of Gareth's eyes crinkled with good humour. Jenny wished he had kissed her, as well as Sal, when they arrived. Her euphoria was threatening to become tearful.

Gareth wagged a finger in the air. 'D'you think they'd sheep-proof our veggy garden? While they're handing out freebies? Siân's had all her greens topped again. Bastard animals. You get trouble with 'em down here, Roy?'

'Had two in the bar last week,' said Roy. 'Ay, serious now.' He stared upwards, as if in recollection. 'Flowers, they were drinking, mind, not greens.'

'What a wit,' said Sal.

'Tell you now,' said Gareth, prodding at her. 'If the opencast

184

gets the thumbs down, it won't be because of anything you or I says. It'll be because it's overlookin' nob-land. There's votes to lose there.'

'An objector from a fishing organization gave evidence today,' said Jenny. 'The Honourable something.'

'That's it,' said Gareth. 'And all up and down the Usk there's Sir this and Lady that, whingeing on about it. Never had that before, see, all the other opencasts are deep in the Valleys. They don't mind shitting on their enemies, do they? But they don't like their own turning against them. That's the only thing might swing it.'

'But they'd still need our arguments, wouldn't they?' protested Sal. 'They could hardly announce that it wasn't being allowed because they'd lose votes.'

'Ay, well, maybe,' said Gareth. 'So you're helping them off the hook, are you?'

'You won't stop 'em.' Roy shook his head emphatically. 'They get their way, those Coal boys. Always do. Always have. You'll see.'

'I do hope not,' said Jenny.

Roy disappeared to serve at the back hatch. 'Let's sit down,' said Sal, nodding at a table to the right of the pub's tiled fireplace. The ashy remains of a wood fire glowed pink in the grate. They walked over and put their drinks down.

'Hey,' Gareth said to Sal. 'Seen your Nathan round the place a few times.' He laughed. 'Quite a character, these days, isn' he?'

'If you mean kind of dark and Tiggerish, I suppose he is,' Sal agreed.

Gareth turned to Jenny. 'Nice for Alex, eh? Used to be best mates, didn't they?'

'Yes,' said Jenny. She nodded, as if to reinforce the point. In fact the last time she'd heard Alex mention Nathan it had been to complain about him. Some incomprehensible grievance about

185

Nathan being deceitful, after Alex had spotted him at Pentre bus stop. Now it occurred to her that Nathan was seeing Lizzie, one to one, and that Alex was jealous.

Gareth drank from his pint and put it down. 'So,' he said. 'Serious now, what'd you two say at the inquiry?'

Sal and Jenny looked at each other. Sal said, 'I told the Inspector that British Coal promises were worthless, and Jen showed them a pretty video of the views from Blaen Dyar.'

Gareth raised his eyebrows at Jenny. 'Where d'you get that?'

'Made it.' Jenny felt her colour rise. 'Alex organized it. A friend of his, Mark, shot the video, and I did a commentary. Turned out OK, I think.'

'Never,' said Gareth. 'Not our Mark from the garage?'

'Er . . . yes.' She tried to sound unjolted. Of course, Gareth would know Mark. And that Mark and Alex were friendly. How stupid of her. 'I must congratulate him when I see him.'

'He's here,' said Gareth. 'The boy's round the back now, playing pool. Saw him earlier.'

'Is he?' said Jenny faintly. 'Oh.' She heard Sal say, 'Well, fancy that,' in a small dry voice. The urge to get up immediately was almost irresistible. She forced herself to stay still, to pick up her wine glass and sip at it. But a huge space had suddenly opened up between herself and Sal and Gareth. Across the distance, she heard Sal telling Gareth, rather loudly and pointedly, it seemed to her, about the afternoon. She couldn't concentrate; excitement flared through the fog surrounding her. Mark was only in the next room. And she was denying herself quite unnecessarily, since she had every reason to see and speak to him.

She picked up her wine glass and drained it. She couldn't sit here, feeling like this, and do nothing.

'I'll get another round. Wine again, Sal? Gareth?'

'Not for me, love,' Gareth said. 'Got to get home soon. Lizzie and Siân both out tonight . . .'

Jenny smiled quickly, not listening, and picked up Sal's glass without waiting for her answer. At the bar she peered across the counter. She couldn't see through the hatch from here.

Roy appeared and said, 'Same again?'

Jenny nodded, pushing the glasses at him. 'But not for Gareth. Er . . . Is Mark Bevan still in the back? Gareth said he was here.'

'He is,' said Roy, reaching for the wine bottle. 'Him and a few more.'

'Um . . . I'd like to buy him a pint. Whatever he's drinking. Could you give it to him? Just say I showed his video today. He'll know what I mean.'

Roy said, 'Right you are, love,' and poured wine into the glasses.

'I've just bought Mark a drink,' Jenny said, when she got back to the table. She avoided Sal's eyes. Mark would come through. People always did, if you bought them drinks.

'We're having one of his pups,' Gareth said. 'You know his Sheba, do you? She's expecting.'

'Yes.' Jenny lifted her voice, making it conversational. 'Alex wanted one too, but I said no. He'll be at college soon and I'm at work all day.'

Sal said, 'Got a dog, has he? What breed would that be?'

'German Shepherd,' Gareth said.

'Christ,' said Sal.

Jenny ignored her. She moved sideways in her seat, so she could watch the door to the back corridor. He must come through soon.

'A cracker, Sheba is,' she heard Gareth say. 'Soft as butter, but looks the business. Could use a dog in my van, I reckon, when I'm out on jobs. The kids are all for it, too.'

'You ought to be careful.' Sal's voice was pettily antagonistic. 'Having young children.'

'Hey, good family dogs, they are.'

Jenny saw the door to the back corridor open. It was being pushed ajar, just a couple of inches. Someone was the other side. Jenny willed the someone to be Mark, for him to hurry up, to stop talking to whoever was delaying him. She shivered violently.

Gareth must have seen it. She heard him chuckle and say, 'Come on, girl. It's steaming in here.'

She shook her head. She was incapable of speech. Her insides were shaking.

Gareth looked across the bar and cried, 'Hey, it's the boy himself. And his shirt. Come to dazzle us.'

Mark was walking towards them, a full pint in his hand. He was wearing jeans and a white T-shirt, and over the T-shirt, the sleeves pushed to his elbows, an unbuttoned rainbow-coloured shirt.

Gareth shaded his eyes. 'Where d'you get 'em, Mark? You're damaging our eyeballs.'

'Jealous, huh?' Mark stood over him, grinning. To Jenny he said, 'Went OK, then, did it? Ta for the pint.'

Jenny could only gaze at him mutely. If she opened her mouth, right now, something huge would flood out of it. He was standing so close that, if she'd wanted to, she could have touched his thigh. She did want to, but managed to stop herself.

She swallowed the flooding sensation and said, glancing across the table. 'This is my friend Sal. She gave evidence today too. Yes . . . I think it went well . . .'

Mark nodded at Sal, lifting his pint.

Sal said, 'Cheers,' and showed her teeth in a ferocious smile.

Mark turned back to Jenny. 'I've got a game to play. Just came to say ta. Catch you later, maybe?' His eyes swept everyone.

'Not me.' Gareth glanced at his watch. 'I gotta go.' He stood up and grasped Mark by the upper arm. 'You looking after that pup of mine, now, boy.'

'Just starting to show,' Mark said proudly. 'Eating for a dozen, she is.'

'Still earning her keep in the garage though, eh?'

'Oh, ay. Got a while to go yet.'

'Four weeks,' said Gareth. 'I know. The little 'un's got it chalked on the calendar.'

'Roy's going to have one too,' Mark said. 'A bitch, he wants.'

'Goodness,' Sal said loudly, making eyes at Jenny. 'He does spread it around, doesn't he?'

Jenny gave an appalled laugh. Sal blinked, as if the outburst had surprised even herself.

Mark looked at Sal very steadily and said, 'You want one too?'

Sal recovered her composure. Her expression became as intense as his. 'I don't think so,' she said.

Gareth looked from Sal to Mark, and grinned. 'Don't mind her,' he stage-whispered into Mark's ear. 'She's sweet as honey, honest. Just gotta take a big bite.'

Sal gave him a pursed-lip look with her head tilted, and Mark relaxed.

'Bye, girls.' Gareth clapped a hand on Mark's shoulder, which had the effect of drawing him away. 'Don't leave it so long next time, eh?'

They both moved off. Jenny watched them disappear: Gareth out the front, Mark into the back corridor. The spring-loaded door swung to after him. She felt bereft.

Beside her, in a furious whisper, Sal said, 'Christ, Jen.'

Jenny didn't reply immediately. She knew Sal was mainly cross with herself.

'What?' she said calmly.

'You know.'

Jenny sipped her wine. 'I think he's beautiful.'

'He certainly thinks he is. God, that shirt.'

Sal had felt Mark's sexuality too, Jenny thought. It had

189

definitely, for a moment, been directed at her. And had enraged her.

'He's beautiful,' she repeated.

'He's a prick. I should have bought you a vibrator. He's got a guard dog, for fuck's sake.'

'Shut up.' Jenny was suddenly furious. How dare Sal refuse to acknowledge her feelings for Mark? How dare she insult him, as if he were a stranger?

'I still want him,' she hissed. 'I need him, and I still want him.' Oh, that is so true, she thought, aching. And a minute ago he was here, beside me, and I didn't even get to touch him.

'Bollocks,' said Sal.

'I'm going to see him again,' said Jenny.

Sal's upper lip curled.

'Don't do that. Why are you being so nasty?'

Sal growled, picked up her drink, and downed it. She replaced the glass and stared without focus at it. Then sighed.

'All right. Sorry. Let's be reasonable. Because it's so dangerous.'

'No,' Jenny said firmly. 'It's not dangerous. Not in the scale of things.'

'OK. Stupid.'

'Not stupid either. Reckless maybe, but not stupid. It's what I need. I know it is, Sal.' She even knew why, now. Because Mark made her whole. Because desiring him, being desired by him, being joined to him, made her whole. She heard herself say, in a low voice. 'I want to see him tonight.'

'Not with me in the bloody house.' Sal sounded alarmed.

'Of course not.'

'Well, then.'

Jenny got up. She shook her head, as if dismissing the idea. 'I'm going to the loo. I won't be a moment.'

She walked quickly towards the back corridor. Her limbs were stiff. Her breasts hurt, like bursting, pregnant flesh. She reached the door and snatched at the handle. On the other side, as the door hissed shut, she turned right, blindly, into the ladies. She entered a cubicle, banged the door shut, and stepped out of her shoes. She had to do everything quickly, and not think. She lifted her skirt and dragged down her tights and pants. At her knees the two tangled. She moaned, yanking at them. When she finally got them off she bundled them into the sleeve of her jersey. Then stepped back into her shoes, smoothed her skirt, and unlocked the cubicle.

There were two doors further down the corridor, one to the back bar, one to outside. She emptied her mind, walked to the back bar door, half opened it, and leant in. The room contained a number of young people. Mark was the far side of the pool table, his elbows propped on the back of a chair, watching another young man aim his cue.

'Mark?' She caught his eyes and beckoned.

He straightened, said, 'Won't be a tick,' to his friends, and walked over to her. She retreated into the corridor so he had to follow. The door clicked shut behind him. She put a hand on his chest.

'Can we go somewhere?' Urgency made her voice so deep she didn't recognise it. 'Now.'

He looked at her hand on his chest, and gave a disbelieving laugh. 'Just like that, eh?'

'I couldn't ring you. I'm sorry. I needed a reason. Please.'

He stared at her. She lifted his right hand and placed it on her breast.

After a moment he said, 'You want to come back to my place?'

'No.' It was difficult to speak. She whispered, 'There isn't time.'

'Your fat friend still here?'

'Yes.' The disloyalty didn't register. Nothing did, except her desire for him.

191

He dropped his hand from her breast. A muscle behind his cheekbone hardened. For a terrible moment she thought he was going to reject her. Then he grasped her elbow and pushed her toward the back entrance door.

It had become dark outside. Six concrete steps led up to the pub's gravelled car park. Mark hustled her up them. A dozen or more car roofs glistened under the white glow of the pub's security light. They walked quickly along the parked lines to the furthest, darkest corner of the car park. Jenny was aware of the pungent, garage smell of still-warm car engines. Then heard the rush of running water, from the fast brook behind the high perimeter hedge.

Mark swung her round, holding her by her forearms. He looked at her closely. 'This isn't sensible,' he said. He was giving her a chance to reconsider. But there was no anxiety in his voice.

'I know.' Jenny gazed at the cars surrounding them. The glass of unlit headlights glinted back at her like silent, watching eyes. Deep and low in her abdomen a womb-fist clenched, unclenched, and clenched again. She stepped away from Mark and lifted the front of her skirt.

'Shit,' he breathed. For a moment he was transfixed, as if to look was enough. Then it wasn't: he started to wrench at his belt. With a choked-off laugh he said, 'Toyota or Sierra?'

Jenny laughed back, a high, dizzy sound. Mark pushed at her, forcing her against a car wing.

'Sierra, then.' He grasped the back of her thighs. Jenny felt herself lifted, a cold metallic slipperiness against her skin. She braced her arms on the bonnet behind her. The metal there was warm. The soles of her feet curled, her insteps cramping. Mark's breath was in her face, his fingers digging into the flesh of her thighs. She closed her eyes.

She was impaled. The ball at her centre split wide. The world dissolved. Myriad threads snaked from the exploding, unravelling ball. Radiated out, like root filigrees, darting, shooting, seeking. Then sprang alive, hummed with light and life.

After a while spaces opened between the threads. In her head, behind her eardrums, in her chest, her armpits, her groin. The spaces began to fill, in rolling waves, with sumptuous fluid; it could be gold, an ebbing and flowing liquid gold. The spaces – no, chambers now – became dynamic and alive, expanding and contracting, yawning wide, sucking the gold in, then contracting, expelling, pumping it into and along the threads, irrigating the rest of her. Until she was saturated, glutted, wholly precious.

There was no end to it. She was gripped so tightly escape was impossible. She would remain like this, nailed into ecstasy, for ever.

Mark's body shuddered. The muscles of her womb convulsed. She heard a groan, and felt his hold on her thighs loosen. She was making a noise too, a whistling sigh.

He withdrew from her. She kept her eyes closed, concentrating on the last golden ebb. She heard him adjusting his clothing.

'Wake up.' He sounded gruff.

She said. 'The car bonnet's warm.' She opened her eyes and pushed herself upright.

He tugged the front of her skirt down and muttered, 'You're crazy.' Then helped her off the car. Her feet, touching the ground, sparked an aftershock of pleasure. Her knees melted.

'You OK?' He steadied her. He sounded embarrassed. 'Sorry,' he said. 'I had to hold you tight.'

'I'm OK.' He thought he'd hurt her. Maybe he had.

Walking back to the building she knew he had. Her thigh muscles felt stiff and shaky. She liked the thought that she would have bruises, reminders of his touch on her.

Before they reached the door she murmured, 'Will your friends ask where you've been?'

'Maybe.'

'What will you say?'

'Been shafting you over a car.' She heard a smile start in his voice.

She smiled too.

She left him in the corridor, re-entered the ladies' and replaced her underwear. She washed her face and saw in the mirror a normal, unfrantic, rational-looking woman. Then returned to Sal, who was sitting with two fresh glasses of red wine in front of her.

Sal said, 'Where the hell have you been?' but looked remarkably unannoyed. Almost good-humoured.

Jenny sat down and picked up one of the glasses. She leant forward and said, in what she hoped was a wicked voice, 'Just took Mark outside for a quickie.'

'Ha ha,' said Sal. 'You've arranged something, have you?'

Jenny sat back and took a mouthful of wine.

Sal took this as assent. 'You're stupid.' She sighed. 'Oh, well. I'm going to have to overlook it this time. We've just had a lucky escape. Frank's been here.'

Jenny gagged on her drink. 'What?'

'He stuck his head round there.' Sal pointed at the back bar door. 'Just after you'd gone. I'm amazed you didn't bump into him.'

'I went to the ladies',' Jenny said. 'He was here? In this bar?'

'He looked round the room, didn't see me because I was hiding behind a beer mat, and went away again. You said he wouldn't come. Wow. It must be love.'

'Oh, shit,' said Jenny. 'Oh, shit.'

'Well, it's all right now,' said Sal. 'He's gone.' She laughed. 'Unless he's lurking out the back still, waiting for you to turn up.'

'Jesus Christ,' whispered Jenny. 'Don't say that.'

'What's the problem?'

Jenny shook her head. 'Nothing. Just . . .' She couldn't cope with a complete invention. 'With Mark being here . . .'

'Oh, I want to apologize for that too.' Sal looked contrite. 'I'm sorry, but I told you if I got pissed I'd be rude to him. I warned you.'

'Did you?' Jenny found it hard to focus on what Sal was saying. Her mind was on unlit headlights, and empty cars. They had all been empty, surely. She pushed the dark, appalling picture away. The cars had been empty. She mustn't frighten herself. She made her lips smile. 'Oh, yes, you did. You're pissed, then, are you?'

'Half-way,' Sal admitted. 'God. Seeing Frank. What a prune. Even I'd prefer Mark.' She snorted, as if this was a vast hilarity.

'Well, thanks,' Jenny murmured.

'Now drink up,' said Sal. 'You've catching up to do.'

An hour later, after three more glasses of wine, Jenny achieved invulnerability. She regretted nothing. What was done was done. What might have been seen, had been seen. Except that it hadn't, of course, because the cars had been empty.

Sal got up to buy yet another round. Jenny stared dreamily around the room, and saw Nathan enter via the front door. Surprising: she'd thought Sal had said he wasn't coming. He pushed towards them through a small crowd of drinkers and leant over Sal's shoulder at the bar.

Sal jumped and said, 'Christ. Don't do that. What're you doing here?'

'Um . . .' Nathan waved at Jenny. 'Hi there. Taking advantage?'

'I beg your pardon? And a pint of Scrumpy Jack,' Sal said to Roy.

Nathan tapped his nose. 'Never mind. You asked me to come. Think of me as a gift horse.'

'Well,' Sal said to Jenny, putting the refilled glasses down on the table, 'fancy. Our very own gift horse.'

195

'Oh, shit, you're pissed.' Nathan looked comically mortified.

'We're celebrating,' Sal said, sitting down. 'What did you expect?'

Nathan gave a short laugh. 'A lift home, actually.'

'You're showing us your mouth, gift horse. This is not a place for lifts home.'

'Have you been out with Lizzie?' asked Jenny.

'Um . . . she wasn't there . . .' Nathan's smile twisted.

'Ah,' said Sal.

Nathan was still smiling at Jenny. 'Alex wasn't in either.'

'He's working. He's meeting us here, ooh . . .' Jenny squinted at her watch. 'Any minute now.'

'He'll have his car, then?'

'He'll have only just come from Aber,' Sal protested.

'He won't mind. I'll pay him the petrol. Ah, great.' As if there was now some point in staying at the table with them, Nathan sat down. He lifted his pint, grinned at Sal, and said, 'Cheers, Mum.'

Alex arrived at ten. Nathan sprang up to greet him.

'Hi, mate. Came round to see you. But you weren't there. So I ended up here.'

'Oh, yeah?' Alex wasn't listening. He looked from Jenny to Sal. 'Well, how'd it go?'

'Brilliant,' said Sal.

'Pretty good,' Jenny agreed.

'Triffic.' Alex looked genuinely pleased. He pulled out a chair and sat down. 'Hey.' He frowned at Nathan. 'Told you I was working tonight.'

'Yeah – dickhead, aren't I?' Nathan sighed ruefully.

Jenny stared at him. Was that all he was going to say? Leave Alex with the impression he'd come to Pentre only to see him? Did he think she and Sal were deaf? Or stupid?

'What?' Alex was frowning at her.

Jenny sat back. 'Nothing.' Oh, God, she was drunk, giving off unintentional messages. And Nathan wasn't, surely, deliberately trying to deceive or confuse Alex. Though he had just done both. And made her feel that she was colluding with him. She stared at Nathan, at his dark, guarded eyes in his silly, puckish face, and wasn't sure.

Sal said with cheerful malice, 'What he's really here for, Alex, is a lift home.'

'Pay for the petrol,' said Nathan quickly. 'Go on. Only take you ten minutes . . .'

Alex said, 'Ah . . .' his face clearing, as if he now grasped what was going on. He looked relieved. He leant back in his chair and said tolerantly, 'Well, buy us a Coke then, Nathe, and we'll see.'

Darling Michael,

It's three in the morning and I can't get to sleep. Sal and I have been talking downstairs and after all the wine I thought I'd fall into a stupor when I got up here, but I haven't.

Sal reckons she's sorted everything for me. In terms of opencasting, would you believe? You're the overburden. Clearly visible, looming barrow-like on the horizon, but half grassed over, you'll be glad to hear, and only a hazard when the wind's blowing. I'm down in the void, digging out the goodies. That's Mark, and Gareth too, I suppose. I said, no way, I'm trying to fill in black holes, not dig them out, but she said, what, with penises? and that it amounted to the same thing.

It doesn't, though, does it? I'm not digging anything out. Not acting out of rapaciousness, or greed. Nor out of malice or vindictiveness. If I'm forced to use the same metaphor, with you as overburden, then I'm the mountain, aren't I? The damaged, bereaved mountain. And all I'm trying to do, I'm sure, is restore myself.

Sal has asked me why I don't have an open relationship with Mark. Tell Alex, and anybody else who matters, and put an end to the furtiveness. I'm afraid I couldn't think of an answer for her, except to say that I definitely didn't want it. Thinking about it now, I find my inability to explain myself disturbing. It means I'm probably keeping secrets from myself. I know what I feel, and that I feel it strongly, but I can't explain why I feel it.

Her suggestion sounds reasonable, on the face of things. Assuming Mark was agreeable – though that's quite an assumption – I can't see much wrong with him as a boyfriend. I think I like him, irrespective of his sexual attractiveness. He's confident, competent, hardworking. Generous. Got a sense of humour. And a brain. OK, he's flashier and definitely more entrepreneurial than I'm used to, but I find that interesting, not at all off-putting. He's younger than me, but so what? No one would lift an eyebrow if our ages were reversed.

And yet I know I don't want him. As an open, acknowledged lover, that is. Or even as a friend. Somebody known. That was what was wrong with Gareth. I mustn't mix things. I've got what I want from Mark already.

I do know this: I don't want other people thinking I've found a replacement for you. No, it's deeper, more personal than that: *I* don't want to think I'm replacing you. Displacing you. That's it. Because I haven't finished my relationship with you. And what I'm doing with Mark is a private matter, between you and me.

Yes. Between you and me. Not him and me. Of course, it has to do with you. I don't know why – it must be part of that secret I'm keeping from myself – but I know it's true.

The climax I experienced tonight was the most spectacular I have ever had. I entered, I swear, a parallel world. You don't know what it's like to trip, and until last night I could barely remember, but I remember now. The dazzling knowledge that the world is much more than it seems. That greater, huger, more intense, more passionate, more colourful and more meaningful things exist. That it is purely the limitations of our senses and intellect that limit the world. A few hours ago I tripped with Mark. I *was* that different universe.

My orgasms are better with Mark than they were with you. No, Michael, I'm not trying to be cruel. I'm hurting me, if anyone, not you. I can't hurt you now, because you're dead. With you, my climaxes were full and satisfying, whole-body sensations, but they were anchored experiences, attached to, and a part of, whatever else we had. Part of a whole. Not the whole in itself.

Tonight, I could have died on that car. Sacrificed the rest of my life for a promise of that ecstasy in perpetuity. I have never felt so focused in abandonment. So single-minded in intent: to lose myself, to become nothing but an erotic, orgasmic entity – unity? – pulsating in the dark.

This is why I cannot resist Mark. Why, although I don't want him, I can't do without him. My body needs him. My need needs him. My senses clot when I think of him. Before he touches me, I'm half-way there. This is what I need. Without knowing why, I know this. He is perfect for me, Michael. Perfect for us.

I must go to sleep. I have to face Frank tomorrow. Oh, God. At best, he's going to complain that I wasn't in the Bridgend when I said I would be. At worst . . . No. I won't contemplate it. The cars were empty, I swear it.

Chapter 19

Jenny had difficulty getting Sal up. She had to march three times into the small spare room to prod the unstirring hump in the bed.

'If you don't want a lift now you can go in with Alex,' she hissed, on the third occasion. 'He's going in at lunch time.'

Sal moaned, 'Nooo,' from beneath the heavy Afghan bed-cover. Only a glimpse of hair was visible, a stiff tousle on the pillowcase. The hump shifted. 'I'm coming. Coffee. Bring me coffee.'

Jenny took her coffee. Then paid a second trip to the bath-room herself to rebrush her teeth in an attempt to expunge the taste of stale wine from her mouth. A headache niggled like a thin worm above her eyebrows. Back down in the kitchen she wrote a note for Alex in huge felt-tip script asking, 'When are you home tonight?' and placed it in the centre of the bare table.

It was nine before she and Sal stepped outside, though the chill that met them made it feel early still. For the first time this autumn there was a dew-mist on the windscreen of the car. White and fine-dropleted enough to be a near-frost. In a few weeks, on crisp mornings like this, Jenny would be examining the road outside the gate for black ice, before descending the hill.

They barely spoke on the short journey into town. Jenny

dropped Sal outside her house and smiled wanly, watching the limp figure hobble up the side alley. Then she drove on to Treherbert & Sons. She wasn't in the building until nine twenty, fifty minutes later than usual.

Up in the office she said, 'Sorry,' to Karen, and slumped, still wearing her coat, into her desk chair. 'I'm wrecked.'

Karen removed her eyes from her monitor. Her smile, Jenny could tell, was meant to convey understanding, but was far too prim at the corners. Jenny bet that Karen, being a young woman middle-aged beyond her years, never got wrecked.

Karen lowered her eyes. 'Is Mr Meredith in now?' There was a surprising delicacy in her voice.

'What?' Jenny immediately tensed. 'Isn't he in?'

'No.' Karen smiled again. 'Did you have a good time last night?'

'I did.' Why was Karen looking like that? 'Too good. And a good afternoon before that.'

Karen turned away, directing her expression at the monitor screen.

'I wasn't with Frank last night,' Jenny said, watching her. 'I was with my friend Sal.'

Karen blinked, then frowned. She turned back. 'I thought . . . Mr Meredith was meeting you . . .?'

'Well, he didn't.' Jenny kept her voice flat. Little cow. Little presumptuous cow. 'Or at least, he apparently tried, but he missed me.'

'Oh.' Karen stared at Jenny with unblinking eyes.

'He hasn't rung in?'

'No.'

'He's never late. And no one's rung him?'

'No. Sorry. We . . . well, we thought, you know, when you were late too . . .'

'For God's sake.' Jenny smothered jangling anxiety under

irritation and snatched up the phone. She dialled Frank's home number. The tone trilled twice, before a female voice said, 'Yes?'

'Mrs Meredith? This is Jenny Parsons, from work. Frank isn't in yet. Is he still at home?'

'My dear.' Mrs Meredith's voice sounded rich and controlled. 'I was about to ring you. Frank is a little unwell this morning. Nothing serious, I'm sure.'

Frank was never unwell. The inside of Jenny's mouth became sticky-dry, the taste horrible. 'Could you tell him,' she said, articulating carefully, 'that I'm sorry about last night. I understand he did pop over to Pentre. We seem to have missed each other. Please give him my apologies.'

'Ah.' There was a pause. The silence seemed to have a rhythm to it, as if Mrs Meredith were nodding her head. Then she said, 'I will, my dear. And I'm sure he'll see you on Monday.'

Jenny said goodbye and put the phone down. 'He's ill. His mother thinks he'll be back on Monday.'

She stood up and took off her coat. The pain above her eyebrows became fierce. She imagined a small horizontal cheesewire slicing off the crown of her head.

She stood still, and the pain lessened. She said, 'I'd better check his diary. Or have you?'

'No.' Karen shook her head. Her eyes were round and dutiful now. 'His office will still be locked.'

'So it will.' Jenny opened her bag and took out her keys. The workshop downstairs was opened up in the morning by a senior operator, but only she and Frank had keys to his office.

'His post is here.' Karen passed her a bundle of letters.

'Right.' Jenny took them and left the room. She crossed the small landing and inserted the key into the lock of Frank's office door.

Momentum failed her. She was assailed, as her hand twisted the metal, by a sense of dread, of calamity waiting beyond the closed door. An intimation of dark private space, of swinging, swaying shadows. She made herself turn the key, push at the door handle.

But the room inside looked normal. A pale, empty, undisturbed room. There was Frank's desk under the window, the surface tidy and uncluttered. Two office chairs. A tall cream steel cupboard and matching filing cabinet. Monitor and keyboard on a white trolley, flexes rolled and wedged into the tray beneath. A framed certificate, a calendar, and three antique street-scene photos of Abercwm on the walls. A neat, colourless room, a little dusty. Nothing personal on display. No scent of Frank, even, in the air. Jenny realized that she was holding her breath, and made herself exhale. She was being silly. What had she expected? Mrs Meredith had just told her that Frank was at home.

She checked his diary, then sat down and opened his post. Nothing she couldn't handle. She picked up the phone and rescheduled a rep's appointment, due this afternoon, to next week.

She put the phone down. The cheesewire was digging deeper into her brain. She had to prop her elbows on the desk and rest her face on her hands.

Why wasn't Frank here? Did she believe in coincidence? Did she believe his absence was unconnected with last night? And if not, what aspect of last night had caused him to stay away? How abominable was the hurt she might have done to him?

There were too many unknowns. Too much she didn't want to know. Speculation, reasoning, were impossible; the components were too slippery and shapeless, and would not adhere.

She got up and gathered the opened letters together. The slipperiness was becoming liquid. Possibilities sloshed around her brain, her grip on them gone. She rejoined Karen.

'Everything all right?' Karen asked, cautiously.

'I don't know.' Jenny sat down. Karen was expecting more, but she couldn't provide it. Her head hurt so much. 'I really don't know,' she said.

Chapter 20

Alex finished work at nine thirty and left the supermarket with two friends, Andy and Phil, whose last day of employment this had been. Both were off to university at the weekend, and both, thanks to the shop-floor send-off they had just received, were already intoxicated. The boys had been forcibly bottle-fed whisky, convinced, till the very last moment, that the pale liquid they were about to ingest was urine. Alex had been reminding himself throughout the day, and especially during the send-off horseplay, that he, too, had a place at university, and that his turn would come. The left-behind feeling would pass. But, just for the moment, while the farewell excitement was in the air, he was indulging in regrets. Friends would be celebrating tonight or tomorrow – their last days at home – and there was, of course, nothing to stop him joining in; except for the enthusiasm-sapping knowledge that he wasn't going anywhere.

He nipped across the road to throw his work clothes into the Escort, rejoined the others, and together they strolled up the high street towards the centre of town. The old Tudor streets, by nine thirty, had already donned their night-time armour: most shop fronts were shuttered or grilled, and the entrances to the two small modern shopping precincts were sealed off with high steel gates. Abercwm's daytime country-town character had disappeared; it was Friday night, and time for the town's youth – and the pubbing and clubbing not-so-youthful – to claim the streets.

Outside the fortress frontage of the old town hall the boys separated. Andy and Phil galloped down a side road; they were joining friends in a bar by Abercwm's cattle market. Alex had arranged to meet Lizzie, and possibly Nathan, at a disco in the King William pub, which was further along the high street. They would all meet up later.

Alex walked on through the pedestrianized town centre, his head down, hands in his jacket pockets. His stride was brisk and purposeful; there was a clear distinction between simply walking from A to B on foot at night, as he was doing now, which was unlikely to attract anyone's hostile attention, and the act of deliberately cruising the streets – especially if you were an out-of-towner – which might. He skirted a huddled crowd of teenage girls outside Woolworth's, too young to attempt the pubs, passing bottles and cans and cigarettes between them. He heard giggling, and a silly high voice calling, 'Hi, Blondie!' after him, which he ignored.

He wondered if Nathan would be at the King William. Nathan professed a horror of discos – the naff habitat of trendies, he insisted – but Alex guessed that he might overcome this prejudice if Lizzie were likely to be there. Nathan, Alex was sure, was pursuing Lizzie. Twice now he'd spotted or met Nathan in Pentre, unexpectedly, and been fobbed off with stories that convinced temporarily, but collapsed on examination. And twice last week he'd rung Lizzie, and then Nathan, to discover that they were both out. Though this latter evidence was weak, he knew; Lizzie was back at school now and often spent evenings at girlfriends' quieter houses; Nathan could be anywhere. But that they had seen each other, one-to-one, without him, was nonetheless incontrovertible; because Lizzie had told him, quite openly, that they had.

207

Mostly he was relaxed about this. Lizzie was his best friend, would always be his best friend, and told him everything of importance that happened to her. He had no romantic claim on her and she was entitled to see whom she pleased. He trusted her always to be open with him and never underhand. When she'd had her crush on the Brynteg boy, he'd known almost too much about it. If she was seriously interested in Nathan, he was sure she would have told him.

At the same time, when he wasn't being relaxed about their association, a very unrelaxed resentment took over. Nathan was not worthy of Lizzie. And Lizzie was remarkably blind about Nathan. Nathan was – Lizzie had said it herself, albeit uncritically – a bullshitter. All attitude and mouth. He didn't deserve Lizzie's friendship. Didn't deserve her attention. And he was a mixer. Alex had a strong sense – though admitting this made him uncomfortable – that part of what attracted Nathan to Lizzie was her attachment to himself. Of course, Lizzie was attractive in her own right. But so was conflict, he suspected, to Nathan.

Outside the King William he checked in his pocket for the familiar shape of his driving licence, though it was rare, these days, for him to be asked for proof of his age. He pushed at the glass-panelled door and stepped into the pub's main bar, a cream and brown room, currently occupied by groups of older men and a smattering of couples. Access to the rear disco was through a door on the back wall labelled 'Garden'.

There was no crowd at the bar, as there certainly would be out the back; he wondered whether to buy his one pint of the evening here and carry it through. As he hesitated, his attention was caught by movement to his right. A hand, flapping. A man was signalling to him. A man sitting on his own behind a trestle table. It was his mother's boss, Frank.

He waved back. Frank's hand flapped again, with more urgency. He was being beckoned over.

He glanced round, with the vague hope that he might spot someone else he knew, whose overwhelming and dragooning welcome would spirit him away. But he saw no one. Frank was still beckoning.

Suppressing a sigh, he walked across to him. Frank looked even older and duller than usual. He stopped in front of the trestle table.

Frank said something, gesturing at the tapestry bench seat beside him.

'What?' Alex leant forward.

Louder, and more distinctly, Frank said, 'Alex, please sit down.' He patted the tapestry.

Alex glanced back at the room, saw no excuse to refuse, and reluctantly walked round the table. He sat down.

Frank opened his mouth, closed it, then opened it again. Alex tried to look unimpatient.

'You and I,' said Frank. 'You and I . . .' He tailed off, shaking his head.

'What?' said Alex. It suddenly came to him that there was a good – though astonishing – reason why Frank looked so dull. He was drunk. Wow. Frank never drank, surely?

'You and I,' said Frank laboriously, 'have something in common. Something very dear, in common.'

'Oh, yeah?' Alex relaxed a little. He was used to drunks in pubs, old strawberry-nosed boys usually. Ruins who wanted to boast about their own youth. How much they'd drunk of an evening. Fights they'd won, or avoided, or orchestrated. How they'd pulled the ladies, even. Crude stuff, often, crudely told, as if they thought this would impress young ears. Normally Alex was good at humouring them.

'Mothers,' said Frank. He nodded, staring into the middle distance, then scowled. He turned, and focused on Alex. 'We have mothers in common.'

209

'Well,' nodded Alex, seriously. 'Everyone has mothers, don't they?'

Frank frowned and looked down at his lap. He shook his head, as if he'd decided not to hear what Alex had said.

'Your mother,' he said. 'We both have, don't we, her interests at heart? Your mother has suffered.'

Alex felt a wave of dislike for Frank. Stiffly he said, 'I've got friends waiting . . .'

Frank rested his hand heavily on Alex's forearm. 'Your mother and I,' he said, 'have been friends for many years. I want only what's best for her. You must understand that. Only what's best . . . As I'm sure you do . . .'

'Yes,' murmured Alex. Frank's hand was still firmly on his arm.

'Your mother,' said Frank, 'is behaving very badly at the moment. I am sorry to have to say this. Very badly.'

Alex blinked. He felt Frank's fingers tighten, digging into him.

'Your mother has been seen,' Frank went on, 'behaving very badly.'

'I have to go.' Alex tried to rise. Frank pressed hard on his arm, restraining him. Alex was suddenly conscious that Frank was a large man. Much larger and heavier than himself.

Frank pushed his face close. 'Your mother,' he hissed, 'has been seen in the car park of a pub, being fucked by a young man.'

Alex stared at him. He had felt Frank's spittle on his face, as he said the word 'fucked'.

'I have seen her, Alex.' With his free hand Frank touched the corner of his eyes. 'With these. These very eyes. Do you have a friend . . .' He corrected himself, '. . . a so-called friend, I should say, whom your mother has known for years? Who is the son of one of your mother's friends?'

Alex tried to swallow. He seemed to hear a cracking sound in his head.

Frank said, 'This is the young man with whom she has been having sex in car parks. I know your mother, and I know this young man. On an earlier occasion she identified him to me. They did it, Alex, on one of the cars. Brutally, Alex. Like animals.'

Frank's lips were wet. Alex wanted to part them with his fist. Split them, sink his knuckles into that filthy, spittle-flecked orifice.

'I can see that I've shocked you, Alex,' Frank continued. 'And for that I am sorry. But sometimes things are intolerable. We have to speak out. Your mother, Alex, is behaving like a whore.'

'Fuck off.' Alex jumped up, wrenching Frank's hand from his arm. Without looking back he stumbled across the room. He yanked at the door marked 'Garden'.

Half-way down the long corridor someone caught at his shoulder.

'Hey.' A big man with an iron-grey pony tail stopped him. He was holding a rubber stamp. 'A pound, butt, OK?'

Alex said, 'I just want to see if my friends are here.' In his own ears his voice sounded loose and uncontrolled. 'I'm not staying.'

'A pound,' the man said. 'Sorry.'

Alex felt like hitting him too. Thumping him, hammering him. Dance music issuing from the double doors in front of them agitated the air. He fumbled in his pocket and found a pound coin.

'Ta,' said the man. He lifted an ink stamp to mark Alex's hand, but Alex brushed him aside. He pushed through the doors.

As he stepped into the back room the music broke over him. It was so loud he felt each beat physically, as if he'd swallowed the source and the sound waves were pulsing from his chest. The room was not large and was dimly lit, illuminated only with red spotlights over the bar to his left and the flashing disco lights below a DJ stage. There was a crush of young people around the bar and in the shadows against the far wall. Three boys with floppy mid-parted haircuts were bouncing around the small dance floor as if on imaginary pogo-sticks. In all, there were probably fifty or sixty young people in the room. An image from a film entered his mind: he saw himself, legs braced warrior-fashion in the doorway, Uzi in his arms, spraying the floor with gunfire. Screams, a crescendo of screams, rising above the music . . .

A boy backed into him, swung round mouthing, 'Sorry, mate,' and then, recognizing him, grinned, 'Hi, Alex.'

Alex grabbed hold of him, put his mouth to the boy's ear, and shouted, 'Seen Lizzie?'

The boy nodded and stabbed a finger over to the shadows at the far side of the room. Alex raised his thumb and attempted a smile. He circled the dance floor.

They were both here. Lizzie and Nathan. As he passed the bar the dazzling effect of the bright lights lifted and he could see them. Lizzie, standing with her back against the rough stone wall, Nathan in front and facing her, an arm propped against the masonry above her shoulder. Lizzie's hair, in the flashes of coloured light, was a gleaming copper halo. Nathan looked spidery and black. To speak, Alex reminded himself, you had to lean in very close.

He guessed that he was almost invisible, with the light behind him. Just a closing male silhouette. Lizzie was smiling at something Nathan had said. Alex watched her face and then Nathan's wiry, energy-filled body, shifting weight from one leg to the other.

He was suddenly choked with self-pity. It hardly mattered whether Frank was right. Though his instinct told him he was.

Because Nathan was here to take things. Anything. Everything. Or, if he couldn't take them, to spoil them.

Lizzie had seen him. Her eyes were widening in welcome. Nathan, not realizing, bent to say something in her ear. Alex saw her eyes flick sideways and her mouth twist to interrupt him. But she was still smiling; her expression was still sparkling.

He'd had enough. He'd thought he needed to see her but now, seeing her, couldn't think why. And he couldn't cope with Nathan. He turned on his heel, pushed his way back through the crowd and almost fell through the disco doors, which crashed shut behind him. The man with the pony tail called, 'Hey, you missed your pass-out!' after him as he lurched on. In the front bar he looked neither right nor left, but made straight for the door.

Out on the pavement he slowed, drawing breath. His chest ached. The music – or the sudden absence of it – had stunned his brain. He fumbled with the front of his jacket, trying to zip it up. His fingers were shaky and incompetent.

He heard the pub door behind him open and close.

'Hey,' said Lizzie, catching him up. Her denim jacket was slung over her shoulder. 'What's up with you?'

Alex looked back at the door, expecting Nathan to appear. He shook his head and started to walk quickly up the high street, the way he'd come.

Lizzie jogged after him, pulling on her jacket.

'What's wrong?' She caught at his arm, slowing him. 'What's bugging you?'

'Nothing.'

She slipped her arm through his. He almost crumpled on the spot.

'It was only a kiss,' she said.

'What?' What was she talking about? He shook his head impatiently.

After a few more yards she said, 'Where're we going?'

213

'I'm going to my car.' He stopped, and looked back. No one else had come out of the pub. 'You just leaving Nathan there, then?'

Lizzie shrugged. 'He'll survive.' She smiled. 'It's me needs the lift home.'

They walked on. Alex said, 'Did you go out with Nathan last week?'

'No,' said Lizzie.

'I rang you. Tuesday and Wednesday. You weren't in. Neither was Nathan.' And neither was Mum, he remembered, on the Tuesday. Rehearsing at Sal's, she'd said, for the inquiry. How did you rehearse a video? In his mind's eye he saw Frank's face. His lips. His wet, obscene, filthy lips.

'I was in Cardiff Tuesday. School theatre trip. And Wednesday was disco night. I have to help on the door.' She paused. 'I expect Nathan has other friends. Other things to do.'

'Yes,' said Alex.

'He's called in a couple of times at home. I told you. No big deal.'

'Did you see him last night?'

'No. He called by, though. Dad said. I was out.'

'I saw him in the Bridgend. He said he'd been up to my place.'

'Maybe he had.'

'Yes.'

They were approaching the crowd of girls outside Woolworth's. One, with frizzy permed hair and wearing a tight calf-length split skirt, hobbled across the paving towards them.

'It's Blon-dee!' she called back to her friends. She ignored Lizzie. 'Hey, Blon-dee, fancy you.' She blew Alex an extravagant kiss.

'Get a life,' Lizzie snapped, and under her breath added, 'Or at least a full-length mirror.'

Alex tried to smile. Lizzie tucked her arm more firmly into his.

'You jealous or something?'

Alex sighed. 'Or something, I think.' He could see his car. He suddenly knew he couldn't face his mother. He saw a mental picture: of her, Nathan, and Sal, in the pub last night. Of Nathan leaping up to greet him. His mother, flushed and tipsy, and looking somehow unmaternal, getting in a muddle over something Nathan had said. He felt a sob catch in his throat. He said in a low voice, 'Can I stay over with you? I don't want to go home.'

'Course.' Lizzie stopped, drawing him to a halt, and studied his face. 'You all right?'

'I don't know.' He couldn't meet her gaze. He didn't know. He was incapable, right now, of any judgement about himself. Or anyone else. He shook his head. 'Something's happened. But I don't want to talk about it. Sorry. I need to think.'

Lizzie was silent a moment. Then said quietly, 'It's OK. No problem,' and led him on.

Chapter 21

Jenny waited to open her eyes on Saturday morning until the bedroom had grown properly light, around eight. She was not convinced, as she gazed wearily up at the smooth slope of grey ceiling above her, that she had slept at all during the night. The hours had seemed never-ending, filled either with persistent, if distant, external noise, or, if the noise had for a while abated, with internal careering, bludgeoning thoughts. The noise had been that of car engines, convoys of them, each a faraway, ear-straining and heart-tensing drone. A drone that failed to change note as it should to indicate the vehicle's turn-off into the village, or on the rare occasions that the note did change causing her pulse to race and her hearing to become super-alert, refused to draw closer or louder. Refused to stop, thrumming, in her drive. Refused, in other words, to become Alex's Escort, returning home.

The thoughts that had filled the gaps between these car engine noises now seemed impossibly wild and confused. Some so bizarre, indeed, that she realized that she must actually have been asleep, or at least dozing, to have entertained them. Now that her eyes were open, most had instantly evaporated.

She lifted herself from the pillows and squinted at the clock. Her tear ducts seemed to have stopped working: her eye sockets were dry and sore. On the floor was a crumpled piece of paper.

It was the note on which yesterday she had written, 'When are you home tonight?' and Alex had pencilled below, 'Late. Taken key.' Jenny saw it now, closed her eyes with a groan, and lay back again.

She got up eventually at nine thirty. Downstairs, after a couple of spoonfuls of breakfast cereal, she admitted defeat and rang Sal.

'Is Alex there? Sorry, it's Jen. I've lost him. Did he stay over last night?'

'Hi there.' Sal sounded tolerantly awake. Not like someone just roused. 'I'm not sure.' Furniture scraped; she must be downstairs. 'Hang on, I'll see.'

There was a clatter as the phone was put down. Jenny waited. She knew that if Alex had killed himself in his car, the hospital or the police would have contacted her by now. And it had been light for hours – a beaten-up body crumpled in a back street would have been reported long ago. And yet . . . Alex nearly always did what he said he'd do. Or rang her, if he changed his mind. He knew she worried, how she felt forced to worry. Her belief that terrible things happened to people who didn't worry. And terrible things, they both knew now, did occasionally happen. She heard the phone picked up.

'No sign of him.' Sal sounded breezy. Genuinely breezy. 'Nathan's gone to work. I think if there'd been two of them I'd have heard. Only one bowl in the sink, too.'

'Damn,' said Jenny.

'He probably found a party last night.'

'He'd have rung.'

'If anything awful had happened you'd have heard.'

'I know.' Jenny's anxiety tipped into irritation. What was it about worries, that they could never come in ones? Why couldn't Alex have waited to behave irresponsibly till after Monday? Till after she'd seen Frank, and resolved things – whatever they were, however appalling – one way or another. She made an impatient noise. 'I bet he was with Lizzie. Perhaps I'll ring Gareth. If she's out after midnight she has to ring home.'

'You do that,' said Sal. 'If he's not there I'll ring Nathan, see if he knows.'

'Oh, thanks,' said Jenny. She cut Sal off and dialled Gareth's number. A child answered. Then Gareth broke in.

'Hello? Jenny, is it?'

'Ah, Gareth. Sorry to bother you. I'm trying to find Alex. He said he was coming home last night but his car isn't here and his bedroom's empty . . .'

'He's here, love,' Gareth interrupted. 'Leastwise, his car's outside. Not up yet. Nor Lizzie. Want me to prod him for you?'

'No, no.' Jenny spoke in a rush, partly from relief, partly instinctively, to protect Alex. Just in case. What was he doing, staying over at Lizzie's? Just a few hundred yards from his own house. Where was he sleeping? Perhaps they'd been talking late, and he'd just dropped off . . .

'Don't wake him,' she emphasized. 'I only wanted to find him. I was worried . . . you know . . .'

'Ay,' agreed Gareth. 'Well, no need. I'll tell him you rang.'

'Thanks.'

Jenny rang Sal back.

'For some reason he stayed over with Lizzie. Mysterious. But anyway, he's safe and sound.'

'Glad to hear it.' Sal was eating something crunchy now. 'Hey Jen,' – Jenny heard the rustle of a newspaper, above the crunching – 'I've got the *Gazette* here. You fancy the cinema tonight? Brynteg's showing *Fantasia* for one night.'

'You've got the video,' Jenny pointed out.

'Not the same as big screen. Ah, go on.'

'You're not going over to Pauline's, then?'

'Tomorrow. Say yes.'

Jenny smiled. Sal's passion for Disney films was endearing.

And infectious. She definitely wanted an early night, but she could go to the cinema and still be in bed by nine thirty.

'Why not? OK.'

'Great. Pick you up at six thirty?'

'Fine.'

Alex didn't come home for lunch, neither did he ring. Jenny gardened most of the afternoon, but couldn't settle to anything. Exhaustion and restlessness were an unproductive combination. She mowed the front lawn – the last cut of the year, she hoped – but lost interest before she reached the side slope. She half weeded a small flower bed. She kept finding herself standing up, staring down the lane, watching for the white shape that would be Alex's car. Except it never was. At four the phone rang. She was moving a rain-filled bucket at the time and sloshed water over her shoes in her haste to get inside. But it was only Nathan. She told him that Alex was at Lizzie's. Or had been, at least, that morning.

By six thirty Sal's red Fiesta was tooting outside the gate, and Alex still hadn't appeared. Or rung. Jenny scrawled a quick note for him.

But climbing into the car she changed her mind.

'Can we stop off at Gareth's? I want to tell Alex I'm going out. He's a sod. He must have known I was anxious this morning. He's never rung back.'

Sal put the car into gear. Cautiously, as they moved off, she said, 'I don't know if it's significant, but when Nathan rang Alex from work this afternoon, Alex wouldn't speak to him.'

'Really?' Jenny looked at Sal in astonishment. 'Are you sure? Messages do get confused down there. The kids . . . you know.'

Sal shook her head. 'He said he spoke to Lizzie. Alex was there and she went to get him, but then came back and said he wouldn't come to the phone.'

219

'Christ.' This sounded most unlike Alex. 'Boy-girl-boy problems, d'you think? I suppose it might explain why he's staying
with Lizzie . . .'

'Nathan sounded exasperated. Whatever the argument is, he
obviously doesn't rate it.'

'But he knows what it is?'

'It's possible.' Sal sighed. 'Never mind. It's between them,
isn't it?'

They'd reached Gareth's house. Sal pulled in behind Alex's
Escort. Gareth himself was in the small front garden, scooping
up children's bicycles. He straightened as he saw them.

Jenny got out. 'Is Alex around?'

Gareth's smile was short. 'Out the back. Playing Mr Moody,
looks like. I'll call him.' He disappeared into the house.

Sal climbed out of the car too. 'Everything OK?'

'Not sure.' Jenny opened the gate and let herself into the
garden. 'I think Alex has outstayed his welcome.'

They heard Gareth's voice shout, 'Alex! Here, now, out the
front.' After a moment Gareth returned. 'He's coming.'

They waited. Jenny felt the atmosphere grow tense. Alex
appeared at the open doorway. He was wearing an unfamiliar
tie-dyed T-shirt – Lizzie's, presumably – over his jeans. He
stopped abruptly, framed in the doorway. His eyes were red-
rimmed and his expression unfriendly.

'We're just off to the cinema.' Jenny wished Gareth wasn't
there, so she could speak more freely. Alex looked ill. Had he
been drinking? 'Don't you think,' she said, as tactfully as she
could, 'that you might go home soon? You look . . . well, maybe
you're overdoing things a bit?'

Alex's gaze rested on her, moved to Sal, and then swung
back again.

'You can talk,' he said.

'I beg your pardon?'

Lizzie's voice, from somewhere in the house, called, 'Who is it, Alex?'

Alex turned in the doorway and called back, 'My mother, the slag, and her fat dyke friend.' He disappeared into the darkness of the house.

Gareth said, 'Little shit,' explosively, and started to follow him. Jenny grabbed his arm. 'No,' she said, controlling her voice. Alex's words echoed in her head. 'No, please.' She turned to Sal. 'I'm sorry, I'm sorry.'

'So what's new?' Sal's mouth was tight.

Jenny moved close to Gareth. 'This is nothing to do with you. Nothing,' she hissed fiercely. 'Alex wouldn't be here if it was. Please, just leave it. I'll deal with him'

'He needs his backside tanned.' The flesh around Gareth's mouth was white.

'Just send him home,' said Jenny. 'When you can. Please. He doesn't mean it. Oh, God.' She waved a hand helplessly. 'I'm going to cry.'

'Get in the car,' said Sal grimly. 'Just get in.'

Jenny nodded, squeezed out, 'I'm sorry,' again to Gareth, and climbed back into the car. Sal slammed herself into the driver's seat, crashed the gearstick, and shot the car into reverse. As they moved off more sedately down the hill Jenny fumbled a length of toilet paper from a roll on the front shelf.

'Well,' said Sal. 'Brilliant. Looks like he knows.'

Jenny wiped her eyes. 'I'm sorry. He was so rude to you.'

'I'm fat. I'm a dyke. You think Mark's been shooting his mouth off?'

Jenny shook her head. 'I don't know. I don't know what's going on. Alex was fine . . .'

Sal said nothing. They reached the main road. She swung the Fiesta left, up the hill towards Brynteg.

'You're going to say you told me so, aren't you?' said Jenny.

A muscle tugged at the corner of Sal's mouth.

221

Jenny looked around, suddenly confused. 'Where're we going?'

'To the cinema,' said Sal. 'I'm not having my evening ruined because your son throws a wobbly about something you could have told him weeks ago. What else would you suggest?'

'You don't think I ought to go home? Wait for him?'

'He looked in a bad mood to me. Give him time to cool off. We'll only be a couple of hours.'

Jenny sank back. Then felt panic rise again. 'But it's not fair on Gareth and Siân. I should have taken him home.'

'He's eighteen, for Christ's sake, not a baby. We'll go to the film, and then I'll drop you home, and if he's still not back you can do your waiting and hand-wringing then. OK?'

'OK,' said Jenny.

Alex splashed his face with cold water over a Belfast stone sink in the back-of-house utility room. Liquid was still pouring down his throat but his eyes had stopped leaking. In the kitchen next door Siân was cooking fish fingers for seven, using two frying pans. Alex could hear whistling applause from her portable television.

Lizzie came up behind him and whispered, 'Dad's furious with you.' She sounded angry herself.

'It's nothing to do with him.' Alex wiped his face on a tea towel.

'It's our bloody house.'

'You two!' Siân's voice trilled through the open door at them. 'You want your tea now, is it, or will you wait?'

'God,' groaned Lizzie.

'She had the telly on,' said Alex. 'She didn't hear.'

'Later!' Lizzie called. To Alex she said, 'D'you want to talk about anything?'

'No.' He knew he did, and that he'd have to, sometime. To someone. But not yet.

Lizzie stared at him. 'You're going to have to go home. Dad won't stand for another night.' She pulled a face. 'Nor will I. God, you were noisy.'

'Sorry. I couldn't sleep.' He'd lain in a sleeping bag on Lizzie's carpeted floor. In a draught, because the door had to be propped ajar – Lizzie's signal to her parents that nothing that they would disapprove of was going on. The night had seemed interminable. He'd only finally dropped off after he'd heard the boys go down for breakfast. He sighed. 'And it's OK, I'm going now.'

Gareth came to the door.

'Hope you washed your mouth out too.'

'Dad,' murmured Lizzie.

'It's all right,' said Alex.

'If you were my boy,' said Gareth, 'I'd leather you.'

'Shut up, Dad. He wouldn't,' Lizzie assured Alex. She turned back to her father. 'He's upset. Leave him alone.'

'I'm sorry,' Alex said. 'I shouldn't have involved you. I'm going now.' He could accept criticism from Gareth. Having Lizzie as his best friend meant her father had laid down the law more often, during his teenage years, than either Michael or his real father had.

He pushed past Lizzie into the kitchen. Siân was bending over the younger of Lizzie's brothers, wiping the child's face vigorously with a damp cloth. She stood up. She was a tall, fair woman with eyes, Alex always thought, that never quite focused on you.

'Thanks for letting me stay over,' he said.

'Off now?' cried Siân. 'No tea?' The radiance of her smile scattered around him. She could as easily, he felt, be addressing the sideboard.

He said, 'No, I must go, thanks,' and went through into the hall. Lizzie followed. He found his jacket and put it on.

223

'I'll ring you,' he said.

'Why did you call your mother a slag?' Lizzie asked. 'That's what this is all about, isn't it?'

'I'll deal with it,' he said.

'I'm not stupid, you know.'

Alex looked away. 'I'll ring you,' he repeated.

He left the house. At the roadside, in front of his car, he hesitated. Left was the hill, and home. An empty cottage, he assumed. Gareth would have said, wouldn't he, if his mother had changed her plans and was waiting at home for him? He turned and looked right. That way, downhill, was the main road. The road to Abercwm and Nathan. And with Sal definitely out.

He climbed into the Escort, then hesitated again. He sighed, a deep, despairing sigh. His mother said he didn't see things. Lizzie said he only saw what he wanted to see. They were right. He hadn't seen this – his mother and Nathan. Nor did he want to see it. He didn't want to be forced into seeing it. Didn't want to have to deal with it.

But. It had upset him and made him angry, and, somehow, he would have to deal with it. He started the car, turned it in Lizzie's drive, and set off slowly down the hill. Half-way down he felt a shift of consciousness, as if he'd just woken up. He was going to Abercwm, was he? Had he actually made a decision to do this? What had decided him? He couldn't remember. Tiredness was cutting up time into chunks.

He reached the junction with the main road and had to wait while slow-moving traffic streamed past. Two other cars came up behind him. If he made a right turn now, towards Abercwm, he would be committed. He would be going to see Nathan.

At the last minute, instead of turning right, he shot across the road, into northern Pentre. Somebody hooted at him; he had been indicating right. He pulled the car up as soon as it was safe, his heart galloping. As if he'd just had a near-accident, though he knew he hadn't.

He'd lost the power to make decisions. Even to think straight. He did want to go to Abercwm. He did want to confront Nathan. But at the same time he didn't want to. Definitely didn't want to. A dangerous state of mind to be in, behind the wheel of a car. He must get a grip on himself.

A red Fiesta parked down the road caught his eye. It wasn't Sal's – hers was a J reg, this was a G – but otherwise it was identical. He stared at it. Sal and his mother told each other everything. Did Sal know about Nathan? Shit. Frank did. Who else? How long had it been going on?

An image sprang to mind: his mother dolled up in velvet, a late summer evening, in their kitchen. Nathan gawping at her as she walked across the room, making a crass remark about toy boys. That was weeks and weeks ago.

He was suddenly overcome. If he didn't do something physical, he would cry. He snatched his hands from the steering wheel. He mustn't drive. He got quickly out of the car and set off down the road on foot, walking fast and vigorously, blinking in the cool air, exercising his feelings away.

He passed the Bridgend pub and then the post office. Then he was at Bevan's garage. He stopped. The yellow 'Closed' sign swung on its concrete base, a couple of feet in from the road. Behind it, on the forecourt to the side of the pumps, was Mark's Hilux. He looked up at the building above the canopy. A window – the bathroom window, he guessed – was open. It looked as if Mark was in.

Something strengthening stirred inside him. Mark had never met Nathan. But Mark, he was almost sure, would not admire him. Mark saw people clearly. He was not easily impressed. And he knew how to get things done.

He crossed the forecourt and rapped on the glass door. A dog barked. He pushed on the door, which swung open, called, 'Mark?' and mounted the stairs. Mark stood in the doorway at the top, wearing just a pair of bright red and green boxer shorts. His hair was wet and he was holding a small white towel.

'Hi,' said Alex.

'How do.' Mark stepped back to let him enter. He rubbed at his hair with the towel.

'Hi, Sheeb.' The dog circled Alex, wagging her tail. He gave her rump a pat before flopping into one of the armchairs.

Mark pushed the door shut with his foot and said, his voice ironic, 'Sit down, why don't you.'

Alex hardly heard him. 'You going out?'

Mark shrugged. 'Later, maybe. Only just got in. Got a big job on. Want a beer?' He crossed to the fridge and opened it.

'Yeah, ta.' Alex told himself that, whatever he eventually decided to do, one beer wouldn't hurt. He watched as Mark bent to remove the cans from the fridge shelf. The white towel hung round his neck. The colours of his boxer shorts were exceptionally loud. If someone had bought him shorts like that he would have buried them in the garden. And yet on Mark they looked right. Stylish, even. How did Mark know, when he shopped, among the multitude of colours and fabrics and styles to choose from, what would suit him? Or maybe, if you had a body like Mark's, everything did. Everything and anything looked right. And maybe, he thought drearily, the converse was also true – that on others, those with lesser, immature, inferior bodies, everything looked unstylish and wrong. A wave of misery broke over him.

'I've had a bust-up with Mum,' he said.

'Oh, yeah.' Mark stood up and lobbed a beer can at him. Alex caught it.

'I've been staying down at Gareth's. With Lizzie.' He pulled the tab on the can.

Mark moved beyond the fridge to look at himself in a small mirror above the kitchen units. 'Oh, yeah,' he said again. He put his own unopened beer can down, shook his head, and finger-combed the short damp hair backwards over his ears.

Alex took a deep breath. 'I called Mum a slag.'

Mark lowered his hands slowly from his hair. He turned round. 'Did you now?' He leant back against the unit and folded his arms across his chest. His biceps looked large and hard and well defined. Alex imagined punching Nathan with those arms.

He swivelled to face Mark full on. It was impossible, looking at him, not to think in physical terms. 'Have you had lots of fights?' he asked.

Mark's eyes were steady, unblinking. 'A few. Not for a while.'

'But . . . you've hit people.'

'One or two've hit me.'

'But you've always won?'

Mark snorted, glancing away. 'Oh, ay.' He shifted his body against the unit. 'You planning to hit someone, then?'

'Maybe,' Alex said.

Mark twisted to pick up his can, and pulled the tab. 'You getting at something particular? Or someone particular?'

Alex nodded. 'Nathan.' He saw something – surprise? confusion? – flicker across Mark's face, so he said, 'The bloke I told you about. My friend from London. My ex-friend.'

'You want to hit him?'

'He's a . . .' Alex shook his head. 'A . . . spoiler.' The word didn't seem strong enough, yet it was exactly what he meant. Someone who played with situations. Pushed and pulled and squeezed them, just out of callous interest, until they broke. 'First he's all over Lizzie . . . and now, and now . . .' He looked away. He could feel himself flushing, but his voice was secure, '. . . now he's screwing Mum.'

He glanced back at Mark, whose body appeared to have frozen.

'Is he.' His face, too, was still and expressionless.

'I want to smash him,' said Alex.

227

'How d'you know this?' Mark asked.

'Someone told me. He saw them. Actually . . . you know . . . together. It's definitely true.' He swallowed. 'Mum's face, when I . . .'

Mark said, 'Shit,' and pushed himself away from the work-surface. He murmured, 'Hang on,' and disappeared into his bedroom. He reappeared carrying a pair of black jeans and a white T-shirt. He slung the T-shirt over the sofa back, and started to pull on the jeans.

'Maybe your mum likes Nathan.' He was concentrating on buttoning the fly. 'You thought of that?'

'I don't fucking care,' exploded Alex. 'It's a bastard thing to do. I'm going to fix him.'

Mark looked up. 'So why're you telling me?'

Alex wasn't sure, now. There had been a reason, earlier. A fantasy reason, he now saw. A fantasy in which Mark, as incensed as himself – for some, now incomprehensible, reason – helped him fix Nathan. As Mark had helped him in the past when he'd needed and asked for help. The repairs to his car; the work on the video recording. It was a fantasy in which Mark was a strength, willing and available for use. A resource.

'If you were me,' he said. 'What would you do?'

'If I were you,' Mark said, 'I'd be gabbing to mates about it and doing fuck all.'

Alex was stung. 'You don't think I've got the bottle?'

'You don't need bottle to hit someone. You want to do it badly enough, you do it. You don't want to, you don't.'

Alex felt suddenly tearful. He wanted to say: but it's all right for you. Alex had never seriously hit anyone. He'd skirmished once or twice, in town. Just fending-off actions, usually followed by swift retreats. He'd never aimed a punch at anyone. Never wanted to. But Nathan had, he bet. Nathan liked conflict. And he collected knives.

He could feel a wobble in his chin. He hoped it wasn't visible. He didn't trust himself to speak.

Mark pulled on his T-shirt and walked round the front of Alex's armchair. He dropped to his haunches.

'You look like shit,' he said. 'Go home and get some kip. If you want to flatten your mate he'll still be there tomorrow.'

Alex sighed. He stared around. Rested his eyes on the dog, now curled in her box by the window. Not asleep, though; her huge soft brown eyes were watching them. In a voice that wavered a little he said, 'Don't suppose I could kip here?'

'No.' Mark's tone was definite. But kind. 'You gotta go home.'

'I don't want to speak to Mum.'

'Don't then. No one's forcing you.'

Alex nodded, and pushed himself up out of the chair. Mark rose too.

'Thanks,' Alex said.

Mark half smiled. 'What for?'

Alex attempted a smile too. 'Not sure. But thanks anyway.'

'Run you home, if you like.'

'It's OK. Got my car.'

Mark nodded. At the door Alex said, 'See you soon, I expect,' and Mark said, 'Yup.'

Alex descended the stairs. At the bottom he shut the glass door carefully and squinted round into the light. Although the sun had set the outside world still seemed very bright. He felt light-headed, his movements floaty. Mark was right. He was in no state to go looking for Nathan. He'd known it earlier, intuitively, but not acknowledged it. Nothing would have changed by tomorrow.

He walked back up the road, his hands deep in his jacket pockets. A gesture, almost, of satisfaction. He was glad he'd been to see Mark. He definitely felt calmer. Mark hadn't seemed shocked or disbelieving. There'd been no fuss, no drama, no requests for details, no judgements. Just matter-of-fact acceptance, and practical advice. He thought about what Mark had said: that if he wanted to hit Nathan badly enough, he'd do it, and that if he didn't, he wouldn't. There was a kind of perfection about this. How much he minded, Mark was saying, and how he chose to react, having decided how much he minded, were matters entirely up to him. There were no rules. No codes he had to abide by. The pressure was off.

He stood by his car, and felt his shoulders sag. Now he was back in control, he realized how tired he was. He needed sleep. He had work again tomorrow, early start. Still, double pay, Sunday. And it would get him away from the house, and his mother. He'd be off at four. He'd visit Nathan then.

Chapter 22

By nine Jenny and Sal were driving home, passing through the high western reaches of the Pentre valley. Up here the main road occupied almost the entire valley floor, the wooded hillsides rising steeply – near-vertically in places – either side. The Fiesta's downhill-facing windscreen was completely filled, above the orange street-light haze, with the dark bulk of the Blaen Dyar plateau ahead.

Some sinister quality to the view reminded Jenny of a scene from the film they'd just sat through. The penultimate Mussorgsky segment, in which the Forces of Darkness had been depicted – in the form of a gigantic over-looming Devil – summoning the human dead of the world from their graves.

'D'you think *Night on Bald Mountain* was trying to tell us something?' She stared up at the hills. In certain lights – in certain moods, perhaps – their pressing mass was forbidding.

'Ah!' said Sal. 'Mr Nasty. Of course. British Coal incarnate. Thought I recognized the sod.'

Jenny nearly smiled. As the car rounded one of the long curving valley bends the southern side of Pentre appeared.

'One of my house lights is on,' she said. 'Oh, God. Alex is back.'

'The Forces of Light triumph,' Sal reminded her. '*Nil desperandum.*'

Jenny felt the onset of panic. 'I can't talk to him. Not tonight.'

'You may have to.' Sal pressed firmly on the indicator stalk. The Pentre junction was coming up. They swung off the empty main road into the village lane.

Half-way up the incline Jenny said, 'Will you come in with me? A coffee . . .?'

'Thanks,' said Sal. 'But I don't think so.'

They passed Gareth and Siân's house. Jenny pressed the back of her head into the seat head-rest and listened to her heart beating.

'There you are.' Sal pulled into the cottage driveway. Alex's car was parked next to the Polo. There were no ground-floor lights on in the house. Just one illuminated window upstairs. Sal leant towards Jenny.

'He's your son, for Christ's sake. Not your husband. You argued the toss with me. So now try it on him.'

'You weren't convinced,' said Jenny.

Sal laughed. 'I'm difficult.'

Jenny sighed and got out of the car. She remained standing on the concrete while Sal turned the Fiesta round, and watched the brake lights disappear down the hill.

She walked round to the kitchen door and found it unlocked. She switched on the light. The brightness hurt her eyes. There were crumbs on the dining-table and a dirty plate, knife and fork in the sink bowl.

Passing through to the rear hall, she switched on the light and mounted the stairs. From half-way up she could see Alex's closed bedroom door. She could hear nothing except her own footfalls and distantly, from the kitchen behind her, the hum of the fridge motor. The cottage felt in limbo. She made herself cross the short stretch of landing and quietly turned the door knob.

The room's centre light was on. Alex was in bed, a bunched-up hump under his black-and-red duvet cover. He was on his front, his long yellow hair swathed across the pillow. She tiptoed round the bottom of the bed, so she could see his face. His eyes were closed, lips slack and squashed against the bed linen. Asleep, or pretending, very convincingly, to be asleep. His clothes lay in a heap on the carpet beside the bed. She strained to catch the sound of his breathing, but could hear nothing. Children were noisy sleepers. But, of course, Alex was no longer a child. She could sense, without watching for it, the rise and fall of the duvet over him; but the action was silent. The room smelt faintly of aftershave and musty socks.

She withdrew, switched off the light, and closed the door. Acknowledged that she was relieved. Then descended the stairs to the sitting room, and poured herself a large gin and tonic.

An hour later she had finished her second gin. Rising from the sofa in the dimly lit sitting room to refill her glass, she realized she was still wearing her coat. She took it off and laid it across the high sofa back.

She knew she ought to go to bed. Tiredness was affecting her perceptions. The world seemed to be slowing down. The room looked softer and darker than it should. And yet this very tiredness that was slowing and softening and darkening the world was also, she sensed, pushing her somewhere new. Lifting shrouds within her. With no energy to contain, or order, or direct her thoughts, they had become loose, roaming, creatively free.

She had come to an end. A swirling, murky, hidden end, but an end nonetheless. A quiet, perhaps as yet unexploded, end. Her son had put a stop to her. What Sal had failed to achieve, with scorn, with persuasion, with argument, Alex had done with one unhappy, red-eyed stare, and a few cruel words. As simple as that. As if when her face was forced towards him, she could, at last, see.

At the sideboard she emptied the tonic-water bottle into

her glass. This time she omitted the gin. She replaced the glass on the octagonal coffee table and sat down again. According to the clock below the hanging wall Buddha, it was now ten thirty.

She must take responsibility for what had happened. The blame, if necessary. She sat up. Good heavens. She had forgotten – how could she? – that there was someone else involved. Someone who deserved to know what was going on, and that an end – of some determination – was approaching. She got up again and crossed to the window sill. Opened the telephone directory. Found Bevan. M. Bevan. There he was, four lines above O. Bevan, Garage Proprietor. She mouthed the number, picked up the telephone and trailed the cable across to the sofa. She pressed the buttons.

She heard two rings. Mark's voice said, 'Yep?'

'Mark?' she said. 'It's Jenny. I need to talk to you.'

There was a short pause. Then she heard his voice say, 'Go fuck yourself,' and the line went dead.

Clumsily, as if she'd never done it before, she replaced the receiver on its base. She heard Mark's words again, and this time made sense of them. 'Go fuck yourself.' She tried to re-hear how he had said it. His tone, the pitch of his voice. Tried to imagine his face, saying it. Tried to work out what he meant.

She glanced upwards in a sudden tremble of anxiety. Had Alex been to see him? Confronted him? She imagined Alex, furious, squaring up to Mark. She started to rise, agitated, then remembered that Alex was here, upstairs. That he had come home, made himself supper, cleared the table, undressed himself, and gone to bed. If he had confronted Mark, he had survived the encounter. He had been untraumatized enough to return home and, once home, behave as normal. And now he was safely upstairs, and asleep.

She settled down again. Had Mark sounded angry? Or upset? She said the words again in her head. 'Go fuck yourself.'

She'd lost his tone. And said it too often in her head now; the words had become meaningless.

She retrieved the phone, which had tumbled from her lap on to the sofa beside her, and stared at it. A strange idea, vague at first, like a ghost, edged into her mind, but solidified, as she looked at it. The phone was here, beside her, in reality. She remembered getting it. But had she actually made that call? The memory of it was fading. Like dreams faded. She was exhausted; was it possible that she had been asleep just now and dreamt it? Invented in her sleep a guilt-inspired, inexplicable phone call?

She was still staring at the phone. It looked secretive. Of course. It knew. She picked up the receiver, held it to her ear, and pressed the re-dial button. Heard a series of clicks. A number rang.

Mark's voice, a little testy, said, 'Yeh?'

She swallowed, and said, 'Mark? . . .' And was cut off again.

She clattered the receiver back on to the phone. She had to get up. She found herself in front of the uncurtained window, pushing the phone away from her along the sill. She wasn't crying, but her chest was heaving as if she was. She swung round. She didn't want to be here. She walked to the door, pulled it open, and then halted in the doorway. She didn't want to be doing this, either. Where did she think she was going? And why?

There was no escape. She would take herself everywhere she went. She closed the door, surprised to find that she still wasn't crying, and returned to the sofa.

On the cushions she sank back with a sigh. Let her heaving chest calm itself. Then clasped her hands together in her lap, and closed her eyes. Repeated in her mind what Mark had just said to her, and forced herself to think.

Darling Michael,

I've reached the end. A mental full stop.

Some things have become clear. Others – Michael, I have lost my grip on them. Something has happened, or is happening, in the world outside, but no one will tell me what it is.

Alex, my beautiful Alex, lies upstairs, asleep. He is upset and furious with me, I know, but that is all I know. For sure. He goes to bed and sleeps, rather than talk to me.

Mark has told me to go fuck myself. This may be perceptive, I've decided, and even constructive, but he means it as an insult. I don't know why he wants to insult me. It is possible that Alex has confronted him with knowledge about us, but why should this turn him against me? He has committed no crime and neither have I. We should, surely, be presenting a united front, not a bitterly divided one.

What is going on? I feel I am sitting here in the calm eye of a storm that I must have created, surrounded by a fog of storm-whipped dust. And beneath the dust is certain damage, though the extent of it is, as yet, invisible to me.

That is the outside landscape. Dark, like the night. Daylight will come tomorrow. I expect. Inside, though, the view is already lighter.

I think, Michael, that this summer I have been grieving not for you, but for me. Yes. For loss of myself. Or rather, part of myself.

Oh, we're all selfish at heart, aren't we? We can't help it: it's how we function. What keeps us alive, ensures we survive.

When you died, I lost you. I grieved, still grieve, for you. For my loss of you. But, in losing you, I also lost part of myself. It's a cliché, I know, that 'He's part of me'. But it's true, isn't it? Aspects of myself died with you. Think about it, Michael.

What were you, to me? Not my co-parent. You were never Alex's

236

father. Never a father at all. God. That's sad, isn't it? But you weren't. Alex had his own father.

You weren't a provider. Well, of course you were, but not one I was dependent on. I provided – still provide – for myself. I coped for years on my own, and I'm as well-off now, financially, as I've ever been. I have not lost a provider.

My friend; yes, of course you were my friend. My friend and confidant. But not my only friend, or only confidant. With your death I have not lost friendship altogether.

But you were my lover, Michael. At the time you died, my only lover. Not a perfect lover – but the perfection or otherwise of your love is irrelevant, a red herring. You were my only lover. When you died, you took me with you. The sexual part of me; the only part of me that was yours, exclusively. And I think I may have been fighting this. Trying to cling on to life. To climb out of the grave. Yes, I think so. The feelings fit. I looked to Gareth first, but he was too much else to me. I couldn't separate the sex out. Too complicated. How can you find yourself – even a bit of yourself – in a person you know is someone else? I needed an unknown: a desirable, controllable blank slate, on whom – in whom? – I could draw myself. Reaffirm, reclaim, complete myself. Mark. My pure, perfect lover. *Go fuck yourself.* Almost right.

So. It is my own partial death I have been mourning, as well as your total death. The two are inextricable. The emptiness I experienced was – is – not imaginary, though I know it is not literal.

But this is now the end. I am decided. It must be. I am hurting people around me. It looks as if I have hurt Mark, somehow. Frank too, possibly. But above all I have hurt Alex, and he is more important to me than anything or anyone else. I must fix on that. For his sake, though you hold in your arms someone precious to me, I must let you go. Accept that I am never going to be as whole as I was, and that you – and your sweet hostage – are gone.

Tomorrow – today, rather – I start to put things right.

237

Chapter 23

Jenny woke from a leaden, dreamless sleep to pale grey light, and the sound of steady rain against her south-west-facing window. She lay still, letting her mind catch up with her body's awakeness and listening to clatters, gushes and scrapes downstairs: the sounds of someone – Alex – in the kitchen beneath her.

He is the bedrock, she reminded herself. Nothing was worth saving or righting without Alex reconciled and restored to her, first.

She twisted her head, wondering what time it was. Her alarm clock said three; she must have forgotten to wind it. She guessed that, since Alex was up, it was late: ten, possibly even eleven. A late Sunday morning, despite the curiously cold grey light. But occasionally, on wet autumn days, this light – a near-dawn light – lasted all day. Something to do with the hills and the low squeezed grey skies.

It was quiet downstairs now. Then a lavatory flushed and, while the water tank in the attic above her was still filling, a door banged. She sat up. That could have been the back door. She listened, straining to hear over the water hiss from upstairs and the thudding in her chest. A car engine started up.

She flung off the duvet, snatched up her dressing gown, and ran downstairs.

Through the sitting-room window she could see the hard standing, and the Escort just disappearing out of the gate. She called, 'Alex!' hopelessly at the window-pane. The rain outside was heavy enough to be bouncing off the sill. The car had gone.

She went through to the kitchen. On the table was a fine scattering of cornflake dust and a sheet of white paper. Written on the paper in pencil, was *Gone to work. Visiting Nathan after. I'll be back.*

Her eyes lingered on the *I'll be back*. She wanted to hear the phrase as she'd often heard Alex say it, with a comically exaggerated Austrian-American accent. 'I'll be back' – a catch-phrase from the *Terminator* films. But couldn't make the mental voice convincing. Was it a reassurance – *and don't worry, Mum, I'm not leaving home again* – or a threat – *and then, Mum, you'll have some explaining to do?*

He'd gone to work. How could he just get up, ignore the fact that she was lying next door, and go to work? Why hadn't he woken her? She glanced at the cooker clock. Good heavens. It was only seven fifteen. She did a mental double take: the world was hours younger than she'd imagined.

She relaxed and rested her hands on the back of one of the dining-chairs. Never mind. She must keep calm.

But I must speak to him, she told herself, before I do anything else. I must hang on to that. Do everything in the right order. He will be back.

Reassured, she rose, made herself a thermos of coffee and returned to bed.

Alex had a breakfast break at nine thirty and after a quick cup of milky coffee made his way front-of-shop to use the customer pay phone. He'd had a nervy couple of hours. The day was moving excruciatingly slowly. His guts were suffering most, twisting themselves into frustrated cramping knots. Today was

239

the day. He wanted to get on, get away from this place, get the day's ordeals over.

He put a ten pence piece in the slot, and pressed out Nathan's number. Sal's voice answered. He asked for Nathan.

'He's not up yet, Alex,' Sal said. 'Can I get him to ring you back? Or take a message?'

Her voice sounded friendly. Sympathetic, even. He said tightly, 'I'm at work. Tell him I'm coming round at four. Tell him to make sure he's in.'

'Fine,' Sal's voice agreed. 'I'll do that. I'm sure he'll be here.' There was a pause before she added, tentatively, 'Nathan knows what this is about, does he?'

Alex made an exasperated noise. What a charade. His anger rose; he suddenly wanted to hurt someone. He heard his voice, knife-thin, saying into the mouthpiece, 'You know why Nathan's come down here, don't you? Bet you don't. Fucking bet you don't.'

'Sorry?' Sal sounded alarmed. Confused and alarmed. 'Down where? Alex? What are you talking about?'

'Why he's here. Staying here in Aber. It's not you, you know. Not because he wants to be with you. It's because his dad's pissed off with him. He got cautioned by the police. You ask him. That's why he's here.'

There was a long pause. Alex put his hand over the mouthpiece, so he could breathe more freely.

After a moment Sal said, in a low voice, 'Why are you saying this, Alex?'

He took his hand away. ''Cos it's true. He told me. You ask him.'

'I didn't mean that.' Her words were soft with reproach.

Alex's stomach turned over. He breathed his way through the sensation. He said, steadily, 'I'll see him at four. You tell him. Make sure he's in. I gotta go.'

He put the phone down. His whole body was shaking. He

240

couldn't remember the last time he'd deliberately tried to hurt like that. He knew he'd succeeded. He'd made himself feel sick. But Nathan deserved it.

At ten thirty Jenny picked up her bedside extension.

'Yes?'

'It's Sal.'

'Hello, Sal.' Jenny propped herself up on the pillows and blinked her eyes wide. She had been dozing. There was a pattering noise in the room. It was rain, lighter now, against the far window.

'I want to ask you a question.' Sal's voice was unusually expressionless.

'A question?'

'You've got to promise me you'll tell me the truth.'

'I always tell you the truth.'

'I do hope so. I still want to hear you promise.'

'Sal? Are you angry with me?'

'Not sure. It depends on your answer.'

'I promise.'

'Have you had sex with Nathan?'

Jenny leant back on the pillows. What an extraordinary question. 'With Nathan? Of course not.'

'You promise?'

'I promise. I haven't slept with anyone except Mark. Well . . . after Gareth . . .'

She heard Sal give a long, fluttering sigh.

'Thank God. Sorry about that. But I had to . . . Listen, Jenny. Have you had your chat with Alex?'

'He was asleep last night. I would've, honestly . . . Then this morning . . . he rushed off to work . . .'

'It's OK, Jen. I'm not criticizing. It's just that . . . I think Alex thinks you and Nathan are . . . involved.'

241

Jenny tried to make herself laugh, but failed. 'Don't be stupid. He can't.'

'I think he does. Alex rang me an hour ago. He's very upset, Jenny. Very angry. With Nathan. I've been thinking about it. About what he said to you and me yesterday, and then to me this morning. It's you and Nathan he's angry with. Definitely. And it's to do with sex. He called you a slag, didn't he?'

'How can he believe . . .?'

'I don't know. I don't know. Put two and two together and made five. But I'm pretty sure I'm right. Nathan thinks it's something to do with Lizzie, but that doesn't make any sense at all.'

'You've spoken about this to Nathan?'

'Not about what I suspect Alex thinks. We've just had a chat about . . . a few things. Hang on a minute . . . shit . . .' Sal broke off abruptly. The phone was put down. Jenny heard a short silence, and then a distant voice raised to someone. Then another silence, before the phone was picked up again. 'Sorry. Just de-bugging the room. No, Jen. I haven't told him what I think, not yet. But I'm going to have to. Alex is coming round here this afternoon. I have to warn Nathan. Tell him the possibilities. I won't make it stronger than that, and I won't say anything about . . . you know. But I must say something.'

Jenny leant back. She was experiencing a horrible feeling in her abdomen. As if it were hollowing out. She recognized a grief pang. She said, 'Should I be doing anything? Only . . . I'm feeling rather odd today. I just want to speak to Alex . . . I don't think I can cope with anything else . . .'

'That's OK. Nathan will sort his end out. Well, explain that he's blameless, at least.' Her voice became sour. 'He's good at that.'

Jenny's chest heaved, in a huge unstoppable sigh.

'Jen?' Sal said sharply. 'What was that? Are you ill?'

Jenny recovered her breath. 'Sorry. No. Well . . . probably

not. But I do feel peculiar. Sal . . .' She nearly sighed again, but managed to suppress it. 'I rang Mark last night. He sounded angry too. He put the phone down on me. I don't understand what's going on.'

Sal was silent. Then said. 'Has Alex been to see him?'

'I don't know.'

'Is it likely? Is Mark someone he'd confide in?'

'I don't know. I don't know anything. Sal . . . what are you saying?'

'Well . . . maybe Alex has told him that Nathan and you . . .'

'Oh no . . . even if he had . . . he wouldn't believe that . . .' But her insides had lurched; she didn't believe herself as she said it.

Sal hissed quietly to herself. 'What a mess.' She paused, then said, 'Will you tell Alex about Mark now? If it's clear he doesn't know?'

'Doesn't know?'

Sal spoke slowly. 'Because I'm sure he thinks it's Nathan, Jenny, not Mark. I just told you.'

'Oh, yes. Sorry. I don't know. I suppose so. I'll have to, won't I?'

'Jen, d'you want me to come over?'

'You're going to see Pauline, aren't you?'

'She'd understand.'

'No. No, thanks. I just want Alex.'

'You're sure?'

'Yes. He left a note. He said he'd be back.'

'Of course he'll be back. Don't worry. I'll ring you this evening, shall I?'

'Yes. Fine.'

They said goodbye. Jenny put the phone down. Alex believed she was having sex with Nathan. At least, that's what Sal thought. And Sal was usually right. And it was possible that Mark believed this too. That she was having sex with Nathan as well as with himself. Was that why he'd been so angry last night? But how could he possibly think that of her? Oh, how stupid everyone was.

She leant back on the pillows. She wanted to weep even more than she'd wanted to last night, but her eyes remained obstinately dry. I feel impotent, she thought. Hollowed out, detached, and impotent. Overlooking, in my hollowed-out, detached and impotent state, a chaotic, wilful world. Oh, God. She closed her eyes.

Chapter 24

Nathan opened the front door to Alex at ten past four. Retreating from him down the hall he said, 'I've not done anything with your mum, and anyone who says I have's a liar, right? Let's get that out the way first.'

Alex said nothing, but followed him down the passageway.

'Nor,' continued Nathan, backing into the sitting-room, 'have I slept with Lizzie. In fact I haven't got laid since I've been down here. So I dunno who's been saying what, but they're wrong.'

Alex stopped in the doorway. He leant his shoulder against the jamb. Tried not to be deflected by what Nathan was saying. He'd imagined this confrontation any number of ways. Nathan belligerent, defiant, apologetic, obsequious. What he hadn't envisaged was out-and-out denial. But how did Nathan know what to deny, if he wasn't guilty?

'A friend of my mother's saw you with her, outside a pub.'

'What friend?' Nathan scoffed.

'Someone she works with. Well.' Alex hesitated. 'Frank, actually.' This felt like an admission, though he couldn't think why.

'Ah. Ah. The Frankfurter. I have never met the Frankfurter. He has never met me. I rest my case.' As if to emphasize this, Nathan sat down on one of the easy chair arms.

Alex loosened and stretched his fingers, which had been clenched into fists. He stared around the room. Nathan must have spent the afternoon drawing. Sheets of paper littered the table, floor and chairs. Pictures of male comic-strip characters, exploding with action.

'Obviously,' Nathan said, 'the Frankfurter's lying.'

'I don't think he was.'

'It wasn't me. If I've never met him, and he's never met me, how could he identify me? What a pillock.'

'He said he'd seen you and Mum some time before, and Mum had told him afterwards who you were. And then he said he saw you again, outside a pub.'

'I haven't done anything, or been anywhere, alone with your mum. Someone's stirring. Honest. I mean, no offence, but your mum . . . and me . . .?'

Alex stared into the middle distance. In his mind's eye he saw Frank's face, Frank's twisted, repulsive, poison-issuing face pushing into his . . .

'Tell you what. You know where this creep lives?'

Alex refocused on Nathan. He frowned. 'Well . . . suppose so.'

'We'll go round there. Prove it.'

Alex gave an astonished laugh. 'What? Is this the bozo you saw with my mum? You're kidding.'

'Wouldn't need to say anything. Just let him see me. You watch his reaction. I promise you, he won't know me.' Nathan stood up. His movements had become vigorous. Even forceful.

'You made a shit of a phone call this morning. You owe me. Let's do it.' He picked up his jacket. 'We're doing it, man.' He pushed past Alex to the front door.

Alex found himself following. He knew he was being hustled, and that he had lost control of the situation, but it didn't seem to matter. The whole point of keeping control seemed to have been demolished.

He banged the front door after him and followed Nathan out on to the pavement. The rain was just drizzle now, soft and cool on his face. He climbed into the Escort and unlocked the passenger door. While Nathan was getting in he took a moment to think. Going to see Frank wasn't a totally stupid idea. Frank was the source. Frank had implanted the poison. Created the enemy – an enemy who, until a moment ago, had had Nathan's face. But was he still an enemy, without Nathan's face? He pushed the key into the ignition, thinking. No. Yes. Shit, it didn't matter. He still wanted to know. A visit might be embarrassing. It might be unproductive. But it was neither stupid, nor irresponsible, nor dangerous. Reassured, he started the car.

They drove through the centre of town and northwards into the residential streets. But turning into Frank's road his nerve failed.

'What are we going to say when he answers the door? We can't just stand there gawping.'

'Leave it to me.' Nathan sounded confident. Grimly confident. Alex's trepidation increased.

They drew up outside Frank's house.

Alex said, 'I'm not sure about this.' The house looked unshakeably solid. He didn't want to risk shaking anything that solid; something huge might fall on them. 'Let's say I believe you. You wouldn't have suggested this, would you, otherwise? Whoever it was, it wasn't you.'

Nathan smiled. 'Just check, then, shall we? No harm done.' He got out of the car.

Alex said, 'Oh, shit,' under his breath, released his seat belt, and climbed out too. A blue Mondeo was parked on the gravel drive.

He caught up with Nathan. 'This is going to be really embarrassing.'

'Ah.' Nathan tapped the side of his nose. His eyes had narrowed to slits. 'But for whom?'

247

He bounded up the wide steps to the door and rang the bell. 'What a morgue,' he murmured, staring up at the house.

They heard the approach of heavy footsteps. The door was opening. A voice said, 'It's all right, Mother, I've got it.' And Frank stood before them. He looked, Alex thought, frailer than he had in the pub. And even older, in daylight.

For a moment no one spoke. Nathan looked from Frank to Alex, smiling, and back again.

Alex finally said, 'Ah . . . hello, Frank.'

Frank said, 'Alex,' gravely, and nodded at Nathan.

Nathan extended his hand and in a ringing English accent said, 'Hello. My name's Nathan. Have we met?'

'I don't believe so.' Frank hesitated, before offering his own hand. Nathan shook it firmly.

'What d'you want, Alex?' Frank turned back to him.

'He wants to know,' Nathan cut in, now speaking in hard Welsh, 'why you told him that I was having sex with his mother.' He gave Frank a fierce smile.

Frank stood very still, with his chin jutting forward and his head slightly inclined, as if the words had been spoken so quietly he wasn't sure he'd grasped them. He looked grotesquely comic, Alex thought, like an old and flightless and soon-to-be-extinct poultry bird.

'You did tell him that, didn't you?' said Nathan. 'Where did he tell you this, Alex?'

Alex nearly didn't reply. Nathan was trying to pull his strings, too. But then muttered, 'In the King William. It's all right, though,' he added.

'I'm not sure it is,' said Nathan.

Frank stepped forward and closed the front door carefully behind him.

'I did not say . . .' He spoke in a harsh whisper. 'I did not say it was you.' He wiped his mouth with the back of his hand. 'Of course I didn't.' He shook his head. His eyes took in

Nathan's wild hair, travelled down his slender black-clothed body. He looked faintly repelled. 'Not you.'

'What did you say, then?' Nathan had registered Frank's expression. His voice took on an aggressive sneer. 'Because, you see, we think it's a pretty shitty thing to do, to tell someone something like that, if it's not true. Wouldn't you say,' he turned to Alex, 'that it's a pretty shitty thing to do?'

Alex wanted, urgently, to leave. He refused to meet Nathan's eye.

Frank lifted his head and stared out over the drive. 'I did not say that the young man in question was yourself. I told Alex that the young man I saw with your mother was someone she had known for many years.'

'And how did you know that?' Nathan enquired.

'Because she told me. I had seen them together on an earlier occasion. In a vehicle, on one of the mountain roads. They were going, she told me then, to make a film, a video . . .'

'Ah, shit.' Alex turned away abruptly. 'Shit. Shit.' He walked, half ran, down the drive. He heard Nathan saying, 'Thank you. Thank you very much.' And then something else in a hectoring tone. He turned out of the garden, stopped by the Escort, and rested his hands on the front wing. He heard a front door bang and running footsteps.

'See.' Nathan's voice was savagely triumphant.

'What have you just said to him?'

'Nothing. Well, told him if he had a problem with your mum he should sort it himself with her, and not tell tales out of school. What a weasel.'

They got into the car. Alex wasn't sure he could drive. He loosened his grip on the steering wheel. 'It was Mark.'

'Yup,' agreed Nathan. 'Your precious Mark.'

'Unless he's lying,' said Alex. 'Unless he made the whole thing up.'

'Uh-uh.' Nathan shook his head.

249

Alex looked at him. Nathan sounded definite. 'How d'you know?'

Nathan pursed his lips, then gave a half-apologetic shrug. 'My mum rang your mum this morning. After you'd rung her. I got to listen in. Went up the stairs noisy and crept down quiet. Didn't know what she was on about at first, but soon cottoned on. And at the end I heard her say "Will you tell Alex about Mark?" '

'What did Mum say?'

Nathan rolled his eyes. 'I don't know, dingbat. I was outside the door, not on an extension.'

Alex stared out through the windscreen. 'I went to see Mark last night . . .' He was going to say more, but ran out of breath.

'Come back to my place,' said Nathan. 'Mum's out all afternoon. Gone to see superdyke in Bristol. You need to think, yeah?'

Alex nodded.

He drove carefully back to the house, then sat in the sitting room while Nathan made coffee in the kitchen. Watching Nathan carry the mugs and a biscuit tin into the room on a tray made him feel like an invalid. He stared at Nathan's face, concentrating on its task.

'D'you know anything else I don't?' Nathan, he realized, had known all day that Mark was implicated. But had said nothing, until Frank's identification.

'Nope.' Nathan set down the tray and handed Alex a mug. 'Here. Don't think so.'

'Only,' Alex said bitterly, 'I feel I'm lagging behind. You knew before we went, didn't you?'

'Not for definite.' Nathan swept up sheets of paper and pens from the other armchair seat and put them on the table. He sat down too. 'And I was only half a day in front of you. Innocent as a baby, I was, till this morning.'

Alex sighed. He sat back and sipped his coffee. Tried to feel calmer. It wasn't Nathan's fault that he'd known.

'When I went round to see Mark last night I told him I was pissed off with you, and why. He never said anything.'

'Grade A bastard,' Nathan said.

'Shit. And he was nice to me.' Alex remembered Mark squatting in front of him, the kindness in his voice. Telling him to go home, sleep on it . . .

Nathan was silent, watching him over his coffee mug.

'Why didn't either of them tell me? Why didn't he? What's so wrong with . . .' He stopped. He heard Frank's words. *They did it on one of the cars. Brutally. Like animals.*

'Presumably,' Nathan said, 'they didn't want you to know.'

'It's fucking my head up,' Alex said.

'They do that.' Nathan gave a sour smile. 'Mums. And dads too, sometimes.'

'I introduced them. I wonder when . . .'

'It started?'

'He must have had his eye on her.' Alex tried to remember earlier exchanges. 'Yeah. He wouldn't let me borrow the camcorder. Offered to do it with her himself. And he asked me, one evening . . . how she was, you know, with Michael dying.' He paused, remembering, feeling his guts churn. 'Bloody hell.'

'He needs a telling off,' Nathan said.

Alex gave a short despairing laugh.

'I'll help you,' Nathan said. 'Serious now. He dumped on me too.'

Alex shook his head. 'You can't give someone like Mark a telling off.'

'Why not? Not Superman, is he? Anyway, I'm not suggesting we lecture him. We do something.'

'Like what? I'm not squaring up to him. I don't want to look more of a dickhead than I do already.'

'Well, what does he care about?'

CATHERINE MERRIMAN

Alex snorted. 'His dog.'

'Right. We nobble his dog.' Nathan caught Alex's expression. 'OK, OK. A joke.'

'It's a bloody great Alsatian. I'd like to see you nobble it. And she's pregnant.' Alex sighed, suddenly deeply sentimental. 'A beauty, she is.'

'I said I was joking. What about his motor? What does he drive?'

'Hilux four-wheel drive.'

'Shit.'

'It's a few years old. And his dad owns the garage. Don't suppose he paid what we would.'

'Even so.' Nathan opened the biscuit tin and removed a chocolate digestive. 'Well, we could nobble that.'

'D'you know anything about cars?'

'Not a lot.' Nathan bit into the biscuit. 'But I could piss into a petrol tank.'

Alex looked away, exasperated. They'd been here before. When they'd discussed actions against the opencast. 'No. This is stupid. It's just talk.'

'Speak for yourself.' Nathan gave a bark of laughter, then collected himself. 'Come on. You're angry with him, aren't you?'

'But this isn't going to help. I mean, if we do something to his car he'll just mend it. And . . . well, it's childish, isn't it? It doesn't solve anything.'

'So what would solve it?'

'I just want . . .' Alex screwed his thoughts up, wondering what he did want. He shook his head. 'I just want to tell him I'm angry, and that I think he's a bastard. For him to hear me say it. I think that's all I want.'

'And what if he doesn't like hearing you say it?'

Alex imagined the scene: him telling Mark, coolly and calmly, what he thought about him, and why. It didn't feel impossible.

252

He nodded. 'I'm in the right. I think he'd hear me out.'

'I'm coming too,' Nathan said.

'No. That's going in mob-handed. And . . .' Alex regarded Nathan steadily, '. . . you're not above mixing it yourself. I'd prefer to be on my own.'

'He let you think it was me.' Nathan was fierce. 'And you dropped me in shit for it. I got a grievance too.'

Alex could see the tension in Nathan's body, the belligerent, almost panicky refusal to be excluded. He was right too: that phone call he'd made to Sal this morning. That shameful call. He felt himself flush. He had hurt both Nathan and Sal. Stupidly. Look at Nathan . . . how could anyone believe that he and his mother . . . he should have thought of Mark. It was obvious, now.

He said, sincerely, 'I'm sorry about this morning. The phone call. Really sorry.'

'Accepted.' Nathan wasn't to be diverted. 'You weren't in the picture. But Mark was. I wanna go with you.'

'OK.' Alex capitulated. He had to give Nathan something. 'Yeah, OK. But I want to talk to him first. On my own. I mean it. You want to say anything to him, you do it after. All right?'

Nathan considered, then nodded. 'Fair enough.'

'You got to give me time. Swear.'

'I'll stay in the car,' Nathan promised. 'No problem.'

'Right.' Alex lifted his mug. 'When we've finished these.'

Half an hour later they were ready to leave. At the sitting-room doorway Alex stared back into the room. The place was a mess: not just the sheets of drawn-on paper now, but dirty coffee mugs, biscuit crumbs and grey graphite-like smears of cigarette ash.

'Shit, Nathan,' he called. 'You going to leave things like this? When's Sal back?'

Nathan clattered down the stairs behind him and pushed past into the room. He snatched up a felt-tip pen and a sheet of paper.

'I'll leave a note.' He walked through to the kitchen and slapped the sheet on to the work surface. Facing up at him was one of his drawings, a comic strip superhero in dramatic pose, reeling backwards, arms outflung, as he took the force of an off-page blast of gunfire. He smirked down at it, inscribed the word 'Mark' on to the costume stripe across the figure's muscle-bound chest, then turned over the sheet.

'Wrongs . . . to . . . right. Back soon . . . to tidy up.' He threw the pen away. 'OK? Now let's go.'

In less than fifteen minutes they were in Pentre. Alex parked the Escort opposite Bevan's garage. He looked across, and felt his shoulder muscles dissolve with anticlimax. Behind the pumps and 'Closed' sign the forecourt was empty. No Hilux across the workshop drive.

'Shit.' He squinted up at the big window above the canopy. No lights on there, either. 'That's his flat. But I don't think he's here.'

'Where'd he be?' Nathan's eyes darted from garage to road.

'Dunno. Pubs aren't open yet. Bet he's working. Oh, shit, yeah . . .' Alex remembered a snatch of conversation from yesterday. 'That's it. He had a weekend job on.' He looked at his watch. Nearly six. 'He'll be back, though . . . soon, maybe. What d'you think?'

Nathan's eyes settled on the building. 'I'm not going home,' he said, staring at it intently. 'Give it an hour, OK?'

Chapter 25

Jenny was eating a Marmite sandwich in the kitchen. She'd finally risen from her bed an hour ago and put on jeans and an old thigh-length cream cotton shirt. She'd actually have preferred to remain in her nightdress – a token, until Alex returned, of her emotional, if not physical, dormancy. But whatever she was going to say to him, she recognized, was probably best not said in night-wear. The soft cotton shirt, which had in the past doubled as a nightshift, was a compromise.

Her Marmite sandwich tasted primarily, though not unpleasantly, of salt. She wondered how long she would have to wait for her son's return. His note had said he was visiting Nathan after work. But that he would be back. It was now, according to the cooker clock, 6.00 p.m.

The outside gate rattled. She rose immediately, listening for the sound of a car rumbling in on to the hard standing, but heard nothing. She stared at the window, willing Alex's head and shoulders to pass by. The muscles across her solar plexus tightened.

There was a rapping noise coming from somewhere in the house. From the front door; she turned, frowning. Nobody, except strangers, or very occasional visitors to the cottage, used the front door.

She walked through to the small dark entrance hall and

255

unlocked the mortice. The door opened with a sucking sigh – the rubber draught excluder at the bottom catching on the tiled floor. A tall man was standing on the doorstep.

'Frank,' she said. 'Goodness, Frank.'

Frank's smile was awkward. He was holding himself oddly too – as if he felt he was too tall for her doorway, though he certainly wasn't.

Jenny said, 'I was expecting Alex,' and then wondered why she'd said it. She started again. 'What are you doing here, Frank?' He did look unusually tall. Because she was barefooted, of course. She'd never stood beside him in bare feet before.

'Can I come in?' Frank frowned down at the ground. 'I'm sorry to . . .'

Jenny hesitated. Found it impossible to say, 'No, not now, I have to speak to Alex . . .'

'Of course.' She stepped back and led the way towards the kitchen. Behind her she heard the click of the front door closing.

In the kitchen she walked over to the kettle and said, 'Glad to see you're better now. Your mother told us you were unwell.'

Frank stopped in the middle of the room. Jenny met his gaze. Her mind trembled. He looked wrong here. Wrong body, wrong face, completely wrong expression.

'I, er . . .' Frank, too, seemed aware of some personal incompatibility with his surroundings. His fingers touched the wooden back of one of the dining-chairs. 'Are you alone?'

Jenny paused, and then said, 'Yes.' She moved away from the work surface. The impulse to boil a kettle for visitors was so reflex she didn't trust herself, if she remained standing there, not to do it. She resettled herself against the washing machine, a few feet away, and folded her arms across her chest, trapping them into inactivity. 'What can I do for you, Frank?'

Frank touched his mouth, his thumb and forefinger at the corners. He pinched delicately at the lower lip.

'I have taken advice from your boys.'

256

'My boys?' Jenny gave a lifting laugh. 'I've only got one.'

Frank frowned and shook his head. 'There were two. Alex and ... a dark ...' He raised a hand and flapped it at the side of his head.

'Nathan.' Jenny stared at him. 'What are you talking about? What advice?'

'Ah.' Frank stepped back from the table, dug in his outside jacket pocket and removed a small spirit bottle containing a clear liquid. It looked like vodka. He placed it on the table top.

'Once,' he said, as if he'd decided on an illustrative story before answering her question, 'I had a problem with this. My mother doesn't know. Or she chooses not to know. It was while I was living in Birmingham, many years ago. I was lonely, I suppose, and I drank. She thinks I'm stuffy now, because I never touch alcohol. But, then, my mother sees people as she wants to see them. And she sees restraint as a weakness. A cowardice. When, of course, it's mainly a strength.'

He spotted a clean upturned glass on the draining board. 'May I?' He walked over to pick it up. 'Will you join me?'

'No.' Jenny watched him pour an inch of spirit into the glass. In a level voice she said, 'Why are you here?'

Frank lifted the glass and drained it.

'I don't think that's a good idea,' she said. 'I really don't.'

'But now,' said Frank, continuing as if she hadn't interrupted, 'I'm coming round to her view. It is the unrestrained people, is it not, who get what they want?' He sighed, as if releasing from within himself the vapour of some deep sadness; but his voice became stronger. 'I misled Alex, inadvertently, because I was too inhibited to speak to you directly. For upsetting and misleading him I am sorry. He and his friend have spoken to me, and I have rectified matters with them, in so far as I can. I see now that directness is important. And that I have, maybe, been too oblique with you all along.'

257

Jenny nearly said, 'Oblique about what?' but guessed she knew the answer, and stopped herself. So Sal was right: Alex had believed that she and Nathan were lovers. Because of something Frank had said, or done. But Frank was saying this had now been put right. Please, Alex, she thought, you must have squared things with Nathan by now, so come back. Now would be a really good time.

'You are still a young woman,' Frank went on. 'And you have a young woman's needs. You have also – excuse me for saying this – a young woman's morals.'

'I beg your pardon.' Jenny's voice shook.

'You take what you want and you doubtless expect others to do likewise. You act on your feelings. Even when those feelings are . . . primitive.' He poured the last inch of vodka from the bottle into his glass.

'Are you drunk, Frank?' Jenny asked.

'Drunk?' He tipped his head, considering. 'I don't think so. Emboldened, perhaps. That is the lure of alcohol, is it not? To be emboldened. To be released from one's timidities.' He caught her eye, and smiled. 'But I'm still being oblique, aren't I?' He took a step towards her, lifted his glass, and drank. Jenny heard the liquid gurgle in his throat. He put the glass down on the table behind him. His hand, she noticed, had only the slightest tremor.

'You came to the village pub on Thursday night, didn't you?' she said.

'I did.'

'And you saw me. In the car park.'

'Yes, Jenny, I did. I was upset. I realized, you see, that you are not the person I thought you were.'

'That person is a person you invented. But I'm sorry. Sorry that you were shocked.'

Frank was silent. Then said gravely, 'Anyone, I think, would have been shocked. I was more than shocked. I was distraught. And angry.'

Jenny blew out. She avoided his eyes. 'I don't belong to anyone.'

'I realize that.' Frank nodded to himself. 'I realize that any understanding we had – that I thought we had – was unfounded. That it had to be, when you could do that. And I realized too that my approach – because of my illusions about you – had been wrong.'

He moved closer and placed a hand on her forearm. 'He is not important to you, is he, that young man?'

Jenny pushed his hand away. Yes, she thought, actually he is, or was. But she wasn't going to explain. She cleared her throat. 'Not in the way you mean.'

'Yet what he wanted, you were prepared to give.'

'It's not like that.'

He was looming over her. She saw shutters in his eyes come down, and knew what was about to happen. His hands reached out for her.

He grasped her elbows, and pinned them to her sides. Forced his lips on to hers.

'Nnng.' She twisted her face away. 'No!' His body smelt cloyingly of sweat and excitement. The sting of vodka was in her mouth.

He pushed his body against hers. 'Did you say no to him? When you allowed him to rape you?'

'He did not rape me.' Jenny heard her words pulsating in the air, like a voice from a dying radio.

'You wanted him to take you like that?' Frank pushed himself harder against her. The control knob of the washing machine was digging into her buttocks.

'Please, Frank.' She could hear panic in her voice. 'You don't know what you're doing.'

Frank let go of her elbows and grabbed at the top of her

cotton shirt. The material gave and two buttons shot, with almost comical force, across the kitchen floor. Jenny tried to lift her leg, to jab her knee into his groin, but his body was too close and heavy. He's going to rape me, she wailed inwardly, and I shall have no redress. Because of what I have done, I have made myself indefensible.

She heard her voice gasp, 'No, please, no!'

Then the enormity of what was happening burst something in her head. As if a membrane had ruptured, releasing a gush of liquid: the salty ocean she'd known was there, swelling inside her, but which she'd been unable, till this moment, to break into. Tears flooded from her eyes.

Frank's hands stopped clawing at her. His weight lifted. He was stepping back, staring into her face, looking utterly dismayed. His hands fluttered between them. 'My dear. My dear, forgive me.' His eyes dropped to her gaping blouse.

Jenny fumbled the material across her breasts. 'Oh, God,' she sobbed. 'Oh, God.' The tears were hot and blinding.

'My dear.' He pulled a chair out from the table. She felt herself being guided into it. 'Please, my dear.' His own voice was breaking.

She put her hands over her eyes, and buried her face in them. Blotted Frank, this confrontation, this awful scene, out. It was over now, anyway. Nothing of significance would happen now. It had ended. Eventually, Frank would leave.

She pressed at her eyes and watched the swirling patterns behind her eyelids. Hot shapes that jumped and flared. Then looked inward and in her mind's eye saw other, more substantial shapes. The outline of three men: Alex and Michael, and yes, Mark too. There they were, shimmering together. Forming, almost, a family group. Michael between Alex and Mark, separating them; but also connecting them.

Connecting herself to them, too, it suddenly seemed.

Aloud she whispered. 'I'm sorry for hurting you. I'm so

sorry,' and didn't mind the thought that Frank, sitting beside her and patting her shoulder helplessly, would assume she was talking to him.

Chapter 26

Nathan hissed, 'This him?' A large red pick-up was driving towards them from the main road.

Alex looked up from his lap, and felt his body tense. He nodded. They watched the vehicle approach, pull into the forecourt across the road and halt, blocking the workshop driveway.

'Right.' Alex told himself that he still wanted to do this. Yes, he did. 'Stay here,' he reminded Nathan. He got out of the Escort and walked across the road. Mark was already beside his vehicle, slamming the driver's door shut.

'Oi!' Alex called.

Mark glanced round. His face was unsmiling. He knows what's coming, Alex thought grimly. He watched Mark remove something from his pocket. Keys; he was unlocking the garage shop. Letting Sheba out. The dog snaked through the half-open door and curved her body round her master's legs.

Alex came up to him. 'Been waiting for you.'

Mark said, without turning round, 'Piss off, Alex. I'm not in the mood.'

He was unshaven, in work overalls. He looked rough. Dirty, even. Not romantic at all. A voice in Alex's head whispered, *They did it brutally, Alex. Like animals.*

He said, keeping his voice steady. 'I want to speak to you.'

Mark said, 'Do you,' and unlocked the frosted glass door. He nodded over to the Escort, where Nathan was still sitting. 'Who's that you got with you?'

'Nathan,' said Alex. 'He's not very pleased with you either.'

'Come again?' Mark gave an offensive, disbelieving laugh. He started to mount the stairs behind Sheba. Alex followed.

At the top, unlocking the flat door, Mark said irritably, 'Ah, go home, Alex. You don't want to come in.'

'I do,' said Alex. 'I'm really pissed off with you.' Saying it made his temper flare. He damped it down. He was here simply to state that he was upset and explain why, coolly and calmly. Trouble was, he hadn't envisaged Mark like this. So unfriendly and abrasive.

The air inside the flat was chilly; it must have been empty all day. Alex marched to the centre of the room.

'Why didn't you tell me?' he asked. 'You could have bloody told me.'

Mark threw a switch on the wall beside his bedroom door before walking to the kitchen area. 'Asked your mum that, have you?' He reached for the kettle.

An odious image flashed into Alex's mind. Mark and his mother, together. Naked. He stared at Mark. At this moment, Mark looked like someone any mother – any woman – should be protected from.

He said, pushing the image away. 'I meant last night. When I came round.'

Mark had a mug in his hand. He banged it down on the work surface. 'OK. You want to hear it from me, do you? Your mum's a goer. Fucked me good. Eh? That what you want to hear, is it?'

Alex experienced a coldness, a draining sensation, moving down his face. Mark was putting the blame on to his mother. Behaving as if he had a right to insult her, for what they'd done.

'How dare you say that,' he said.

263

'Ah, fuck off,' said Mark.

Like animals, Alex heard in his head. Mark's fault. Had to be. Dragging his mother down to his level.

'You're a bastard,' he hissed.

There was a faint grumbling noise in the air. It came from the dog, prowling between them. Mark said, without looking at her, 'It's OK, girl.' And then gave Alex a spiteful smile. 'Actually, thought you were the bastard.'

It was like a slap. It came to Alex that their friendship had been a sham all along. That under the surface Mark despised people like him. Which would include his mother. Mark had been predatory. Men like Mark were. His mother was Mark's victim.

'You started it,' he said. 'You must have. It's your fault. You set it all up.'

'Yeah, yeah,' Mark scoffed.

'My mum . . . shit, Michael only died . . . she's a widow . . .'

'My heart bleeds.'

'I fucking hate you.'

Mark seemed suddenly to lose patience. He pushed past Alex towards the front of the room. 'You spoken to her, have you Alex? Your mum.'

'Don't need to.'

Mark stopped by the hi-fi rack. 'OK for some, is it, and not for others? Not my fault your mum's a nympho.'

Anger and frustration made Alex want to cry. What was Mark talking about? And how dare he be angry? Why couldn't he just admit that he was in the wrong? What was he doing now? He was yanking at flexes. What the hell . . .? He'd just punched the television on.

Fiddling with something on the shelves, Mark said, 'What're you doing with that cunt, anyway?'

What cunt? Alex felt stupid. And being confused was frightening him. His fists clenched. He wanted to hit Mark, to shut him up. A plump bearded figure on the television screen descended studio steps. A crowd clapped and whistled. The picture seemed to have caught Mark's attention. He made a harsh noise; it could have been a laugh.

'You want to see me fucked good and proper, Alex? See me taken for a ride?'

Alex stared at him. And then at the television. Strained to work out the connection. He couldn't get it, though an ominous pressure, a horrible sense of premonition, was building in his chest.

Mark stepped away from the television. He had something in his hand, and a wire trailed from it to an object on the shelves. 'Tell me when to stop,' he said.

The thing in his hand was a remote control. The object on the shelf a camcorder. Alex's brain made a revelatory leap.

'Stop!' he roared, and rushed forwards.

The dog was suddenly in front of him, low on her haunches, barking up into his face, an ear-cracking volley of sound. Her huge trembling wolf teeth were inches from his leg.

'Stand still!' Mark shouted. Alex froze.

'All right, it's OK, it's OK.' Mark carefully put the remote control back on the shelf. The dog barked again.

Alex tried to keep still. But his body kept flinching. He couldn't help it. He whispered, 'Oh, shit, oh, shit.' The dog's ears were flat to her skull. She was going to bite him.

There was a crash downstairs. The wolf head in front of him swung round. The raised spine of black hair on the dog's shoulders swelled, became stiff and spiky. Someone was pounding up the stairs. The dog streaked for the half-open flat door.

'Stop her!' It was Nathan, Alex knew. He must have been just outside the lower door, waiting for an excuse to rush up. He yelled, 'Nathan! Sheba! Sheba!'

Mark was moving almost as fast as his dog. But several yards behind.

Outside the door there was a scuffling noise, a heavy thump and a gasping shout. And then, suddenly, a high noise, a thin continuous cry, which seemed neither human nor animal. Nathan staggered backwards into the flat, knocking into Mark, who pushed him violently aside, towards the kitchen units. Something dropped from Nathan's hand on to the carpet.

The crying noise was still outside. Nathan was gasping, not crying. Hugging his chest. Alex ran to the door.

Mark was kneeling over a black furry heap on the landing. Sheba, somehow cut down. His hands were sweeping frantically over her, patting and pushing at her, as if trying to hold her together. The dog was making the crying noise. A toneless, mindless, hopeless sound. Blood was spreading out fast beneath her. Already the step below the landing was wet and scarlet. A spasm twitched the dog's legs.

Mark lifted his face and said in a terrible voice, 'Want me to smash that cunt for you now?'

Alex suddenly understood. Everything. He could see straight through the slate-coloured fury in Mark's eyes into his mind. He knew why Mark was so angry with his mother and with Nathan. The awful mistake of it paralysed him.

Mark had his arms under the crying dog and was lifting her. His face seemed to be crying too, or maybe it was just the physical effort of raising her. On the linoleum where she had lain there was a sticky pool of blood. He started to carry the animal downstairs.

Alex stepped back into the flat, away from the crying noise and the lake of spilled blood.

He heard laughter. For an appalling moment he thought it was Nathan; no, it was the television set left on. Nathan's face was white and stiff.

'She bit you.' The black T-shirt above Nathan's heart was wet and shiny.

Nathan nodded fast, swallowing hard.

'I think you've killed her.' Alex stared at the knife on the carpet. It was long and thin and shiny. A fishing knife. Nathan had come with him to confront Mark, armed with a lethal, razor-sharp, flesh-cutting knife.

'Didn't mean to,' Nathan whispered. 'I heard the fight. Was just holding it. Happened so quick. She came right up at me.'

Alex said nothing. There was no point. He went over to the television and turned it off. The camcorder lay on the shelf. He hesitated, then pressed the eject button on the side of the machine, removed the tiny video cassette from beneath its transparent cover and pocketed it. He turned back to Nathan.

'He thinks he wasn't the only one. With Mum. He believed me last night. When I told him that you and her . . .'

Nathan took a moment to comprehend. Slowly his mouth sagged open. 'Oh, shit.' His lips pulled into an uncontrolled, grotesque attempt at a smile. 'Cock-up all round.'

'Yes.' Alex didn't want to think about what this said about his mother. Or rather, Mark's opinion of his mother. He refused to feel naïve for not guessing. He was right. Of course his mother would only have one lover.

Mark was returning. They could hear fast footsteps on the stairs. Somewhere, very distantly, the injured dog was still crying.

'You gotta tell him.' Nathan sounded panicky. He started to gulp in air. 'Oh, shit, he's gonna . . .'

Mark strode into the flat. His overalls and hands were red with animal blood. Nathan shrank back against the kitchen units.

Alex said quickly, 'Mark, Nathan never did anything with my mum. I got it wrong. Last night . . . I'm sorry. I misled you, I'm sorry . . .'

Mark's eyes flicked at him, barely noticing. He was making for his bedroom. He pushed through the door which swung to behind him.

Alex felt cold. He wasn't sure Mark had heard him.

Nathan hissed, 'What's happening? What the fuck's he doing?'

Alex's heart hammered in his throat. He felt an overwhelming urge to run away. To run and run and run.

He made himself walk to the bedroom door. He heard a metallic click. Gently, he pushed the door open. Mark was sitting on the side of his bed, a shotgun broken across his knees. He was pushing a cartridge into the single barrel.

'There was only you,' Alex said steadily. 'Not Nathan. Only you. I promise. You didn't need to be angry. Neither did I. I thought you'd deliberately made a fool of me. So did Nathan. I'm sorry. Sheba . . . Shit, Mark.' He couldn't stop his voice crumbling. 'I'm so sorry . . .'

Mark snapped the gun straight. Then lowered it back to his knees. He stared down at the decorated stock.

'Mark?' Alex said. 'Can you hear me?'

Mark looked up at him. Outside, the dog was still crying. The noise seemed to flicker in his eyes.

'OK.' Mark's voice was flat and dead. 'Heard you, Alex.'

He stood up, pushed past into the main room, and walked up to Nathan. Nathan, blinking furiously, tried to reverse into the units.

Mark kept the gun stock under his arm, the barrel pointing at the floor. He pushed his face close to Nathan's and hissed, 'Get the fuck out of here. I see you again, I promise you, you're dead.'

For a moment he stood motionless, as if fighting the impulse to kill Nathan now, on the spot; then pulled abruptly away and left the room.

Nathan sagged sideways on to the units. His whole body was shaking. He gasped, 'Oh, shit, Jesus.'

Alex walked over to him, grabbed his upper arm, and pulled him away. 'You heard.' He didn't care that he sounded unsympathetic. 'We go, now.'

He ran, with Nathan stumbling behind him, down the stairs. Neither Mark nor Sheba was at the bottom, or anywhere on the garage forecourt. But they could hear the crying noise coming from behind the building; from the rear yard. And just after they passed the petrol pumps, they heard the shot.

June

—◆—

12 June 1994

My dear Michael,

Today I found all last summer's letters. They were in among a bundle of opencast papers in my desk. I'm sitting in the garden under our silver poplar tree and I've just finished reading them. Reminding myself that the woman who wrote them was me. Dear God. Dear God. And they end so abruptly: in the middle of a dark cathartic night.

I'm going to bring you up to date. Draw the curtains back and let the light in for you, before closing them permanently again. Yes. A rounding up and a signing off, for you and me.

First, the news at the forefront of everything at the moment – and the reason I was digging out my inquiry papers. The Welsh Office have just announced the result of last September's inquiry, and, guess what, there is to be no opencast! It was announced in the *Western Mail* last Thursday, and all objectors received 150 pages of 'judgement' in the post on Monday. Everyone is astonished. Delighted, of course, but mostly astonished. The Secretary of State cited environmental reasons. In particular, his (or rather, his Inspector's) lack of faith in British Coal's ability to restore the mountain after an opencast,

273

because the site is so huge and exposed. An unsuccessful restoration, the judgement says, would be a catastrophe, and wasn't worth risking.

Cynics (i.e. Gareth) claim the outcome would have been different if the site had been deep in the Valleys, and not overlooking Green Welly Wales. But cynics do like to have it both ways, don't they? A week ago he was pooh-poohing any chance of saving the mountain at all. I felt, when I heard the decision, peculiarly light-headed. As if a weight pressing down on my head – that I had scarcely, till then, been conscious of – had been suddenly lifted, and my brain was reacting as limbs do when relieved of pressure by trying to float upwards. I felt proud as well. That Sal and I had contributed, albeit in such a very minor way, to the winning side. I even shed a tear or two. Sal says (mostly to Nathan) that it is proof that idealistic political action is not a dinosaur activity, and that right can sometimes prevail.

Yesterday, for our own personal satisfaction, Sal and I drove to the Vale of Neath to visit one of the biggest opencast mines there. The idea occurred independently to both of us. A closing ceremony, if you like.

I've seen opencasts before, Michael, but nothing could have prepared me for this. Yet it was only half the size of what they had planned for Blaen Dyar. We stood on a viewing platform – yes, they cater for sightseers – and stared down, it seemed, into the very bowels of the earth. A post-apocalyptic view. Monster vehicles which look tiny down there, like children's toys, labour on narrow terraces of black rock. You can smell the coal, a sour, damp, ancient smell. The men who work the site are rendered insignificant by the scale. The coal goes to fire power stations: neat slices of the world cut away by vast machines for consumption by other, even vaster and more voracious, machines.

Sal was in ecclesiastical mood. In her most sonorous Valleys' accent she declared that we had 'seen the voids of hell and were glad we were not sinners'. I swear, Michael, you could have interred a small city in that hole. I wished I had brought flowers with me. I had an overwhelming urge, standing on that platform above the void, to scatter flowers into it.

I have been up to Blaen Dyar, on my own, and told it how lucky it is. That's when I shed my tears. The heather isn't in bloom yet, but everything else is much as it was last summer. Except me. There's talk of a celebratory bonfire party up there in a fortnight, in Black Cliff Valley. The plan, ha ha, is to set fire to the coal, so that British Coal – or their successors, when they're privatized – can never try for it again. I think, having missed my chance with flowers in the Vale, I can't let a bonfire pass without some symbolic gesture. I'd thought of making a burnt offering of my opencast papers, presented in a meaningful manner, but torching these letters would actually make much more sense. I do have to destroy them sometime, Michael.

Alex will be back for the bonfire. He got to Australia just after Christmas and rings me at eight every other Sunday morning. That's late afternoon over there. He's bringing an Aussie boy, Zane, back with him for the summer. They met through one of Alex's casual jobs, distributing flyers for a Melbourne night club. Alex can surf now, he tells me, and has clearly matured, because he's had four gold letters spelling ALEX studded into his left ear. He says body piercing is really big out there. He's managed to live almost entirely on his earnings, so he's still got eight hundred pounds left from last autumn, which'll help postpone his student loan when he gets to Plymouth. I've missed him terribly, but not, to be honest, as terribly as I feared I might. He's alive and well and he's coming back to me, after all.

Which brings me to Mark. Yes. Oh, Michael. If this is my final, valedictory letter to you I have to write about Mark. But what can I say? I can't, even now, excuse myself.

Still, he's alive and, I hope, well too. He has a new German Shepherd dog. Called Gypsy, I believe. He bought her as a pup just before Alex went to Australia.

Of course, I went to see him after Sheba died, to apologize. Alex had told me exactly what happened. I just turned up at the garage, so he couldn't refuse to speak to me. The meeting was less hostile

275

than I'd prepared myself for, but oddly formal. I should have guessed how he'd react. He listened to my apology in complete silence and then dismissed it by saying that actually he blamed himself. That if he hadn't misread things so badly none of it would have happened. So conveniently obliterating my part in his life, and Alex and Nathan's. He told me Sheba would have killed Nathan if Nathan hadn't mortally wounded her – which I really doubt, when Mark himself was there to intervene; though I suppose Nathan might have been much more badly bitten. But I knew I was listening to what Mark wanted to believe about the incident. What he felt he could handle. He needs to believe that he's responsible for the things that happen in his own life, even when the things are bad, and that the hurtful actions of others can't touch him. Very male. Poor Mark.

I came away from the meeting upset. Which maybe he intended. I always underestimated him. Perhaps he understood that not having your wrongdoings acknowledged, when you want to apologize for them, is a real punishment. And I felt I'd ended up liking him a lot more than he liked me, which also hurt. I liked him, I think, for the person he actually was, not just for the person I wanted him to be. But what was I to him, even when things were going well, beyond an easy, flattering sexual opportunity?

Sheba's death was a tragedy, but not a human tragedy. Anyone who can shoot their own fatally injured dog must be, at heart, unsentimental about animals. Gareth has told me he'd done it before, when other dogs or livestock were dying. Although I left our meeting upset, I also left with the feeling that life would go on; and that while Nathan and I might remain unforgiven, he attached no great blame to Alex, which I was relieved about. I know that their paths crossed several times, without incident, before Alex went to Australia.

But I don't see Mark at all now, as I didn't before last summer.

Nathan is still working at the Ruckshop, but is off to the States soon to help out at one of their summer camps. God knows what the Yanks will make of him. He's a truly mercurial character. Both Sal and I have tried being furious with him, but he simply buckles contritely wherever you attack him and then reforms immediately afterwards, perfectly intact and seamlessly bright again. Sal promised not to tell his father that he'd carried a knife to a confrontation, and pulled it, in return for the forfeiture of his entire knife collection, to which he agreed without further argument. He took the lot round to Aber police station and, I suspect, rather enjoyed the drama of turning in so many lethal weapons. And he now has a girlfriend, called Gina. She looks remarkably like him – bird-framed, darkly stylish, and seems to tiptoe everywhere. They look like a pair of spectral twins.

I bumped into Mrs Meredith the other day in W. H. Smith's. The first time I've spoken to her since last summer. She told me how much Frank was enjoying Hereford. I'm still at Treherberts, you know. Frank and I both resigned on the Monday after that dreadful weekend, and to avoid chaos the younger Treherbert intervened, offered Frank a senior post in the Hereford branch, where there was a vacancy, and me Frank's job, on a temporary basis. He has spies, I can only assume, who told him something about our relationship. Anyway, we both accepted. I did Frank's job till November, when the manager post was advertised; I tried for it but was unsuccessful. Asking to be permanently rewarded for inconveniencing the business was probably pushing my luck. So I'm back in my old job, and my new boss is a Mr Scott Thomas, a married forty-year-old with two young children and a weight problem, but, I have to admit, an excellent manager. When I met Mrs Meredith she was as sweepingly gracious as ever. I don't know how much she knows of what happened last autumn, but it can't be nothing; I found the encounter disturbingly unreal.

I am, however, generally much calmer these days. And feeling, ninety per cent of the time, optimistic. It's easier to let go of some-thing when you have seen it clearly and know what it is, and the quieter energy that remains I have been directing outwards. I have the garden under control this year – my lupins and tubs are magnifi-cent – and I attend a photography class at the leisure centre every Monday evening. I've developed an interest in landscape photography and have taken a panoramic shot of the tiered terraces of Abertillery, sunlit under their lumpy mountain tops, that I reckon Lowry would be proud of.

Only a couple of things can still choke me up: thinking for any length of time about you, obviously; and thinking about Mark. But I would call that normal, given the unhappy conclusion to both relationships, and not pathological.

I'm going out to Aber with Gareth and Lizzie tonight to hear Siân sing in *La Belle Hélène*. Lizzie has refused to let Rob, her new boyfriend, accompany us – she says she doesn't know him well enough to be excruciated in his presence. Lizzie knows about me and Mark – I gave Alex permission to tell her – and apparently she said stoutly, 'And why shouldn't she? Good for her.' Which was sweet of her but shows Alex didn't tell her the whole truth.

And guess what, Michael, I almost forgot. News you will definitely regret missing. Wales won the Five Nations Cup last winter! Yes! Not a clean sweep, I'm afraid, but still, they got it.

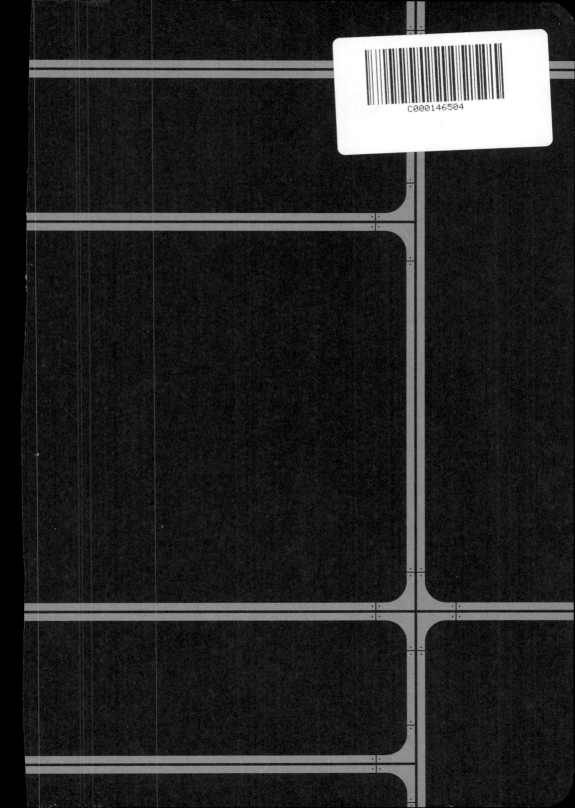

FifthMan
c/o Allford Hall Monaghan Morris
Morelands, 5–23 Old Street
London EC1V 9HL, UK

ISBN 978-1-9161204-2-6

First published in 2021 by FifthMan

Editor: Emma Keyte

The Post Building
Daybook

This is the journal of a project to create
architecture out of infrastructure. The Royal Mail's
West Central District Office, built in the 1960s to
serve London's WC postcode, was a Midtown
monolith, a machine for sorting letters with its own
stop on the underground mail railway. Later the
vacant, factory-like volumes became the scene
of fashion shoots and raves.

Now, the new-out-of-old Post Building has become
a characterful theatre for city life. The retained
frame has been given a super-scaled industrial
wrapping; the remarkable volumes have been
repurposed. An internal promenade leads from the
ground-floor public room through a glazed kinetic
core to one-acre floorplates with a new sandwich
of uses – as offices, shops, social housing, gyms
and roof gardens.

Internal view of the West Central District Office as found: a building on a spectacular scale, with huge volumes and a robust structure.

The Pirelli Tower penthouse, designed by Gio Ponti and photographed in 1960. From the thirty-first floor, the aluminium and glass curtain wall gives panoramic views over the lower-rise city below.

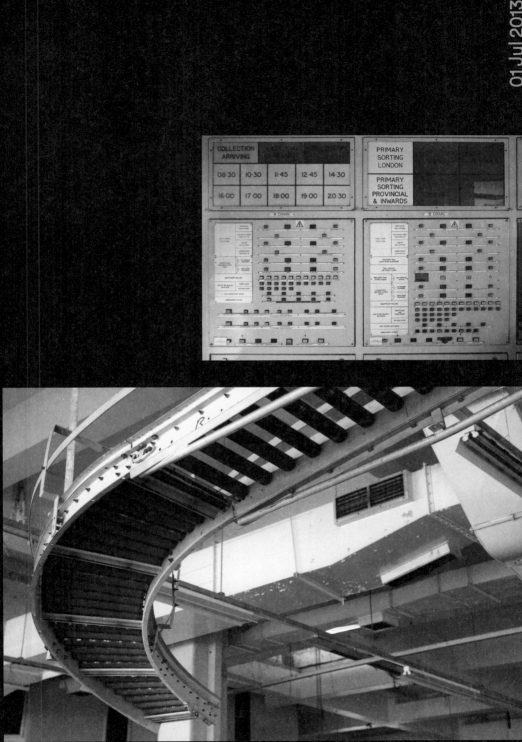

01 Jul 2013

Feasibility study sketches establishing a strategy
for the building's adaption and re-use, maximising
area with minimal interventions to the fabric.

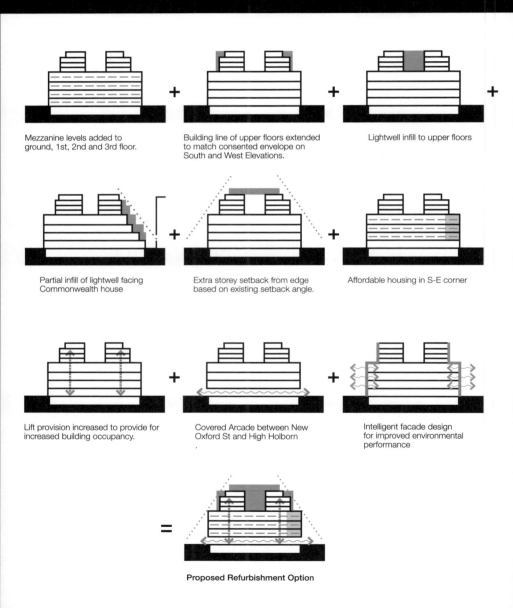

Mezzanine levels added to
ground, 1st, 2nd and 3rd floor.

Building line of upper floors extended
to match consented envelope on
South and West Elevations.

Lightwell infill to upper floors

Partial infill of lightwell facing
Commonwealth house

Extra storey setback from edge
based on existing setback angle.

Affordable housing in S-E corner

Lift provision increased to provide for
increased building occupancy.

Covered Arcade between New
Oxford St and High Holborn
.

Intelligent facade design
for improved environmental
performance

Proposed Refurbishment Option

The Agas map of London, first printed in 1561, showing a bird's-eye view of the city. The site of The Post Building, in the parish of St Giles, is still – literally – in the fields.

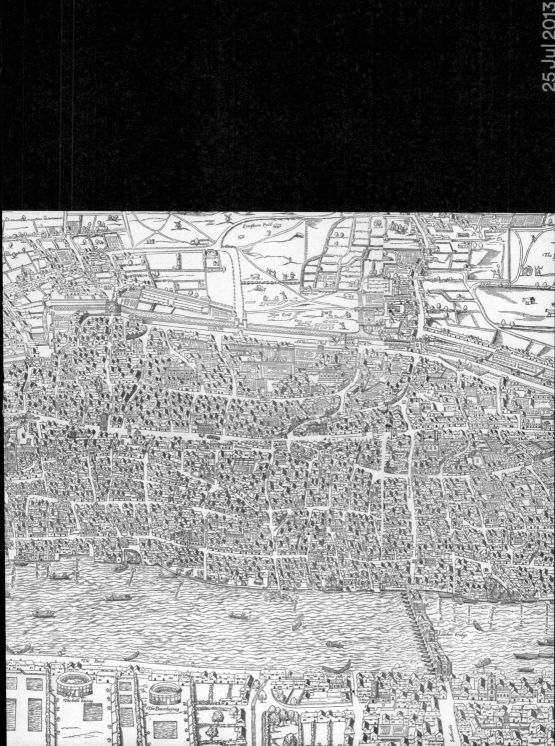

Fynfburie Fyld

The

S. Giles

Mora Fyld

All Halowes in ye Wall

Cryched

London bridge

The Bull

The bolle bayting

The Beerebayting

Barnes fielde

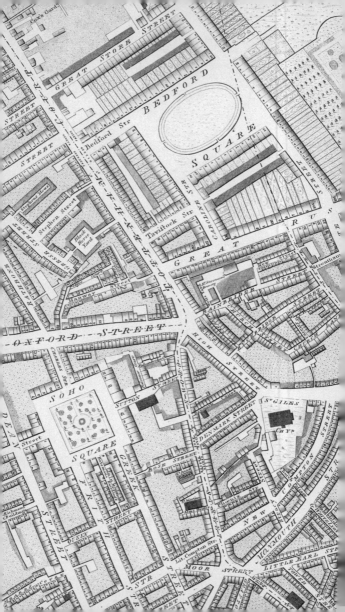

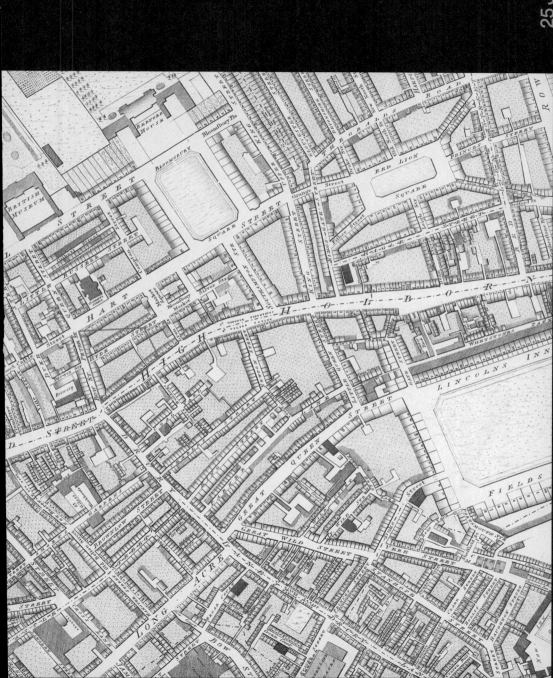

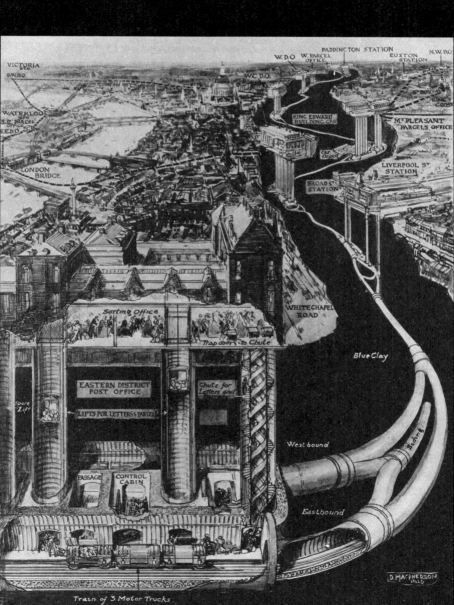

A 1926 illustration showing the route of the underground mail railway in London from the Eastern District Post Office to Paddington Station. The West Central District Office, which occupied the site of The Post Building, appears just to the right of St Paul's dome.

1970s map, published by the Post Office, of the Mail Rail system. The tunnel that runs beneath The Post Building was in use until 2003, the platform connected to the floors above by a series of shafts originally used as lifts. Both tunnel and platform have been left intact during the works above.

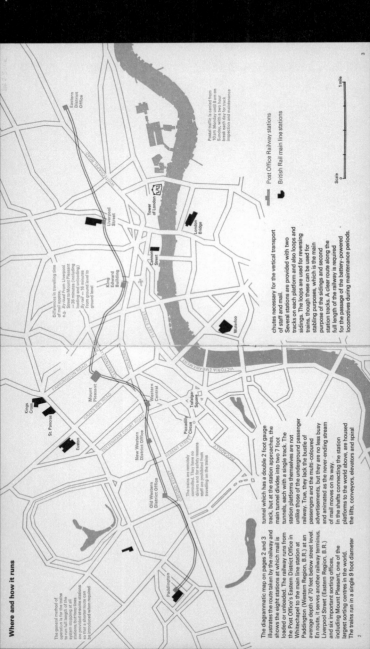

A mail operative loads a train during the 1970s. Construction of the Mail Rail tunnel network began in 1917, and the railway was opened ten years later in 1927.

Diagram from a 1960s publication describing the sorting process from post van to platform.

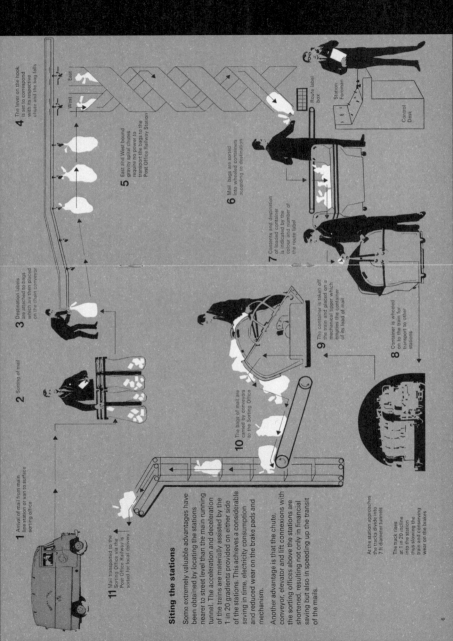

A customised Austin-Morris personnel carrier takes workers from the West Central District Office in 1971.

13 Sep 2013

Cutaway diagrams illustrating the layout of
machinery on each floor of the building, and
the Mail Rail link below street level.

London WCDO Mechanisation

First Floor, Second Floor and Third Floor

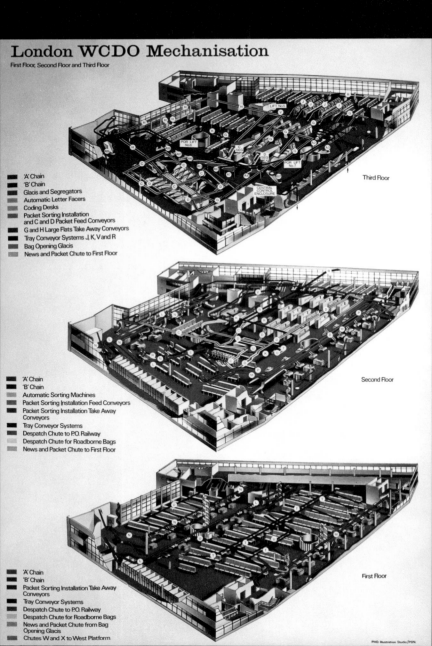

'A' Chain
'B' Chain
Glacis and Segregators
Automatic Letter Facers
Coding Desks
Packet Sorting Installation
and C and D Packet Feed Conveyors
G and H Large Flats Take Away Conveyors
Tray Conveyor Systems J, K, V and R
Bag Opening Glacis
News and Packet Chute to First Floor

Third Floor

'A' Chain
'B' Chain
Automatic Sorting Machines
Packet Sorting Installation Feed Conveyors
Packet Sorting Installation Take Away
Conveyors
Tray Conveyor Systems
Despatch Chute to P.O. Railway
Despatch Chute for Roadborne Bags
News and Packet Chute to First Floor

Second Floor

'A' Chain
'B' Chain
Packet Sorting Installation Take Away
Conveyors
Tray Conveyor Systems
Despatch Chute to P.O. Railway
Despatch Chute for Roadborne Bags
News and Packet Chute from Bag
Opening Glacis
Chutes W and X to West Platform

First Floor

PHO. Illustration Studio/PBN.

London WCDO Mechanisation

Post Office Railway, Basement/Sub-Basement and Ground Floor

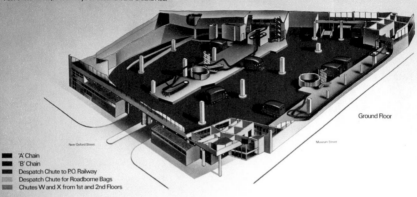

Ground Floor

New Oxford Street

Museum Street

- 'A' Chain
- 'B' Chain
- Despatch Chute to P.O. Railway
- Despatch Chute for Roadborne Bags
- Chutes W and X from 1st and 2nd Floors

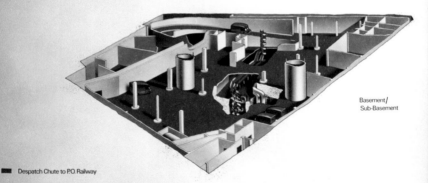

Basement/
Sub-Basement

Despatch Chute to P.O. Railway

Post Office Railway

Despatch Chute to P.O. Railway

Early proposals suggested an undulating
upper-level volume quite distinct from the
repurposed floors below.

A 3D-printed city plan, with newer streets – New Oxford Street and Bloomsbury Way – breaking through the original, dense grids of Bloomsbury and St Giles, to create angled views and the significant corners sketched opposite.

Images of the interior as marketed to potential
tenants. With a strategy built around the generous
volumes offered by the building, a makeshift
basketball court was constructed to demonstrate
the internal scale, and a mezzanine floor mocked
up between floor and ceiling.

The Carson Pirie Scott department store (1899) in Chicago, designed by Louis Sullivan and Daniel Burnham. The deep reveals across the façade give a sense of solidity despite the large windows, and an opulently ornamented, curved tower on the corner marks the main entrance.

Palazzo Pitti in Florence, designed by Luca Fancelli in 1446. A robust Renaissance palazzo studied for the scale, opening and variation of its façade.

Donald Judd's studios at 101 Spring Street in
New York – a cast-iron building designed by
Nicholas Whyte in 1870. Judd wrote in 1989 that
the façade of the building "is the most shallow
perhaps of any in the area and so is the furthest
forerunner of the curtain wall".

Study drawings exploring scale, opening, variation, and the differences between each elevation of the building according to function and orientation.

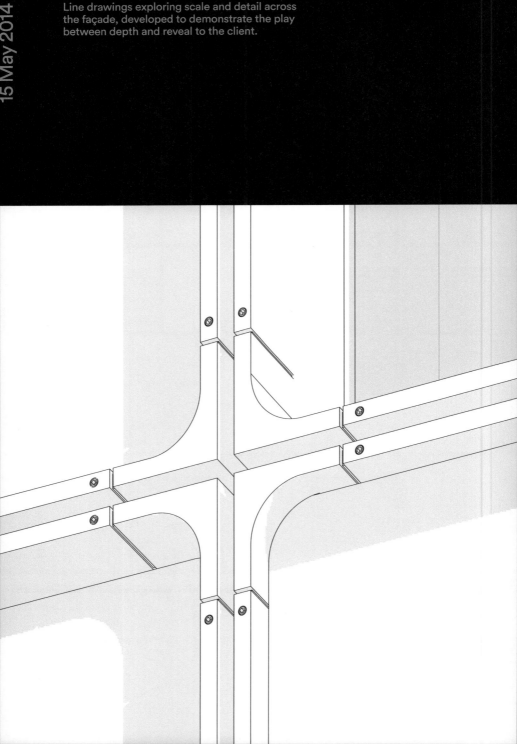

15 May 2014

Line drawings exploring scale and detail across the façade, developed to demonstrate the play between depth and reveal to the client.

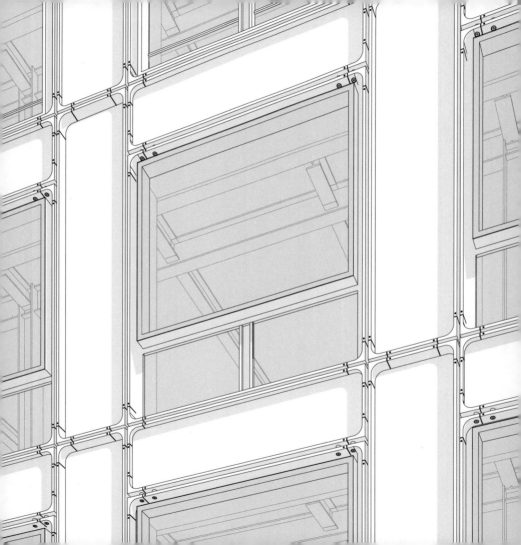

Drawings exploring an angled view, looking at
how the lines of each machined component would
look when viewed obliquely, from a distance or
at close quarters.

Peter Behrens' AEG Turbinenhalle (1909) in
Berlin, an urban factory and – like The Post
Building – a very large building in a dense grid.
The mitigation (and celebration) of scale was
a focus for investigation.

Mies van der Rohe's S. R. Crown Hall at IIT (1956).
A more abstract idea of a factory, and differing in
its external expression.

Mies van der Rohe's Seagram Building in Chicago (1958), with its curtain wall of bronze and dark glass, offered a reference for a monumental building in metal.

Louis Kahn's Center for British Art at Yale (1977) celebrates the natural variation and contrasting, self-finished qualities of concrete, glass and matt steel.

Detail of tunnel construction on the westbound platform of the Mail Rail. The robustly-engineered machinery and components of the former sorting office, and its below-ground infrastructure, provided cues for the new building's look and feel.

Precedents for the construction, materials and styling of the building's industrial wrapping. A heavily machined casting from the Reliance Foundry, and Jean Prouvé's Standard chair, designed in 1934.

21-31 New Oxford Street

Tray Junctions
1:2.5

Visualisation looking through the façade into the
retrofitted space from the outside. The office floors
take advantage of the building's inherent volume,
here with a mezzanine added.

19 May 2014

he 10th Avenue overlook, a
or how an old industrial building
habited.

19 May 2014

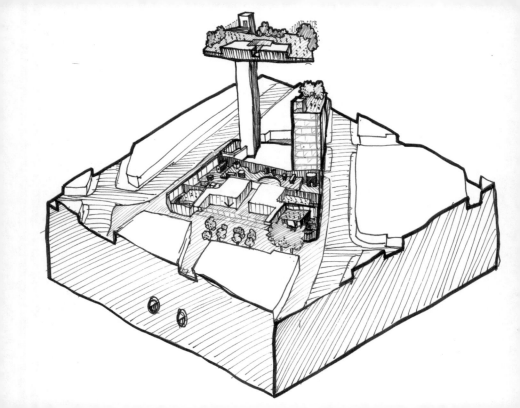

and arrangement of infills on each elevation. The larger windows of the office floors contrast with those of the residential apartments, above a base of retail.

City elevation. The Post Building, with its one-acre
elevations, takes its place in a streetscape
of buildings of many different styles and eras.

26 Aug 2014

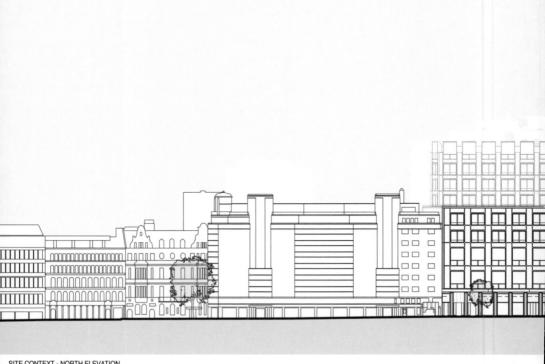

SITE CONTEXT - NORTH ELEVATION

MUSEUM STREET

crank line

WEST CENTRAL STREET

Roof level view, with Hawksmoor's stepped tower at St George's, Bloomsbury, the domed roof of the British Museum, and University College London's Senate House aligned in an axis of religion, academia and culture.

GIN LANE.

Gin cursed Fiend, with Fury fraught.
Makes human Race a Prey.
It enters by a deadly Draught
And steals our Life away.

Virtue and Truth, driv'n to Despair,
It's Rage compells to fly,
But cherishes, with hellish Care,
Theft, Murder, Perjury.

Damn'd Cup! that on the Vitals preys,
That liquid Fire contains,
Which Madness to the Heart conveys,
And rolls it thro' the Veins.

Publish'd according to Act of Parliament Feb. 1 1751.

Visualisation of the residential entrance on High Holborn. The apartments – including 21 affordable homes – are positioned on this south elevation to maximise sunlight, looking onto both the street and an internal lightwell. Each has a winter garden, protected from noise and pollution, and there is a private roof garden for the residents on the eighth floor.

Plan of a typical two-bedroom apartment, with the
winter garden leading off the main living space.

Wardrobes:
Built-in cupboards
to all intermediate
bedrooms

Front door:
Painted plain-faced
solid core door
PAS 25/24
Automatic boxing
multi-point lock, with
euro cylinder

Lighting:
Arup Lum1 A

RSL Bayonet lamp
holder enclosed in
flush shade. Low
energy pendant.

Living room and circulation:
Kamdean
French Oak
VGW65T
Vinyl tiles

Bathrooms:
British Ceramic Tile
Note ceramic, black
BCT403361 with dark grey grout
331x331mm

Bedrooms:
Mr Tomkinson
Twist Wool Mix Carpet
Tungsten

Wintergardens:
Ecodek
Composite decking

Ironmongery
Dline

Walls:
Matt emulsion
Off white, TBD

Timber models showing the building's elevation onto New Oxford Street, Museum Street and High Holborn.

New Oxford Street

North Elevation
Scale 1:75

21-31 New Oxford St.

Museum Street

West Elevation
Scale 1:75

21-31 New Oxford St.

High Holborn

South Elevation
Scale 1:75

21-31 New Oxford St.

The huge bookstack of Gordon Bunshaft's
Beinecke Rare Book and Manuscript Library
at Yale (1963) rises up through the centre of
the building, a distinct volume within the
greater whole.

Sketch illustrating the structural concept of raft and core. The foundation – an acre of concrete raft two metres deep – was retained during the demolition, saving around 1,600 tonnes of carbon. Above it, the lightweight, exposed steel core is effectively a building within a building, acting as a giant bridge truss to spread structural loads across the raft.

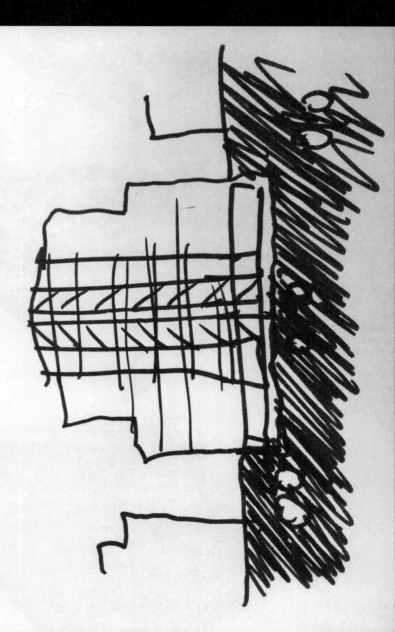

A multi-storey stack of Farnsworth houses (Mies van der Rohe, 1951) collaged into the building to visualise the core. Occupying a hole cut through the centre of the building, it has a comparatively domestic scale.

CGI view into The Post Building's main entrance and west elevation. From the industrial wrapping, the building is detailed with increasing refinement and texture as you move inside.

Rave in The Post Building in late 2010. After the Royal Mail sold it in the late 1990s, the post-industrial shell became a venue for corporate parties, experimental theatre performances and fashion shoots – as well as a more informal destination for ravers and urban explorers.

Celebrations for AHMM's 25th anniversary
in the building, a few months before the partial
demolition began.

25 Jun 2015

Marketing brochure focusing on the scale of the building as a selling point. Tenants were encouraged to make the most of the unusually large volumes in their fit-out.

04 Sep 2015

Principles and ideas for fitting-out

THE POST BUILDING

BROCKTON | OXFORD

"It has a volume and generosity that you don't normally discover; it's something you'll never be able to build again"

SIMON ALLFORD
ALLFORD HALL MONAGHAN MORRIS

VOLUME

Volume to think big and aim high, cultivating the ideas of the future.

CONNECTIVITY

Unparalleled connectivity to transport, culture and people to access London's great talent.

DESIGN

Design to liberate creative expression. Nurturing productivity, prosperity and wellbeing.

apartment in Paris (1929). Le Corbusier's
surrealist view of the roof terrace, overlooking
the Champs-Elysées, places domestic items
in an outdoor setting.

The walled garden at Scampston Hall in North Yorkshire, designed by Piet Oudolf and completed in 2004 as a series of rooms, each with its own character and planting.

07 Sep 2015

CGIs visualising the outdoor terrace at the top level of The Post Building as a series of bookable meeting rooms, with views out across the city.

together in the acre-sized roof terrace, accessible
to the public via a dedicated entrance.

0   5   10   ○

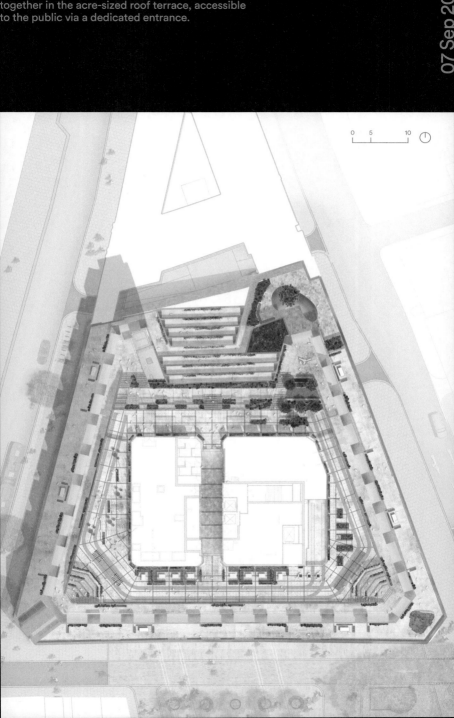

Plan showing the extent of the demolished
(red hatched) and retained (grey) structure by
engineers Arup. The old Mail Rail tunnels below
the site limited the possibility for new piling, so
the building's existing raft foundation was kept,
along with as much of the existing column grid
as possible.

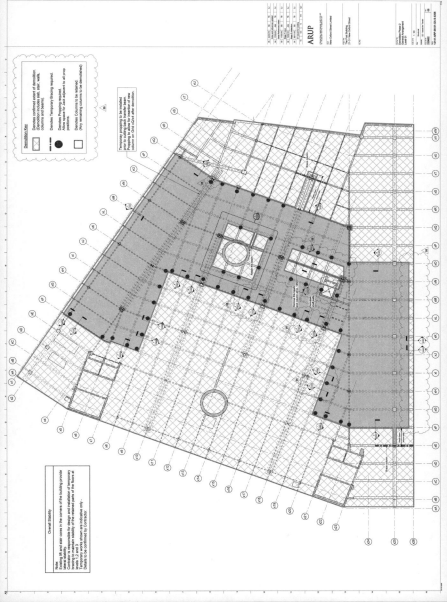

22 Mar 2016

Webcam sequence showing the partial demolition of the building.

28 Jan 2016

17 Feb 2016

07 Jun 2016

28 Jun 2016

29 Sep 2016

31 Oct 2016

31 Dec 2016

28 Feb 2016

17 May 2016

15 Jul 2016

16 Aug 2016

29 Nov 2016

31 Dec 2016

Mockup of the façade system developed by
the cladding contractor, Metallbau Früh, at its
headquarters in Freiburg, Germany.

ornamental door handle made by Anton Früh, grandfather and namesake of the Anton Früh who now runs Metallbau Früh, a family business with a tradition of high quality metalwork.

Ticking-lined suitcase, inspiration for the core wrapping.

28 Oct 2016

giving way to a softer, lined interior to the lift car.

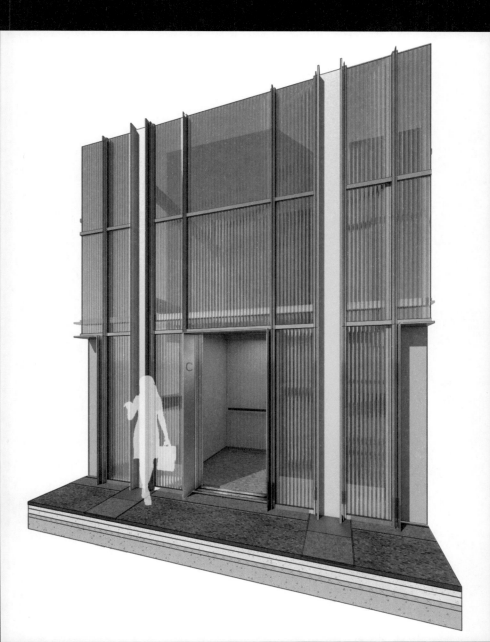

Samples testing different aggregate mixes and pigments for the floor tiles in the reception and lift lobby.

Working drawing of the lift car interior. The finish is
Richlite, a composite made from resin and recycled
paper, cut to reveal its inner layers.

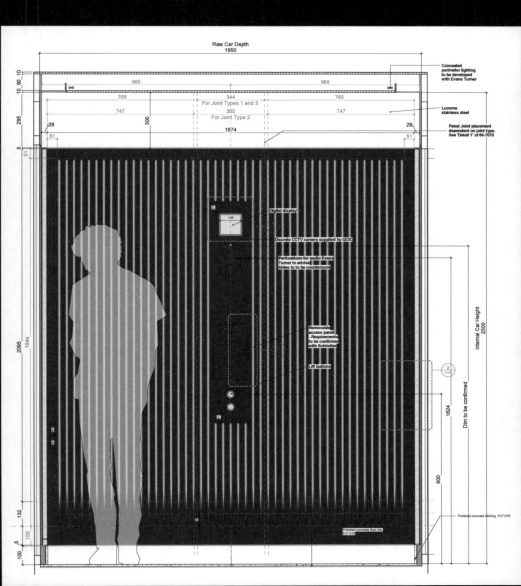

Raw Car Depth
1950

965   965

765   765
344
For Joint Types 1 and 3
747   380   747
For Joint Type 2
1874

28   28
51   51

Concealed
perimeter lighting
to be developed
with Evans Turner

Luceme
stainless steel

Panel Joint placement
dependent on joint type.
See 'Detail 1' of 66-7070

Digital display

Discrete CCTV camera supplied by QCIC

Perforations for audio Evans
Turner to advise
Holes to to be countersunk

Removable
access panel
- Requirements
to be confirmed
with Schindler

Lift buttons

106

Internal Car Height
2500

Dim to be confirmed

2

1624

900

Polished concrete skirting. FLF-016

Polished concrete floor tile
FLF-016

2095   1944

295   300

132   100

5   5

10 90 10   00   00

Demolition shots, taken as the raft foundation was
slowly revealed.

13 Nov 2016

The original blue helical gravity chute, undergoing restoration at metalwork specialists Southdown Construction.

Mockup by the steelwork contractor BHC to show the quality of the structural frame connections.

22 Dec 2016

Demolition shots. The forest of original rust-
coloured columns was an important influence for
the woven artwork designed to line the lobby.

11 Feb 2017

Site shot, with temporary grey-blue steelwork
supporting the retained, red-oxide-coated
structure during demolition.

TYPICAL GUSSET PLATE DETAIL

BHC

MEDWYN PARK, EDINBURGH ROAD,
CARNWATH ML11 8HE.
TEL. (01555) 840006
FAX. (01555) 840008
www.bhc.co.uk
enquiries@bhc.co.uk

CLIENT:
ARUP

PROJECT:
THE POST BUILDING

TITLE:
CORE - ELEVATION X8 AND 1F

TP8-BHC-000-XX-EL-X-26-2000

ISSUE PURPOSE
A

DRAWN: BR
            17.08.2016

CHECKED: SK
            15.08.2016

REV: C02

CORE ELEVATION - GRID xE

CORE ELEVATION - GRID x8

STEP LEVEL

Temporary and permanent steelwork in the
basement, with bracing to support the retaining
wall alongside the new structure.

15 Jul 2017

Tolerance drawing for the lift shafts, calculating the splay needed to take up the slack and allow for tolerances as different materials – primary steel, glazed screens and lift door architraves – interface within the core. Cedric Price spoke about 'aiming to miss', the art of designing in anticipation of future events. In a steel-framed building at this scale, there are generous tolerances to work to.

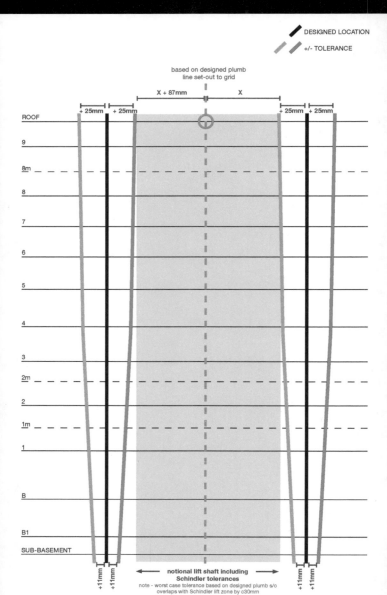

DESIGNED LOCATION

+/- TOLERANCE

based on designed plumb
line set-out to grid

X + 87mm   X

+ 25mm   + 25mm   + 25mm   + 25mm

ROOF

9

8m

8

7

6

5

4

3

2m

2

1m

1

B

B1

SUB-BASEMENT

+11mm +11mm   +11mm +11mm

notional lift shaft including
Schindler tolerances
note - worst case tolerance based on designed plumb s/o
overlaps with Schindler lift zone by c30mm

Temporary bracing to a column, adjusting it
so that it is in the correct position to comply
with the tolerances allowed.

Steel columns, photographed during construction. Although the frame is rationalised as much as possible, several different column types were needed to deal with the exposed junctions between old and new, some with an almost classical look to their bases and capitals.

Webcam sequence showing the construction
of the structural steelwork. The horseshoe of the
retained structure, and the concrete raft below
it, are slowly obscured as the cores are formed,
with the new grey steelwork around them.

31 Dec 2016

08 Feb 2017

29 Apr 2017

27 May 2017

29 Aug 2017

13 Sep 2017

01 Mar 2017

31 Mar 2017

27 Jun 2017

29 Jul 2017

01 Oct 2017

31 Oct 2017

Ceiling setting-out plan for the services that interface between old and new on one of the office floors. Like the infrastructure of the old sorting office, the new services are exposed throughout the building.

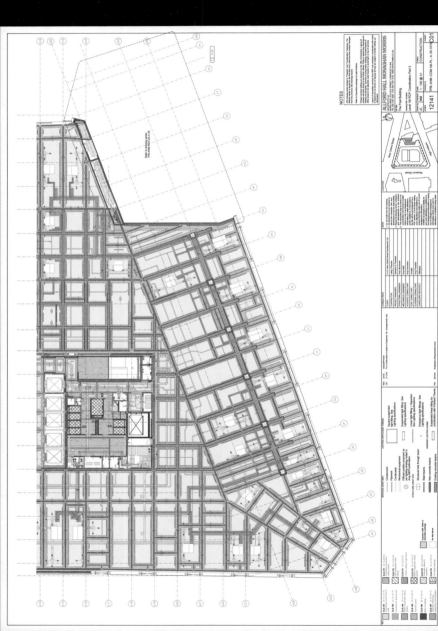

The fumoir at Claridges Hotel in London. The washrooms were inspired by a tour of West End hotel lobbies, bars and cloakrooms. The one at Claridges, with its etched, art deco mirrors and Lalique glass, has been a haunt for discerning drinkers – and smokers – since 1929.

Visualisation of The Post Building washrooms. The building's common parts are moments of luxury and texture within the robust, protective envelope, and here the lighting, back-lit reeded glass and mirrors strike an intimate datum in a very high space.

21 Feb 2018

A jacquard loom, dating from 1920. A bespoke textile was commissioned to infill the frame of the building in the main reception, screening the core behind. The jacquard technique uses punched data cards similar to those used by the Royal Mail for sorting post to different distribution centres.

19 Mar 2018

our Elements of
e describes how
kely to have originated
om the fences and
e.

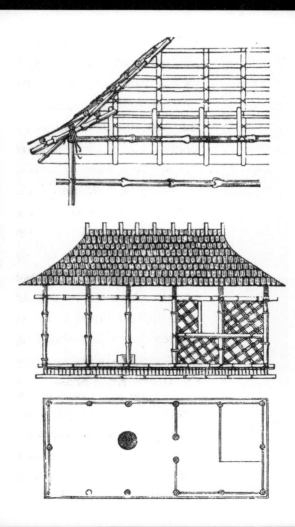

11 Apr 2018

Kees Boeke's 1957 picture-essay Cosmic View:
The Universe in Forty Jumps. The essay plays
with ideas of exponential scale, zooming from
a human figure to the edge of the known universe,
before rewinding to look at atomic particles.
The textile needed to work on multiple scales,
bold enough to be viewed at a distance but
with interest and texture close-up.

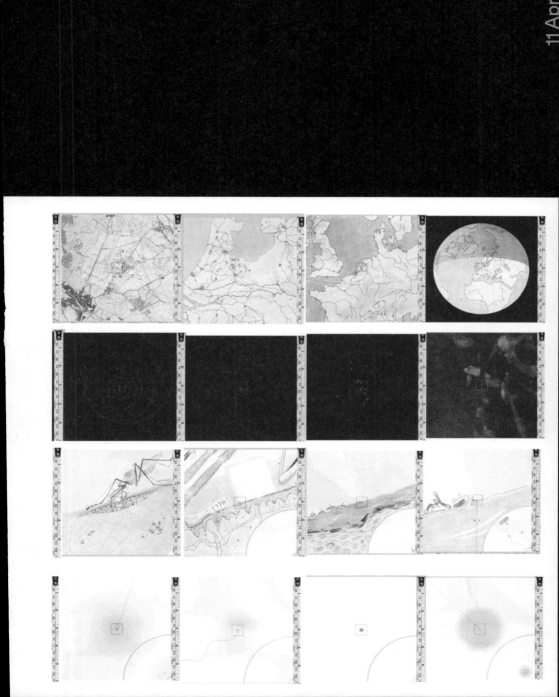

Paolo Uccello's The Hunt in the Forest (1470),
designed as a spalliera painting to be set within
the architecture of an aristocratic room and viewed
at shoulder height. Its composition, drawing the
viewer's gaze from a distance and also working
in close-up, was a reference for that of the textile.

16 Apr 2018

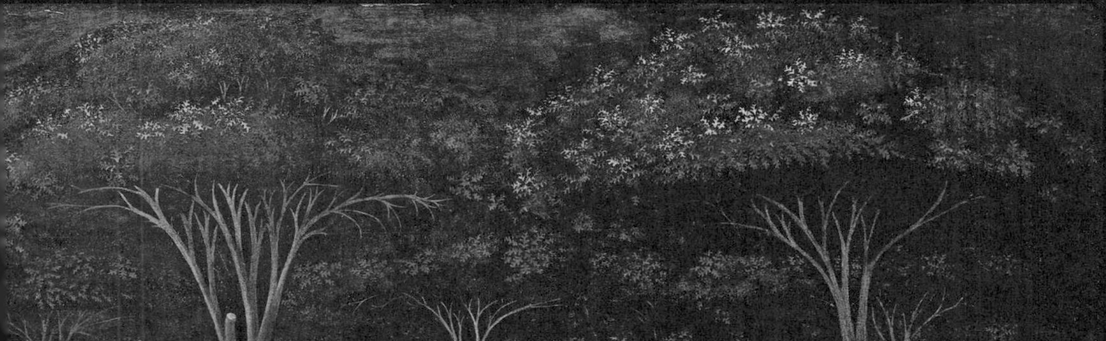

Swatches, sketches and yarn wrappings. In the textile design, an abstraction of the original oxblood red structural elements of the building frame areas of blue and green which represent light and the newly added structure.

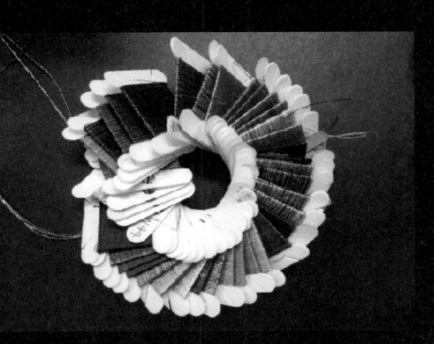

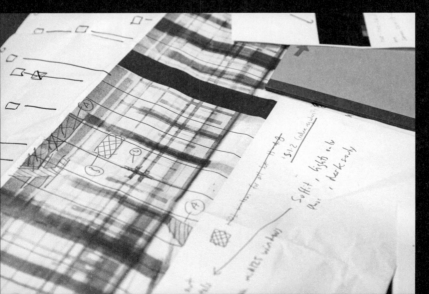

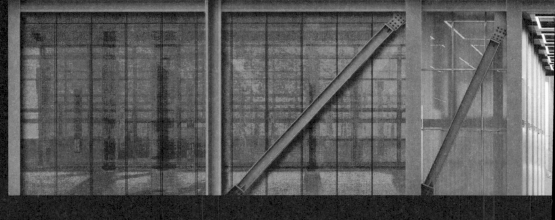

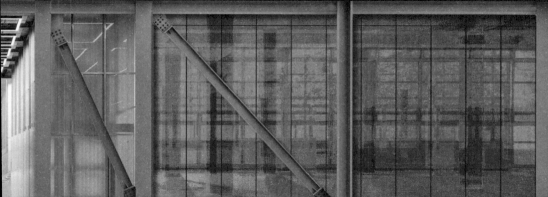

Matthew Murphy of AHMM collaborates with textile designer Ismini Saminidou to develop prototypes at TextielLab at Tilburg in the Netherlands.

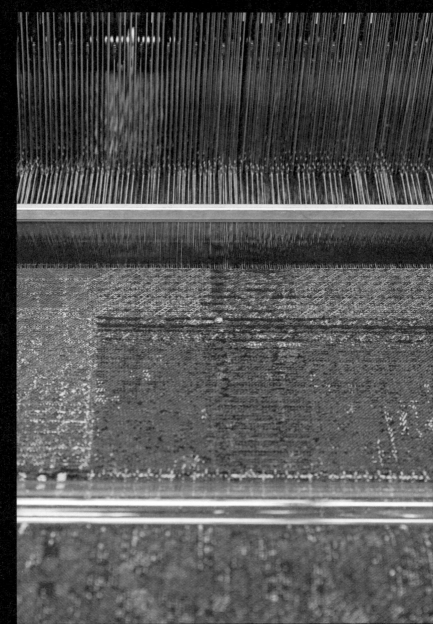

Weaving the textile at TextielLab. The fabric was woven on a jacquard loom using the same principles as the nineteenth-century ones, with the old punch cards replaced by computer files.

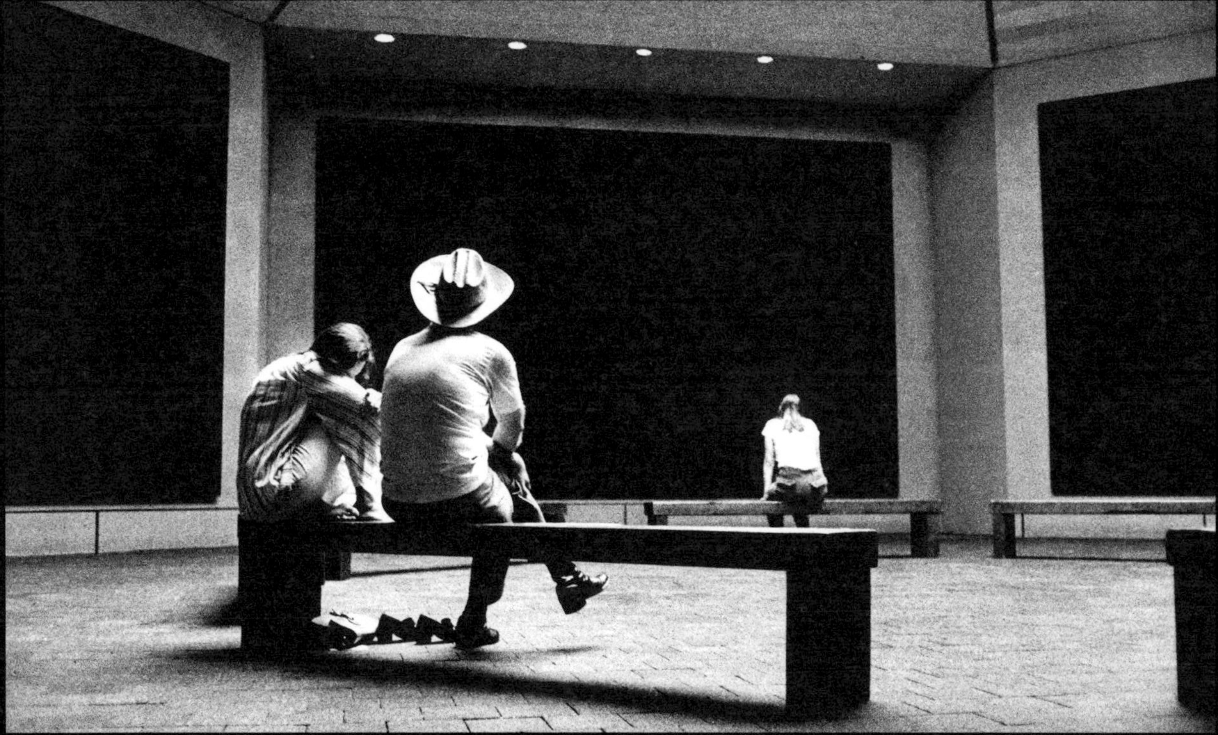

17 D

Assembly of the reception desks at Quest Joinery. The dark red Richlite tops (added later) sit on a base of vitreous enamel fabricated by AJ Wells on the Isle of Wight, who also produce signage for stations on the London Underground.

15 Feb 2019

Construction images showing the installation of
the exposed services on the office floorplates.

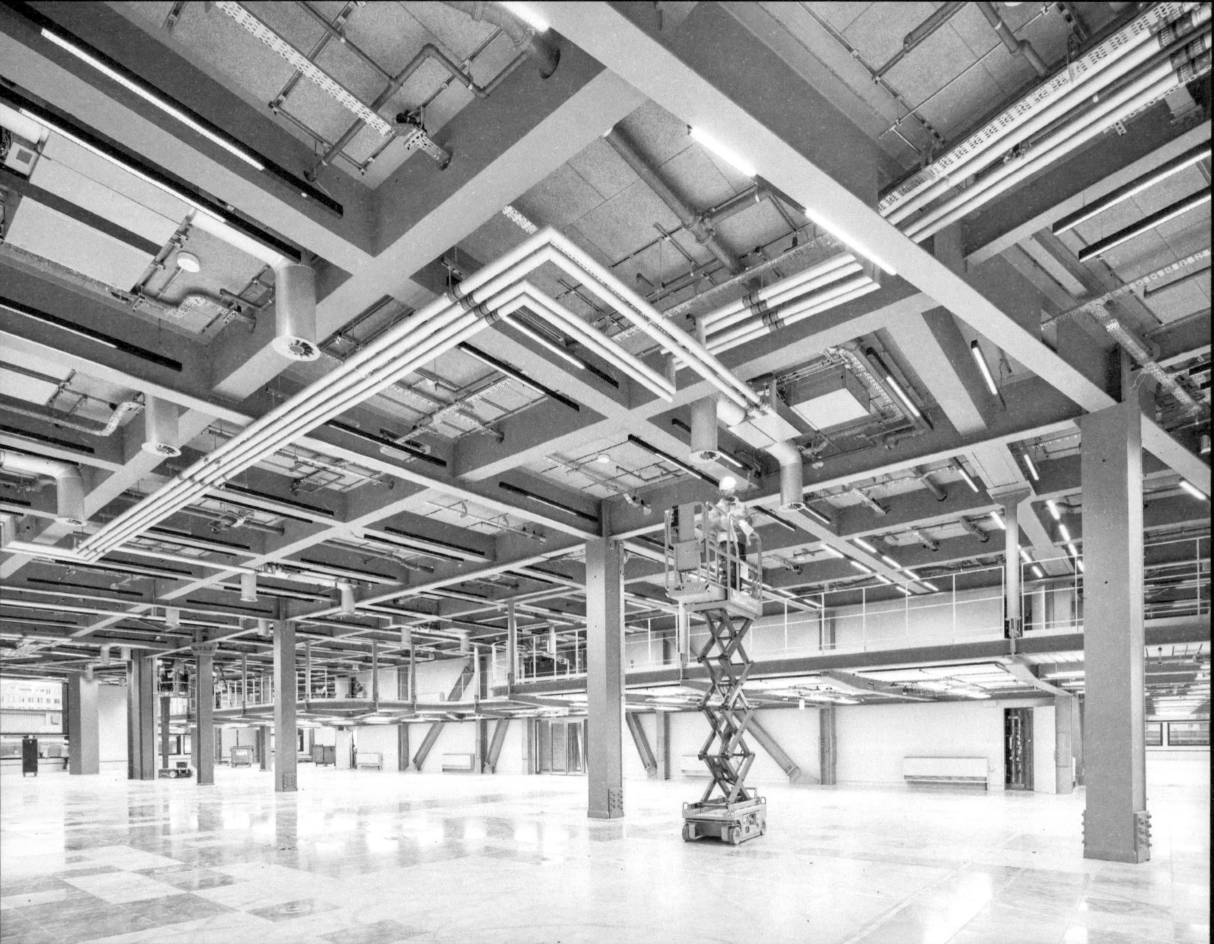

15 Feb 2019

Webcam sequence capturing the wrapping of the building in its new envelope.

28 Nov 2017

28 Nov 2017

16 Dec 2017

28 Apr 2018

20 May 2018

28 Sep 2018

17 Nov 2018

28 May 2019

28 Jan 2018

31 Mar 2018

26 Jun 2018

25 Aug 2018

29 Mar 2019

28 May 2019

Roof view. The residential terrace under
construction, and workers on the terrace
of the neighbouring office building.

27 Feb 2019

Timothy Soar's images of the building, complete,
in March 2020.

03 Mar 2020

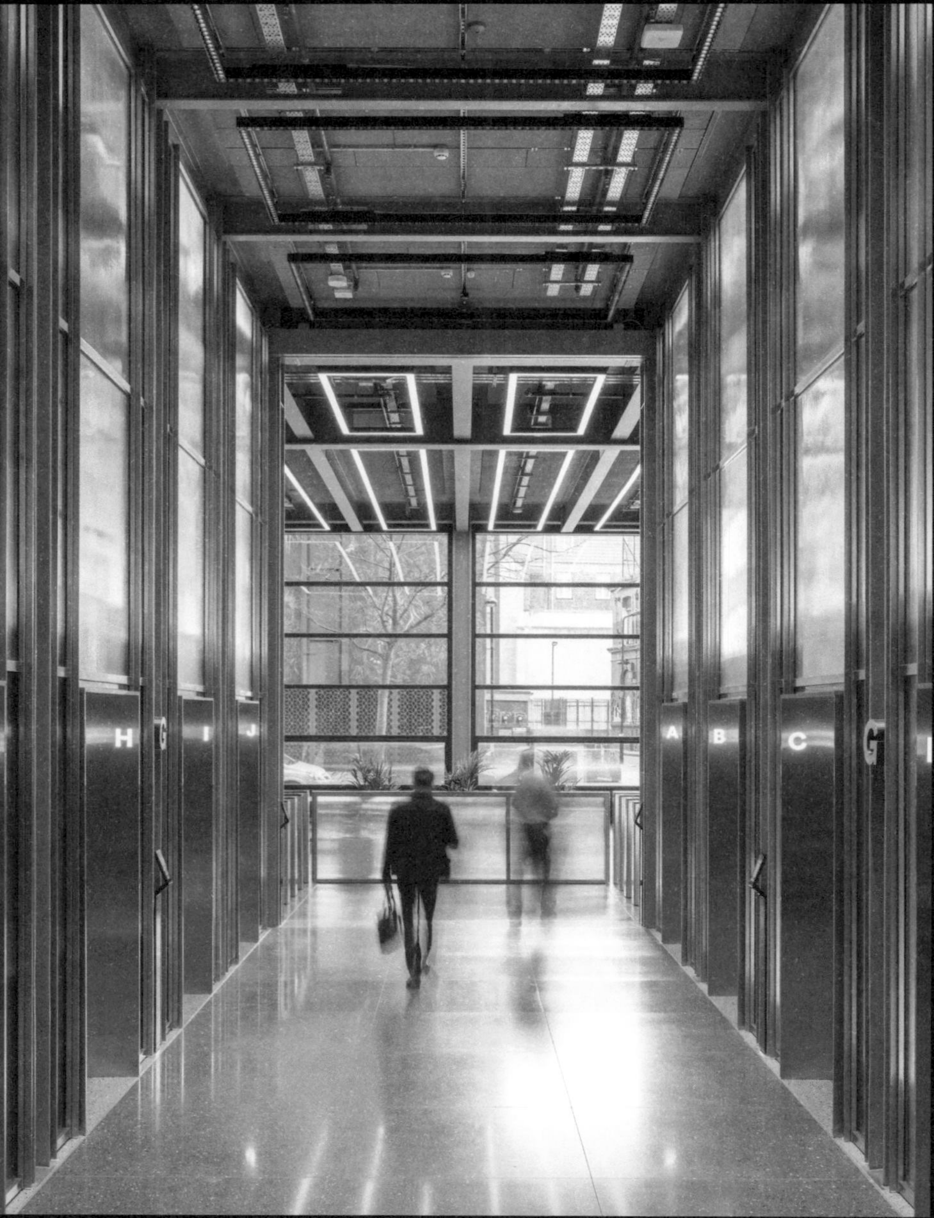
H
G
I
J
A
B
C
G

03 Mar 2020

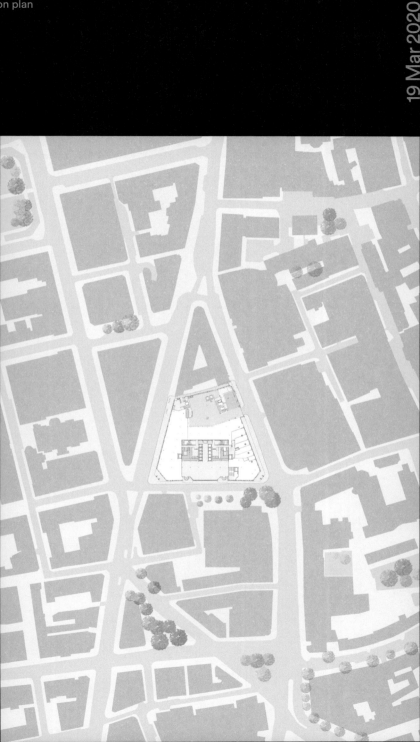

19 Mar 2020

Ground floor plan

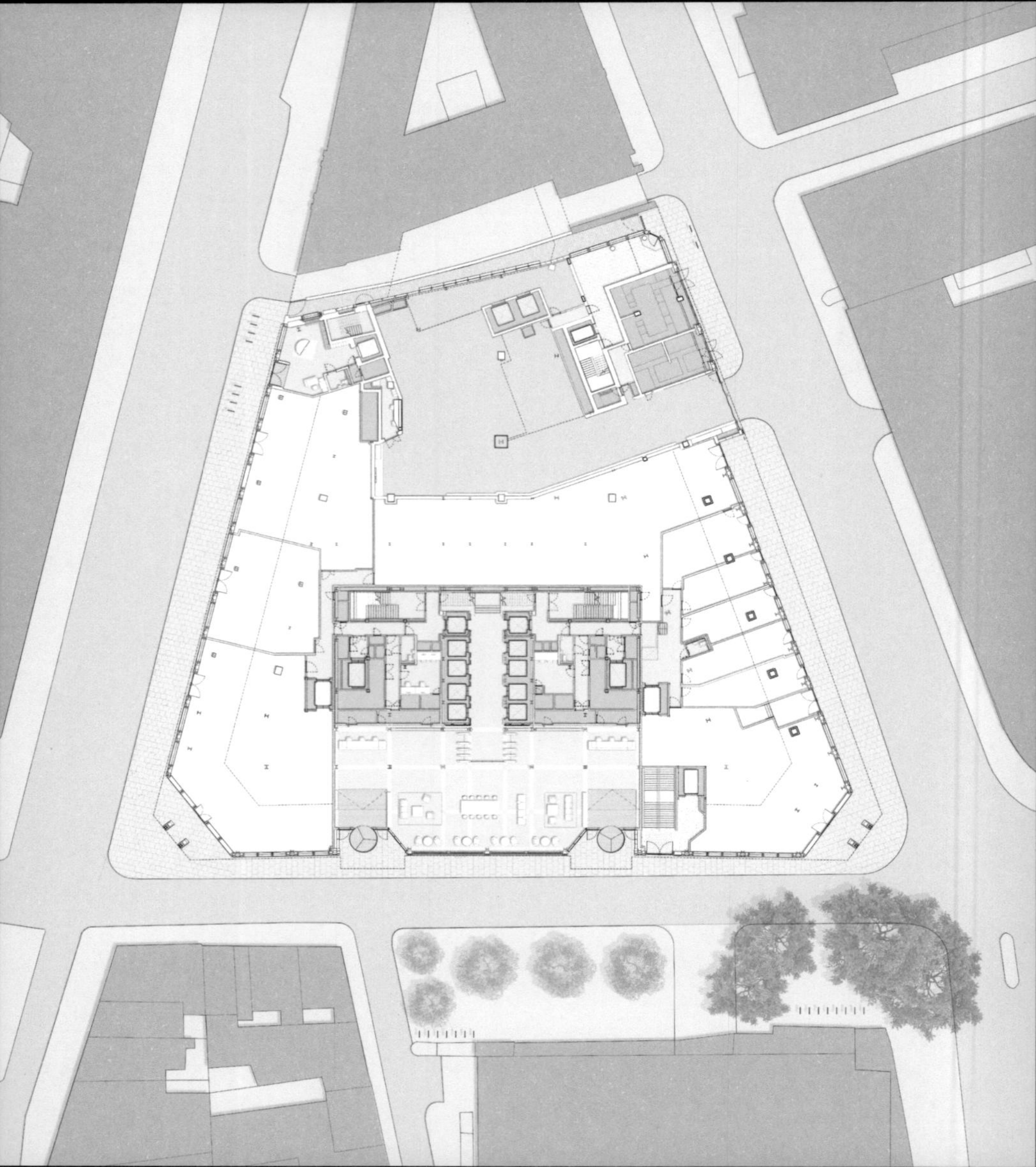

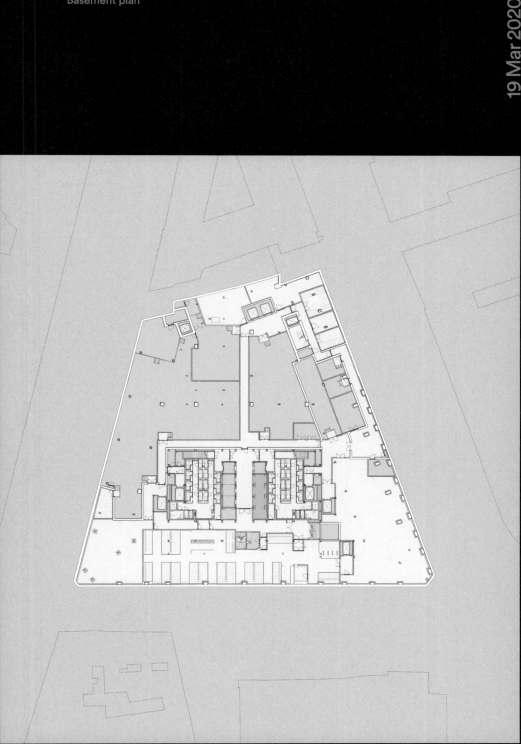

Typical lower floor plan

Line of mezzanine above

19 Mar 2020

Roof plan

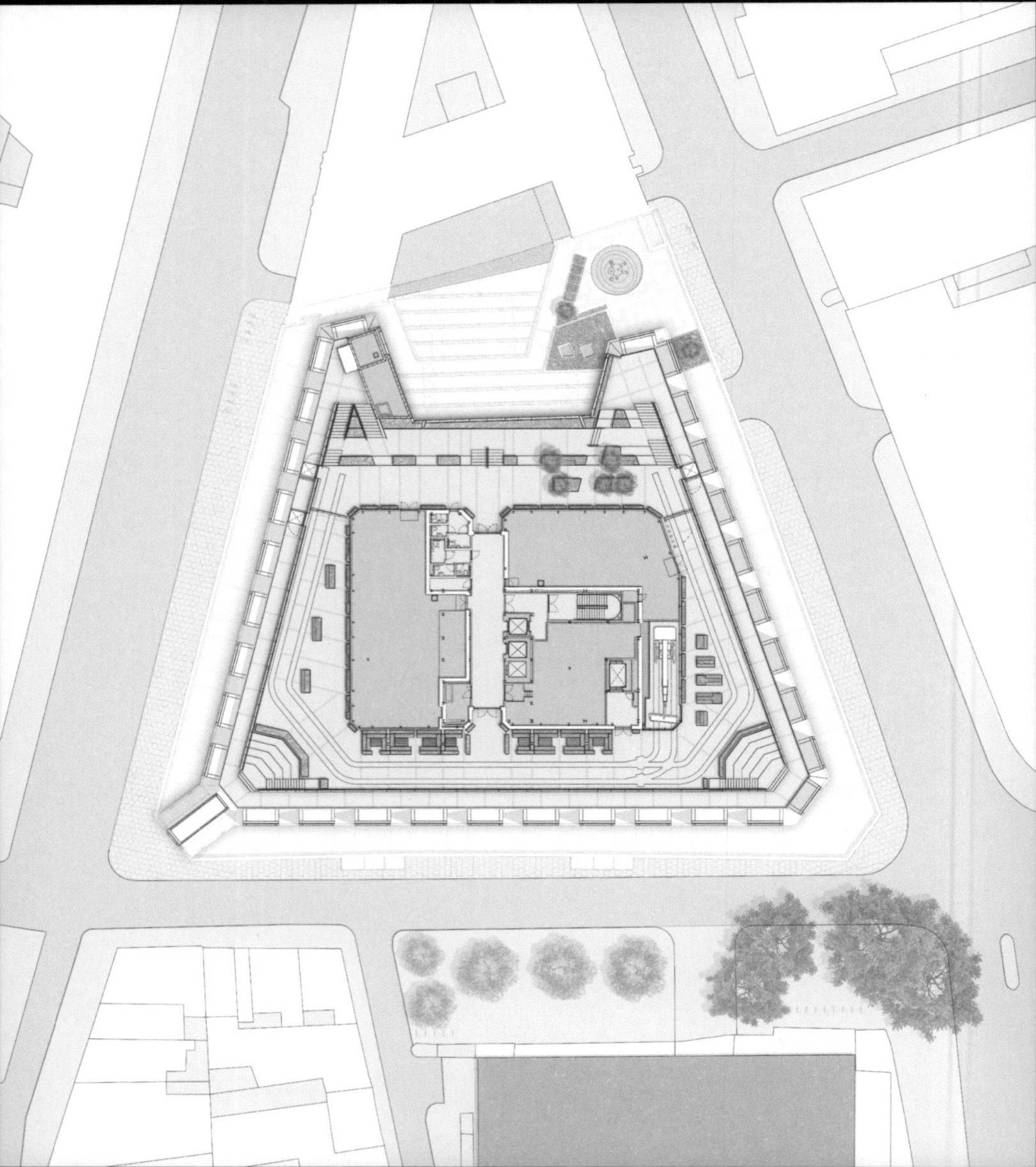

Top-left post:

HAYESDAVIDSON
Posts
Follow

hayesdavidson
London, United Kingdom

Liked by dicanio_jones and 302 others
hayesdavidson Our image in The Post Building brochure. @ahmmarchitects... more
View all 3 comments
4 September 2019

hayesdavidson
Japan

Top-middle post:

TOP POSTS
#thepostbuilding

bhc_ltd · Follow
London, United Kingdom

29 likes
bhc_ltd Throughout the re-development of the Post... more
1 September 2017

Top-right post:

TOP POSTS
#thepostbuilding

i_like_patterns · Follow

20 likes
i_like_patterns Site stuff... more
17 March 2018 · See Translation

Bottom-left post:

MOST RECENT
#thepostbuilding

una_grana · Follow
London, United Kingdom

THE POST BUILD

51 likes
una_grana THE POST BUILDING ... more
4 May 2018

llacitton · Follow

Bottom-middle post:

MOST RECENT
#thepostbuilding

eb7immersive · Follow
Centre Point

37 likes
eb7immersive Blue hour looking West towards... more
14 February 2019

nicolaosborn · Follow

Bottom-right post:

MOST RECENT
#thepostbuilding

BBUK bbukstudiolimited · Follow

21 likes
bbukstudiolimited Roof garden recently completed... more
28 July 2019

ahmmarchitects

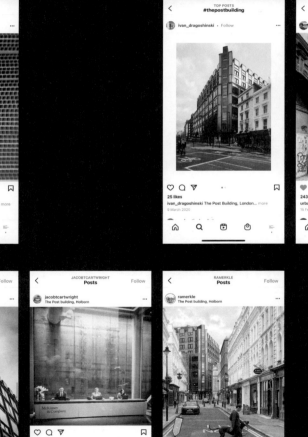

Timothy Soar photographs from September 2020.

MOTORCYCLES

07 Sep 2020

Photography by Timothy Soar.

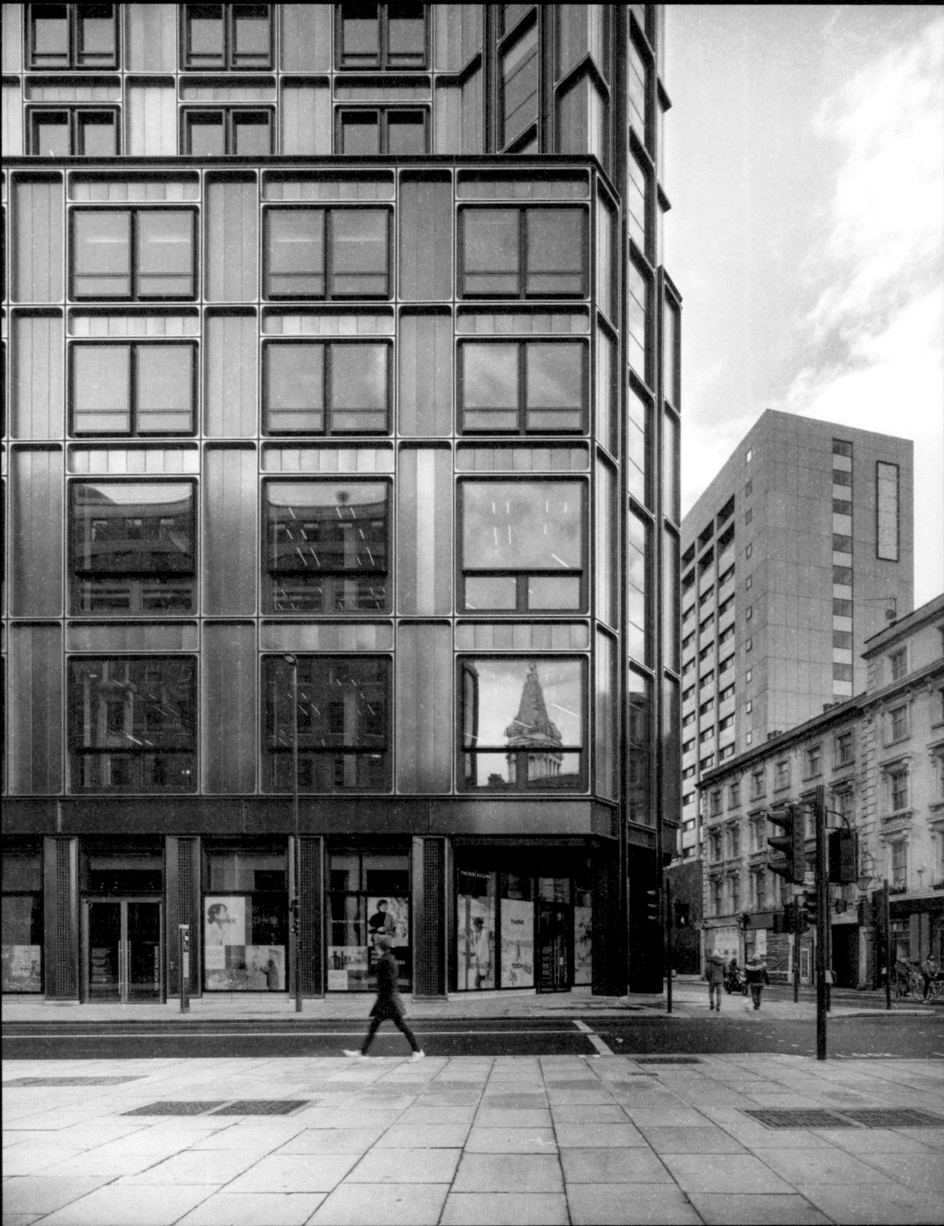

05 Feb 2021

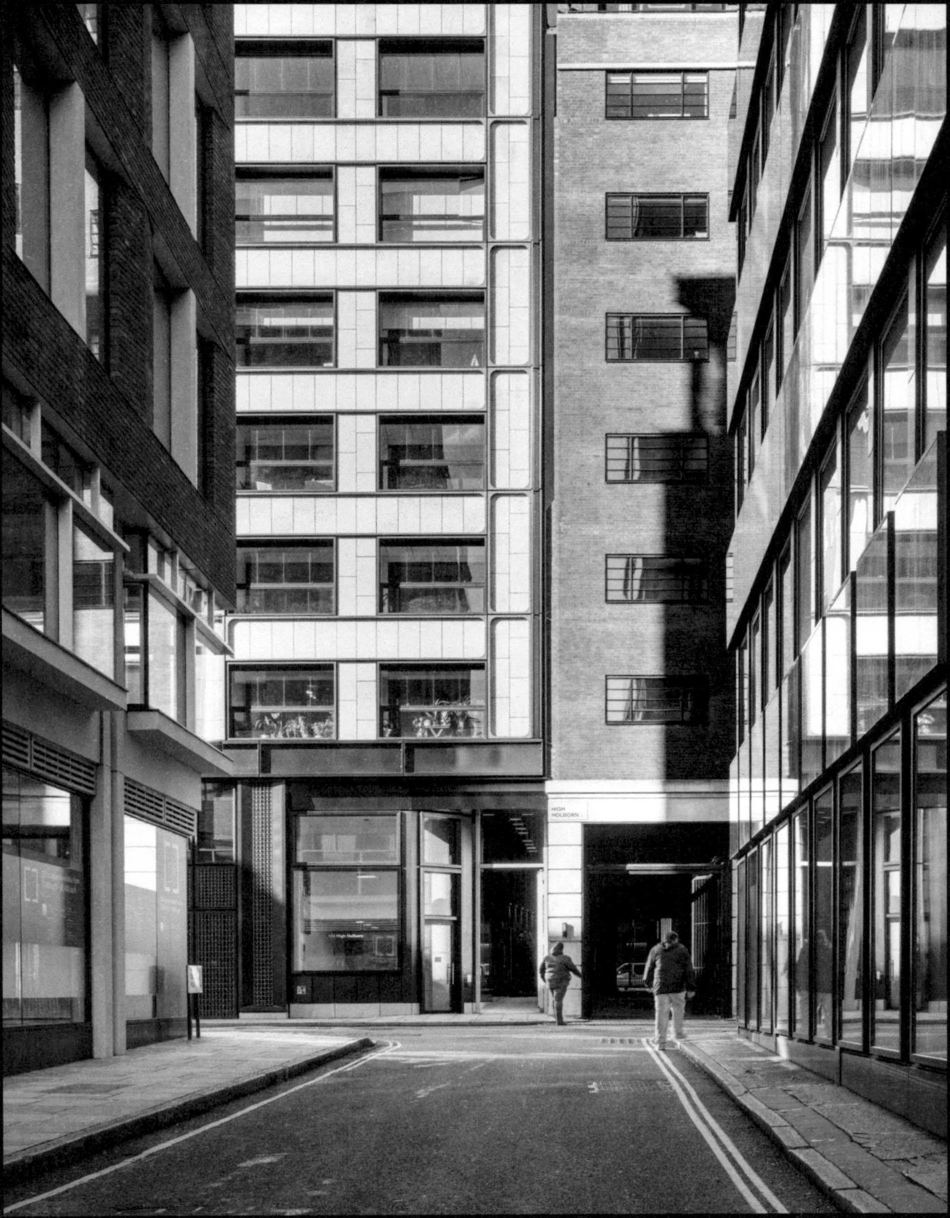

Image credits

01 Jul 2013	West Central District Office in 1969, Postal Archive
	Internal view, Rob Parrish
	Pirelli Tower penthouse in 1960, Archivio Paolo Monti/Fondazione BEIC
	Internal views and machinery details, Rob Parrish
	Feasibility sketches, Allford Hall Monaghan Morris
	Rooftop view, Rob Parrish
25 Jul 2013	Agas map of London, 1561, London Picture Archive
	Horwood map of London, 1799, London Picture Archive
13 Aug 2013	Illustrated London News of 1863, Mary Evans Picture Library
	Cutaway illustration, 1926, Postal Archive
13 Sep 2013	Network map, 1970s, Postal Archive
	Tunnel view, 1970s, Postal Archive
	Sorting diagram, 1960s, Postal Archive
	Personnel carrier, 1971, Postal Archive
	Floorplate drawings, Postal Archive
01 Nov 2013	Cutaway sketches, Allford Hall Monaghan Morris
28 Nov 2013	Sketch views, Allford Hall Monaghan Morris
12 Dec 2013	Marketing suite views, Allford Hall Monaghan Morris
17 Mar 2014	Detail of Carson Pirie Scott store, iStock
	Carson Pirie Scott department store, Chicago History Museum/Getty
	Detail of Economist Building, Jaume Prat
	Economist Building, Architectural Press Archive/RIBA Collections
	Palazzo Pitti, CSP_karkozphoto/age fotostock
	Donald Judd House and museum, 101 Spring Street, Museum of the City of New York/Getty
15 May 2014	Façade drawings, Allford Hall Monaghan Morris
19 May 2014	AEG Turbine Factory, Berlin, Roland Halbe/RIBA Collections
	S.R. Crown Hall, Illinois Institute of Technology, Aksel Coruh
	Seagram Building, Iñaki Bergera
	Yale Center for British Art, Kalle Söderman
	Westbound sign, Postal Archive
	Steel casting, Reliance Foundry
	Standard chair, Jean Prouvé, Galerie Patrick Seguin
	Samples board, Allford Hall Monaghan Morris
	Interior view, Rob Parrish
	Visualisation, Allford Hall Monaghan Morris
	High Line overlook, Brandon Baunach/Flickr
	Collage, Allford Hall Monaghan Morris
06 Aug 2014	Sketch, Allford Hall Monaghan Morris

26 Aug 2014	Bay studies and elevation, Allford Hall Monaghan Morris
11 Sep 2014	Sketches, Allford Hall Monaghan Morris
20 Nov 2014	Model, Allford Hall Monaghan Morris, photographed by Rob Parrish
16 Jan 2015	Rooftop view, Allford Hall Monaghan Morris
	Gin Lane, 1751, William Hogarth, Private Collection/Bridgeman Images
03 Feb 2015	Visualisation, Hayes Davidson
	Apartment plan, Allford Hall Monaghan Morris
06 Feb 2015	Models, Allford Hall Monaghan Morris, photographed by Rob Parrish
04 Jun 2015	Maison du Peuple, Clichy, 1939, Jean Prouvé, Simon Guesdon
	Beinecke Library at Yale, Ezra Stoller/Esto
	Sketch, Allford Hall Monaghan Morris
	Farnsworth House, Library of Congress
	Collages, Allford Hall Monaghan Morris
	Dollhouse, Frans Hals Museum, Haarlem
	Visualisation, Hayes Davidson
25 Jun 2015	Rave in Museum Street, PA Images
	AHMM 25th anniversary party, Matt Chisnall
04 Sep 2015	Marketing brochure, DN&Co
	Visualisation, Hayes Davidson
07 Sep 2015	Aerial view, Hayes Davidson
	Le Corbusier sketch, 1929, Fondation Le Corbusier
	Garden at Scampston Hall, with thanks to Scampston Walled Garden
	Visualisations, Hayes Davidson
	Landscape plan, Allford Hall Monaghan Morris
22 Mar 2016	Demolition plan, Allford Hall Monaghan Morris
28 Jan—	
31 Dec 2016	Webcam images, Site-Eye
29 Jul—	
19 Aug 2016	Mockup and manufacture images, Allford Hall Monaghan Morris
28 Oct 2016	Suitcase with ticking lining, Alamy
	Lift drawings and samples, Allford Hall Monaghan Morris
13 Nov 2016	Construction images, Timothy Soar
22 Dec 2016	Helix and steelwork images, Allford Hall Monaghan Morris
11 Feb 2017—	
17 Feb 2017	Construction images, Timothy Soar
08 Jun 2017	Steelwork drawing, BHC
15 Jul 2017	Construction image, Timothy Soar
15 Sep 2017	Tolerance drawing, Allford Hall Monaghan Morris
21 Oct 2017	Construction images, Timothy Soar
	Services drawing, Allford Hall Monaghan Morris
31 Dec 2016—	
31 Oct 2017	Webcam images, Site-Eye
21 Feb 2018	The Fumoir, Claridges Hotel
	Visualisation, Hayes Davidson

19 Mar 2018	Worker making carpet with jacquard loom, Corbis Historical/Getty
	Caribbean hut from Gottfried Semper's The Four Elements of Architecture, 1851
11 Apr 2018	Spread from Kees Boeke's Cosmic View, 1957, published by Faber and Faber
16 Apr 2018	Paolo Uccello's The Hunt in the Forest, 1470, Ashmolean Museum, University of Oxford/ Bridgeman Images
27 Apr 2018	Wrapping samples. Ismini Saminidou
03 May—	
30 Oct 2018	Visualisations, Allford Hall Monaghan Morris
28 Nov 2018	Images at the TextielLab loom, Allford Hall Monaghan Morris
17 Dec 2018	Rothko Chapel, Houston, 1977, Romano Cagnoni/Getty
	Richlite manufacture, All CNC and Shape Studio, with thanks to Surface Matters
	Reception desk fabrication, Allford Hall Monaghan Morris
15 Feb 2019	Construction shots, Timothy Soar
28 Nov 2017—	
28 May 2018	Webcam images, Site-Eye
27 Feb 2019	Sleeping farmer, Allford Hall Monaghan Morris
03 Mar 2020	Completed images, Timothy Soar
19 Mar 2020	Presentation drawings, Allford Hall Monaghan Morris
29 Jul—	
04 Sep 2020	Instagram images by @hayesdavidson @dr.berman.tal @jack_lomond @bbukstudiolimited @jacobtcartwright @ramerkle @alessandraricardipetro @ramonekersey @marce_chaconb
07 Sep 2020	Completed images, Timothy Soar
18 Sep—	
28 Sep 2020	Completed images, Rob Parrish
05 Feb 2021	Completed images, Timothy Soar

Team

Client	Brockton Capital and Oxford Properties
Project manager	Gardiner & Theobald
Quantity surveyor	Arcadis
Engineer	Arup
Main contractor	Laing O'Rourke
Lighting	Pritchard Themis
Landscape architect	BBUK (terraces) and Gillespies (public realm)
Wayfinding	Cartlidge Levene
Textile designer	Ismini Saminidou
Steelwork contractor	BHC
Cladding	Metallbau Früh

Architect	Allford Hall Monaghan Morris
	Simon Allford
	Will Lee (project director)
	Matthew Murphy (project architect)
	Francesco Belfiore
	Stefan Rust
	Javier Cardos
	Maria Perez Sarasibar
	David Kahn
	Juan Morillas
	Ling Leng
	Harry Casey
	Joshua Broomer
	Victoria Casal
	Wolfgang Frese
	Laura McDonnell
	Michelle Price
	Angel Ruiz-Peinado Sanchez
	Adrian Lau
	Alison Bounds
	Marion Clayfield
	Chikako Kim Kanamoto
	David Murphy
	Joseph Davis
	Gosia Malus
	Amritpal Matharu
	Paul Jenkins
	Alanna Wylde
	John Randall
	Jonathan Hall
	Paul Monaghan
	Peter Morris

Facts and figures

Location	100 Museum Street
	London WC1A 1PB
Completion	May 2019
Area	43,500m² (gross)
Outcomes	11 floors of Grade A office space
	4,500m² retail space
	21 affordable homes
	3,000 new jobs
Sustainability	Re-use of 4,600m³ of concrete
	(= 1,600 tonnes CO_2)
	BREEAM Excellent
	LEED Gold Standard
	Code for Sustainable Homes Level 4
	300m² photovoltaic cells